ROCKY ROAD

A SONS OF SCANDAL ROMANCE

BECKY WADE

Romances by Becky Wade

Dedication

*All my gratitude to the three outstanding female doctors
out of Presbyterian Hospital in Dallas
who treated me for breast cancer.
Dr. Archana Ganaraj, surgeon
Dr. Jaya Juturi, oncologist
Dr. Jessamy Boyd, radiation oncology*

*I feel fortunate to have been paired with you because you're as
compassionate as you are smart and experienced. "Thank you"
feels too small, but thank you just the same.
You're an inspiration.*

Chapter One

Though they'd never met, Jude Camden was an expert on Gemma Clare.

Minutes from now he'd introduce himself to her, which made him feel the way he'd once felt toward standardized tests in high school. Lots of duty mixed with purpose.

It was February sixteenth in the state of Maine and today's sunny weather would have been enjoyable for this time of year if not for the biting, angry wind. Fortunately for him, he always dressed appropriately for the weather because he never left home without first studying the forecast. Flipping up the collar of his dark gray pea coat against the gusts buffeting him, Jude walked past the trendy shops and restaurants of Bayview, Gemma's small, historic hometown.

When people thought about Maine, they usually thought about the coast. Many had little familiarity with inland towns and cities like Bangor, where Jude lived and worked. Or Bayview, which was named for its view not of an ocean bay, but the bay of Pushaw Lake. Bangor was a forty-minute drive from the coast and Bayview was twenty additional minutes north of

Bangor. He loved to fish, so he'd come to Pushaw Lake numerous times. But he didn't love to shop, so this was the first time he'd bothered to visit the town's center.

He watched the address numbers climb until he reached Gemma's store and stopped. A sign creaked on a wooden arm jutting from the white-painted facade of an old brick building. Carved gold letters on the sign read *Perfumes by Gemma Clare.*

Time to get down to business. Steeling himself, he entered through a hot pink door.

He saw no one. But a fragrance—flowers and citrus—welcomed him the way a dust storm might welcome a traveler to the Arabian Peninsula. The scent barreled over him, incredible, unlike anything he'd smelled before. Rich and complex . . . Maybe too much of a good thing? Like serving a person a forty-ounce steak or a bucket of wine.

Other than the lack of people, the interior looked as expected based on the online photos he'd viewed. Wood floor. A ceiling that exposed the cement underbelly of the floor above plus ductwork and metal pipes. White walls. Shelves holding clear glass bottles of perfume, body cream, shower gel, candles. Labels in bright pastel colors. The feminine environment gave him the uncomfortable feeling that he'd breached a space men rarely visited.

"Hello?" came a woman's voice from behind the swinging double doors that divided the retail space from the space at the back.

"Hello," he answered.

He knew that Gemma employed one person, Stella Russo, her aunt on her father's side, age fifty-eight. He also knew that Gemma worked the shop floor in the middle of every weekday so the older woman could take her lunch break. He'd purposely arrived during the lunch hour on a Wednesday in hopes of catching Gemma alone.

A flash of movement at the double doors caught his eye. He looked up in time to see a woman peek out. "Ah!" she said, then disappeared before he'd had a chance to meet her eyes or register anything about her other than her long, red hair. Fortunately, that one distinctive detail was enough to confirm her identity. This was Gemma. "One second," she called.

He crossed to a shelf and opened a tester bottle of bath gel named Relaxation and Berry. As he was holding it up to his nose, Gemma burst through the double doors carrying a huge gift basket.

When she spotted him, her eyes went big with alarm. "*No!*" she yelled.

He startled. *No?*

"No, no, no!" She rushed toward him with the gift basket. "Put that down!"

"In my defense, it was labeled as a tester—"

"There's citronella in that! Let me take it from you!" She jostled the gift basket to the side to free one of her hands. Doing so caused the basket to slip. She bobbled it. Its top edge, covered in a pink bow, smacked the shower gel he was holding. A glob of it flew into the air and landed on the side of his jaw.

She steadied the gift basket and froze, gaping at him with wide-mouthed horror.

Gelatinous liquid curved down his throat.

What in the world had just happened?

Gemma set the basket on the floor and raised her palms toward his neck. "Oh my goodness, oh my goodness! Don't panic." She jerked the bath gel from him and set it aside. "You'll be fine. I'll just—" She reached up and swept the goo off his skin with her fingers.

He was too stunned to speak. Too professional to lose his cool.

With her other hand, she pulled up the hem of her long

cardigan and wiped the area. "Don't panic!" she exclaimed again, then sprinted to the back of the shop.

Jude looked from side to side. Was he being set up? Filmed for some type of social media challenge?

She returned, a tornado of orange-red hair and charisma. She now held a wad of paper towels, wet at one end. Once again, she took it upon herself to scrub at his jaw and neck.

He couldn't make sense of her huge overreaction. Or her complete disregard for his personal space boundaries.

"Lie down on the floor," she demanded.

He gave her a slow, incredulous blink. "No, thank you."

"That might help calm you!"

"I'm calm."

"Should I take you outside for—for fresh air? Will that help? Or should I call an ambulance? Both?"

"None of the above."

"Anaphylactic shock is serious business! That gel has *citronella* in it. I can't believe it made contact with your skin! This is all my fault. But also somewhat your fault because the ingredients are clearly listed on the back label." She resumed scrubbing his neck with the paper towels. "And two days before your wedding, no less! I'm so terribly sorry. There. I think I got it all." She paused for a split second to bite her lip, then physically turned him toward the door and gave him a push.

He took one step forward, then resisted going farther.

She continued to exert pressure against his back. "If you won't lie down, I'm going to insist you go outside. Getting away from your allergens can only help matters, surely. If you have a red, swollen face for your wedding, Amber is never going to forgive me. Outside! Please!"

Just then the door swung open to admit a blond man around Jude's age wearing the sort of heavy-duty face mask that came with a built-in vent.

Gemma's hands abruptly fell away from Jude, then she came to a stop next to him. She faced the newcomer with an expression of blank incomprehension.

For a long moment, no one spoke.

"I'm here to pick up an order for Amber," the newcomer said.

Gemma clicked her teeth closed, eyebrows lifting high. Another awkward pause. "*You're* Brent?"

"Yes."

She winced, cutting a guilty look at Jude.

He'd been the victim of a case of mistaken identity. Laughter threatened to burst upward and out of him. He called on his steely control to keep it down. If he laughed at her, Gemma might dislike him for it, and he was here to gain her cooperation. Amused, he reached down for the gift basket. "I believe this is yours." He handed it to Brent. "Congratulations on your wedding."

"Thanks, man."

"Yes, *huge congrats*," Gemma said. "Have a happy, allergic-reaction-free wedding!"

"Just making sure." Brent angled his chin toward the basket. "There's no citronella in these products?"

"None at all," she assured him. "No worries on that front."

"Have a good day."

"You too," Gemma said as he let himself out.

As soon as Jude was alone again with Gemma, she faced him. Now that he was seeing her straight-on and she was no longer a blur of panicked motion, he was able to get his first good look at her.

The numerous photos he'd seen of Gemma had revealed that she was beautiful. Yet, somehow, they'd failed to prepare him for the strength of her beauty in three dimensions.

She was much more vivid than a regular person. Her skin

was luminous white, dotted with pale freckles. The bright green cardigan, white top, and jeans she wore showed off impressive curves. Her dainty nose, pink lips, and pretty chin gave her the appearance of sweetness. But her eyes told the rest of the story. They were the color of liquid silver. Bold, intelligent eyes that currently communicated self-deprecation.

Her looks stunned him a little, making it hard to think clearly—

"I'm guessing," Gemma said, "that you, sir, are not a soon-to-be groom with an allergy to citronella."

"I am not."

"And yet I accosted you with my hands, sweater, and paper towels." She smiled, shaking her head. "When a blond man showed up at my shop exactly when I expected a blond man to pick up an order, I assumed you were Brent."

"Understandable."

"Amber is one of my regulars. She's told me a lot about Brent and the wedding, but I've never met him."

"Until today."

"Yep. I won't blame you if you run out of here screaming."

"I think there's been enough screaming in the last five minutes."

She laughed. "You must have thought I was absolutely crazy. I'm really sorry. To express the depth of my apology, I'd love to give you any item in this store."

"Thank you, but I'm actually not here to shop."

"Oh?" Confusion tweaked her forehead.

Her smile was like summer to him. Sunny and bright. He was hungry for more summer in his life—especially during Maine's literal winter—and was sorry already because he knew telling her the name of his employer would erase that smile. He pulled free his wallet and flipped it open to show his badge. "Special Agent Jude Camden, FBI."

The warmth that had been living beneath her expression drained. "FBI?"

"Yes."

"You're telling me that I attacked an FBI agent?"

"*Attacked* is too strong a word. It was more like you cleaned my neck really, really well."

She wrinkled her nose. Scratched the side of her head. "May I see your badge?"

"I don't pass my credentials over. But feel free to look as long as you'd like."

She scrutinized his ID. "Badge number?"

Smart question. He couldn't see the numbers on his badge from this angle and a fake FBI agent likely wouldn't have memorized the numbers. He rattled off the digits, watching her irises move as she tracked the same numbers on his badge.

"Do you have a business card?" she asked.

Ordinary people didn't take this much time confirming his identity, but he understood it coming from her. This wasn't her family's first dance with the FBI.

He passed over a business card.

She studied it, then tucked it away as three grandmotherly women let themselves into the shop. "Welcome," Gemma said to the women. More quietly to him she said, "What brings you here today, Agent Camden?"

"I came by to speak with you privately."

"With me?"

"You're Gemma Clare, correct?" He asked not because he needed confirmation, but to prove to her that he wasn't mistaking her identity the way she'd mistaken his.

"Yes, I'm Gemma."

"You're the one I came to speak with."

. . .

Gemma kept her body motionless even as her thoughts began to whirl like an amusement park ride. "Would you mind waiting in the back while I help these ladies?"

"Not a problem."

The FBI had come knocking.

The FBI. Had come knocking.

She led Agent Camden into the multi-purpose room, which contained shelving units for product followed by a kitchenette that faced a long table and chairs.

"Anyone back here but us?" he asked.

"No."

"What about up there?" He motioned toward the staircase to the second floor.

"No. I'll be back shortly." She fled, glad that her customers' arrival had bought her time to think.

Except, no. It turned out to be impossible to think while selling perfume with *FBI, FBI* chanting within her head. Her brain kept plotting routes of escape as if . . . What? She was going to sprint down the pavement outside? Squeal away on her Vespa scooter? Disappear to another country with funds she didn't have?

She didn't need an escape route. She'd done nothing wrong. Nothing, that is, other than mistake him for an allergic groom. Had she *actually* mopped shower gel off of his jaw and neck? Had she *actually* spun him around, placed her hands on his back, and tried to shove him out of her store?

Indeed.

What could he possibly want?

Right before the ladies departed, a young woman arrived. She was buying a gift set for her sister's birthday and had lots to say about how her sister claimed she'd bathe in Gemma's perfume if she could, that's how much she loved it.

Bathing in perfume? See. Hard to focus.

She wrapped the purchase and bagged it. The young woman left.

Gemma locked the shop's front door and flipped the sign from *Open* to *Closed*. Steadying herself with a deep inhale and exhale, she walked to the back of her shop.

She kept her store uncluttered and rigorously organized. But the area in the rear was much more *her* . . . colorful and cozy. Seeing it through Agent Camden's eyes, she noted the funny photos of herself mounted on the corkboard that celebrated her adventures, friends, and travels. A buffet of visual inspirations intended to help her flesh out the perfumes she had in progress littered the table. Two throw blankets had fallen like empty parachutes where she'd left them.

Agent Camden sat on one of the rickety, girly chairs at the table. Though the chair was too small for his frame, he didn't look uncomfortable. On the contrary, he looked like a male model posing as a debonair businessman for a *GQ* ad.

Instead of sitting across from him—which would be too much like those police interrogation scenes in movies—she leaned against the kitchenette's counter.

He tracked her with cool, observant poise.

He had a rare kind of face. Hard in all the right places and soft in all the right places. Eyes of striking pale green. FBI agents didn't make exorbitant salaries, but everything about this one read as rich. He wore his stylish dark blond hair short on the sides, semi-long and finger-combed up and back on top. He'd set his pea coat aside. His white business shirt and blue tie were both pristine except for a dark, wet spot on the collar left behind by the shower gel or the paper towels or both. His charcoal suit pants, which had likely cost more than her monthly rent, accentuated the lines of his lean torso and long legs.

She had a sudden, wild urge to pinch a wrinkle into his shirt, loosen his tie, and mess up his hair.

He pressed to his feet, unwilling, it appeared, to let her tower over him. As soon as he became the taller one, she felt crowded even though the table remained between his position and hers.

"We know," he said, "that your cousin Cedric is trying to sell the recipe and manufacturing secrets behind the Rhapsodie perfume empire. And we know he asked you if your boyfriend might be able to find a buyer for those secrets."

That set her thoughts back to whirling. *Cedric. Rhapsodie.* A dozen questions occurred to her. She caught one by the tail and voiced it. "How do you know that Cedric asked if my boyfriend could find a buyer?"

"We've been monitoring Cedric's phone."

She tried to remember what, exactly, she'd said to Cedric in response to his inquiries. "I've been stalling Cedric to buy myself time to think what to do, but I have no intention of helping him sell Rhapsodie's secrets." She pressed away from the kitchenette, crossing her arms and making herself as tall as her five-foot-five frame allowed. "Am I . . . in trouble?"

"No. But if Cedric misappropriates a trade secret used in foreign commerce, he'll be in violation of the Economic Espionage Act, which will put him in trouble with the Federal government."

Stupid, greedy, selfish Cedric.

"As I'm sure you're aware," he continued, "Cedric Bettencourt has been involved in numerous illegal activities, both in his native France and in the United States, since he graduated college nine years ago."

"I'm aware."

"Because your father was Cedric's accountant here in the States, your father's now serving time for embezzlement, tax evasion, and money laundering."

Her temper flared, lifting her chin a fraction as her usual

confidence returned in a rush. "Yes. And are you aware that it was the FBI that brought those charges against my father?"

"Yes."

"And the FBI who has so far allowed Cedric—the kingpin behind *all* the illegal activities—to go on living happy and free in the south of France?" Bitterness toward Cedric and the FBI had been lodged like a hot marble in her stomach for years. She'd never been able to digest it, never been able to get rid of it.

"We've had our eye on Cedric for a long time. We would have arrested him along with your father if we'd had evidence against him that would stick."

"Essentially, what the FBI did, when they put away my father, was cut off one arm of an octopus. But Cedric is the *actual* octopus."

"I agree with that assessment. You don't contend though, do you, that your father was innocent of the charges?"

"No. My father made mistakes that ended up costing him, and my mother, and the rest of us a lot. I'm big enough to admit that his verdict was somewhat fair. But it's maddeningly *unfair* that Cedric hasn't been punished when his mistakes have been far worse and far more frequent. If the FBI had put Cedric in prison, he wouldn't be able to sell Rhapsodie's secrets now."

"I wish we'd had enough evidence against Cedric to bring charges against him years ago. We didn't. We still don't. However, when Cedric asked you if your boyfriend might be interested in buying Rhapsodie's secrets, he created an opportunity for us."

"What type of opportunity?"

"An opportunity for an agent to go undercover as the representative of someone in the perfume industry here in the US who has the finances to buy what Cedric's selling."

"You'd be that agent?"

"I would."

She narrowed her eyes, thinking. "Representing a fictional perfume industry magnate."

"Who would, of course, insist on remaining anonymous. Yes."

"And you'd collect audio and video evidence of Cedric violating the Economic Espionage Act?"

"Exactly."

"Cedric is smart, and his right-hand man Vincent is even smarter. Why would they consider selling their secrets to you?"

"Because I'll gain their trust."

"By?"

He slipped his hands into his pockets. "Posing as the boyfriend of someone they already trust." He gave her a meaningful look.

Her heart kicked. In a flash, she comprehended why Agent Camden had come. After what they'd done to her father, he —*they, the FBI*—wanted her help. That was rich.

Enduring the emotional swings she'd been through since his arrival was like trying to balance on the deck of a ship pitching wildly from side to side. First, her panic over an allergic reaction. Then relief when she'd realized no one was going to go into anaphylactic shock on her watch. Followed by unease when he'd identified himself as FBI. Now defensiveness and disbelief as she tried to grasp his proposal. He was asking to pose as her boyfriend.

"Cedric has known for months," he said, "that you have a wealthy boyfriend who works in the perfume industry. Right?"

"Yes."

"But you've never posted your boyfriend's picture on social media."

"I have one Instagram account that I use for the business. That's it."

"As far as we can tell, you haven't shared Chaz's name or picture with anyone."

It was true. This stranger from the FBI knew that Chaz was her boyfriend's first name and knew the contents of her social media.

Gemma relished dating. She was very pro-boyfriend. But every time she'd hurried to introduce a new boyfriend to her family, she'd lived to regret it after their break-up. At every family gathering, her brothers delighted in laughing about the ghosts of her boyfriends past. So, a few years ago, she'd decided to keep boyfriends separate from her family until her dating relationships successfully passed the six-month mark. She'd been dating Chaz for five months. "I like to keep the early stages of my romantic relationships private."

"Chaz doesn't live here."

"No. He lives in New York."

"Which suits my purposes. And you're still on good terms with Cedric, despite what happened with your father."

"Yes."

"Which also suits my purposes."

"In my heart of hearts, I'm furious with Cedric." She rubbed her forehead, then dropped her hands. "But Cedric is powerful. I have to be practical." She was the oldest child in her family, followed by three rambunctious, daredevil brothers. Early on, she'd learned not only to fend for herself but also how to run defense between her brothers and their collective death wish. The sense of responsibility that had been sowed in her at a young age had served her well when her father had gone to prison, her mother's health had tanked, and she'd become her mother's caretaker, too. "It was practical to remain on good terms with Cedric."

He held her gaze. "I get it."

She had the strange sense that perhaps he did. Agent

Camden was more FBI droid than human person, though, so she wasn't about to let herself soften because he'd shown one glimmer of empathy. "Are you proposing that you . . . become Chaz?"

"No. If this operation moves forward, I'd become your boyfriend using the name Jude McConnell, an alias prepared by the Bureau."

"You'd keep your first name?"

"We often do when we go undercover. It's second nature to all of us to answer to our own names. Also, in the event that I cross paths with someone who knows me while working the op, and they call me Jude, my cover won't be blown."

"And when Cedric researches Jude McConnell online? He'll find your photo and details about Jude McConnell's life and career in the perfume industry?"

"The short answer is yes. The Bureau's excellent at back-stopping an alias."

She started pacing back and forth. "What would my role in all of this be?"

"You'd tell Cedric that your boyfriend has a buyer for the secrets. Then we'd set up a meeting where you'd introduce me to Cedric and endorse me."

"And, during this meeting, I'd be playing the role of your girlfriend and you'd be playing the role of my boyfriend?"

"Yes, but in a . . . platonic way." His lips thinned, the first sign of discomfort she'd seen in him. "And only when you and I are both in Cedric's company—which will hopefully only happen once."

"Hopefully?"

"If Cedric wants to meet with both of us on more occasions and it would raise suspicion to refuse him, then we'll meet with him on more occasions." He gave an elegant shrug. "It's sometimes difficult to anticipate what the subject of an operation will require. We'll both need to be flexible and respond to situations as they develop."

"And how much time outside the meeting with Cedric will be required of me?"

"Should you agree to cooperate on this, you and I will spend time preparing. We'll need to agree on the details of our relationship and learn all the information a boyfriend and girlfriend would know about one another so that we can fulfill our responsibilities believably."

Fulfill our responsibilities believably. He was quite a formal person, wasn't he? She was thirty and pegged him as near her age . . . maybe a year or two older. He spoke and held himself, though, with the proficiency and composure of an older man. "Ballpark number of hours this will take?" she asked.

"Unsure. A handful of in-person planning meetings and quite a bit of email or phone correspondence."

Gemma stopped pacing. "When would we begin?"

"We're prepared to go immediately on our end."

"What am I supposed to do about my actual boyfriend?"

"You can continue with him as normal, so long as you keep his identity secret from your family and your involvement in this op secret from Chaz and everyone else. He'll have to stay away while you and I are interacting with Cedric. And it's imperative that he not share any information or photos pertaining to his relationship with you."

"What happens if I do this," she asked, "but you don't end up arresting Cedric? Would Cedric still find out that I was working with the FBI?"

"Not if we can help it. If the op fails, it will likely be because Cedric backs out. In that case, you can tell him you broke up with Jude McConnell and go on as usual."

"And if you succeed at arresting Cedric? What would be required of me then?"

"You'll officially be classified by us as a cooperating witness. Whether or not you'll need to testify in the future will depend on federal prosecutors."

She chewed her lip, deliberating. "I need time to think."

"Certainly. We can give you four days. This case is time sensitive because we don't want Cedric selling his secrets elsewhere before our op is underway."

He was so *collected!* If she were to start a fire right now, she suspected he'd give her a look of disdain and then snuff out the blaze without even rolling up his sleeves. Which, irrationally, made her want to start a fire. "I'll show you out."

He gathered his coat and soon she was unlocking the shop's front door for him.

"Good day," he said as he passed by.

Who said "good day" in this century? "Beware of citronella," she called.

He nodded in appreciation of her parting remark while thrusting his arms into his pea coat.

The brunette who walked by him on the sidewalk gave him a double take.

FBI, FBI.

God, help me.

What was she going to do?

Chapter Two

FBI agents appreciated many things. Law-abiding citizens. Humor. Courage. Coffee. Promptness. Teasing. Hard work. Team players. Witty operation names.

Jude was handed two of those things—teasing and coffee—when he returned from his meeting with Gemma to his field office inside Bangor's Federal Building. The 1968 structure had been built in a style considered modern in its day. It was boxy and large enough to house the court, the Social Security Administration, the IRS, and more.

After updating his case agent on his interaction with Gemma, he settled at his desk in the bullpen and opened a folder on his computer named Operation Scent-sible—the title his superiors had given the investigation into Cedric. His keyboard clicked as he added to his notes about Gemma. Thinking of her reminded him how mortified she'd looked when the bath gel had hit him in the face. His lips twitched up.

He'd been breathing in the scent of that gel ever since. Flowers and fruit, clean and slightly powdery. It smelled great but also very feminine. His best hope was that none of the other agents smelled it on him.

Focus, Jude. Type.

The FBI of the twenty-first century required a great deal of documentation. He was thorough and organized, the type of agent who met and exceeded the documentation requirements with every case. No subject of his was going to go free because he hadn't crossed his t's and dotted his i's.

During his high school and college years, he'd planned on a career as an attorney. That choice had been correct in some respects. He'd known himself well enough to understand that pursuing justice was his calling.

But once he'd graduated from Columbia Law School and gone to work as a prosecuting attorney, he realized his choice of profession was also incorrect in some respects. He was firmly ethical, born with a guiding sense of right and wrong. Which was strange, given the personalities and behaviors of his parents. So strange that he had to wonder if he'd developed that sense of right and wrong *because* of the personalities and behaviors of his parents.

As a prosecutor, he'd struggled when guilty people had gone free despite his efforts and when people he suspected to be innocent had been put away because of his efforts. For two long years, the unfairness of it had scratched at him.

He'd reached two conclusions. One, trial work was not for him. Two, when law enforcement did their job well—when they gathered excellent evidence according to the rules—that multiplied the likelihood that justice would be served.

He came to see that what he really wanted was to be the one gathering evidence. He'd applied to the FBI and been accepted, an accomplishment in its own right seeing as how only five percent of the twelve thousand or so people who applied to the FBI annually made it to the Academy in Quantico.

Upon graduating from that five years ago, he'd ranked his preferred field locations. His first two picks had been New York and Philadelphia, both in the FBI's "Top Twelve" largest field offices. He'd been assigned to his third choice, Maine.

He'd listed Maine because this was where he'd been born and raised. This was the state he knew the best, loved the most. He hadn't lived here year-round since leaving home for college and had valued the chance to work less than an hour and a half from his hometown of Groomsport—where his mother, father, and brothers still lived.

Maine had a lot going for it. However, it wasn't exactly a hotbed of Federal crime, so when an interesting case like Scent-sible landed on his desk, he was even more motivated than usual to handle his workload well. He'd passed Undercover School two years back. Since then, he'd only been assigned to a couple of short-term UC ops run out of the Boston office. Scent-sible was his first UC op run out of his home office and his first international UC op.

Only he and one other agent in this office were cleared for undercover work. The other guy was in his fifties and much more senior. Jude had been chosen for this op because it would have been a stretch to sell Cedric on the idea that Gemma had a boyfriend the age of her father. Also, Jude spoke decent French, which might prove beneficial. Also, Cedric was rich and well educated. Jude's bosses had remarked that Cedric would be more likely to relate to someone as rich and well educated as he.

Across his college and career years, Jude had done every-thing in his power to be recognized simply for the quality of his work. Even so, with his employers and friends, he'd never been able to escape his famous last name or his upbringing. His bosses knew his history and had given him this assignment, in part, because of it. He intended to succeed with this case not because of birth, but merit—

An administrative assistant named Riley approached his desk. "Here are the files you requested on the Carter case and the Westheimer case." She handed them over, blushing.

"Thanks." Carter and Westheimer were open-and-shut cases. But even Jude's open-and-shut cases required him to comb through large amounts of data from surveillance logs, phone transcripts, and more, so that relevant facts could be presented to a judge and jury.

"You're welcome." Riley remained, clenching her hands together like an anxious old woman even though she was in her late twenties. She had a long blond bob and the sort of pretty face that would probably make it easy for her to snag a boyfriend. He wished she would. Then she and her boyfriend could be infatuated with each other. Instead, Riley had nursed a crush on him for years.

"How are you?" she asked with the seriousness of a person inquiring about the state of his eternal soul.

"Fine."

"Will you be going to the sports bar after work Friday?"

"I don't know yet. Maybe."

"Anything else I can do for you?"

"No, thank you."

Still, she lingered.

He tapped the files. "This is all I needed."

"'Kay." She smiled at him dreamily.

He shifted his attention to his computer and went back to work on his notes about Gemma.

Finally, Riley drifted off.

Gemma had been angry that the FBI had put away her father but let the far more prolific criminal, Cedric, go free. He could see her point. But now that he'd offered her a chance to rectify that by helping put Cedric behind bars, he didn't doubt that she'd set her animosity toward the Bureau aside and agree to work on this case. As soon as she did, the two of them would be tied together, a likelihood that filled him with a satisfaction he didn't want to study closely.

Gemma was larger than life somehow. Interesting, talented with perfume, colorful.

He was greedy to see her again even though greediness was out of character for him and ridiculous in this situation. Gemma was his cooperating witness and could never be anything more to him than that.

The FBI frowned on friendships and strictly forbade romances between agents and their informants and witnesses.

Breaking that rule would mean putting his job on the line.

Gemma was not a turncoat.

The aging floorboards of her one-hundred-and-fifty-year-old house wheezed as she paced a circular track around the first floor. Kitchen, dining room, living room.

After her conversation with Agent Camden, she'd cast herself onto her work to-do list with ferocity. At closing time, she'd tried to talk Aunt Stella into dinner out. But Aunt Stella, the party pooper, had said she'd promised Uncle Arnie a romantic evening. So Gemma had done an hour and a half of desperation-fueled shopping, spending more than her allotted monthly antique-buying budget. At that point, she'd still been facing too many empty hours. So she'd gone to a kickboxing class at the gym. Sweat had run down her face, her chest had heaved, yet the class had brought her little peace.

She'd come home, showered, made and eaten a late dinner.

Now there were no distractions left. She'd always dealt with sadness or pressure or worry best when she had things to do. When she ran out of things, there was only insomnia left. That, and pacing.

It went against her grain to help the FBI catch one of her family members in the act of committing a crime. Gemma loved her family deeply. In fact, her love and devotion to them had defined much of her life. If the FBI had asked for her assistance in catching any other family member, she'd have turned them down flat. Cedric, though, was the family's one very bad apple.

Her great-grandfather and Cedric's great-grandfather had been siblings. Then her great-grandfather, Paul Bettencourt, had abdicated from his family's perfume empire and relocated from France to America for love.

For generations, the American and French branches of the family had made the effort to attend reunions every three or four years. They'd alternated locations. The Americans would host a reunion in Maine, then the French would host a reunion in the French Riviera.

According to her mom, Gemma and Cedric had gravitated to one another from the start. He was only a year older than she and they'd both been active and adventurous. During reunions, they'd hunted for imaginary treasure, put on plays, battled one another at board games. She had a vibrant memory of him—a good-looking, brown-haired, brown-eyed kid— standing on top of a rock and striking a victorious pose against the sky.

By their late elementary years, she and Cedric had become pen pals when Great-Grandpa Paul had encouraged her to learn the lost art of letter writing. The letters crisscrossing the continents had given Cedric a reason to practice writing in English and given her a reason to dream that she could one day be as fashionable and successful as his side of the family.

She paced another circle. Living room, dining room, kitchen.

Her house was small—the second story contained just a bedroom and bathroom—but fabulous. Perfume was art but so were many things. Interior decorating was art, and she loved the creative way that she'd melded antiques, ceramics, flowers, paintings, and rugs inside her home.

Usually, these surroundings soothed her. Tonight? Not so much.

When she and Cedric were in middle school, they'd ceased writing letters and switched to communicating through texts. They'd chatted, joked, encouraged. They'd sent each other pictures of milestone moments.

Then, seven years ago, her father had been arrested. He'd remained loyal to Cedric, never turning on him, staying close-mouthed. It was only when Cedric's name had come out in evidence during the trial, that Gemma had understood the depth of the illegal actions Cedric had asked her father to take. She'd been brutally disappointed in her cousin and childhood friend.

Cedric had shot her one text expressing his sorrow and concern for her. She'd responded, saying that she was fine. *In no way* had she been anything close to fine. Cedric had left it at that.

His family existed in the upper echelon of society and industry. His grandfather had been awarded the Legion of Honour pin by the French president, for pity's sake. The French Bettencourts had chosen to remain in denial regarding Cedric's involvement in her father's crimes, finding it easier to pin all their censure on Gemma's father, Angelo. They'd conveniently forgotten that Angelo had been a favorite of theirs. He was gregarious and affectionate with a deep, booming laugh. Gemma would always love him. But the French Bettencourts had only loved him up until the moment when they'd become ashamed of him.

Her father's arrest had disconnected Gemma from the affection she'd once had for Cedric. Yet, as she'd told Jude, she'd never disconnected contact. If she'd made an enemy of Cedric, she'd feared the hurt he was capable of causing her mother, grandmother, and great-grandmother. They all treasured their French relatives. Gemma didn't want them excommunicated because of her.

So she answered Cedric's occasional texts and calls. She'd spoken with him at the last two reunions. Twice, when he'd insisted she meet up with him during his frequent trips to New York, she'd done so. Their interactions over the past seven years had assured her that he'd become more ruthless and ambitious over time, not less.

Two months ago, when he'd contacted her to ask if her boyfriend might be able to find a buyer for Rhapsodie's formula and process, she'd been horrified. But she had not been shocked.

Perhaps Cedric assumed she didn't care much about Rhapsodie perfume, given that she'd never displayed her love of it to him. Perhaps he assumed that she was as materialistic as he because she'd worked very hard to begin her own small line of perfumes.

He'd misjudged.

She might be the poor American relation, but she would always and forever be Paul Bettencourt's great-granddaughter.

Gemma came to a stop at one of the windows facing the lake. This part of her home projected out over the water on stilts. The view revealed moonglow on the ice-encrusted surface frosted with snow. Above the spiky line of dark trees at the opposite shore's edge arced a canopy of stars and gauzy clouds.

Paul had passed away ten years ago, but he'd raised Gemma on bedtime stories of Rhapsodie's centuries-long, illustrious history. She easily pulled up a memory of him tucking her in at night in the bedroom where she'd stayed when she'd been young and a frequent guest for sleepovers at his and Gracie's house.

He reclined on top of the covers and, smiling, Gemma looked up at him from where she was stuffed under the sheets like cheese beneath the flour tortilla of a quesadilla. The door to the hallway was ajar, buttery light spilling across the dim carpet.

"Will you tell me about the perfume again?" she asked.

"Ah, my favorite story." Pleasure marked his French-accented English.

"Mine too!"

He settled more deeply against the stack of pillows, his hands interlaced on his lean stomach, his leather slippers crossed at the ankles. "Back in the 1600s, a group of French nuns invited a woman into their convent to set up an apothecary. An apothecary in those days was similar to what we call a pharmacy. This particular woman was named Marion Doulcet and she was an expert in herbs. She knew how to make glorious things from plants. Medicines to heal. Perfumes to enchant. Her life, though, had been difficult and so it was a tremendous opportunity for her to have a place of her own inside the convent. She was cared for there, given plenty of food to eat, a small private bedroom. Once she was safe, the creative space inside her grew and grew until it was large enough to fit an inspiration straight from God."

Gemma balled a hand under her chin, waiting.

"Marion began following that inspiration and blending fragrances. Changing the recipe. Blending. Working late into the night. Working early into the morning. Until, after three long years, she finished her God-given masterpiece named . . ." The gentle motion of his hand invited her to finish the sentence.

"Rhapsodie," she whispered reverently.

"That's right. She bottled it and sold it to the villagers. For most, the world was small back then. Long-distance communication was not easy. Many people never traveled to other countries. Selling her perfume to her community would have been Marion's expectation and almost certainly she would have been content with that. But if that's all she'd ever done, these many years later we wouldn't know her story or the scent of her perfume. But we *do* know her story and the scent of her perfume because of one thing . . ." He made another *fill in the blank* gesture.

"God had a plan for Rhapsodie."

"Yes, God had a plan for Rhapsodie," Paul said.

She loved how he said the word in its French way. The musical *R* and *S* and *dee* sounded foreign and glamorous. When she spoke the word, she tried to mimic the way he said it and never got it exactly right.

"The word *rhapsodie* is spelled different in French and English, but in both languages, it means a creative piece containing powerful emotion. Usually a rhapsody is a piece of writing or music. But Marion could not write or play music. Her skill was with herbs and flowers. So she used the talent she'd been given to make a creative piece containing powerful emotion out of *scents*. Marion Doulcet created a perfume that had the ability to lift people's spirits because it brought something lovely into their daily lives. Does bringing something lovely into the world have value?"

"Yes."

"Correct. The few people in the village who smelled Rhapsodie told the people they knew. Who told the people they knew. Who wrote about the perfume in letters. And those people wrote about it in more letters to the people they knew. And that's how the legend of her perfume spread. Men and women began coming from all over France to the convent's apothecary to buy Rhapsodie. Then they started coming from the countries beyond. They wanted to experience Rhapsodie for themselves."

"Because it's the best perfume in the world."

"I, of course, agree."

Great-Grandma Gracie stuck her head inside. Her reddish-gray hair looked silky in the hallway light. "You two doing all right?"

"Yes, love," Paul answered. "Never better."

"Sweet dreams, Gemma."

"Sweet dreams, Great-Grandma."

Gracie's head vanished into the hall.

"Her whole life long," Paul said, returning to his tale, "Marion gave all her earnings from Rhapsodie to support the work of the convent. Eventually, she married and had one daughter. Like you." He tapped Gemma's nose.

Her adoration of him glowed warm in her chest. Her cozy spot and his soft voice and the darkness were making her eyes heavy.

"To protect her creation," he said, "Marion never did allow anyone to write down her recipe or process. She kept it all in her head until the time came to tell those secrets to her daughter. Marion asked that the secrets be handed down within the family that same way and that no less than a third of the profits always be given to God's work."

"And that's what happened."

He nodded. "In all the generations since, her family—my family—the Bettencourts, have honored her requests. Two hundred years ago, it was decided that no more and no less than two family members would know the secrets at any given time. Whenever one of those two dies, another is chosen to receive the information. That person must stand in a church before family and employees and swear their commitment to keep Marion's secrets private before they can be entrusted with them."

"I want to be one of those people."

"I know you do, *ma cherie*. But when I left France and the company, my brother and his line became the ones who'd inherit the secrets because they're the ones who run the company."

"Does it make you sad? You could have been the one running it, the one with the secrets."

"I'm very, very proud of my heritage, Gemma. And of Rhapsodie. But no. It does not make me sad. When I met Gracie, I knew that my destiny was different. My destiny was with her, here. I don't regret my decision. Not for one second."

"It makes *me* kinda sad," she said because he never minded when she admitted such things. "If you'd stayed in France, I'd get to grow up and learn the secrets and run the company."

"If I'd stayed in France," he said gently, "I'd never have married Gracie and we wouldn't have had our daughter Colette and she wouldn't have had her daughter Simone and Simone wouldn't have had her daughter, you. This way is better because you exist, Gemma. And the world needs a Gemma Clare. You have Marion's blood in your veins, and you also have her gift, never forget that. I've introduced all my children and grandchildren and great-grandchildren to fragrance, but *you* are the only one who's shown a love and a talent for it."

Even when she was very little, he'd encouraged her to smell things. Wild blueberries. Root beer floats. Steak. Lobster. Tree bark. They'd go on walks, and he'd pick leaves and rub them between his fingers and they'd both inhale the scents.

He and Gracie had given her a perfume-making set and she and Paul had spent a lot of time playing with it. Making perfumes. Laughing.

"If you want to," he continued, "one day, you will do something better than run Marion's company and make Marion's perfume. You will make your *own* perfumes and run your *own* company. And that is precisely as it should be."

Then he'd kissed the top of her head and she'd closed her eyes and coasted to sleep, carried by his love and his belief that she was special.

Gemma blinked, seeing again the frozen lake before her. Tears warbled her vision. He had been *so* good to her. She missed his love and his belief.

Cedric's father was currently CEO of the Bettencourt company but Cedric, his oldest son, had been tapped as his successor. Two years ago, Cedric had made the public oath in a church, after which his father had taught him Rhapsodie's age-old recipe and method. It was still shared through oral retelling only. Never was it written down on paper or in digital format.

Over the centuries, Rhapsodie's renown had grown to worldwide proportions. It was a work of uncontested brilliance and had become one of the most exclusive and expensive fragrances in existence. The Bettencourts had become the captains of a powerhouse business. Over time, they'd added more fragrances to their line. They offered ten perfumes now and they were all very, very good. But Rhapsodie was by far the most successful, famous, and excellent of them all.

Gemma was, and always had been, fiercely proud of Rhapsodie.

Her great-grandfather could never have imagined a situation that would require Gemma to step in and guard Marion's masterpiece. Yet, he'd prepared her for that role just the same, grooming her through his lessons, his bedtime stories, and the honorable way he'd lived his life.

Her fear of making an enemy of Cedric remained. And, God help her, she earnestly did *not* want to rupture the relationship between the American and French branches of her family. But Cedric had sunk so low that he was willing to betray Rhapsodie. And she'd been presented with an opportunity to prevent that. She was going to have to set aside her bitterness toward the FBI and deal with whatever consequences came for her and her family down the road.

Because the thing that mattered most was this.

Cedric must be stopped.

The following morning, it took Gemma less than a minute to compose a text to Agent Camden short on letters but long on consequences.

GEMMA

I'm willing to serve as a cooperating witness in the case against Cedric.

She stared at what she'd typed, her finger hovering over the button that would send it away. At last, she lowered her finger. *Whoosh.*

It seemed like an earthquake should strike or thunder boom in response. Yet only the usual comforting sounds of her home surrounded her. The creaking wood, the chug of her old heater.

Agent Camden responded almost immediately.

JUDE

Very good. I think we should meet after dark at your house to plan and prepare. What days and times work for you? I'd like to get this started as soon as possible.

GEMMA

Monday at six?

That would give her four days to gird herself mentally.

JUDE

That works. I'll park at a distance. Please leave all exterior lights off and keep interior light to a minimum until I enter.

Chapter Three

Jude arrived early everywhere he went. Fishing outings with friends. Social gatherings with his FBI buddies. Meals with his family. When he was on the clock at work, he showed up for things even earlier.

Prior to his meeting with Gemma, he parked on the street across from a convenience store twenty-five minutes before he'd told her he'd arrive. He'd picked this location, a ten-minute walk from her address, because he didn't want his car spotted at her home. And was extra-early because Gemma had been on his mind for days and he wasn't about to let anything make him late for tonight's appointment with her.

However, a man couldn't sit in his car on a dark street like this one without making people wonder. So he stocked up on a few items at the convenience store, left his purchases in his car, then set off downhill toward her house.

He arrived one minute ahead of schedule. He'd learned through his research that she lived on the lake. But he hadn't expected her house to be so old or so tiny. Gray wooden shingles framed the white windows and door. None of the walls or eaves looked square. The whole thing was crying for a home inspector to inform Gemma that her house needed major renovation.

He knocked.

Waited.

Gemma had followed his suggestion and turned off outdoor lighting. To anyone watching, he'd look like a dark shadow against a dark house. Even so, he felt like a quail sitting on a fence rail in front of a hunter.

Was it taking her a long time to let him in or was his impatience pulling time long? He'd been telling himself that she could not be as compelling as he'd made her in his memory. Even so, he'd looked at the clock repeatedly during this long, long day.

Gemma swung open her door.

He stepped quickly inside. "Good evening."

"Good evening." She closed them in. Her long-sleeved T-shirt read *Yellowstone National Park* across the front. It wasn't skintight but it also wasn't loose. Beneath that, she had on bell-bottom yoga pants. Her socks had miniature mountains printed on them. She'd parted her hair in the middle and tucked it behind her ears on both sides. From there it hung slightly wavy to several inches past her shoulders.

"Now that you're here may I turn the lights back up?" she asked. "If there's one thing that will make my neighbors suspicious it's me rattling around in my home in very dim light."

The only illumination came from one lamp on the kitchen counter and four candles on the kitchen island. He panned the space, confirming that she'd drawn curtains and shades. "Yes. Feel free to turn on as many lights as you'd like."

"Hallelujah!" She went around switching on overhead fixtures and several lamps. Soon the interior was blazing.

Like when he'd visited her store, scent hung in the air. This time, it came from the candles—these smelled like rosemary and pine—and also from the pesto sauce sitting in an open blender next to a bubbling pot on the stove.

Her decorating style reminded him of the stylish antique stores his mother liked to force him to go into with her. A collection of patterned dishes in shades of white, green, and blue filled a wall of shelves. Every flat space held plants or objects or magazines. He counted four throw blankets scattered around, which made his hands itch to fold them and stack them in a basket.

Gemma came to stand in front of him.

He knew she'd inherited her intensely red hair from her mother's side of the family. But Gemma's Sophia Loren–type build seemed straight from her father's Italian side. She was fit but not scrawny. Both strong and soft.

Impossibly, she was even *more* compelling than he'd made her in his memory.

"Would you like something to drink?" she asked.

"No, thank you."

"Have you eaten dinner?"

"Not yet."

"I'm making pasta and I always make lots so that I can eat leftovers for lunches. There's plenty for you, so we'll eat together."

"No, thank you."

"I just got home from work and I'm hungry and I'd really prefer to eat my dinner without an FBI agent sitting there staring at me."

"I'm on the clock."

"Yes, but agents have to consume food at mealtimes while on the clock."

For his sanity, it would be best to keep his work objectives at the fore. "For this meeting to be as productive as possible, I'll need to focus."

"Eating with me will not make this meeting any less productive. C'mon. I insist."

"No, thank you."

She stuck her hands on her hips. "Agent Camden—"

"You can call me Jude."

"*Jude.* Is the rapport between us going to be combative? Or is it going to be agreeable?"

He sized her up. "Can things only be agreeable if I accept everything you insist on?"

She laughed, which caught him off guard. She had a great laugh—genuine and a little husky.

It occurred to him that he was looking at her mouth. He lifted his attention to her gray eyes. No help there, though. They were lively and direct.

"Things are going to be combative," she said with an upward tilt to her lips, "if you refuse to do the things I insist on when those things are easy and harmless for you to accept. Eating with me is easy and harmless." She lifted her eyebrows in a challenging way.

She was his cooperating witness. If Dixon or Shannon saw him sitting down with her over dinner, this meeting might appear too casual and intimate for their taste. It was shaping up to be too casual and intimate for *his* taste. Thing was, it didn't look like he was going to get far with Gemma if he kicked things off by declining her offer.

Cooperating witnesses and informants were all unique. They needed different things from their contacts in the FBI and an agent had to be flexible. Dixon and Shannon would understand. "All right. I'll eat."

"Excellent. You drain the pasta and I'll set the table and get us drinks."

"Only non-alcoholic drinks for me."

"Oh? *Shocking.*" She moved like a whirlwind around the small space, her hair swinging.

He hesitated in front of the boiling pot. "Where do you keep your strainers?"

"If you rustle around in this cupboard"—she tapped a lower cupboard with her toe—"you might find one."

Her cupboard was overstuffed, but he located a strainer and they worked on their respective jobs. He noted for the first time that she had music playing. Some sort of mellow, instrumental soundtrack.

"I thought I'd begin," he said, "by filling you in on the backstory for my alias."

"Actually, I'd like to learn some things about the real you first. I'm most comfortable working with people I feel that I know."

"Learning about the real me will make your role more difficult."

"Why?"

"Because details about me will blur with details about my alias." He drained the pasta. "When Cedric asks you questions, you'll be more likely to slip up."

"I'm confident that I'll be able to keep Jude Camden and Jude McConnell straight in my head."

Ordinarily, civilians were obliging and deferential to FBI agents. He was used to them doing what he asked. He wasn't used to pushback on everything he said. "I still think it's best if you know me as Jude McConnell only. There's no reason pertaining to this case for you to know me as Jude Camden."

"I disagree."

She couldn't see his scowl because his back was to her as he moved fettucine into the bowls she'd set out. Was she taking the opposite side purely to frustrate him?

"I'm never going to be able to pretend a sense of ease with you," she continued, "if I have no idea who you are. I don't even feel easy about having dinner with you in my home without knowing who you are. Is ice water fine?"

"Yes."

"I'm guessing there's more to you than just an FBI badge. Unless you're actually a robotic soldier like Arnold in *The Terminator*."

In truth, there wasn't much more to him than his badge. He spent time with his dog, his family, and his friends. But his job had become the largest and most central thing in his life.

"*Are* you a Terminator?" she asked when he didn't reply.

He met her gaze. "I feel like this is a good time to admit that yes, I'm a T-800 sent here from the future."

Her face revealed grudging respect. "You're familiar with that movie."

"Yeah. I'm an old movie buff."

"Me too. We officially have one thing in common. What else can you tell me about yourself?"

"Nothing that pertains to the case."

She stood beside him and poured pesto over the pasta. He looked down. The sliver of space separating his arm from her feminine one was enough to heat the skin on that side. He stepped away.

She grated parmesan onto the pasta. "It didn't take you long to switch back to combative."

"I'm just doing what's best for the case. When in doubt, I will always do what's best for the case."

She salted and peppered the food, then looked across her shoulder at him. "Very well. You've left me no choice but to Google you."

"Please don't do that."

Her eyes widened. "Is there something juicy to find if I Google you?"

"No."

"Yes!" she crowed. "I can tell there is." She swept into the living room, grabbed her laptop off an armchair, and opened it on her kitchen island.

His spirits sank. He'd much prefer for her to have no idea who he was. For starters, that would enable her to view him as a person and not as a scandal. Also, he'd meant what he'd said earlier. Knowing the real him would force her to juggle his story and Jude McConnell's story in her head. But short of jerking the computer away from her, there wasn't anything he could do to stop her.

She rolled her bottom lip in as she read information on the screen. "Oh." Then, "*Ohhhh.*"

He studied the angles of her lowered profile, the way her hair curved as it hung forward near the keyboard.

Finally lifting her head, she peered at him with interest. "You're one of *those* Camdens."

He gave her an expression he hoped read as patient.

"Felix Camden is your father?" she asked.

"Yes."

"My mom loves celebrity gossip. She's followed the exploits of your family for decades."

"Ah."

"I see lots of pictures of your brother here." She moved a fingertip on the laptop's touchpad. "Jeremiah, is it?"

"Yes. Jeremiah's a public figure. He was a professional driver."

"Okay, but why aren't there any pictures of you at all?"

"Because I always hated media attention. When I was ten years old, I asked my parents to make sure that my photo wasn't printed on websites or in magazines or newspapers or books. My parents' attorneys went to work to protect my privacy."

She consulted the screen again, then jutted a hand in his direction. "You're the second son. You're Prince Harry!"

"No. Definitely not."

"Here's what I know about your family. Your ancestor was a Gilded Age titan." She set both palms on the counter. "Your dad was a famous NFL quarterback when he married that supermodel. What was her name?"

"Isobel O'Sullivan. But why don't we talk about the details of my alias—"

"I just saw Isobel O'Sullivan in a magazine a couple of days ago. *That* was your father's first wife?"

"It was."

"Felix and Isobel's marriage was broadcast live on TV and millions of people tuned in, including my mother. They were everyone's fairytale couple of their era. Then a few years later, he had an affair with Isobel's sister. This all happened before I was born, but even I know the scoop."

All of this had happened before Jude was born, too. Which hadn't saved him from living under its storm clouds all his life.

"What's your mother's name?" she asked.

"Fiona."

"Right! So Isobel's younger sister Fiona has an affair with Felix and gets pregnant. Isobel finds out. The *whole world* finds out. Isobel divorces Felix. Felix marries Fiona. And Fiona goes on to have children. Your brother. *And you.*"

"Correct."

She stared at him incredulously.

He looked back, showing none of what he felt, including regret that he'd only known her for what seemed like five minutes before she'd discovered this about him.

"Your parents didn't stay married," she went on, "because

in the end Felix had another affair, with a housekeeper, and conceived another child."

He nodded.

"I have *so many* questions."

"Which I would prefer not to discuss at this time. Is that an easy and harmless request that you can accept?"

She released a huff of appreciation. "Touché. Fine, I'll exercise self-control and won't ask—for now—any of the deep, prying questions I want to ask about the nitty-gritty of the emotions involved in all of those relationships."

"Thank you."

"But I would like to know why you're not living in Bermuda off your trust fund and spending your time partying and playing pickleball."

"Do I look like someone who parties and plays pickleball?"

"No. Not in that tailored shirt and suit pants. But you definitely do look like the trust-fund type. Do you have a trust fund?"

"That's a very nosy question."

"You're about to become my fake boyfriend."

"Jude McConnell is about to become your fake boyfriend," he corrected. "I won't divulge financial details." Namely, that all Camden descendants received one lump sum from the family trust at the age of twenty-five. "But I will say that we're not to waste the money that comes to us through the Camden family sitting on a beach in Bermuda. We're expected to use it in entrepreneurial and charitable ways."

"If you're expected to be entrepreneurial, then why didn't you become a business tycoon or a doctor or a lawyer? I would've thought that's the career route a Camden would've taken."

"I *am* a lawyer."

Her head pulled back. "A lawyer who works for the FBI? Why?"

He hesitated.

"The truth, please," she added.

"I like doing what I can to make sure the good guys win," he answered honestly.

"Huh." She appeared to think that over. "Even though you weren't recognizable to me, you're from a well-known family. I'm guessing that you're recognizable to some Mainers as part of the famous Camdens. What if we're out somewhere while you're posing as Jude McConnell and you're recognized?"

"The chances of that aren't as large as you might think. I purposely keep my family connection quiet. Only my friends and co-workers know I'm part of the famous Camdens. But if I were to be recognized, I'd handle it."

She drummed her fingers. "When we put you forward as the representative of the buyer of Cedric's secrets, Cedric and Vincent will look into you closely. I can totally picture them doing a reverse image search of your face online. If they do, we can't have them learning that you're really Jude Camden."

"Agreed. The Bureau has a department called A/FID, which stands for *alias or false identification*. They're the ones who crafted my alias. They'll run a thorough reverse image search of my face and make sure all the hits that come up in response are for Jude McConnell."

They held eye contact.

"Okay," she said. Then, "Let's eat."

They carried their bowls to the table and sat across from each other. With plants and clutter between them as a centerpiece, they started on the food. He didn't usually eat a meal made of nothing but carbs, sauce, and cheese. He was more of a protein, vegetables, chocolate guy. Still, the pasta was delicious. Maybe not good for him. But good.

She'd claimed that eating would not make this meeting less productive. But it was hard for him to concentrate with her across from him, pasta flavors in his mouth, candle smells, and music.

"I cannot believe," she said, "that I'm going to pose as the girlfriend of a Camden heir for this FBI operation."

"You're posing as Jude McConnell's girlfriend and Jude McConnell has nothing to do with the Camdens."

"Right, but Jude McConnell *is* Jude Camden and it's becoming clear to me that we have a more important problem than getting our details about your backstory straight."

"Which is?"

"You are not the type of person I would date." She circled her fork in his direction. "For one thing, your social circle probably includes the Vanderbilts and Hiltons."

"And yours includes the Bettencourts," he pointed out.

"The Bettencourts have to interact with us because they're related to us by blood."

"Chaz is wealthy."

"Chaz is wealthy because his dad owns three car dealerships. You're the type of wealthy that owns half of America. Every time I've interacted with people in your tax bracket, I've found it difficult to relate to them. They're not usually very . . . normal."

"I'm normal."

"Of course *you'd* think that. The rest of us don't. All that to say, the altitude of your social circle as well as your personality are going to make a supposed romantic pairing between us tricky to pull off."

"What's tricky about my personality?"

"You're too strait-laced for me. Very controlled and tidy." She reached across and moved his water glass to the wrong side, then pointed his knife away from his plate. She glanced at him expectantly. "Does that bother you?"

"It's fine."

She waited.

He smiled coolly.

She took a bite, chewing slowly, as if taking time to taste the food before swallowing.

He'd never met a woman who commanded his attention to this degree. She was just eating pasta, yet he was transfixed by her expressive features, quick movements, and the way her dark lashes emphasized her light eyes.

She swirled more fettucine around her fork. "I go for guys who are self-confident and adventurous. Charming. Spontaneous. Guys who love squeezing the enjoyment out of life. Are you any of those things?"

"I'm confident. I like to think I have at least a little of those other qualities in me."

She angled her head doubtfully. "Are you going to pretend to be my type of guy for this operation?"

"That would only be of value if Cedric knows the type of guy you usually date."

"He does. He met several of my high school and college boyfriends. Since my dad went to prison, I've only introduced him to one boyfriend—at a family reunion. But my type hasn't changed."

He refolded the napkin in his lap. "I'll come across as more believable to him if I stick close to my own personality, but I can tweak a few outward things."

She leaned against her chair's back. "Am I the type of person you'd date?"

"No."

"Are you in a relationship right now?"

"No."

"What kind of woman appeals to you?"

He had a bad habit of going for damsels in distress. "Sweet, calm types."

"What are we going to do about this? We're clearly not right for one another."

"I'm not worried about it. I think Cedric will see between us what he expects to see."

For the rest of the meal, she gave him a crash course on her prior relationships. Then stated, "Here's a list of outward things you can tweak. Clothes that will help you dress looser."

He didn't hate the sound of "a faded jean shirt over a T-shirt" or "a ring" or "statement sneakers." But he did hate the thought of "a turtleneck," "a beanie," and "a long necklace." *A long necklace?*

By the time they'd finished the meal and she announced that she was tired and ready for a bubble bath and a book, they hadn't covered a single detail regarding his alias.

Gemma Clare had a mind of her own. She was feisty. Funny. Stubborn. She wasn't easily swayed off her ideas and didn't seem interested in sitting back and following his lead.

He refused to call this strange meeting a failure because he loathed failing. He was going to call this progress because at least he'd learned information about her that might be useful to the operation.

They cleared their plates.

"I'll text you to let you know when I'm free to meet again," she said.

"Within the next couple of days?"

"Yes."

"Okay." He was reluctant to go and not just because they had far more to discuss.

"Jude?"

"Yeah?" He gathered his coat.

She angled her chin toward his place setting on the table. It took him a fraction of a second, but then he understood what she wanted him to see. Unknowingly, he'd put his water glass back in the correct spot and straightened his knife.

The wry, narrow-eyed look she gave him said, *I have you pegged.*

Chapter Four

Once Jude left, Gemma had time to do the thing she'd been dying to do through most of dinner—more research on him. She curled up on her sofa under a throw blanket and read article after article about the Camden family. They were one of Maine's premier families. Their Irish ancestor, Finbar Camden, had migrated here after arriving on American shores in the 1800s. He'd begun with one modest bank. Then grown that into a mighty dynasty of banks that the Camdens still owned. His sons built on their father's endeavors, taking the empire across the nation. It had been on to bigger and better things for them ever since.

The Camdens had produced their first elite athlete in Jude's father, Felix. Twice, he'd quarterbacked teams to Super Bowl victories before becoming a commentator.

Like many New Englanders, Gemma was a Patriots fan. Not the rabid type. The type who enjoyed getting together with friends at a bar while the game played on TV. But even her type of fan saw Felix on TV now and then, wearing luxury suits and giving his opinions during halftime presentations.

Felix was in his sixties now. Still remarkably good looking, eloquent, smart, charismatic. It seemed he hadn't married again since his divorce from Jude's mother. A lot of people held his sins against him, but based on her internet surfing just now, an even larger number of people had either overlooked his sins or viewed his sins as awe-inspiring.

Now that she knew Jude was Felix's son, as she studied close-ups of Felix, she could see the similarities between father and son. Both men were tall and athletic with dark blond hair. Both had angular faces and those rare, noteworthy, pale green eyes.

She'd compared Jude to Jeremiah's pictures, too. The brothers looked a lot alike, though in photos Jeremiah communicated an I'm-gorgeous-and-I-know-it boldness. Jude's demeanor was cautious, impassive.

Her rabbit hole informed her of the tragedy that had befallen Jeremiah when his wife died young and suddenly—falling from a cliff. Up until that point, Jeremiah's life had appeared charmed. After that point, she couldn't imagine the hardship and grief he'd suffered.

Upon concluding her research, she squirted her own Luxury and Cream scented bubble bath into her tub and submerged herself neck deep. She loved her home state. That said, winter was not her favorite season. She was the type who bloomed beneath sunlight and skies the color of robin's-egg blue. In order to survive this time of year, she treated herself to a warm-up courtesy of a bath almost every night.

She swished her toe through a hill of glossy bubbles. She'd had a few hours now to absorb the revelation that her assigned FBI agent was Felix Camden's son. Yet she was still *amazed*. Still struggling to believe that a Camden son had entered into her ordinary life here in Bayview.

The things she'd noticed about Jude at the start, his refinement and expensive looks, now made sense. This was not a cop turned FBI agent. This was not a military guy turned FBI agent. This was a man from a privileged family turned attorney turned FBI agent.

How fascinating that he hadn't followed the Camden blueprint. He wasn't running meetings in a skyscraper's board room or charging a zillion dollars an hour via his private practice.

He was camera-shy. A media recluse. For a person of his pedigree, working as a special agent was humble work.

He'd said he'd chosen his profession because he wanted to make sure the good guys won. He almost certainly viewed her father as a bad guy. But Gemma had learned that life was often more complicated than good and bad. Had her father broken laws? Yes. Was he good? Yes. Her dad had read hundreds of books to her, cheered from the sidelines of her soccer games, and pumped his fist every time he'd beat her or her brothers at Chinese checkers. His dinnertime stories had kept them all laughing. He was a loving husband to her mom.

Her phone pinged from the floor next to the tub. She peeked over the lip and saw an incoming text from her boyfriend, Chaz.

CHAZ

Hope you're having an ABSolutely great day.

He'd attached a shirtless picture of himself at the gym that prominently displayed his abs. He was giving the camera a comical Flynn Rider expression.

Gemma smiled. Chaz frequently sent her shirtless pictures with puns. She enjoyed this form of communication not so much because she found it sexy. More because she found it amusing.

GEMMA

Shirtless at the gym? Isn't that against the rules?

CHAZ

Only if your abs don't look as good as mine.

GEMMA

Well, that explains that.

CHAZ

Thinking of you, babe. Miss you.

GEMMA

Ditto.

She'd said ditto because that was the mannerly thing to say. But did she actually miss him? In the type of way that deducted enjoyment from her day? No. Dating long distance got a bad rap, but to her surprise she'd found she liked it.

She lowered in the tub, warm water lapping her collarbones.

She'd met Chaz at a perfume convention. They'd struck up a friendship that they'd continued through texts and phone calls. After three months of that, he'd asked if he could come for a visit to see if there was the potential for more between them. She'd said sure.

During that visit five months ago, she'd felt just enough chemistry with Chaz to move him out of the friend zone into the boyfriend zone. Her attraction to him buzzed along at a pleasant level. It wasn't so overpowering that it scrambled her brain, which was nice. She could relax around Chaz. She could think. Plus, he lived in New York, which meant she always had things on her calendar—her getaways there, his trips here—to look forward to.

Together, she and Chaz had admired the Christmas tree at Rockefeller Center. Visited every floor of Macy's two-million-square-foot flagship store. Sampled the places that claimed the city's best bagels and pizza. Bought discounted tickets for Broadway shows just hours before curtain time.

When Chaz came to Maine, they hiked. Packed picnics. Went out on her rowboat. Shared meals at expensive restaurants that she never ate at except when he was picking up the tab.

The dynamic between them was simple and relaxed. Simple and relaxed was all she had the mental capacity to deal with. In her dating life, anything *other* than light felt too hard.

When she and Chaz were apart, her thoughts were free to focus on her perfumes, her business, and the welfare of her family. Truthfully, she preferred to focus on those things. So her relationship with Chaz gave her the best of both worlds. A boyfriend *and* the autonomy to concentrate on her priorities.

The soapy water unloosened stress deep inside her and she closed her eyes in order to better concentrate on the sensations.

Her phone pinged a few more times but she was too relaxed now to check it. Besides, her thoughts were already tugging back toward Jude Camden.

Jude would never have stripped off his shirt at the gym, not even for a quick selfie, if it meant violating a rule.

When Gemma entered her great-grandmother's room two days later, three generations of redheaded female relatives greeted her with, "Gemma!" in unison.

"Everyone!"

Today was her great-grandma Gracie's one hundred and second birthday. Thus, Gemma hugged Gracie first. Nowadays, Gracie secured her hair in a loose bun on top of her head that was almost entirely silver, with just a hint of soft red to it. Gracie's embrace smelled of rose body powder and felt like soft, pillowy skin.

After Gracie, the DNA pendulum had swung toward brash with Gracie's daughter Colette. Colette's hug smelled like grass clippings and felt like sinew. At seventy-five, she still made her living playing poker. She had short, puffy hair tinted a peach color never naturally found on a human head. She was a straight-talking, hard-drinking woman with a heart of gold who'd been serving as her husband's caregiver for a decade.

The DNA pendulum had swung toward timidity with Colette's daughter Simone, Gemma's mother. Mom had always been gentle and uncertain. Following Dad's arrest, she'd plunged into a season of such extreme stress and heartache that she'd suffered a stroke.

Simone had been just forty-eight at the time, which hadn't stopped the stroke from doing vicious damage. Gemma had spent several days in her mother's hospital room, terrified that she was about to lose both parents in one brutal chapter. Her father to prison, her mother to the stroke. Had that happened, she'd have been the only one left to parent her younger brothers.

God had brought Mom through, but she'd required language, physical, and occupational therapy for years. She'd eventually resumed her job as a secretary at Bayview's Visitor's Bureau. But, to this day, she had difficulty concentrating, spoke slowly, walked with a cane, and tired easily. She didn't pay much attention to her left side and so sometimes bumped into walls or failed to see obstacles in her path.

Mom's hug smelled like pears and felt like slender limbs. She'd styled her reddish-auburn hair into bangs, then blow-dried the rest straight to her shoulders.

After Mom, the DNA pendulum had come to rest right back where it had started with Gemma, who was basically a clone, she'd been told, of what Gracie's personality had been in Gracie's younger years.

"Let's head out!" Colette boomed. "I'm ready for birthday brunch."

The older ladies positioned their purse straps over their arms. Then Gemma assisted Gracie and Colette assisted Simone as they made their way toward the exit of Marigold Manor, Gracie's long-term-care facility.

Gemma's transportation was a Vespa, so whenever they rode together, they piled into Colette's car and Gemma served as their de facto chauffeur. Gracie had flunked her bid to renew her license back in 2012, Colette drove too fast for the others' taste, and Simone drove too fearfully for the others' taste.

Gemma was perfectly comfortable behind the wheel. It was her pride, not her nerves, that took a hit when they went places as a group because Colette's car was an embarrassment on wheels. Grandma Colette had allowed a local company to wrap her ten-year-old Ford Fusion in advertising in exchange for seventy-five bucks a month. Both sides were emblazoned with images of a juicy orange cut in half, a Vodka bottle, and a cocktail-in-a-can named Orange Thunder. The slogan urged customers to, "Get your citrusy buzz on!"

Yes, they'd ended their slogan with a preposition. Hard to say what was worse, that or the giant, cartoonish images.

Once they'd helped Gracie and Colette into the car, Gemma steered Orange Thunder to a historic church that had been converted into a restaurant named Faith Foods. Here, they served breakfast until two in the afternoon five days a week. The pews and stage were gone. In their place stood tables covered in white butcher paper and bouquets of fresh flowers.

A teenage hostess greeted them with, "Welcome to our congregation of food!" and showed them to their table. "Are you all related?" she asked when they were seated.

They smiled en masse and Gemma sensed their shared pleasure. Redheads of four generations caused a stir wherever they went, and they all relished the attention. There were variations between them—Colette proudly the heaviest and Simone proudly the thinnest—but they did resemble one another.

"You betcha," Colette answered. "This is my mom, daughter, granddaughter." She pointed them out.

"Wow!"

"It's my mom's birthday," Colette continued. "She's one hundred and two."

"Oh, how wonderful!"

"We'll take the free birthday cinnamon roll, please."

"I'm sure your server will be happy to help you with that—"

"And I'll have a mimosa. STAT."

"I'll let your server know. Here are your church bulletins." She handed out menus made to look like old-fashioned, folded bulletins.

They'd be eating brunch family-style, so they hotly debated which dishes to order until their server, a gawky twenty-something guy, approached bearing Colette's mimosa. She grabbed it from his hand before he had the opportunity to set it before her.

He cleared his throat and his Adam's apple shuddered. "Hello, ladies. My name's Grant and I'll be your deacon"—he gave a tortured wink, then continued the script, deadpan—"that is, *server*, for today's heavenly dining experience."

"We're delighted to be here," Gracie said encouragingly.

"What food requests do you have for the big guy upstairs?" Another awful wink. "And by *big guy upstairs* I mean our head chef."

As usual, Colette spoke for them. "We'll have the sausage casserole, the monkey bread, and the fruit plate. Plus, a carafe of coffee and two glasses of orange juice. And another mimosa. STAT. Plus, it's my mom's birthday, so I want to make sure she gets the free cinnamon roll."

Gemma scooted closer to Gracie and took hold of her hand. "Has your birthday been a good one so far?"

"Oh yes." Gracie patted her cheek. "I love you, sugar."

"I love you, too."

"God has been good to let me see my great-grandchildren grow."

Parents had to be sensible and enforce things like bedtimes and vegetables and curfews. Colette had been the type of grandma who'd made her grandkids mocktails and taken them to Bingo nights. But Colette was not maternal. So the unconditional-love role had been wide open for Gracie and Paul.

"What can we do to make this birthday even better for you?" Gemma asked.

"Just one thing."

"Of course."

Gracie squeezed her hand. "Remind me of my love story."

Gemma tilted her head questioningly.

"I have a grand love story with Paul," Gracie went on. "I know I do, and I know that it's precious to me, one of the most important things in my life. Yet now . . ." Her mouth tweaked, and her white eyebrows drew together. "I can't remember most of it. I want my story back, Gemma. I feel incomplete without it."

Gemma's heart cracked with sympathy. Gracie had been diagnosed with Alzheimer's two years ago. Shortly after, Colette and Grandpa Stevie had moved in with her. That arrangement had worked out fine until six months ago when Colette had found her mother attempting to feed owls in her nightgown one block over at three in the morning. Into long-term care Gracie had gone.

So far, Gracie's diagnosis had not changed her wonderful disposition. She was still kind, still optimistic by nature. However, age and Alzheimer's had faded aspects of her. Her courage, her confidence, and her sense of humor were all depleting as more and more of her memories were lost to her. Loving her felt like a race against the clock.

"You're asking about your love story, Mom?" Grandma Colette asked.

Gracie nodded.

Gemma kept hold of her hand.

"You moved to Washington, D.C., during World War Two," Colette told her, "to work in a factory that made weapons. You met a handsome young Frenchman named Paul Bettencourt at a dance. He was in Washington as a diplomat at the time, representing the interests of the provisional government of Free France, formed by generals Charles de Gaulle and Henri Giraud. You fell in love but your first duty and his first duty was to serve your countries. You were both aware that he'd be called back to France eventually. And sure enough, he was."

She paused to take a sip of mimosa and Mom picked up the thread of the story. "You parted from Paul, afraid that you'd never see him again. Your goodbye was very romantic . . ." Her words came more slowly as she clearly ran out of verbal steam. "And heartbreaking."

"As soon as the war ended," Gemma said, "and he'd fulfilled his responsibilities, Paul returned to America and found you here in Maine. He professed his undying love and asked you to marry him. You professed your undying love to him and accepted."

"You and Dad married at a church in Caribou," Colette said, "up north where your sister lived."

"You treasured Maine and your family here," Gemma went on. "This is where you wanted to live and raise your children. Great-Grandpa said that he'd have been happy living anywhere in the world, so long as you were there. So he gave up the fancy career he could have had in the Bettencourt family company back in France and the two of you settled in Bayview. He was a high school teacher. You worked as a statistician."

"Nine months after the wedding," Colette said, "Warren was born. Then me. Then Marie. Then Joseph."

"You had a very long, happy marriage," Mom assured her.

"That's your love story in a nutshell," Grandma Colette announced.

Gracie rubbed her lips together thoughtfully. "What else do you know about our love story during the war years?"

The other three women exchanged glances. "Not much more," Colette answered. "That's about it."

Gracie's posture deflated. "I have a feeling, here." She set a weathered hand over her heart. "That there is much more to it, that there are things I ought to know, things I've forgotten."

When Gemma was little, she'd counted on these women to know things for her that had been impossible for her young mind to grasp. How to protect her. How to care for her. Now it was her turn to know things for Gracie that were impossible for her old mind to grasp. Not only was Gemma's love for Gracie motivating her to fulfill Gracie's request, but she understood, to the center of her being, that Paul would expect nothing less of her.

She pictured her great-grandpa's kind, elegant face looking at her with expectation. He wasn't here to love Gracie in a tangible way anymore. He was relying on them to stand in the gap.

"My memory is failing me," Gracie said softly.

"I'll be your memory," Gemma said to her. "That is to say, I'll do everything I can to find out more about your love story during the war years so that I can share the details with you."

"I'll help, too," Simone said.

"And me," Colette promised. "What about your diaries? I think you started keeping diaries when you were a teenager. Those would be an excellent source of information."

Hope lit within Gracie's expression. "My diaries."

"Where are they stored?" Gemma asked.

Gracie straightened in her seat, causing her bun to teeter. Several long seconds went by. Finally, she admitted, "I don't know where the diaries are stored. You don't know either?" she asked Colette.

Colette shook her head. "Every once in a while, I'd see you writing in a leather-bound diary. But, as far back as I can remember, your diaries were never kept in an ordinary, accessible spot. Stevie and I have been living at your place for two years now and I haven't run across a single one of them."

"It's . . . distressing to think they might have been lost."

"I'm sure they're somewhere safe," Simone said. "We'll just need to figure out where."

"Other than the diaries," Gemma said to Gracie, "do you have any suggestions about where to look for information about your love story?"

"Hmm." Gracie looked up and to the side.

The rest of them waited. When Gracie remained silent, Grandma Colette asked Mom about Ronan's struggles in his college math class and the conversation swung to other topics.

Gracie did not join in. Nor did she consume more coffee or OJ. In the middle of chitchat, Gracie suddenly stated, "My desk."

At once, Gemma understood she was answering the earlier

question. "We should look for information about your love story in your desk?"

"I think so."

"Where in your desk?" Colette wanted to know. "And what are we searching for exactly?"

Gracie looked up and to the side again. "I don't know. But I believe there might be something important inside my desk."

Colette drained her second mimosa and craned her neck, looking for their server so she could order a third.

"We'll search your desk," Gemma assured Gracie.

"Thank you. Gemma, sugar?"

"Yes?"

"I want . . . I *dearly want* to know everything about my story with Paul."

"I understand. I'll do my best."

Chapter Five

When Gemma ushered Jude inside her house on Friday for their second after-work, after-dark meeting, the sight of him hit her first. His thick hair, the thoughtful set of his lips, the beautifully sculpted *V* of his jaw. More than six feet of lean, muscular man dressed in a crisp business shirt and suit pants.

Quickly on the heels of all that, she noted his cologne. It had base notes of oakmoss, tobacco, and smoky vetiver. It mingled with his body chemistry brilliantly, producing an excellent masculine scent.

"Good evening," he said. Stiff and proper as usual. "Welcome."

He took off his coat while she went around turning on lights and lamps. She hated gloomy houses at nighttime. She was very much an every-light-burning-until-bedtime person.

Returning to where he'd positioned himself in the kitchen, she said, "Clam chowder. It's what's for dinner."

His mouth tightened. Clearly, he didn't like that she was interrupting his business meeting with a meal again. The fact that she was interrupting his business meetings with meals on purpose had not seemed to occur to him.

She and Jude Camden were like a fox and an eagle. In nature, they would not coexist. Which meant she was going to have to work to establish a rapport between them. Or, at the very least, establish the ability to *act* as if they had a rapport. They were never going to achieve that sitting across from each other with notepads and pens in their hands.

"What can I do to help?" he asked, apparently deciding not to fight her on dinner this time.

"Nothing. It's all ready to go. Take a seat." She ladled chowder into thick antique ceramic bowls. They settled into the same places at her table they'd occupied the last time.

For a few quiet minutes, they sampled the soup. Thanks to all the cream and salt she'd added, the laws of the universe dictated that it *must* be delicious. And it was.

He pulled a neatly folded sheet of paper from his pocket and handed it to her. "Since you weren't interested in discussing my backstory the last time we met, I've printed it out for you."

She was tempted to respond with a mocking, "*Thank you Agent Camden, sir!*" and a salute. But she valiantly held that back.

While continuing to savor her soup, she glanced over the page. It contained a slew of dry information. His fictitious self had been born to a Henry and a Harriet and raised in Rhode Island. "Apparently you're the only child of two doctors."

"Right."

"Jude McConnell didn't go to an Ivy League school?"

"Tufts is an excellent school."

"Ever heard of my alma mater?" she asked. "Costa University online degree program?"

"Yes, because I studied your background extensively."

"I wasn't quite as smart as Henry and Harriet."

"You're plenty smart enough to achieve anything you want, Gemma."

"Oh?" She regarded him with surprised interest. "You view me as smart?"

"You took college courses while working full time. Then spent the next several years serving as the primary breadwinner for your family. You found a way to keep your mom and brothers living in their house. You invented a line of award-winning perfumes and you're now running your own successful business. Yes, I view you as smart."

"I run my own *very small* business."

"You run your own successful business," he repeated.

She consulted the paper. "Jude McConnell got a business degree and interned at House of Cordell Fragrance. After you graduated law school, they hired you and you've been working there ever since. Is House of Cordell going to back up this information?"

"Yes. It's all arranged. Cedric will assume the buyer I'm representing is House of Cordell. But he won't ask me that directly because he knows I'd never divulge my buyer's identity."

"My own bio is more interesting than Jude McConnell's but not nearly as interesting as Jude Camden's." She set the paper aside to review at a later time. "How about we build a story around how we met?"

He straightened in his seat like, *finally*. "Let's do. I've thought of a plausible scenario."

"'Kay. What is it?"

"We met at my gym in New York when you were there for vacation."

"No. I never go to the gym when I'm on vacation."

"Cedric doesn't know that about you, though. Does he?"

"I have another scenario in mind. I met Chaz at a perfume conference in Las Vegas eight months ago. So you and I can pretend we met at the very same time and place. I'm imagining that my friend and I—"

"No friends can be involved. We can't mention anyone who Cedric can then reach out to later to confirm."

"Fine. Then, I, by myself, without a friend, wanted to go on the gondola ride at The Venetian hotel and casino. You and I were put on a four-seater gondola with a middle-aged couple from Kentucky wearing fanny packs."

"I chose to spend my time in Las Vegas going on a gondola ride with strangers?"

"Not you. *Jude McConnell.* Our gondolier was a stout man with the voice of an angel, and we chatted easily—you and me. *So* easily, as if we'd known each other forever. While the gondolier sang, we floated down the man-made canals and the couple from Kentucky took pictures." She set down her silverware and scooted back her chair. "When the canal opened up into a mini-harbor type of thing, I stood up and sang along." She rose to her feet and threw out her arms.

"I like the gym scenario—"

"But I was so swept away by the moment that I lost my focus and my balance." Leaning to the side, she pedaled her arms. "And accidentally plunged into the water." She dropped to her hands and knees and crawled under the table, emerging next to Jude's chair. "Overwhelmed with affection and concern for me, you leaned over and plunged your hand into the depths."

"I think the canal water is three and a half feet deep—"

"You leaned over and plunged your hand into the depths," she said again.

He reached down.

Gemma grabbed his forearm. He wrapped his strong

fingers around her forearm in turn. Huh. She really didn't hate the way that felt. "When our eyes locked," she continued, "we both felt a deep soul connection. Then you easily lifted me back into the boat." She popped to her feet. They let go of each other. She circled back to her seat. "At which time you declared, 'You're as light as a feather!'" She moved her hand in a *say that line* motion.

"You're as light as a feather."

"You took off your jacket to give to me so I wouldn't be cold, then stripped off your sweater—"

"I stripped off my sweater?"

"Yes, to wrap around my wet hair, of course. Go ahead. Let's practice. Strip off your shirt." She smiled with mischievous challenge. This partnership might turn out to be more entertaining than she'd expected.

"I will absolutely not be stripping off my shirt. In fact, none of this sounds like something I would do."

"But this is exactly what Jude McConnell did. Jude McConnell is very chivalrous."

He wrinkled his nose. "Did I have a T-shirt on under my sweater?"

"No. At this point, you were sitting in the gondola shirtless."

He appeared disgusted by this prospect. "In front of the people from Kentucky?"

"Shirtless," she confirmed. "And the lady from Kentucky turned her camera in your direction but you didn't notice because you were enamored with me."

"Yes. Because I never can resist women who fall out of boats."

"My actions showed you how free and fun-loving I am."

"Your actions showed me that you have bad balance and worse judgment."

"You admired how . . . unhindered I can be."

"Unhinged, did you say?"

She laughed.

He didn't laugh. He didn't even smile, not really. But his lips did edge up on one side. Also, she thought she detected a flare of humor behind those jewel-green eyes as well as something that looked like . . . admiration? Reluctant fondness?

"I love our gondola story," she said.

"It's not believable enough."

"And I think its uniqueness is the thing that makes it believable. It's the sort of meet-cute that ends up leading people to their ideal match."

"I don't know what a meet-cute is."

"It's the charming way people first meet their lifelong loves. You can't meet your lifelong love doing pullups at a gym."

"You absolutely can."

"Did you meet one of your girlfriends at the gym?"

"Yes."

"No wonder you're no longer together. So anyway, where was I? I haven't finished our tale."

"Oh, good," he said, deadpan.

She reached around in her brain for where she'd left her story the way she often had to reach around in the dark for her slippers. "Ah! We're sitting in the gondola and I'm shivering adorably. I look like a gorgeous mermaid, slightly moist."

He winced.

She tilted her head. "What's the wince about? I know it can't be about me looking like a gorgeous mermaid."

"It's that word."

"Which word? Was it—"

He made a *stop* signal with his hand. "Don't say it out loud." He spelled out the letters. "M-O-I-S-T."

"You have word aversions?" she asked with delight.

"I do."

"Will you please tell them to me?"

He didn't reply.

She ate chowder, waiting.

"I don't want you torturing me with them," he said after a time. "And I don't want to have to say them out loud."

"You don't have to say them out loud. You can type them in a note." She slid her phone across the table.

He reacted as if she'd slid a squirrel toward him instead of an ordinary, three-year-old cell phone. "No, thank you."

"*Please*, Jude. For the sake of the operation. This is exactly the realistic kind of detail that I would know about you if I was your girlfriend. Word aversions would've become an inside joke between us. It would be a *thing*. This is our third conversation, but this is the first personal detail that seems like it belongs to a real human being that I can attach to you."

His forehead grooved. "Is there a criticism about me in there?"

"Yes." She cleared her throat. "If you tell me your word aversions and a few other personal details about yourself, then I will tell you personal details about myself." This seemed the way to deal with Jude Camden. Negotiate as if everything was a business transaction.

He thought about it, then bent his head and typed on her phone. After a few minutes, he pushed the phone back to her.

Silently, she read his list. *Moist, livid, scuttle, jiggle, cacophony, congealed, luggage, gal, greasy.* This intelligent attorney and composed FBI agent shuddered at the word *jiggle*? This information was gold.

"All right." She attempted *not* to look like she was bursting at the seams with this new, bribe-worthy data. "And now personal details? What do you do for fun?"

"I hang out with my friends and my family. I play sports—"

"Which ones?"

"Racquetball in the winter and golf in the summer."

"Other things you do for fun?"

"I really like to fish."

"Lake or ocean?"

"Both."

"Okay. Go on."

"I eat clean. But I do have one serving of chocolate a day. I love chocolate."

"What Enneagram number are you?" she asked.

"I don't know."

She leaned forward, placing her elbows on the table. "It's sort of a no-no in Enneagram land to diagnose other people's personality numbers but you're definitely a one."

"And you are?"

"A seven. I'm sure you'll do your homework later and research what that means. When you do, you'll have access to my inner workings." She carried her empty soup bowl to the sink.

"And now for some personal details about you?" he prompted, holding her to her end of the bargain.

"As you can see, I love hunting for antiques and packing my house with my finds." She gestured to her collection. "I go to kickboxing class three times a week, which I *love* and also *hate*. I sometimes eat dessert for breakfast or breakfast for dinner. People who park at a gas pump and then go inside when there are cars waiting for open gas pumps are my pet peeve. I prefer old-fashioned paper maps. I can look at a map before I take off on my Vespa and get where I'm going without a single wrong turn."

She rinsed her bowl and opened the dishwasher. He brought the rest of the tableware—his bowl, their silverware, glasses—to her. Nice manners for a man who'd doubtless been raised with servants to clean up after him. She pre-washed the items. He held out a hand for her to pass each piece to him so he could slot them inside the dishwasher.

When done, she flicked the dishtowel over her shoulder and closed the dishwasher door with her foot. "Have you had your serving of chocolate today?"

"No."

"Are you saving it for later so you can drown your sorrows in it after having to spend time with me?"

"Nope."

She rustled around in her freezer.

"Dealing with you," he said from behind her, "is not as hard on me as you seem to think it is."

"Glad to hear I don't force you to drown your sorrows in chocolate." Geez, she really needed to get rid of half the stuff in this freezer. Items were packed in like bees in a beehive. "You're not one of those lightweights who only eats milk chocolate, are you?"

"I am not."

She straightened, holding a container of Rocky Road. "This is very chocolatey. It is not for chocolate novices."

"Good, because I'm not one."

She scooped ice cream into two dishes.

"I typically put more time between dinner and dessert," he noted.

"Very moderate of you." She handed him his ice cream. "Willing to live a little with me?"

"Yes. Willing."

They remained standing in her kitchen as they dug into their ice cream. Gemma was not the type to indulge in guilt regarding the enjoyment of dessert. For two reasons. One, she loved her body exactly as it was. Some men preferred skinny women and Gemma had no difficulty recognizing those types.

Men who valued the curves she took pride in were the ones who became boyfriends. Two, it was Gemma's nature to enjoy things worthy of enjoyment. Tastes, smells, sights, textures, experiences.

Rocky Road ice cream was definitely worthy of enjoyment. She delighted in its cold, rich flavor and nutty, marshmallowy consistency. She could tell Jude was doing the same, which gave them a point of connection. "Since Jude McConnell and I met when Chaz and I met, I vote we model our fake relationship after my relationship with Chaz."

"How so?"

"We travel to see each other every six weeks or so. We talk a few times a week. We text daily."

He looked unimpressed. "Wouldn't I want to see you more than once every six weeks?"

"You live in New York, and I live here."

"Right, but if I'm really into you, I'd miss you. I'd make more of an effort."

"Nah. We're independent and busy doing our own things. Plus, it's expensive to travel."

"I have money."

"But you don't have Jude Camden money. People with Jude McConnell money don't flush it down the drain traveling."

He hesitated, then gave a nod. "All right. We see each other every six weeks, talk a few times a week, text daily."

This ice cream was divine. If it wasn't socially unacceptable to moan, she would have moaned. "At our last meeting, I expressed concern that Cedric would recognize that you're not the type of guy I usually date. But I now think that might be okay so long as we act as if we find each other's differences endearing. You're self-controlled." She pointed at him, then at herself. "I act like I find that endearing. I'm outgoing and spontaneous." She pointed at him. "You act like you find that endearing. If Cedric comments on the fact that we're dating off-type, I'll say that it's an opposites-attract kind of thing. What do you think?"

"I like that better than having to wear a turtleneck."

"So even though you're not into me in real life, you think you can sell Cedric on the idea that you find me endearing?"

He held her gaze a beat longer than normal. "I can. I'm trained at undercover work, remember."

"So how come I feel like I'm the better actor here?"

His lips did that upward slant again. "Empty conceit?"

She smiled broadly. Banter was her love language.

For a few seconds, he appeared to go into a mini trance. Then seemed to snap out of it and set his empty bowl aside. "I should go."

"'Kay."

Silence. A subtle charge hummed in the air between them.

"We're going to need to spend," he said, "a lot more time talking through your backstory and mine."

"Can we do most of that over the phone from now on? I can't be expected to feed you every night."

He gave her a look like, *I never expected you to feed me.*

She winked.

"Yes," he answered. "We can do most of our talking over the phone from now on."

"Excellent."

As she accompanied him to the door, her hand shot out. She squeezed a piece of the shirt fabric covering his hard chest, then whipped her hand back to her side.

He froze, peering at the wrinkle she'd just given his shirt. His eyes rose to hers.

"Sorry," she said. "I couldn't resist. You're so pressed."

"I like it that way."

"I see. So if I were to do this . . ." She squashed another piece of shirt fabric between her fingers, leaving an even bigger wrinkle. "You wouldn't like it?"

"No."

They were standing very close. Oakmoss definitely formed one of the base notes of his cologne. She'd always been a sucker for oakmoss. "But you did not lose your cool."

"No."

"And you can roll with the unexpected."

"Yes."

"Very good, Jude. One suggestion for the future. If I do something charming and unexpected like that in front of Cedric—"

"Wrinkling my shirt classifies as charming?"

"—You're supposed to find it *endearing*, remember?"

He looked down his aristocratic Camden nose at her.

"Repeat after me," she said, motioning to herself. "Endearing."

"Endearing," they said together in slow unison.

"As are you," she told him, pinching his shirt one last time for the road. "So endearing!"

Jude had stolen something from Gemma.

Actually, two things.

Before knocking on her door last night, he'd flicked through the envelopes in her mailbox. Two of them had tripped his curiosity, so he'd slipped them into his jacket pocket. He'd been within his rights to do so. A judge had granted the FBI a search warrant pertaining to Gemma's communications so that they could, if they chose, supervise their cooperating witness. The last thing the Bureau wanted was to invest manpower in this operation only to have it ruined when Gemma went behind their backs to warn Cedric.

After he'd arrived home, he'd steamed open the envelopes' flaps so that he'd be able to stick them closed and return them to her mailbox on Monday without arousing her suspicion. It was now midday on Saturday and he half-regretted taking them because they were taunting him. He was getting ready to leave to play racquetball and should be thinking about that. Instead, he was thinking about this.

Eating a piece of avocado toast, Jude paused in front of the letters. They rested face-up on his kitchen island.

His five-year-old yellow Lab, Mabel, came to stop beside him. She gave him a look that said, *Again? Staring at those letters again, buddy?*

"Yeah," he admitted.

Mabel was still panting from the fifteen minutes they'd just spent outside, him throwing a tennis ball, her bounding through the snow to retrieve it. He played fetch with her at least once a day, no matter how freezing or wet, because she was one of the best things in his life. They were two of a kind—him and Mabel. Both of them mature and calm and responsible. Both had made it their mission in life to better the world.

He narrowed his eyes at the letters. They were from debt collection agencies regarding Gemma's mother's debts. He knew her mother was fragile, and it seemed clear that Gemma was fielding financial correspondence for her family in an effort to shield her mother from stress and pressure. That was admirable of Gemma. But what kind of stress and pressure had this put on her? He'd happened upon these two envelopes, but they probably indicated just a few of the debts Simone Clare was trapped under. It couldn't be easy for Gemma to have debt collectors hounding her.

Since opening the letters, he'd been worried. Worried for

the Clare family and for Gemma. So much so that he hadn't slept well.

What could he do about this?

He and Gemma had a business relationship. These papers represented personal matters that went beyond the scope of that. At the Academy and in-service training, it had been drilled into him that agents were not to become friends with their confidential informants or their cooperating witnesses. Getting emotionally involved was an occupational hazard.

Despite the wisdom of that, the need to act on the Clares' behalf was nagging at him. As an attorney, he had knowledge that could help them.

While his mind ran down potential responses to the letters, his vision cataloged the details of his surroundings. He'd built his modern cabin three years ago on the bank of the Penobscot River. The wooden floors were stained the same medium brown as the support beams on the high ceiling. Large windows let in views of river and forest. His kitchen cabinetry was so dark a green that it almost looked black. He owned high-quality furniture, but not too much of it because he liked space, clean lines, a lack of clutter.

His thoughts pulled back to Gemma. It was like his brain had been infiltrated and set to think about nothing but her. Her sense of humor. Her smile. Her smarts. Her forthright personality. Her curves. She was unfiltered, one-hundred-percent genuine.

Last night she'd said, "*Even though you're not into me in real life, you think you can sell Cedric on the idea that you find me endearing?*"

Her comment had taken him by surprise. She thought he wasn't into her when he'd never been *more* into a woman he'd just met. It would have been a disaster if she'd detected that, though. So he'd told himself he should feel relieved that she couldn't read him well. The skill he'd learned young—to appear impassive even when chaos was happening inside him—was still protecting him all these years later.

So how come he didn't feel relieved?

Irritated, he walked toward his bedroom. Mabel trotted beside him. Her kind face seemed to ask, *What's the matter?*

Gemma Clare was the matter.

She'd gotten under his skin.

Chapter Six

"This is the desk Mom was referring to the other day at brunch." Grandma Colette pointed her martini glass at the piece of furniture sitting against a wall in her living room. "She recommended we look in here to find additional details about her love story during World War Two. I already went through it, though. Didn't find anything except the stuff that's been in there for ages. Stevie and I also looked in every closet and cupboard for her diaries. Came up empty there, too."

It was Sunday and Gemma had come straight here from church. No way was she leaving without searching the desk herself. However, going against the grain with Colette always took the diplomatic skills of a government executive assigned to Russia. "While I'm here, I'm happy to go through the desk one last time. That way, you and I can both tell Great-Grandma that we tried."

"I think you're wasting your time," Colette said.

"Hanging out with you, Grandpa, and Mom is never a waste of my time."

Colette grunted acknowledgment, letting Gemma off the

hook with relative ease, then frowned at her daughter. "Simone, you look like you're about to fall over. Sit down over there with your father."

Skinny, hard of hearing, and almost always smiling, Grandpa Stevie had assumed his Sunday afternoon golf-watching position on his recliner.

Mom obediently followed orders, perching on the end of the sofa near Grandpa.

Gemma faced Gracie's rolltop desk. Gracie and Paul had lived in this historic, Greek Revival–stye house—with its triangular roofline and columned porch—the whole time Gemma had been growing up. She could still taste the frothy root beer floats they'd sipped while sitting out back in the summertime. Vanilla ice cream fizzing and melting in their glasses, her great-grandparents had passed memories on as if she was their own personal time capsule.

Like the prodigal son in the Bible story, Paul's French family had given him a lump sum when he'd decided to go his own way. Paul had explained to Gemma that he'd invested most of that in this house soon after Warren was born. Paul had talked about the sleep he'd lost in the early days, wondering if he'd spent the money wisely. But then he and Gracie had lived here for sixty years. Now their daughter and son-in-law lived here. This home had proven itself to be a golden asset.

Every room and piece of furniture stirred recollections of Gracie and Paul, and the desk was no exception. Gracie had often sat here writing letters, balancing the checkbook, talking on her pale blue landline phone, jotting down messages on one of those old-school, *While You Were Out* notepads.

Gemma began her examination of the desk by checking places Colette likely hadn't. She stretched out on the floor and studied the desk's underbelly. She didn't see anything unusual but went to the trouble of running her fingers over all the surfaces, just in case. Next, she pulled out the shallow drawer at the center, got below the desk again, and looked up. Nothing.

Back on her feet, she grunted with effort as she angled the desk to the side so she could look behind it. Nothing. She eased the rolltop section closed and back open three times, watching and listening for anything out of place.

Gemma sat in Gracie's wooden chair with the padded seat and removed the contents of each drawer. Scrutinized every item. Repeat. Repeat. Repeat. The back of the piece, above the horizontal surface of the desk and below the rolltop, contained slats, cubbies, and miniature compartments. The most central of those compartments had a knob and keyhole. Gemma tugged on the knob, but it didn't budge. "I'm not able to open this compartment." Gemma swiveled toward Colette. "Do you know where the key might be?"

"What?" Stevie asked.

Colette never responded to her husband's frequent *what's*. "There's never been a key for that. It's just decorative."

Gemma gave her a look like, *What if it's not just decorative and contains a clue?*

Alcohol sloshed over Colette's glass as she set it on the coffee table. Her liver was as hardy as Popeye and Gemma was convinced Colette would outlive them all. Colette approached, then planted her palms on her knees to study the compartment. "If you want to confirm that it's just decorative, I'm willing to break it open."

"We shouldn't damage the desk," Mom said worriedly. "It's an antique. A family treasure."

"Simmer down now," Colette said. When she used that phrase she meant, *No matter what you say I'm not going to change my mind.*

Colette left the room. Mom fretted. Stevie smiled benignly.

Colette had an extensive tool collection she used to fix

plumbing issues, car issues, and everything in between. She'd once reroofed a section of the house after a tree had fallen on it. She returned with a tiny crowbar, which she slid beneath the top lip of the compartment. She began to exert force. The wood creaked and squealed.

"I really don't think," Mom said, "you should damage that desk—"

"Simmer down now."

"What?" Stevie asked.

It felt wrong to damage the desk. At the end of the day, though, if there was no key, Gemma was willing for Colette to damage it for the greater good.

One more squeal, then the top third of the small door broke off. "Wood glue will fix that right up." Colette wedged two fingers inside, rooted around, and brought out a strip of paper. "Well well well." Her peachy hair drifted in the warm air coming through the vent as she unfolded and read it. She handed it to Gemma.

"What does it say?" Mom asked.

"I don't know," Gemma answered. "There are hand-written numbers and letters in groups, but they don't spell anything." The bright white paper looked to have been snipped off a plain notepad or piece of printer paper. It wasn't brittle and the ink wasn't faded. She walked the paper over to her mom, who held it up so Grandpa Stevie could see it, too.

The four of them stood in positions that formed the points of a square. Gemma and Colette standing, the other two sitting.

"It's some kind of code," Colette said.

"Could it be shorthand?" Mom wondered. "Did Gracie use shorthand at her job?"

"Not to my knowledge," Colette answered. "But maybe? I think shorthand was popular back during her working years."

"Isn't shorthand made up of non-alpha-numeric symbols?" Gemma asked.

Mom shrugged. "I don't know."

"You could call Dot," Stevie suggested to his wife. "She was an expert at shorthand in her day."

"Good thought." Colette dug her phone from her purse and dialed.

The rest of them listened as she and her longtime friend exchanged greetings. "Look, Dot, I just found something unusual among my mom's things. A piece of paper with writing on it that's in some type of code. If I take a picture of it and send you the picture, can you let me know if it's shorthand? And if it is, can you translate it?"

She listened for a few moments, nodding. "Great. Thanks. Bye now."

It took Colette no time to snap a photo of the scrap of paper and text it to her friend. And very little time for Colette's incoming text notification to chime. Colette slid on her reading glasses and peered at her phone. "It's not shorthand."

"How strange," Mom said.

"I'm guessing," Gemma speculated, "this piece of paper *is* what Gracie intended for us to find in her desk. But now I'm wondering why this was locked away, hidden. Why she wrote it in code. And how she knew this code if this code isn't shorthand."

"Could Paul have been the one who wrote on the paper?" Stevie wondered.

The three women shook their heads. "This is definitely Mom's handwriting," Colette said.

"Where do we go from here?" Mom asked.

"To Marigold Manor," Gemma suggested, "to show this to Gracie."

Thirty minutes later, Colette, Simone, and Gemma circled the chair where Gracie sat, awaiting her reaction to the slip of paper.

"I told you to look in my desk," Gracie said, seeming to want extra confirmation on the chain of events. "Which you did. And you found this there?"

"Yes," Colette answered.

"Very good. Well done, all of you." Gracie turned an expression of pink-cheeked admiration up at them. "I think this *is* what was niggling in my brain." She smoothed the paper again and again with bony fingers. "I can picture myself sitting at the desk and writing this out."

"What does it mean?" Colette asked. "What type of code is this?"

Gracie pondered that while commercials ran on her silent TV screen. "I'm afraid I can't recall."

"Until we found this," Gemma said, "we hadn't realized that you knew any codes."

Gracie released a sound of amusement. "*I* didn't realize I knew any codes. How mysterious of me."

"Do you have a sense of *why* you would have hidden this in your desk?" Mom asked.

"No. I wish I did."

"Does anyone know someone who's knowledgeable about codes?" Colette asked.

"I might," Gemma said. Jude was FBI and if anyone had code experts on the payroll, it was them.

Fiona Camden loved having her sons under her own roof, the way she did tonight. It was her favorite thing. Even ahead of an excellent manicure, perfectly done Botox, and a full-body massage by a strong-handed man named Hans at Groomsport Country Club's spa.

When Jeremiah and Jude weren't under her roof, which they almost never were these days, her worried subconscious liked to remind her that the two most important people in her life were missing. When her sons were physically here again, the way they had been for all those years when they were little, those anxious reminders were vanquished. Jeremiah and Jude brought a unique dynamic into her home. One of deep familiarity, humor, love, comfort, *family*. A sense of completeness.

Jude helped her carry the last two serving platters to the table. Tonight, she'd seated her guests in the dining room of her storybook cottage of a house. Like the rest of the rooms, the dining room testified to the beauty of a monochromatic color scheme. The table, chairs, curtains, rug, and paint surrounded them with shades of white, cream, and blush. The centerpiece and place settings were elegant. The meal of cioppino, sourdough bread, and salad would hit just the right warm note on this very cold Sunday.

"Do you all have everything you need?" Fiona asked.

They replied that they did.

She really was an excellent hostess.

Artfully, Fiona took her place at the head of the table and draped her linen napkin across the lap of her gray cashmere sweater dress. "I'll say grace." She'd been raised in an Irish-American family and grace before dinner was nonnegotiable. She finished the prayer with, "Amen." Then looked up to smile at the faces around her.

Jude asked Jeremiah's girlfriend, Remy, about her current

wood sculpture in progress, and the talk flowed easily from there as they passed the dishes.

Fiona preferred even numbers for dinner because, clearly, symmetry was best. Tonight, however, she had seven. In addition to Jeremiah, Jude, and Remy, Fiona's friend Burke was present. As was Remy's elderly friend Wendell and his girlfriend, Marisol.

Everyone complimented the food, and she pretended humility in the face of their praise.

She really wasn't feeling humble about anything tonight because she—she!—had raised these two sons. *You're welcome, Remy. You're welcome, woman-who-Jude-will-marry-one-day. You're welcome, future, beloved grandbabies.*

Jeremiah was one of the most eligible bachelors in America—

She was being too modest. He was one of the most eligible bachelors in the world. Remy Reed was a quirky, unknown wood sculptor who spent most of her time on one of Maine's remote islands.

Looking at the two of them sitting side by side at her table, though, you wouldn't know that Jeremiah was the famous one and Remy the anonymous one because Jeremiah treated her like the sun rose and set for her. It was extraordinary. He loved her and had fixed the full power of his focus and determination on her. Fiona had never seen him like this, not even when he was dating, engaged to, and newly married to Alexis. God rest her soul.

Fiona tended to be suspicious by nature and back when she'd first met Remy, she'd thought she might be after Jeremiah for his money. Luckily, she'd only voiced that concern to her son once. Not only had she been wrong about Remy, but had she continued to harp on that, she'd likely have driven a wedge between herself and Jeremiah.

"Remy," Jude said, "Jeremiah was miserable, sad, and lonely after he met you and before you agreed to be his girlfriend. So thank you for taking one for the team and becoming his girlfriend." He raised his glass. "Cheers."

"Cheers," they all said, Jeremiah loudest of all. Everyone lifted glasses and clinked rims.

"You're very welcome," Remy told Jude.

"He's back to being his old self," Jude said.

"Bossy and pampered?" Remy joked wryly.

"That," Jude said, "plus arrogant and difficult."

"I think you mean irresistible and one of the best drivers in F1 history," Jeremiah said.

"Plus generous, confident, and good," Fiona added loyally. "He's a prize."

"A consolation prize, maybe," Jude said under his breath.

Remy laughed.

Jeremiah pitched the bite of bread he'd been about to eat at Jude, who caught it in his mouth mid-air.

"No throwing food at the table," Fiona scolded automatically.

"Speaking of people coming back to their old selves," Remy said, "it's wonderful to see you doing so well, Wendell. You already know this, Marisol, but you've made Wendell very happy."

"Oh! He's made me very happy. My Wendell is wonderful."

"Marisol is the best woman in the universe," Wendell declared, never one to miss an opportunity to overstate things.

"Cheers!" Another round of raised glasses.

When Remy came to the mainland, she stayed with Wendell, who was in respectable shape for a man of eighty who required frequent dialysis. He had a pointy face, tall frame, and a fondness for patterned sweaters. Tonight, his sweater had cows on it, and it looked like something a person would choose for an ugly sweater party, but he was wearing it without a trace of irony.

Remy had told Fiona that she wanted Wendell to mingle more with the community for the sake of his mental and physical health. So Fiona had graciously (but also cagily—to court Remy's favor) been inviting Wendell and Marisol to gatherings from time to time.

Marisol had a short, plump body and no fashion sense. However, she was so cheerful that she practically shone. Her dark, twinkling eyes were set in a round, olive-skinned face. She wore her pure white hair in a twist at the back of her head.

Wendell gave Marisol a peck on the lips.

They were very cute, those two. Also oblivious to the fact that it might make others uncomfortable to be in the presence of eighty-somethings who acted like infatuated teenagers.

Jeremiah took Wendell and Marisol's kiss as an invitation to lean over and whisper something to Remy, whose cheeks turned rosy.

The two besotted couples were making Fiona feel her singleton status in an unpleasant sort of way. She'd purposely chosen to sidestep romantic love in big ways—like her divorce from Felix. And small ways—like when Burke had mentioned three months ago that he'd like to date her, and she'd gently nipped that idea in the bud. Typically, when she considered her singleton status, it was in an empowering, this-is-how-I-like-it sort of way.

"Jude," Wendell said, "are you dating anyone?"

"Not at the moment, no."

"Really?" Marisol asked in surprise. "You're so handsome!"

"Not as handsome as me," Jeremiah whispered.

"Women must be waiting in line to be your girlfriend," Marisol said.

"There's no line," Jude said kindly to the older lady.

"Jude's busy at work," Fiona stated. "He hasn't taken the time to notice all the women who are interested. Jude, I can think of three women off the top of my head who would be perfect for you. Give me the word and I'll set you up."

"No, thank you."

Neither of her boys had ever let her set them up with any of the fabulous people she knew. Had they failed to notice that she understood them better than anyone in the world? Had they failed to notice that she had very discerning taste? "There are many impressive and beautiful women in my circle."

"I'm not really interested in women in your circle," Jude said.

Her eyes rounded. "You two are *from* my circle! It's reverse snobbery to say that people in my circle aren't good enough for you."

"It isn't that they're not good enough for us," Jeremiah said. "It's that they're shallow and not very nice."

"What!" She needed to keep in mind that her sons enjoyed the sport of needling her. "You haven't even met the women that I'd like to introduce Jude to. It's shallow and not very nice of you to stereotype without giving them a chance." She flourished a hand toward Burke. "Burke is in my circle!"

Burke grinned at her. "Right. And I'm nice *and* not shallow."

"Exactly." Thank goodness she'd invited Burke. It was a welcome change to have someone sensible take her side.

"I concede," Jeremiah said, "that Burke is the best person from your circle that I've met in years."

"I agree," Jude said.

"Thank you," Burke said warmly to her sons.

"You are also very handsome," Marisol told Burke, unwilling to miss the chance to praise someone.

Marisol wasn't wrong. Burke, who was sixty-four to Fiona's fifty-eight, was fit and strong. He had the kind of appealingly rugged face that photographers like to feature in black-and-white portraits, thick pale gray hair, and a short beard the same shade of gray.

Fiona had met Burke back in their PTA days when their kids were in elementary school together. She'd thought of him then as Nice Dad. He'd always been good looking, too. But he just wasn't the type of man a woman would christen Sexy Dad because he'd been *such* a devoted husband and father. And so personable. Laid back. A good listener. He put everyone—including her—at ease.

His wife had passed away a few years ago and he'd recently moved back to Groomsport. When they'd resumed their friendship, Fiona had been surprised to realize there'd been a Burke-sized vacancy in her life.

Prior to his homecoming, she would have sworn her life already held all the friends it could contain. She'd spent years investing in phone conversations, meet-ups, and special occasions with friends near and far. She'd brought more gifts for birthday dinners and wedding showers and baby showers than she could count. She had friends from her volunteer organizations. Co-worker friends at her company. Country club friends who played golf as poorly as she did but enjoyed the chitchat and cocktails afterward immensely.

But it was only since Burke had reentered her life that she'd remembered what it felt like to click deeply with a person. They'd been hanging out more and more, and now she understood that she'd been in dire need of a friend like him without even knowing it.

Around the time she'd rekindled her friendship with Burke, she'd decided to try to mend fences with her estranged sister, Isobel. Thus Burke had been her sounding board as she'd talked through the thorny issues between herself and Isobel and the potential actions that might reopen conversation between them.

Fiona understood very well that her actions of thirty-five years ago were, technically, unforgivable. She'd had an affair with Isobel's then-husband. In doing so, she'd destroyed the close bond she'd shared with her older sister. Back then, she'd been so stupid with love and desire that she'd been willing to sacrifice Isobel for Felix. She'd lived plenty long enough since then to bitterly regret that choice.

Now, her hope of establishing a dialogue between herself and Isobel hung on the three things that may have softened her sister. One, time. Two, Isobel was a Christian who believed in grace. Three, Fiona had gotten her comeuppance when Felix had ended up betraying her, also, with the housekeeper.

Recently, she'd worked up the courage to send Isobel a letter. In it, she'd expressed how sorry she was. The letter had come straight back marked *Return to Sender*. Isobel had refused it without even reading it. Which had been a setback but not a shock. A disappointment but not an end to Fiona's hopes.

Back when Fiona was eight and Isobel nine, their amateur astronomer dad had taken the family to see a total solar eclipse of the sun in South America. She and her sister were the second and third in a line of siblings that totaled seven. They'd become wealthy women, but they hadn't started out that way. They'd started out in a big, messy, wonderful, middle-class family.

She and Isobel had stood side by side while the South American eclipse had turned the world dark around them during the middle of the day. It had been one of the most wondrous experiences of her childhood. In the awestruck aftermath of the eclipse, they'd turned to each other and made a solemn pinky-promise to experience together the total solar eclipse that was coming to their very own Maine neighborhood decades in the future.

Those decades had come and gone. Maine's eclipse would occur in seven months and Fiona wanted, very much, to make good on their pinky-promise and watch the eclipse together. In part, she wanted that because she missed her sister. In part, she wanted that because their parents weren't getting any younger. Her mother and father hadn't had all seven of their children in one room for three-and-a-half decades. It would mean the world to them if she and Isobel could reconcile enough to attend the same family functions.

At present, she was taking time to ponder next steps on the Isobel front.

"Are you dating anyone?" Marisol asked Burke.

"No. I'm not."

"Also busy with work?" Wendell asked.

"I'm retired. I have room in my life for someone."

Even though Fiona had steered Burke toward friendship when he'd expressed an interest in her, she'd been secretly pleased ever since. It was lovely to know that he found her desirable.

"And you, Fiona?" Marisol asked.

"Am I dating anyone?" Fiona said. "No."

"Is there any chance that you might one day get back together with your ex-husband?" Wendell wanted to know.

"Yeah, Mom," Jeremiah said before she could reply. "Maybe it's time for you and Dad to reunite."

"We can be one happy family again," Jude said.

Hilarious. So much time had gone by that they could joke about it. The divorce had *not* been funny at the time. "How can I state strongly enough the impossibility of me ever reuniting with Felix . . . Let's see. If he was the last man on Earth is a cliché." She snapped her fingers. "How about this? If I had to choose between living on a remote island or reuniting with Felix and having access to spas—I'd choose the island."

Burke looked like she'd handed him a gold bar.

Fiona glanced at Jude. After Felix broke her heart, Jude was the one who'd gotten her through the worst years of her life. At the time she'd been too proud and too lethargic to seek out a mental health expert. Which meant her depression hadn't been addressed, which meant Jude's high school years had been brutally hard.

"This cioppino is one of the most delicious things I've ever tasted," Wendell announced. He'd butchered the pronunciation by calling it *see-oh-peeno*. Her sons knew the correct way but neither corrected him.

"I'm so glad you're enjoying it."

"And I love this salad," Burke added.

"And the bread's wonderful, too," Remy told her.

"I purchased it at Savory, that bakery you like."

"Thank you." Remy smiled at her.

Pleasure sparked inside Fiona. She was at a disadvantage with Remy because she did not like any of the things, other than Jeremiah, that Remy liked. Remy enjoyed carving wood, roughing it in a rustic cabin, and reading fantasy novels. It was good that Fiona had learned of Remy's affection for bread, because at least they had this to build on. Sourdough. Relationships had been built on less stable foundations than that.

"Can you tell us anything about your current case?" Jeremiah asked Jude. He posed this question at every family gathering.

"I can tell you that this case is an unusual one."

"How so?" Fiona asked.

"I can't say. It's top-secret at this stage."

"Nothing makes me want to know details more than when

I'm told those details are top-secret," Fiona stated. "Can you at least tell me whether or not the case is dangerous?"

Jude considered that for a moment. "It's not currently dangerous to me physically."

Fiona cocked her head. "The way you phrased that makes me think the case *is* dangerous to you in other ways. Care to tell us what those are?"

"I plead the Fifth."

How curious. Was this case somehow emotionally dangerous? Mentally dangerous?

"I went through a time when I didn't think my prayers were having any impact." Wendell patted Marisol's hand. "But look what God brought into my life. Now I suspect my prayers are all being carefully considered. I'll pray for you and your case, Jude." Wendell closed his eyes. "Lord God."

Oh? They were praying right here and now? Fiona shut one eye.

"Please protect Jude as he goes about his business for the FBI," Wendell continued. "And, Lord, if I might be so bold, please bring love matches into the lives of Jude, Fiona, and Burke."

A sound of displeasure stuck in Fiona's throat.

"In your time and in your way, Lord. May it be so. Thank you, God." Wendell picked up his spoon and resumed eating.

"Now that Wendell's prayed for love matches for you three," Jeremiah said with a grin, "your fate is set. Ready or not, you're all about to lose your heart."

Chapter Seven

Like almost every other person her age on planet Earth, Gemma preferred texting to talking on the phone. Except, as it turned out, when it came to Jude Camden.

His calm, manly, educated voice was the auditory equivalent of a fudgy brownie. She loved the timbre of it. Plus, he didn't interrupt, and he didn't monopolize the conversation.

On Monday, the night of their first scheduled phone call, she caught herself smiling as they talked over his fake backstory and her real one while she unloaded dishes and folded laundry. When she completed those chores, she carried the phone into bed, flipped the covers up over her crisscrossed legs, and simply focused on the conversation. She almost always multitasked while talking. But this time, the conversation was plenty engaging on its own. To be the object of this particular man's time and focus was a little . . . dazzling.

He was Felix Camden's son and Finbar Camden's descendant, and Jude could have been a bit of a celebrity for those things if he'd wanted to be. The fact that he'd kept his pedigree quiet made his family connections more interesting to her, not less. Imagine, her, Gemma Clare, being in on that secret-ish information. Like Lois Lane knowing Clark Kent was Superman, Gemma knew that FBI Agent Jude was from the famous Camdens.

When he said he should let her go because an hour had passed, she was astonished to learn that much time had gone by. "While I have you," Gemma said, "may I ask a favor unrelated to our case?"

"Yes."

"My relatives and I recently found a mysterious code in my great-grandmother's desk." She briefly explained to him Gracie's desire to be reunited with her own love story, and how Gracie's mention of her desk had led them to the handwritten code. "I'm wondering if you know someone at the FBI who could provide information about it."

"I know a cryptanalyst," he said. "If you'll take a photo of the code and text it to me, I'll run it by her."

"Thank you, Jude."

"You're welcome, Gemma."

The strip of paper with the code on it rested on her bedside table. She snapped a picture and—*whoosh*—sent it off.

Gemma heard back from Jude the following afternoon.

JUDE

My cryptanalyst friend thinks your great-grandmother's code is a cipher used in World War Two.

GEMMA

A cipher? Interesting. Thanks. Any chance your friend can tell me what it means?

JUDE

No, that type of code hasn't been in use in
decades. She recommended you reach out to
a man named Everett Rusk. He's a professor
and expert on WWII codes.

A few seconds later, a text followed containing Everett Rusk's phone number.

Gemma dialed Professor Rusk and was pleasantly surprised when he answered right away. She identified herself and her purpose. He responded with interest and explained that he taught history at Maine's largest university, the University of New England. He told her he'd make time to meet with her if she wanted to bring the code, which had her rushing to her desk calendar. "I can be there Monday afternoon," she told him.

"Excellent. I have you on the schedule for three o'clock."

On Thursday morning Jude spent far too much time writing and editing a brief text to Gemma. He was careful and a perfectionist with all his communications. For some reason, though, he obsessed over every letter and punctuation mark when he communicated with her.

He had a ton on his plate today—audio evidence to review, cases to prepare for, investigative work outside the office. He couldn't afford to burn this many minutes on a text to Gemma.

He made himself quit fussing with it and hit send.

JUDE

Supervisory Special Agent Dixon Martin and my case agent, Shannon Bailey, would like to introduce themselves to you. Do you have time to meet with them briefly tomorrow afternoon?

GEMMA

Yes, but why do they want to introduce themselves to me? Have I already messed up? Is this like getting called to the principal's office?

JUDE

You haven't messed up. They just want to put a face to their names and answer any questions you may have. Did you get called to the principal's office a lot growing up?

GEMMA

Teachers threatened to send me to the principal's office a handful of times, but I only had to actually go once. The time I ripped Audrey Templeton's book report in half in second grade.

JUDE

You ripped it in half because?

GEMMA

She said my hair was ugly and called me ketchup head.

He chuckled. The agent at the next desk looked up questioningly. Jude swiveled his back to the guy.

JUDE

Sounds like Audrey Templeton had it coming.

93

GEMMA

I acted rashly but regret nothing. I'm guessing you've never been called to the principal's office.

JUDE

Only to receive awards.

GEMMA

Ha! Figures. Talk during our phone call tonight about when and where to meet with the agents tomorrow?

JUDE

Yes.

The information he relayed to her through their nightly phone calls was dry. But the information she relayed to him, the information about her life that a boyfriend would know, fascinated him. Every detail he learned caused five more questions to spring into his head.

He kept his eye on the clock during their talks and ten minutes before their hour was up, two halves of him would go to war. One half, telling him to enjoy talking to her while he could. One half, depressed that it was almost over.

Their phone calls were the best part of his day.

Vespa scooters were not the most practical form of transportation during a Maine winter.

For one thing, Gemma's scooter left her unprotected from the elements. For another, she couldn't drive on roads covered by more than an inch or two of fresh snow.

For those reasons she frequently borrowed Orange Thunder from Grandma Colette when driving long distances or on more challenging terrain. She hadn't come in Orange Thunder today because she hadn't known that the meeting with Jude and his FBI bosses would call for challenging terrain . . . until now.

She brought the Vespa to a stop, eyeing the private drive that would take her the rest of the way to her destination. A snowplow hadn't cleared it, so she'd have to cross the remaining distance on foot. If she engaged in an unplanned aerobic workout and power-walked, she'd get there on time. She left her helmet behind and set off.

On this first Friday of March, moody clouds formed swirls against a pearl-gray sky. Pine trees lined both sides of the drive like a closely packed crowd at a concert, all of them wearing mantles of snow. She could hear a burbling creek but couldn't see it.

Her breath started to huff.

Interesting that they'd chosen this secluded spot between Bangor and Bayview. Did they own this land? Or was it owned by an FBI supporter who'd given them permission to use it?

She flipped the fur-trimmed hood of her jacket up over her cap to further warm her head and ears. Her duck boots provided a good bit of protection but wouldn't keep her feet warm long-term in these conditions. Already, she could feel the cold creeping over her toes.

She rounded a bend and three distant figures came into view standing next to a black Ford Bronco and a Suburban.

The creek Gemma had heard earlier made its appearance in the meadow, running parallel to her as she walked. Ice clung thick to its sides, but a lifeblood of moving water flowed down its center over smooth, brown rocks.

"Good afternoon," Gemma called breathlessly as she approached. She would not apologize for being late because she was not late. She was precisely on time.

A middle-aged woman and a man in his fifties waited for her wearing work attire and more formal coats than the one she wore. Jude, too, was dressed professionally in a gorgeous black wool coat over a suit. Her eyes met his and an unexpected jolt went through her. Maybe because, for the past four nights, she'd had his voice in her ear? That was probably the reason. It had been a week since she'd seen him in person. She'd grown accustomed to talking to him on the phone and had gotten to know him much better that way. But now she felt oddly unaccustomed to being face-to-face with him.

"I drive a scooter." She came to a halt before them. "I left it behind a little way back since it's not designed for off-roading." She didn't want them to think her eccentric enough to have walked here all the way from Bayview.

"Gemma," Jude said, "I'd like you to meet Shannon Bailey, case agent for our operation. And Dixon Martin, Supervisory Special Agent."

She exchanged "nice to meet yous" and handshakes with them.

"Thank you," Dixon said, "for your involvement in our operation."

"You're welcome."

Shannon's face was round, unembellished, no-nonsense. Dixon's face was aging, endearing, wise. Jude's—serious, thoughtful, dignified. The wintry weather had coaxed color to his cheekbones.

"This mission is important to us," Dixon told her. "We'll be working hard to ensure its success and we're here to support you in any way we can."

In the presence of these two strangers, she felt the connection between herself and Jude strongly, as if they were linked by a glowing red thread. She was far more aware of him than

Dixon and Shannon, even though she wasn't looking at Jude. It didn't matter. She could *feel* him there.

"Do you have any questions for us?" Shannon asked.

Jude had answered all of her questions thoroughly. But since he'd given her a heads-up that Dixon and Shannon would be open to questions, she'd come with a few for them. "What will happen if our cover is blown while we're meeting with Cedric?"

"We'll have four to five friendlies nearby—inside and outside the restaurant," Shannon said. "If your cover is blown, we'll be listening, so we'll know. And we'll act accordingly."

Yikes. Four or five agents on site and Shannon listening. Quite an audience.

"Cedric doesn't go anywhere without his henchman, Vincent," Gemma said. "And frankly, Vincent's scary. Just so you're aware, he'll no doubt have a weapon on him. What happens if things turn violent before the friendlies can intervene?"

"I'll protect you with my life," Jude said.

His simple words packed a powerful punch, momentarily stealing the air from her lungs.

"Violent situations resulting from a blown cover are very rare," Dixon told her.

"Also," Shannon said, "you and Cedric are cousins and he views you as a friend. Should Cedric and Vincent discover Jude's affiliation with the FBI, you will claim that you had no idea. We do not expect that Cedric will allow you to be injured."

"And Jude? Will Cedric allow him to be injured, do you think?"

"We can't predict the future," Shannon answered. "Our agents understand the risks and have been trained to manage them."

For the first time, she felt the weight of what Jude was risking to do this. And just how much his risk depended on her capability. She glanced at him.

No doubt any kind of backdrop would complement Jude's eyes. Spring flowers. Summer skies. Autumn foliage. But something about the snowy backdrop of today suited his green eyes, reminding her of pale emeralds on a bed of white velvet.

Her body responded with a thrum of heat.

Oh, no no no. She was accustomed to listening to her body and following its lead. Often, the body was smarter than the brain. Just . . . not this time. Why had physical attraction to him come online now? At the worst possible time? In front of his bosses!

She had a boyfriend. Also, she was good at gauging people, and she knew Jude wasn't interested in her in *that way*. He was as capable as a person could be, and more uptight than a White House press secretary. He'd said he'd protect her with his life. But not because he had a crush on her. Because it was his job to say that. To do that.

She did not want him injured. And she definitely did *not* want to have any hormones for him.

"Other questions?" Dixon asked.

She heard herself ask, "How should Jude and I handle PDA in our roles as pretend boyfriend and girlfriend?" She had not given her brain permission to speak that.

"PDA?" Shannon asked.

"Yes. We'll have to sell Cedric on the idea that we have chemistry and we'll have to do that, in part, through outward affection. Right? In order to appear convincing?"

"No," Jude said. "It will be enough to treat each other in a way that communicates closeness."

Gemma pursed her lips with skepticism, then turned an inquiring look on Dixon.

"To be clear," the older man said, "we are in no way asking or obligating you to display physical intimacy. We'd never want to make you uncomfortable."

"What about physical intimacy that doesn't make me uncomfortable?" Gemma asked. "Cedric has seen that I'm physically affectionate with my past boyfriends. If Jude and I stand around stiffly without touching, Cedric will know something's wrong."

The agents didn't look convinced.

She was outnumbered here. The outsider. The youngest. Some might feel cowed by their superior experience and sheer . . . *FBI-ness*. But there was something in Gemma that had always risen up stubbornly when in the position of underdog. "I think Jude and I need to agree on what type of physical affection we're both okay with."

"What are you suggesting?" Jude asked tightly and she could read exactly what he was thinking. *Really? You're asking this now, in front of them?*

"I'm suggesting handholding for sure. And it would be good to have prior permission to touch your fingers, forearms, shoulders, and chest when the spirit moves."

Jude bristled. "No to the chest. Handholding is okay and it's fine for you to touch anywhere on my arms."

"Can I touch your face?"

"Cheeks only."

"Waist?"

"No."

He looked so adorably uncomfortable that she had to tamp down a burst of inappropriate giggles. "If we're sitting next to each other, can I sidle up to you?"

A gap of quiet, while he thought it over. "So long as you remain sitting beside me on your own seat, then yes."

"How about a friendly peck on the lips?"

"No," Shannon and Dixon said in unison.

"Hugging?" she asked.

"That's all right with me," Jude said, "so long as it's brief."

"How many seconds can the hug last?" she asked with a straight face.

"No more than three," he shot back, equally deadpan.

"Can I touch your hair?"

"Same rule applies. For three seconds or less."

"Can I adjust your clothing?"

This seemed to stump him. "In what way?"

"Like . . . to loosen your tie or help you remove your jacket or push up your sleeve."

His expression asked, *Why would you want to do that?* "The three examples you've given are all okay. But let's limit it to those three."

"What about pet names? Is that fine?"

"What did you have in mind?"

"Honey?"

He gave a taut sigh. "A little of that goes a long way, but I'm not opposed to you using honey from time to time if you think it's necessary."

"I do."

"And you, Ms. Clare?" Dixon wanted to know. "What are you comfortable with?"

"All of the things Jude just agreed to. And he can call me sweetheart."

"I'll allow the signs of affection you just discussed, but no others." Shannon, who probably wasn't much fun at a kegger, did not appear to find Gemma amusing. "We have extremely strict rules against romantic relationships among our agents and witnesses, informants, suspects, and fellow agents during the course of an operation."

"Understood," Gemma told her. Though, actually, she

didn't understand how Shannon had made the leap from their chat about crafting *the appearance* of a romantic relationship, to warning her against an actual one.

"I've participated in and run a number of operations," Shannon went on. "Sometimes, when you go undercover, the line between what is real and what is acting can blur. If this operation is going to be effective, neither of you can allow that to happen. I need you both to remain clear-headed and discerning at all times. We can't have either of you straying too close to a boundary."

No one spoke.

"Thoughts?" Dixon asked Gemma in a fatherly tone.

"Um, yeah. I get it."

"Very good," he said warmly. Him, she liked.

"Is there anything else?" Shannon asked.

Gemma thought it over. "No. That's all. Thank you for your time."

"You're welcome," Dixon said.

She wanted to say, *Bye, honey!* to Jude and give him the approved three-second hug, but she knew no one would find that funny but herself.

She walked back in the direction of her scooter with an image of Jude saying, *"I'll protect you with my life"* replaying over and over in her head.

She'd never had a real boyfriend who'd had that type of mentality toward her. Remembering Jude, and how he'd looked saying that, sent what felt like the streaking tail of a firework all down the center of her. Heat and sparkles.

Oh, no no no.

She had a boyfriend! And she'd literally *just* received a stern lecture from the FBI about why she couldn't stray too close to a boundary.

. . .

"I'm pleased," Dixon said to Jude after Gemma vanished from view. "She has spirit, which makes me think she also has the bravery to pull this off. Plus, there's good rapport between you two."

"I'm concerned." Shannon gazed at Jude. "Your rapport with her is almost too good. To be frank, it feels like actual chemistry."

Jude's muscles tensed. "We're both simply doing our part to fulfill our assignments. It's taken us several conversations to develop even the small amount of rapport we have."

"You'll be careful?" she asked.

"Absolutely."

Chapter Eight

Gemma was a hometown girl who never wanted to live far from her family and thrived best in the community where she'd been raised. But none of that disqualified her from loving travel of all kinds. Short overnight road trips like this one to the city of Portland to meet with Professor Rusk. Long, rambling overseas trips.

She'd once spent two months backpacking on a shoestring budget across Europe. She'd once explored Asia for three enchanting weeks. Her blood always seemed to hum through her body at a faster pace while off on adventures.

Since opening the shop two years ago, she'd traveled less than before because she'd been funneling profit back into the business. Also, she employed just one other person, Aunt Stella, her father's sister. If Gemma left, that dumped a lot of responsibility in Stella's lap. To compensate for that, when Gemma was away, Stella closed the shop on the weekends and each weekday during her lunch break. Which was fair, but also resulted in decreased revenue.

All that to say, even this overnight to Maine's largest city felt like a treat. She'd been justifying it by telling herself that this was not only something Gracie needed her to do but also something that would boost Gemma's creativity. Over her years working with perfume, she'd learned that if she intentionally sought out smells, inspiration followed.

She planned to hit several sensory meccas while in Portland. Flower shops. A friend's woodworking studio. A coffee roasting company. A chocolate shop, a German bakery, a lighthouse standing sentry near the icy sea. She'd even make a stop at her favorite pizza place, which was always filled with the savory scents of yeasty dough and spices.

Following Professor Rusk's instructions, she parked on campus at 2:50 p.m. on Monday and located his office. In reply to her knock, a voice from within called, "Come in."

The professor rounded his desk to exchange introductions. He was around the age of sixty and a few inches shorter than she. His disheveled salt-and-pepper hair sprang coarse from his scalp. The cotton of his gray button-down shirt had formed tiny lint balls, indicating its age. His yellow-and-white-striped bowtie hung askew.

Gemma liked him on sight, though he was nowhere near as pressed as Jude—

Was she now comparing every person she met to Jude?

No. Certainly not.

Their operation hadn't even started in full force, and Jude was already intruding into her life too much. But in a way that was increasingly, confusingly pleasant. She'd taken to crafting her schedule around their weeknight calls.

Gemma had resented the FBI ever since they'd put her father behind bars and let Cedric skip off into the sunset. But now that she was linked to the FBI through Jude, he'd become an ally.

Sort of? Cedric, Rhapsodie, Jude, her father, and the operation aroused a jumble of conflicting loyalties in her.

She took a seat across from the professor, whose office looked like a set from *Harry Potter*. The window framed a view of walkways flanked by lampposts and bare trees. Every other inch of space was jammed with books, papers, and quirky objects.

"Thank you very much for taking the time to see me," Gemma said.

"It's my pleasure."

She reached into her purse. "Here's the piece of paper I told you about over the phone."

He accepted the code written in Gracie's hand, then perched a miniscule pair of reading glasses on the tip of his nose. "Remarkable. Yes. Very." He placed the scrap of paper on top of a closed hardbacked book entitled *Leningrad: The Epic Siege of World War II*. "How old is your great-grandmother?"

"One hundred and two."

"What type of education or work experience did she have before the war?"

"She was a statistician. She went to community college for two years and then to work for a healthcare company. She wasn't there long before war broke out."

"And then?"

"During the war, she lived in Washington, D.C., and worked in factories that supported the war effort. She was a real-life Rosie the Riveter. After the war, she went back to work for the healthcare company. She was there her whole career except for the years when her kids were small."

Professor Rusk steepled his hands. "She supported the war effort while in Washington, D.C., to be sure. But if she's the one who wrote out this code, I very much suspect she did not do so in a factory, as she led her family to believe."

Gemma lifted her eyebrows.

"This cipher is one of many used in the Asia-Pacific theater. Factory workers would not have been familiar with it."

"Oh?"

"Many women who were gifted in statistics, math, and puzzle solving were recruited by the military in the early 1940s. They targeted some college-educated women with letters. Others they found through newspaper ads and meetings with recruiters. The women they hired were brought to Washington, D.C., and put through a challenging training course. Then they went to work decoding intercepted communications. Essentially, they were tasked with cracking the enemy's code and giving the United States an advantage."

Goosebumps lifted on Gemma's arms. Gracie had always loved puzzles of all kinds. "How wonderful."

"Yes. The Code Girls, as they're called, were highly intelligent, dedicated, and outstanding at their work. We now know that a woman was responsible for cracking the 'purple' cipher used to send messages to high-ranking Japanese officials. Another woman cracked the code that gave us the locations of Japanese supply ships, which our troops then sank. Their accomplishments were many but mostly went unacknowledged at the time. In part, that's because men took the credit for their successes."

"My family is close. If Gracie was involved in this—in code-breaking—why didn't she share that with us?"

"The military impressed on the women that secrecy was of the utmost importance. And it was. They drilled that home. Ever heard the phrase *Loose lips sink ships*?"

Gemma nodded.

"That's the phrase they used to highlight how damaging it could be to the lives of our soldiers if the women didn't keep every aspect of their job strictly confidential. The women were genuinely worried, and not without cause during the war years, that talking about their work could result in the loss of life."

"I see. In that case, why wouldn't she have told us that she was a Code Girl after the war?"

"Their involvement in World War Two remained classified until recently. Over the decades, the Code Girls as a whole have proven to be incredibly discreet and humble. They kept quiet. In fact, almost all of them passed away without ever saying a word about their code-breaking work to anyone. Which is a shame for academics like me. When we spoke on the phone, you said that your great-grandmother has Alzheimer's?"

"Yes."

He pressed to his feet, hardly taller standing than sitting, and hunted through his messy bookshelves. When he faced her, he held a book in each hand. "You're not a student in any of my classes, but may I recommend some reading?"

"Certainly." This didn't look like her usual fodder—antiquing books, home decor books, *People* magazine.

"These two books about the Code Girls are excellent. I suggest that you have a conversation with Gracie about her service. In the event that she doesn't recall it or isn't willing to speak about it, these books will broaden your understanding of her heroism."

"Thank you. Let me jot down the titles and authors." Gemma opened a note on her phone and typed.

"It's incredible," he said, "that you have a Code Girl in your family. It's rather like discovering you're the owner of a treasure you never knew you possessed." He stood the books upright on his desk and resumed his seat. "Former Code Girls are tremendously rare."

"Gracie has always been a treasure to our family, but I'm thrilled to learn that she's also a treasure in terms of American World War Two history. My guess is that she doesn't remember her time as a Code Girl, because she doesn't remember her love story, which took place in the same era. But I'll certainly discuss this with her."

He picked up Gracie's handwritten code. "I don't suppose you have any idea when she wrote this note?"

"No, but it looks fairly recent to me."

"To me, too. Who do you suppose it was meant for?"

"We found this in a locked compartment of Gracie's desk. None of us have a key so we had to break in to get it. Because she'd hidden this note so well, my guess is that she wrote it for herself. Like a reminder note?"

"Ah. She wrote a note only she could read, then locked it in her desk and hid the key." He bent, opened a drawer, and dug through papers. "It seems logical that she might have utilized one of the last codes she worked with during her time in D.C." He plunked a file on the desk and opened it. "These are codes from that era. Let me just line these up with what she's written and see if any of these can make sense of her note."

Gemma waited while he looked back and forth between Gracie's writing and the keys to the codes. Minutes tracked by and her hand kept wanting to compulsively reach for her phone so that she could fill the time with distraction. This was what life had come to. People, including her, couldn't sit quietly anymore, simply thinking thoughts. Absurd! She kept her hands intertwined in her lap.

"Ah," he eventually said, "I think I have it." He tapped the paper. "Using this key here, I've translated the code to say *Box in northwest corner under dormer.*"

Gemma chewed her lip, thinking. Of all the deep, earth-shattering things Gracie could've written and kept in her secret compartment, this seemed weirdly pedestrian. "There are dormer windows . . . in the attic of the home she and my great-grandfather shared. Perhaps she's referring to an object stored there?"

"Perhaps." He slid Gracie's note across to her. "I'm a scholar, which means I'm curious by nature. This has captured my imagination. I'd be grateful if you'd keep me apprised of what you find."

"Yes, I'd be glad to." Over the phone, she'd asked how she could compensate him, and he'd assured her he did not expect compensation. It would be nice to pay him back in some small way.

"Please don't hesitate to reach out to me if there's any other way in which I can be helpful or provide context for your grandmother's story."

"I'll do that. I can't thank you enough."

"Sharing this with me and giving me a chance to crack a World War Two code is thanks enough, believe me. If you'll wait a few moments, I'll photocopy this key. That way you can take a copy home with you, in case you find additional ciphers."

When Gemma returned to Orange Thunder following her meeting with the professor, she checked her phone and found a text from Jude. Just the sight of a text from him gave her a happy little jolt.

As a business owner, she'd come to value suppliers and freelancers who had Jude's get-the-job-done personality type. In her private life, though, his was not the personality type she'd gravitated toward in the past. She loved entertaining experiences, stimulating sights and sounds. She steered clear of people like Jude because they could drain a gathering of its enjoyment.

Which made the happy little jolt perplexing.

For all intents and purposes, Jude was a business associate. She'd prefer to think of him the way she thought of Mike, the guy who made the labels for her products. She liked and appreciated Mike but, appropriately, his texts did not give her happy little jolts.

JUDE

Would you be able to give me a quick introduction into perfume making? Jude McConnell works on the financial side of things at House of Cordell. But he'd have gained an understanding about perfume and perfume making. That's knowledge your cousin Cedric has and would expect Jude McConnell to have. I've read books about it, but there's no substitute for talking to an expert.

GEMMA

Certainly. Join me at the shop after close of business one day this week and I'll give you a crash course.

She'd been planning to return to her hotel room in time for their call tonight, but seeing as how he was like a business associate, and she was on a getaway, that suddenly felt too extreme.

GEMMA

By the way, I'm on a quick trip to Portland. Can we skip tonight's call and resume tomorrow?

JUDE

Yes. I'll call you then at the usual time.

She was visiting one of her favorite cities. Her business associate had just let her off the hook for tonight's scheduled phone call and she should feel glad about that.

Instead, inexplicable disappointment drifted down her like flour through a sifter.

"I was a Code Girl?" Gracie asked the following evening.

"It looks that way," Gemma answered.

All the co-conspirators on task Reunite-Gracie-With-Her-Love-Story were present in the living room of Gracie and Paul's former home, now Colette and Stevie's house.

Gemma had spent last night in Portland and the day sightseeing there. Ten minutes ago, she'd returned to Bayview and parked Orange Thunder in Colette's garage. The others had gathered here earlier for dinner and been awaiting her arrival. Almost as soon as she'd hugged each of them, she'd begun relaying the conversation she'd had with Professor Rusk and passing along his translation of Gracie's note.

"I don't remember working as a Code Girl," Gracie confessed.

"Do you remember working in a factory making weapons?" Colette asked.

"No."

"What?" Stevie asked.

"The idea of you as a Code Girl makes a lot of sense to me," Colette stated from her standing position near the fireplace. When Gracie was here, Colette always insisted her mom sit in her recliner, the one next to Stevie's. "You've never been the slightest bit handy, and it's always been all but impossible for me to imagine you working in a factory like you said you did. But math? You're unbelievably good at math. The government would've wanted you to use your skills for their cause."

"It reminds me of that British movie," Simone said. "The one with Benedict Something-or-other in it."

"*The Imitation Game.*" Gemma nodded. "But unlike the people in that film, it sounds like you," she said to Gracie, "might've been involved in an effort that was made up of dozens and dozens and dozens of women."

"Extraordinary," Simone murmured.

"Girl power." Colette pumped the air with her fist, then went to the drink cart against the wall and poured gin and vermouth into a martini shaker. "Box in northwest corner under dormer. Huh. The attic is the only floor of this house with dormers."

"That's *if* the note is referring to this house," Simone said.

"One way to find out. We go upstairs and check." Colette added ice, then rattled the martini shaker vigorously. The noise of a martini shaker had always been the soundtrack of Gemma's visits with her grandparents. Colette looked to Stevie and raised her voice. "Do you think the box Mom's referring to in her note might still be located in the northwest corner?"

"I'd think so," he answered. "The northwest corner is very deep back in there behind many, many boxes. I've added boxes while we've been living here but I haven't moved any of the existing ones."

"Were any of Gracie and Paul's belongings ever taken to a storage facility?" Simone asked.

"Goodness, no. I'm too cheap for that and I know Mom is too, because I pay her bills. We're happier piling dozens of boxes in the attic." Colette strained liquid from the shaker into a glass, expertly sliced off a peel from a lemon, pinched the back of the peel over the glass, then ran it around the lip. A hearty sip, followed by "Ahhh." Then another hearty sip for good measure before she set the glass on the drink cart and clapped her palms. "Who's coming upstairs with me to find the box?"

"Me," the rest of them answered.

"Not you, Simone," Colette shot back. "You have a dust allergy on top of everything else. And not you either, Mom. I don't even want you walking up the stairs let alone blundering around in a dark attic." Hard to know why she'd asked who was coming if she was just going to veto half of them. "Stevie, put *Murder, She Wrote* on for them and meet Gemma and me up there."

Gemma followed Colette's sizeable rump as they ascended the staircase. In the second-story hall, her grandmother pulled the cord dangling from the ceiling, which brought down the attic stairs. An icy blast of air flushed over them.

Colette swore. "I'll go get our jackets and some flashlights. You turn on the light in the attic. See it there?" She pointed toward a lone bulb.

"Yep."

Colette made her way back to the first floor while Gemma climbed the creaking stairs to the attic. The light bulb rasped on as if exhausted. It smelled like wood and age up here, but her overwhelming impression was simply: COLD. When she let out an angry, "Brr!" her breath frosted the air.

Stevie had been right when he'd proclaimed that any box in the northwest corner was going to be hemmed in by numerous other boxes. This attic stored items left over from Gracie and Paul's and Colette and Stevie's decades of life and marriage and family. Gemma began pushing/shoving/lifting boxes out of the way to form a path toward that corner.

Soon Colette joined her, bearing warm layers. And Stevie, bearing flashlights. Reorienting the boxes and bins was like playing a life-sized game of Tetris. Gemma worked as quickly as possible because she was determined to reach her house before tonight's call with Jude. Colette did a lot of heavy lifting, too, while issuing bossy instructions to Stevie regarding how to light the space.

After fifteen frigid minutes, they approached their targeted corner of the attic. Time had caused the cardboard boxes here to sag. Gracie's labels, handwritten in marker, had leached pale.

Gemma and Colette hefted a box containing quilts out of the way, then a box containing photo albums, which at last revealed the space squarely below the dormer. A box, approximately two feet by two feet, sat there patiently. Unlike the rest, it wasn't labeled. The three of them pressed close—all shivering.

Gemma leaned down and opened its flaps. The beam of Stevie's flashlight revealed a stack of letters—the old-fashioned, trifold, Airmail kind bordered by red, blue, and white. A pale pink ribbon held the letters together. Below that, clothing?

"I'll carry this downstairs," Colette said, "so that we can look through it where it's warmer."

"I'll get it, love," Stevie suggested. God bless her grandfather, still calling his wife "love" in the face of all the scolding he'd just received.

"No, I've got it," Colette insisted. Stevie's diabetes had grown more and more difficult to manage in recent years. Colette was his nurse and there was no way the nurse was going to let her patient carry a box.

They returned to the living room and a temperature warm enough to sustain human life. Colette set the box on the coffee table and Simone helped Gracie up.

"Oh," Gracie breathed when she came to stand over the box. Reverently, she lifted the letters.

The rest watched her, waiting.

"From Paul," she said with wonder, unfolding the top one. "This is dated June of 1944. He sent it to me from France."

"That was the month and year," Colette said, "when France was liberated from the Nazis and his assignment in D.C. ended."

Gracie's eyes swam with tears. "My Paul."

Simone squeezed her forearm.

"There's more here," Gemma said. Another piece of paper, not bound with the letters, rested on top of the clothing. "Your marriage certificate."

"Is it, now?"

"Yes." Gemma passed it over.

Colette pulled out the next item—a man's vest. Then a man's striped tie, white gloves, a white pocket square, a silk flower boutonniere. Simone lifted out a slip and crinoline, followed by a wedding dress.

"Mom." Colette beamed. "I haven't seen your wedding dress in a long, long time."

More happy tears filled Gracie's eyes.

"What?" Stevie asked.

"Well done, Gemma," Simone said. "Your sleuthing led us to these wonderful items."

Gracie tugged Gemma forward to give her a kiss on the cheek. "Thank you, sugar. You're so clever."

"You're welcome." Gemma was delighted to have unearthed this family gold—letters, a marriage certificate, clothing from Gracie and Paul's wedding day. Yet this felt more like a first step than a final destination. "Why do you think you might have written a note concerning the whereabouts of this box in code, then locked the code in your desk?"

"I've no idea," Gracie said.

It seemed like the type of thing a person would do if they had something to hide. Yet the box didn't appear to contain anything secret. Nothing here needed protecting from the rest of them. Or did it?

"Once you've had some time with these items," Gemma said to Gracie, "I'd love to borrow the box so that I can go through everything one at a time. Read all the letters, etcetera."

"Yes," Gracie assured her. "Absolutely."

Chapter Nine

"What's your faith life like?" Gemma asked Jude over the phone on Wednesday night.

As always for their phone calls, he and Mabel had situated themselves in his home office. He had his computer open to take notes as well as a pad and pen ready.

"If I was your girlfriend," she went on, "I'd know whether you believed in God, and I'd know whether or not you attend church."

"It's complicated."

"I'm listening."

Frowning, he considered the nighttime view through the floor-to-ceiling window. No rain was falling on the trees outside, but lightning had been streaking at regular intervals across a distant corner of sky. "I grew up going to church services regularly with my family. It . . . meant a lot to me. I was the one who nagged my family members to go whenever they were on the fence."

"Aww. I'm betting you were a kid who was too hard on

himself. I can see how it must have been a relief to hear about grace week after week."

"Yeah." Her insight into him took him aback. He'd never thought about it exactly that way, but she was right. He was hard on himself, now and when he was young. Grace had given him a vacation from all the striving. "My dad was our church's most famous member and, I'm sure, their largest financial supporter. Keep in mind, though, that he never attended much. During the football season, he worked weekends. During the off-season, he'd only go to church for holidays or special occasions. My mom and my brother and I were the ones who were involved. We were part of the community. We had friends there."

"I have a bad feeling about where this is going," Gemma said.

"When it came out that my dad was Max's biological father, the church leaders and members immediately swept his actions under the rug. I could have chalked their forgiveness of Dad up to compassion and accepted it if . . ."

"If?"

"If they'd taken care of my mom and me after the scandal. We really needed them then."

"No one called or came by?"

"At first, a few of Mom's church friends did stop by. They suggested my mom needed to pray harder and have more faith in order to feel better. They made things worse because they were basically finding Mom deficient in a situation brought on by my dad's infidelity."

"That makes me ragey. Did you guys try to resume church services?"

"Yes. But we got the sense that our presence made everybody else uncomfortable, which made us uncomfortable. It was like they were afraid that if Dad showed up the same Sunday we were there, that might make Dad unhappy. And they didn't want to risk that. It was clear that they were okay with us disappearing and never coming back. So that's what we did. We disappeared from their congregation."

A few seconds went by. Jude was on the verge of saying Gemma's name to make sure she was still there when she spoke.

"So your church left you, a fourteen-year-old boy, to take care of your mom?" Anger was clear in her tone.

"To be fair, my mom's situation was messy back then. She wasn't well mentally, and it was hard to know how to be there for her. My dad also left me to take care of her. So did her so-called friends who weren't from the church. My mom's parents and siblings were the only ones who stuck close."

"That is *not* how that should have gone down, Jude. When things get messy in someone's life, that's when the church community should step in, not away. Even if it is hard to know how to be there."

Privately, he agreed.

"I hate hearing that's what happened to you and your mom," she said. "I'm sorry."

No one had ever said sorry to him on behalf of the church. Gemma'd had nothing to do with it. She definitely didn't owe him a sorry, so he didn't understand why it meant so much to hear her say that. Maybe because she'd hit a nerve with this topic? He'd never made peace with the way their church had abandoned them.

"What's the state of your faith and your mom's faith nowadays?" she asked.

"After my mom's mental health improved, she joined a different church in Groomsport and has been going there for years. I still believe in God, but I haven't been a regular at any church since."

"Sadly, one of the biggest obstacles to Christianity is the way some Christians treat people. It shouldn't be that way, but it is. I get why it's almost impossible for people to separate God from the hurt the church caused them."

Her words impacted him like an arrow. They were true. He'd felt let down by the church and so he'd also felt let down by God. "This is an area where it doesn't make sense for McConnell and me to be the same."

During one of their first phone meetings, they'd agreed that he and Jude McConnell would overlap in as many areas as possible. He and his alias had to be different when it came to family, hometown, college, and career. But for the sake of simplicity and clarity, Jude and his alias would share the things they could share—hobbies, preferences, movie favorites, forms of exercise, and more.

"McConnell's parents were never divorced," he continued, "and were never the subject of a scandal. So McConnell wouldn't have experienced what I experienced with church members. Let's just say that McConnell went to church a lot as a kid but is busy and so doesn't go that often anymore."

"All right."

This talk was getting so personal that it was making him desperate to change the focus to her. "What's your faith life like?"

"My family also went to church a fair amount growing up. Unlike you, I wasn't the one who nagged the others to go. I was the one who nagged them not to go because I found it boring. The lessons from church only penetrated skin-deep."

"Ah."

"But then my own mom's life got messy. Really, our whole family's life got messy when my dad was arrested and Mom's health deserted her. Our church friends were incredible to us. They took turns at the hospital with Mom so I could go home and sleep. They fed us. They hosted my youngest brothers for weeks in their homes because Nicolas and Ronan were too young back then to stay home alone for extended periods."

Just because his experience with the church when he'd been going through a crisis had been bad, he'd never have wanted the same to be true for her. "I'm glad."

"I was more scared than I'd ever been in my life," she said. "Dad was gone and I thought that my mom might die. I begged and begged God to get my mom through the stroke. He did, of course. But an unexpected thing happened."

"Which was?"

"He got *me* through it, too. My prayers were all for her. Yet He graciously carried me. For years. He was and is my source of strength. We became pretty close, God and me." She paused for a moment. "Does the fact that I'm a Christian surprise you?"

"No." For all her outward energy and his outward calm, she was the one who had real peace at the core of her.

"I wish I'd been your mom's friend after her split from your dad," she stated. "If I had been, I would have stepped right into that mess and I would have helped you."

Gratitude and affection for her broke free in his chest. "I believe you would have."

Selfishly, though, he was glad she was not the age of his mom's friends. The world needed her just the age she was and just the way she was.

Two nights later, Jude knocked on the alley door at the rear of Perfumes by Gemma Clare for his lesson in perfume making. He hadn't seen Gemma in person since last Friday, when they'd met with Dixon and Shannon, which felt like an extended drought of time—

Gemma swung the door open and waved him in. Then indicated her mouth, calling attention to the fact that she was chewing something.

Waiting on her to finish chewing was a blessing because, as usual, he found it challenging to adjust to Gemma in the flesh. Even the air around her—which smelled like pineapple cake this evening—seemed to spark with vitality.

She made him feel the way he'd felt standing in the Uffizi Gallery in Florence looking at the Venus figure in Botticelli's painting *Primavera*. Intrigued. Spellbound. Willing to stay in place for hours, studying what was before him.

Gemma swallowed, scooped up an open box of chocolate truffles, and held the box out to him. "Would you like one?"

"I've already had my chocolate for the day."

"How about walking on the wild side and enjoying *two* servings of chocolate today?" She rustled the box.

There were a lot of things in Jude's life that he desired but resisted because they weren't good for him. Consuming too much alcohol, relying on painkillers to numb anxiety, bingeing TV, sitting around instead of exercising, Gemma herself.

Something about her made him want to rebel against his own self-control. If he was going to be self-destructive and rebel against his own self-control while under the influence of Gemma, chocolate was by far the least harmful mistake he could make. He took a truffle.

"Bravo, Jude!"

"And here you thought I was a prude," he said wryly.

She laughed.

He loved the sound of her laugh even more than he loved truffles.

He took a bite and tasted silky dark chocolate flavored with slivers of nuts and coffee beans.

"Let's head up to my studio on the second floor." She

popped another truffle in her mouth before leaving the box behind and ascending the stairs. Halfway up, she paused.

He came to a stop a few steps below.

More chewing as she looked at him. Beneath the freckles, her skin was like white porcelain. She wore a navy sweater, wide jeans, and red-orange sneakers that matched the color of her hair. Her side ponytail somehow looked fashionable instead of untidy. She swallowed. "I keep forgetting to mention this on the phone, but thank you very much for asking your friend at the FBI about my grandmother's coded message."

"You're welcome. Was Professor Rusk able to help you?"

"He was. Gracie's code said *Box in northwest corner under dormer*. The box in the attic under that dormer held letters between her and my great-grandfather and clothes from their wedding day. It made her happy to see those things again."

"Good."

She braced a hand on the banister. "I often get asked for perfume recommendations, as well as free samples of perfume, body cream, and bubble bath. Do you often get hit up the way I hit you up? For FBI perks?"

"FBI perks?"

"Yeah like, *Hey, can you help me out by running some fingerprints?*" She did an impression of a male mafia voice. "Or, *Hey, can you wiretap my cheating girlfriend's phone?*"

"I don't get hit up often for FBI perks, but my brother was recently in a situation where my connections did come in handy."

"Really? Which brother? Jeremiah the racecar driver? Or Max the business tycoon?"

During their conversations, Gemma had made it clear that she'd put in time researching his family. Which left him both pleased and uncomfortable. "Jeremiah."

"Oh? How did you assist?"

"He was looking into the circumstances of his wife's death, and I knew someone who could help."

"That's so vague, Jude! What were the circumstances of his wife's death? What did you discover?"

"In the interest of his privacy, I can't go into it."

"You!" She shook her fist. "So circumspect!"

"I just ate a second helping of chocolate."

"Too circumspect," she insisted.

His lips twitched with amusement. "You should thank me for that—"

"I'm annoyed with you for that! I want all the juicy details!"

"—because if someone asks me for juicy details about you," he said, "you can be sure I'll protect your privacy."

"You helped your brother, and you helped me, and you like doing so, I can tell."

He shrugged.

"Understated and humble you are," she declared.

"Is there a reason why you're now speaking like Yoda?"

"Nope. No particular reason." She continued up the stairs and made her way through the door there. "This is my inner sanctum. I bring very few people here."

"Thank you for bringing me."

Gemma's studio was about twenty-by-twenty feet with walls of brick and flooring of scuffed wood. A painting of the sky at dusk covered the ceiling with pinks and oranges, soft grays, gold, clouds. She'd added a few rhinestones to it that sparkled like stars.

Only one wall, the one overlooking the alley, had a window. That window was huge, however, with black lines dividing the glass into rectangular panes. All the commercial structures on this historic street were at least two stories high. But on the far side of the alley, a neighborhood of old homes sprawled. He could make out roof lines, trees, smoke rising from chimneys. "Would you mind closing the blinds?"

"Oh! That's right." With a tug, she freed a bamboo roman shade that zipped down to cover the glass.

Her desk, in front of the window, reminded him of the type architects used. On both sides of it rolling carts held vials upon vials of liquid.

"I sometimes come up here with my laptop," she said, "when I need quiet to work on the business side of running the shop. But most of the time I do that type of work downstairs so I can keep this as a creative zone."

"Where does the manufacturing happen?"

"When I started making perfume and selling it online, back in high school, our family's kitchen was my manufacturing hub. My mom and dad and brothers would all pitch in. That continued until around the time I opened the shop. The business had grown enough by then that I contracted with a company in Bangor. They handle my manufacturing and shipping."

"I see."

"FYI, Cedric and Chaz both work for large companies who don't contract out manufacturing like I do. Their companies have their own plants."

Jude leaned over the notepad on her desk. Scribbled words covered the top page.

"Every fragrance of mine," she said, "begins with a bolt of inspiration. It goes from my imagination to this notepad where I brainstorm and mix and match ideas."

"Where does the bolt of inspiration come from?"

"Both from memory and the present. I've always had a very sensitive nose. My great-grandfather, Paul Bettencourt, was raised with the Rhapsodie legacy. Centuries of perfumers had come before him, and he'd been trained in perfume since birth.

He saw potential in me when I was young and began to pass his training on to me." She pushed her hands into her pockets. "All of us associate our experiences and the emotions of those experiences with smells. Some of those experience-emotion-smell combinations are worthy of becoming perfume."

"You take experiences and emotions and boil them down into a physical bottle of perfume?" He was a consumer of creative work. He purchased and greatly admired art, books, and music. But he couldn't imagine having the ability to make any of those things himself.

"I try to. Once I flesh out my thoughts on the notepad, I begin working with these vials. They contain fragrance notes." She reached for one of the carts. "Scents are extracted from flowers and all kinds of other materials."

"Like what other materials?"

"Balsam. Spice. Grass. Fruit. To name a few." She unscrewed a vial and held it to his face.

"Vanilla."

"Yes. One of the most recognizable scents. For many people, this scent evokes a comforting emotion. It's cozy. It makes us feel secure—maybe because when we were growing up our house was filled with this scent when, for example, our mom was baking cookies." Deftly, she returned the vial to the cart and unscrewed another for him to smell.

"Citrus?" he guessed.

"Tangerine, to be specific. Smelling citrus is like smelling sunshine. It's uplifting. One more." The citrus returned to its spot, and she held another out to him.

He sniffed. "I'm not sure what that is."

"Pink pepper. It's spicy and it tends to invigorate us and make us want to embrace adventure."

"Huh." Pink pepper was just a smell. It did not make him want to embrace adventure.

Gemma pushed up her sleeves. "Big cosmetic brands often take their inspiration for a new perfume to one of the great perfume houses in France. They meet with an evaluator who helps them articulate and refine their ideas. Then the evaluator communicates with a perfumer, also called a nose. The nose works with all these aromas"—she indicated the carts—"and many, many more in a lab. He or she experiments and gradually cultivates the fragrance. It's an art form. The great noses are brilliant because they have a gift for combining separate notes into the perfect blend. When that happens, we say that an *accord* is reached. The separate notes become one, masterful whole."

He hoped this lesson went on for days because he could happily watch her for that long.

"There's no client or evaluator here," she said. "There's just me, the perfumer, following my own imagination and taste." She grabbed strips of paper from her desk and led him to a glass shelving unit that displayed all of her perfumes. "You smelled individual scent notes just now. Here's a finished fragrance." She sprayed perfume onto a strip of paper, fanned the paper in the air for a few seconds, and held it up to him.

He breathed it in.

"This is Relaxation and Berry, the fragrance you were smelling the day I leapt to the conclusion that you were about to perish on my shop floor from a severe allergic reaction."

"It's nice to smell it without being attacked."

"You said that *attacked* was too strong a word, that I'd just cleaned your neck really, really well."

"I said that to be polite, seeing as how we'd just met. You definitely attacked me."

She grinned. "I definitely did." She snapped the cap back on Relaxation and Berry. "The inspiration for this one was bath time when I was little. My mom would stick me in the tub with bubbles. When I got out, she'd wrap me in a fresh towel. For me, this one smells of clean skin and belonging."

"I recognize your inspiration in the scent. But this is a very sophisticated, mature take on bath time."

She looked at him the way an elementary school teacher would look at her star student. "That was my intent. Be aware that what you're smelling here"—she held up the paper—"is the perfume's top note. It's deceiving to judge a perfume based on its top note only. I advise all my customers to test a perfume by applying it, then living with it for hours. If they do that, they'll be better able to decide if the perfume is perfect for them. Too often people enter a perfume shop and buy based on the top note alone. The top note is like the outer petals of a rose. Fleeting. The middle note and base notes are the inner petals. A person is going to spend most of their time with those latter notes, so it's best if they make sure they love how the middle and base notes mix with their body."

She took a new bottle off the shelf. "My brothers were almost always nearby when I was a kid. But once a month or so, I'd have my mother, grandmother, and great-grandmother to myself when we'd have high tea together. A few times a year we'd splurge and have high tea at a restaurant. The rest of the time, we'd gather at one of the homes for tea and sandwiches and scones. I loved those tea parties and created this perfume with that inspiration." She sprayed a fresh strip of paper. "It's called Luxury and Cream and has notes of tea and strawberry. My challenge was to find aromas that would also communicate the *feeling* of high tea. Fancy. Crisp like a linen napkin. A ritual inherited from nobility."

He took the paper from her and inhaled. "I'm impressed." He inhaled again. "Is there a specific way that experts smell perfume? A series of steps?"

"When we go to a symphony, we take in the details of it

with our sense of hearing while letting our thoughts and emotions expand. Perfume is a symphony, too. One that we take in with our sense of smell. Like with music, we experience it more fully if we let our thoughts and emotions expand."

"I don't know how to do that."

"Take your time with a perfume. Draw in several breaths and allow yourself to focus on it. I often decrease my other senses by closing my eyes or silencing sounds." Her eyelids drifted shut and she demonstrated by breathing the fragrance, then staying very still.

He froze, staring down at her. She wasn't looking back so he was free to study the way her eyelashes rested against the top of her cheekbones. The delicate shape of her lips. The arch of her brows.

His mouth went completely dry.

Time stalled. He was distantly aware of the painted sky above them and the fragrance of her perfumes all around.

Why hadn't he met her some other way? Any other way? At any other time? As it was, she had a boyfriend. And even if she didn't, he couldn't act on his feelings for her because of the FBI. The operation that bound them together was also the thing that cast him as the rule-following professional. He wished it wasn't so. He didn't want to play this role with her.

Her eyes snapped open, and time lurched back into motion.

She reached for another strip of paper and another bottle of perfume as if everything was normal, as if she hadn't just devastated him. "This is my newest fragrance. It's inspired by Maine, but I purposely avoided the most obvious notes of ocean and evergreen. With this one I was trying to communicate big dramatic skies and rugged coastline. Nature and freedom and wild blueberries and home."

Jude took his time with it, as she'd instructed. "You

captured Maine's soul. Gemma, you're as brilliant at this as any of the great noses you mentioned earlier."

Her face softened. "That's a lovely compliment. Thank you. But no. In all humility, I'm not at the level of the great noses. I'd like to be one day." She grasped another bottle. "This one's my best seller. I was twenty and wildly infatuated with a boy when the inspiration for this one came to me. It took me years to nail the blend."

"Years?"

"Yes. My work on this far outlasted my crush on the boy. It's called Hope and Spice and its fragrance evokes attraction. It has notes of musky amber, incense, and guaiac wood. When I finally brought it to market, women went crazy for it. Over and over they've told me that their boyfriends and husbands find it addictive and irresistible. A few of them jokingly call it a love potion."

"But your goal with this wasn't to attract men?"

"No. I'm all about creating scents that are true to me, that I love. And I'm all about helping my customers find the one that they love. If the scent they pick ends up enslaving men, that's just a side effect." She sprayed and held up the paper.

The scent hit his nose. Deep and delicious. He ran a hand through his hair, then cupped the back of his neck. The magnetism he felt toward Gemma hovered close to the surface when he was near her, but now he felt overwhelmed by its rushing, heady power. Blood pounded against his temples.

"Does it smell like infatuation to you?" she asked, a knowing glint in her gray eyes.

"Yes," he said simply, voice hoarse.

She returned the bottle to its shelf. "As you can see, I have several other fragrances. But that's enough for you to get the gist. I'll email you a list of the perfumers and brands responsible for the most famous scents of the last fifteen years. It would do you good to read up on them and also on the scientific process of extracting scents and fusing them with an alcohol base. That involves molecules and compounds and the like."

He felt drunk.

"Also, I highly recommend you gain some firsthand experience with Rhapsodie. You should be very familiar with the scent and history of the perfume your fictional buyer is purchasing. Do you know anyone who owns a bottle?"

"My mother does." Research he could manage. What he couldn't manage was another sniff of Hope and Spice. "I should be going," he said abruptly, taking several steps toward the stairs. "I don't want to infringe on your time any more than I already have."

"Oh. Um, okay."

"Shannon, Dixon, and I agree that you and I have prepared enough. We're ready for you to contact Cedric and express your boyfriend's interest in brokering a deal for Rhapsodie's secrets."

"Really?"

"Yes. Please work up a sample text message to Cedric tomorrow and forward it to me for approval before sending." He retreated down the stairs.

Her footsteps followed.

He opened the door to the alley, glancing back to give her a nod. "Good night."

"Good night."

Bemused, Gemma watched the door shut behind him. Her lips curved upward slowly, smug satisfaction burning within her like a pilot light.

Her perfume had profoundly impacted Jude Camden. For the first time, his astonishing control had fractured. She'd taken his big, fit, masculine body and that privileged upbringing and that incredible brain power honed by the best education America offered. And she'd turned it all to putty in her hands through the power of her fragrance.

Verbal instruction could only give him the tiniest peek behind the curtain of perfume making. But absorbing a perfume into your lungs? Letting it affect you emotionally? That was a far, far better lesson. In her studio just now she'd paired the right person with the right fragrance. Hope and Spice had made him *feel*, and perfume's ability to make people feel was precisely the thing that drove her passion for her profession.

She went into motion, doing what she mentally referred to as "putting the shop to bed" for the night.

Each of her fragrances was somebody's favorite. You never could predict for sure which one was going to stir a person's soul. But in this case, her money had been on Hope and Spice, which was why she'd saved it for last. When men smelled her artistic interpretation of attraction in liquid form, they tended to like it. And even mighty Jude was not immune.

Jude Camden. So ironed and correct and polished. It was almost impossible to shake him, but it turned out that she liked him shaken. Even though he was FBI and off-limits, she liked him in general lately.

From now on, she knew exactly which fragrance she'd wear every single time she was around him.

The following morning Gemma followed through on Jude's request that she formulate a text to Cedric.

It was a Saturday and despite that they'd only communicated on weekdays up until now, his reply came in quickly.

She opened a message to Cedric, typed the approved text to him, then paused before sending. She eyed the half-eaten poppyseed muffin and coffee on her kitchen island.

This text might set her cousin's demise in motion. It definitely would, at the very least, set the operation with Jude in motion.

Cedric deserved incarceration, for more reasons than his willingness to betray Rhapsodie for money. It wasn't that she regretted the choices that had led her here. She was still clear on her reasons and she stood behind them. It was just . . . The act of sending this text had weight. She couldn't do this and expect zero consequences. With this text she'd push over the first domino in a line of dominos that would take Cedric, Jude, and herself who-knows-where.

She bent her head and prayed, asking God to use this operation for good, for the cause of justice. When she finished, she checked and double-checked her text to ensure she was sending it to the right person and that she'd phrased it exactly the way Jude had approved. Then, heart pounding, she sent it. "Lord God, have mercy," she whispered.

She let her blood pressure and breath steady, then texted one word to Jude.

GEMMA

Sent

JUDE
Kindly contact me as soon as you hear back.

An hour later, Gemma received a reply from Cedric.

CEDRIC
Very good! I'll think on it.

She took a screenshot and sent that to Jude.

JUDE
Great. Don't press it. Acknowledge Cedric's text as quickly as you normally would in the way you normally would, with a brief text in return, or an emoji, reaction, etc.

She held her finger over Cedric's text and selected the thumbs-up reaction.

The dominos had begun to fall.

Chapter Ten

On Sunday, Fiona's doorbell rang fifteen minutes before Jude had told her he'd be coming by. Fortunately, this did not catch her unawares. She tended to run a hair behind schedule because excellence in preparation required time. But Jude was always, *always*, at least fifteen minutes early, God love him. Thus, she planned on him being twenty minutes early so that if she was running five minutes behind, their timelines would align perfectly, as they had today.

She opened her door and was assailed with the same emotion she typically experienced upon coming face-to-face with one of her sons. Bottomless pride. She might not be perfect, but she had done some things right in the mothering department because she'd raised two of the best and most accomplished men.

She hugged him. The surprise she felt at how big and tall her boys had grown was evergreen. They'd been this size for around twenty years now and she'd yet to rectify in her mind their current strong builds with her memories of them when they were little. How could *her* Jude—the quiet, wary towhead who'd known his entire alphabet at the age of sixteen months—be this large person?

"Hi, Mom."

"Hi." She patted his face. "So good to see you."

He was dressed as casually as she ever saw him, except for when he was on his way to the gym or the beach or wearing pajamas. His pale green crewneck sweater emphasized the color of his eyes. His jeans were faded, his leather lace-up shoes well-worn.

"If you're ready now to head to the country club for lunch," she said, "I'll just grab my things."

"Actually, there's something I wanted to do here first. Research. For a case."

"Oh?" He was notoriously close-lipped about his cases. Even after they'd been declassified it was more difficult to pry details out of him than to pry a Prada purse from a fashionista.

"I'm looking into the world of exclusive, high-end perfume. I know you own a few scents like that, and I think it would help me if I could smell those perfumes. And if you could tell me what you know about them."

"Certainly!" She loved it when people asked for her insights. She especially loved it when her sons did so.

She preceded him through the house. "I'll set up a smelling flight for you. Like a tasting flight at a winery, only for the nose." He followed her into her spa-like master bathroom. She directed him to sit on the upholstered pink stool.

His expression communicated that sitting there insulted his masculinity, but he went ahead and sat there anyway.

Fiona told him about the first perfume, supplying insider tidbits about its history and the names of the celebrities who'd worn it. She sprayed a pump on a tissue and handed it to him.

She'd expected him to toss the tissue right away. Instead, he spent silent time considering it.

"You're taking this seriously," she observed. "If you'd like, I can go get some coffee beans for you to sniff in between fragrances to cleanse your palate, so to speak."

"Sounds good."

She swept into the kitchen, then sailed back to her bathroom and handed him the container of her best arabica beans.

She spoke about each of the perfumes in turn, finally coming to the last one. "This is the most special of them all." Picking up the hand-blown glass bottle, she cradled it like a proud dog breeder showing off her prized puppy. "This is Rhapsodie. In my opinion, this is the most magnificent perfume ever created. It's also the most expensive of the perfumes I've lined up here and very difficult to purchase. They make a limited quantity of these each year, a quantity that's far, far below the demand. There's a wait list a mile long to purchase one. Even with my money and connections, it took me seven years to get a bottle."

Jude appeared appropriately respectful.

"This has been worn by countless famous people," she continued. "It was Marie Antoinette's favorite and is said to have been the favorite of every French queen and noblewoman of taste through the generations. In more recent eras, it was given by the French government as a gift to Audrey Hepburn and became her signature perfume."

"I see."

"There's no way I'm going to waste a spray of this on a tissue, but I will flagrantly spray it on my wrist." Jude asked so little of her that she'd never turn down a request of his that was in her power to grant. Plus, it had been quite some time since she'd smelled Rhapsodie herself.

She carefully applied the fragrance, making sure that if any droplets fell anywhere, they'd fall onto her clothing and not be wasted on the floor.

Rhapsodie contained complex florals, certainly. Grasses and fruit zest, maybe. But she couldn't distinguish any one thing. It was a study in contrasts. Lush and yet snappy. Bright but not light. Classic yet modern. It made her think of French couture and confidence.

She extended her arm to Jude and waited for his proclamation.

"I can see why it's so popular," he said.

"Yes. Its genius is instantly recognizable—"

A knock came from her front door.

"Who's here?" Jude asked.

"I don't know." An electronic gate at the road only permitted those who knew the code up Fiona's drive. She'd given her code to close friends and family only, so she never received knocks from Girl Scouts selling cookies (sadly) or door-to-door salesmen (not sadly). "Maybe Burke?" Burke dropped by unexpectedly more than her other friends ever had.

She made her way to the entry, Jude trailing. Warm gratification rushed through her when she saw through the door's inset window that it was indeed Burke.

For the second time in a half hour, she answered the knock of a handsome man.

"Hi," he said, smiling directly into her eyes.

"Hi. Jude's here."

"Yes." Burke turned his friendliness toward her son. The two men shook hands. "I saw your car. You doing okay?"

"Just fine, thank you."

"I don't want to intrude," Burke told Fiona. "I was at Java Junkie and saw that they had the gluten-free, sugar-free nut bar that you love."

"Ah!" she exclaimed. "These bars are almost as rare as living T-Rexes. They'll never tell me in advance when they're going to make them because they only make them on the chef's whim."

"Right. So when I saw them, I bought out the store." He raised a white paper sack. "Here you are."

"Thank you." She accepted the bag from him. Her male friend was now delivering gluten-free, sugar-free treats to her door, which made her think she was training him exceptionally well. "My taste buds and the circumference of my thighs thank you."

"You're welcome." He sniffed. "What's that smell?"

"The most fabulous fragrance in the world." She held out her wrist. "Rhapsodie."

His eyebrows rose high. "That smells amazing."

"I agree."

"Well. I'll be on my way."

"We're going to lunch in a minute," Jude said. "You're welcome to join us."

"No, no," Burke said. "Thank you, though. You two enjoy your time together."

He closed the door behind him.

Jude faced her. "What's going on with you and Burke?"

"Nothing. We're friends."

He frowned slightly. "How come you're friend-zoning him?"

"Because I don't want a boyfriend." She walked into the kitchen and started transferring the nut bars to a canister to keep them fresh.

"Maybe keep an open mind. If Burke was your boyfriend, having a boyfriend could be good."

"Are you advocating for Burke because you think your life will be easier if I have someone else in my life to bear the burden of my drama?"

"I'm advocating for Burke because I think a relationship with him would be nice for you."

"And nice for you if I have someone else in my life to bear the burden of my drama." She winked at him to remove any sting from her words. Her sons viewed her as high-maintenance, but she preferred to think of herself as a loving mother who had high standards. "You don't have to worry about me, you know. I'm doing just fine, aren't I?"

"Yes."

"I don't lean on you too much."

"No."

That hadn't been the case when he'd been in high school. He was now thirty-two years old. She was a mentally healthy business owner now. Yet she could not erase the damage that had been done. Jude's sense of duty toward her had been grooved into him as surely as stitches in fabric. "I'm sorry, Jude. That you had to take care of me after Dad left."

"It's okay," he said at once.

They'd had this exchange many times. On each occasion, Jude reassured her. Yet this topic always left her feeling heavier inside, not lighter.

◦ ◦

Monday, Gemma caught herself eyeing the clock as it neared the time when Jude used to call for their weeknight prepping sessions. He wouldn't be calling. He'd brought an end to the preliminary phase of their case when he'd given her the go-ahead to contact Cedric.

Gemma enjoyed her days best when they were full. And today had been brimming with activity, conversations, productivity, exercise, creativity, food, *life*. Yet knowing Jude wasn't going to call made all of that feel less full.

She could still communicate with him, though. It wasn't mandatory to sit around feeling the lack of something.

GEMMA

It's been more than two days since I texted Cedric to say my boyfriend was interested and eager to meet with him. Is it less likely with every passing day that Cedric will take the bait?

It gratified her to see alternating dots appear almost at once.

JUDE

Not necessarily. He said he wanted to think on it, which isn't surprising. He might think on it for several days. We'll bide our time.

GEMMA

Kay. What chocolate did you have today?

JUDE

That information is not relevant to our case.

GEMMA

It absolutely isn't. So . . . what chocolate did you have today?

JUDE

A chocolate chip croissant. One of the best foods on earth.

GEMMA

I'm guessing it wasn't greasy?

She giggled because she'd just used one of his word aversions.

JUDE

Gemma!

GEMMA

I'm sorry. I try not to use my knowledge of
your word aversions for evil.

JUDE

Try harder.

She was still giggling.

GEMMA

Good night.

JUDE

Good night.

Her phone pinged and she checked it eagerly. More from
Jude? No, from Chaz. He'd sent a glamour shot of himself
holding a hamburger bun.

CHAZ

What did the bread say to the baker?

GEMMA

I don't know. What?

CHAZ

You knead me.

She texted back cheerful words, even as a voice inside her
pointed out an uncomfortable truth. Jude was the one she'd
needed a connection with tonight. Jude was the one who'd
brought her genuine amusement just now.

Jude, who wasn't destined to be anything to her, *ever*, other
than her fake boyfriend.

⚬⚬

Two nights later, Cedric still hadn't contacted Gemma.

Though snuggled under a throw blanket on her sofa at home, a spot which should have mellowed Gemma's spirit, she was battling a restless, discontented mood.

Maybe Cedric hadn't responded to her text about her boyfriend because he'd thought better of his terrible plan to sell trade secrets. Maybe Cedric was so oily that no law enforcement agency would ever be able to grasp hold of him.

Yesterday Jude had texted to say that if much more time went by without contact from Cedric, he'd ask her to follow up with her cousin. But he was willing to wait longer before taking that step because he preferred to let Cedric initiate.

That businessy text was no match for the living connection of his voice over the phone. One of those things was a feast, one of them a saltine cracker.

Rain drummed against the roof and pattered the window-panes. Gracie's cardboard box of mementos waited next to the sofa and Gemma lifted the stack of letters off the top of the contents. Placing them in her lap, she gently untied the pale pink ribbon. She could do nothing about Jude and Cedric at present, but maybe there was something she *could* do for Gracie. Best to funnel her thoughts toward the letters.

Earlier today, Gracie had called and invited Gemma to come by and retrieve the box. At the end of the workday, Gemma had driven her Vespa to Marigold Manor and stayed to share a cup of tea with Gracie, whose demeanor had been uncharacteristically anxious.

"The letters between me and Paul are beautiful but distressing," Gracie said. "I don't know what to make of them."

"Why are they distressing?"

"It's clear from the letters that something went wrong between us." Her hand shook and she wrapped the fingers of her other hand around it. "I don't remember what went wrong. I can't imagine . . ."

Gemma had anticipated that the letters would answer Gracie's questions and bring solace. It was disorienting to learn that, in some ways, they'd had the opposite effect. "If something did go wrong, you have to rest in the fact that you and Great-Grandpa Paul overcame it and went on to a fantastic life together."

"Yes, but did I do something to cause him pain when he was a young man? I can hardly bear the thought that I did something to cause him pain."

"I'll read the letters," Gemma had told her, "and do everything I can to get to the bottom of this."

She thumbed through the first few and noticed two black-and-white photos tucked into the pile.

The first one showed Gracie and Paul with the Washington Monument in the background. They stood very close, their hands resting on one another's lower back. Both were dressed beautifully, as had been the norm in the forties. Gracie had on heels and hose, a pleated skirt, a tailored shirt. She'd caught the front of her hair back in a barrette, the rest she'd worn down and curled. Paul was dapper in a cable-knit sweater and trousers. They were both strikingly attractive, their faces youthful and smooth, their demeanor hopeful. Though Gemma had only known Gracie and Paul when they were late in life, she easily recognized the younger versions of the people she loved. She flipped the photo over. Gracie had written *October, 1943* on the back in faded blue ink. An intricate hand-drawn doodle in black ink formed a border around the date. Flowers and hearts connected by swirling leaves.

The second photo captured the two of them holding hands on a crowded train platform, a suitcase waiting near his feet. This must be their goodbye. Paul was looking at Gracie gravely.

She was looking toward the camera as if the photographer had just called her name. Her eyes appeared puffy and, beneath her brave smile, Gemma saw grief. The writing on the back of this photo read *June, 1944.*

Carefully, she unfolded the earliest and top-most letter, written that same month from Paul to Gracie. His words made clear that they'd fallen in love during the time they'd spent living in Washington, D.C.

Gemma now believed that Gracie had been working there as a Code Girl. The letter didn't mention that, though, and Gemma had to wonder if even Paul had been privy to her true purpose there. Likely not, if the Code Girls had taken their vow of silence as seriously as Professor Rusk claimed.

In the first letter, Paul noted that their nine months together had been precious to him, despite the terror and sorrow of the war raging across the globe. He'd been recalled to France after France's liberation from the Nazis, while Gracie had remained behind to fulfill her responsibilities in D.C.

> *I miss you, Gracie. You're with me when I wake in the morning. You're the one who motivates my days. My work, my errands, my eating, my sleeping. I get through them all because of the memory and promise of you. The thought of seeing you again as soon as all of this comes to a close is the fuel that gives me strength to wait until you're in my arms again. I love you with all of my heart.*

Like so many young couples of that era, her great-grandparents had been deeply in love and separated by war.

In the next five letters, written both by Gracie and Paul, they reported details of their lives and expressed their love and their joy in receiving letters from the other. The five letters spanned a two-month timeframe. Careful reading made it obvious that more letters had been written by the couple during those two months. Gemma concluded that these were the only five from that period that had survived eight decades.

After the first two months of their separation, a strange thing began to happen with their letters. For some reason, Paul was not receiving Gracie's letters. And Gracie was not receiving Paul's letters. Instead of responding to each other's questions, they were both longing to see a letter from the other, both imploring the other one to write.

Gemma grabbed her phone and googled information on mail between America and Europe in the latter part of World War Two.

Apparently, US intelligence offices intercepted incoming or outgoing mail that they thought might contain sensitive information. How much more vigilant would they have been with the mail of an American Code Girl?

She googled the end date of the World War Two conflict. For America, it ended in the Pacific, September 2, 1945.

Gracie would still have been hard at work codebreaking when her letters with Paul had been interrupted in the fall of 1944. Perhaps her correspondence had come under suspicion for some reason and intelligence offices had held her incoming and outgoing mail? The fact that these letters existed among Gracie's keepsakes supported that theory because some of the letters—*these* letters—had been given to their rightful owner eventually.

As fall of 1944 turned into winter of 1944, Gracie and Paul wrote more worry and desperation into their letters. They were each yearning for information from the other, yet each seemed to be conducting a one-way conversation.

Gracie, do you still believe in me? Do you trust my love and fidelity? I'd give my life for you. I love you so. Letter from Paul dated November of 1944.

Paul, I'm so very, very worried that you've moved on from me. Do you know how often I write? Do you hear from me? It seems most likely that you do.

I wholeheartedly trusted in our love, in us. How long should I wait before I conclude that you returned to Europe and came to your senses and wondered why you'd gotten so carried away with an American girl? Did you decide that it's too difficult to maintain a relationship with someone separated from you by culture and miles and ocean? Did you deem me not worth the effort? Did you meet someone else who stole your heart?

As you see, I can imagine your reasons but that doesn't help me accept the truth. It doesn't stop the pain and grief and anguish. Letter from Gracie, December 1944.

Please write to me, Gracie. I beg you. I am ruined. Alone. Terrified that I've lost you. If your devotion has moved on from me, write to me and tell me so because, as it stands now, I fear that something awful has happened to you. I can go on living if I know, at least, that you are well and whole. Letter from Paul, December 1944.

No wonder Gracie had been distressed by these letters when Gemma had seen her earlier today. A stone had gained weight in the center of Gemma's own stomach as she'd read. Their despair and heartbreak were jagged to experience, even all these years later, even knowing they had found their way to a happy ending.

At the time they'd written these letters, these two twenty-somethings hadn't known the future and Gemma could feel their stress lifting off the ink and creating an electrical presence in the room—buzzing and upsetting.

The last nine months of letters, from January to early September of 1945, had been written only by Paul. None by Gracie.

Had Gracie given up on him?

Reaching into the box, Gemma unearthed their marriage certificate. They'd married in Caribou, Maine, in January of 1945.

Gemma stilled. January 1945. How was that possible?

Paul had still been in France at that time, writing these tormented letters. Gracie would still have been in D.C. at her Code Girl post.

"*Something went wrong between us*," Gracie had said to Gemma today. She'd been absolutely right. Something had gone dreadfully wrong between Gracie and Paul during the final year of America's involvement in the war.

But what?

And how, exactly, was Gemma to dig up the truth?

Two days later, Gemma received a text from Cedric.

Her body jerked at the sight of it as if she'd stuck tweezers into an electrical outlet.

CEDRIC

Can your boyfriend join us in Bangor next
weekend? If so, Vincent and I will take the jet
and meet up with you then.

His text had arrived in the middle of her workday morning. She was sitting at the desk in her second-story studio, experimenting with notes of Casablanca lily and pomegranate.

For a couple of minutes, she did nothing but absorb the magnitude of his message and what it might mean.

Jude had been waiting, in hopes that Cedric would initiate, and that strategy had paid off.

It was Friday and Cedric wanted to meet next weekend. A week from now.

She set aside her fragrance-testing blotter paper and teat-pipettes. Her vision rested on the familiar view of rooftops and treetops as she dialed Jude. Today's soft sky looked like a water-color in shades of gray.

"Jude Camden speaking," he said even though he knew who was calling him and even though she knew who she was calling.

"Cedric just reached out through a text." She read Cedric's message aloud to him.

"Very good," he said in a matter-of-fact tone. "Please wait an hour before replying to make it feel believable that you've had time to call me where I work in New York, and I've had time to confirm that I'll be able to travel to Bangor. You can tell Cedric next weekend works, but that you do have some plans on your calendar. It will strike him as suspicious if you act as if your entire schedule is clear for him. *Do* you have some existing plans?"

"I do."

"What are they?"

"Kickboxing class Saturday at ten, then a baby shower for a

friend. Sunday night my brother's getting an award and we're going out after for a family dinner."

"Okay, go ahead and communicate your schedule to him. If it turns out he's only available when you're busy, tell him you'll see if you can reschedule your plans since the chance to see him is such a rare one. Then let more time pass, then tell him you were able to make it work."

"Got it."

"Please show the usual amount of excitement regarding this chance to see him again. No more. No less."

"Okay." Her cousin Cedric was a criminal and now here she was, in the thick of an honest-to-goodness FBI operation. *An. FBI. Operation.*

"Gemma?" Jude's voice was smooth and masculine. The sound of her name on his lips slid into the center of her, where it formed heated swirls. She'd missed that voice.

"Yes?"

"You've got this."

He sounded so certain that she believed him. "I've got this. I'll text him back and let you know what he says." They disconnected.

She followed Jude's recommendations to the letter by waiting, then sending Cedric a text saying she was looking forward to seeing him, telling him that her boyfriend could join them, and listing her schedule for next weekend.

CEDRIC

How about Friday? Can you two join Vincent and me for dinner then? What is your boyfriend's full name, by the way?

Cedric was likely asking for her boyfriend's name so that he could have him thoroughly checked out before making the effort to travel across the Atlantic. *Here's hoping Jude's alias is airtight.*

GEMMA

> Sure! Friday's good. His name is Jude McConnell. Now that I've told you that, you'll have to assure me that you won't speak his name to anyone in the family. If you do, word will spread like wildfire, and I'll never hear the end of it.

CEDRIC

> Your secret is safe with me.

But, obviously, Rhapsodie's secret was not.

CEDRIC

> Let's eat at 5 your time because that'll be 10 for us. What restaurant?

She took a screenshot of their text message exchange so far, texted it to Jude, then dialed him. When he picked up, she asked, "Which restaurant should I choose?"

"A restaurant in Bangor where we'll be unlikely to see people we know."

"Cedric likes fancy food. He doesn't appreciate budget-friendly restaurants."

"He'd probably like Artisanal. Have you been there?"

"Nope."

"It's good and the location is conducive to having multiple agents on site."

"I'll pitch that one." She hung up.

GEMMA

> How about Artisanal? The food's delicious!

His reply was slow in coming. She envisioned him

checking Artisanal's ranking and viewing photos to see if it was up to his standards. Jude had picked it, so she had no doubt it would be up to Cedric's standards.

CEDRIC

Sounds good. See you then.

She took another screenshot of the last few texts and sent it to Jude.

JUDE

Well done, Gemma.

Why did a simple "well done" from Jude feel like a trophy she wanted to set on a shelf to dust and admire?

GEMMA

What should we do over the coming days to prepare for the dinner?

JUDE

In my eyes, we're already prepared. If you want, we can talk Thursday night to review.

GEMMA

Yes, definitely want to talk Thursday.

JUDE

Okay.

On a shaky huff, she sat back in her chair, then raised both hands in front of her.

They were quivering.

Monday morning, Gemma swung by the house she'd grown up in.

Her red-headed brother Hugo, now twenty-six, lived in an apartment of his own. But her youngest red-headed siblings, Nicolas and Ronan, ages twenty-three and twenty, still lived at home. Every morning followed the same pattern with those two. They'd hit snooze on their alarm clocks until the last possible second. Then they'd rush to scarf down breakfast, rush to get ready, then rush out the door a few minutes behind schedule.

She found them in the "scarf down breakfast" phase of their morning.

"Gemma! Can you make me pancakes?" Ronan asked as soon as he caught sight of her.

"No, indeed. Shockingly, I didn't swing by to cook for you two people."

"My eggs," Nicolas said, holding out a spoonula to her. "Can you take over with these real quick while I get some orange juice?"

"Also no. Good morning, though."

"Gemma!"

"Is Mom up?"

"No."

Gemma had both expected and hoped to hear that her mom was not yet awake. Since the stroke, she'd needed more sleep than before. Her tendency to rise late suited Gemma's purpose today since she'd come on a clandestine mission.

She sailed past the kitchen mayhem into the messy den/office space of their home. Starting seven years ago, after Mom's hospitalization, she'd spent a great deal of time sitting at the desk in this room, attempting to keep her family afloat. To this day, she acted as a buffer between her mom and bill collectors whenever she could. That task resembled nothing so much as running to one fire to douse it with a bucket of water only to spot another fire burning.

In the right bottom desk drawer, she found the file she sought. She flicked through it until she came to the item she was after—her parents' marriage certificate. She laid it on the desk, then pulled out Gracie and Paul's marriage certificate and arranged them side by side.

Gracie and Paul's certificate had no seal and was a fill-in-the-blank-style document. It had printed sections, but all the personalizing details had been added by hand.

Were these certificates different because one was much older? Because they'd originated in separate counties? Or, as Gemma feared, because Gracie and Paul's was a fake?

Her sense of unease regarding Gracie and Paul's certificate deepened. She wasn't ready to foist her worry on her relatives, though. Her mom was weak, Grandma Colette was volatile, and Gracie was one hundred and two. She'd very much like to cushion this conversation with more facts. Hopefully kinder facts. In order to do that, Gemma needed to uncover additional details.

But how? What was her next step?

Chapter Eleven

The rubber was about to meet the road.

The night she and Jude had been prepping for had arrived. In no time, they'd sit down for dinner with Cedric and Vincent. And when they did, they'd need to convince the two Frenchmen that their romance was real. Anxiety buzzed in Gemma's stomach as she steered her Vespa toward the strip mall parking lot Jude had chosen as their meeting spot.

She'd told Jude once that she had the ability to study a paper map, then get to her destination without consulting directions along the way. It was a challenge she enjoyed, a skill she took pride in. Before setting off from Bayview to Bangor just now, she'd studied her map extra-hard, not wanting to get lost. She could just imagine herself saying, *Sorry that I'm late to your very important case, Jude. I looked at my paper map but forgot the route halfway here and ended up in New Hampshire.*

Jude would have a conniption and she was looking forward to seeing him in person too much to ruin it by giving him a conniption. Two long—very long—weeks had passed since they'd been face-to-face during their perfume-making lesson.

The strip mall should be just up here on the left and . . . yes, it came into view exactly when expected. Navigation was always easier when it was light out, like it was now on this mild, sunny day in late March.

After turning into the lot, she spotted Jude exiting a sleek silver Mercedes sedan. He stood, watching in stillness as she whizzed closer. Despite the pressure riding on the coming dinner, seeing him again sent simple happiness cutting through the static.

If a poet and a male model were to merge into one human being, that human would look like Jude Camden. He was as contemplative as he was beautiful to look at. Modest. Reliable. *Good.*

She came to a stop in the parking spot next to his, stepped off the Vespa, and removed her helmet. Her hair cascaded free. "You listened to what I said the night I listed the clothing that would help you dress looser."

"I listen to everything you say, Gemma."

"You do? I don't even listen to a quarter of the things I say."

He gave a subdued smile. "Since I'm going to be different from your past boyfriends in temperament, I figured a few outward adjustments to make me look more like them wouldn't hurt." Along with a pair of great-fitting dark gray jeans and his pea coat, he had on retro-style green and white Adidas shoes.

"Statement sneakers," she noted.

"Yeah."

"A ring."

"I didn't have one, so I purchased this." He held up his hand, displaying a cylindrical platinum band.

"A faded jean shirt, open down the front, rolled up at the sleeves, and a white T-shirt underneath!"

"That suggestion of yours was oddly specific, but check."

She beamed, pleased all out of proportion that he'd taken a few of her recommendations to heart.

His expression was circumspect, but intensity lit his eyes. She had the sense that he was cataloging every aspect of her.

She cleared her throat. "Can—can you pop your trunk, please?"

He did and she stashed her helmet there.

"Is this car new?" she asked.

"Two years old."

"Yours?"

"It's a Bureau car, confiscated in a bust."

"And if Vincent sees the license plate and runs it?"

"Jude McConnell will come up as the owner."

"If Vincent gets a look at your credit card or wallet tonight?"

"Every item in my wallet, including my credit cards, belongs to Jude McConnell." He held the passenger door open for her, then went around and slid into the driver's seat. "It's not enough to substantiate an identity only on the internet through search engine results, LinkedIn profiles, and so on. It's still important in this day and age to get every physical detail right." He was a perfectionist.

Everything's going to be all right, she told herself. *She* was going to be all right because this was Jude's operation, and he could be trusted. He'd look out for her, and he'd take care of business.

Gemma was wearing her Hope and Spice perfume and Jude had to wonder if she was messing with him on purpose. Had she comprehended his reaction to this perfume and decided to use it against him?

If so, why? To make him crazy for the fun of it?

Maybe.

Gemma Clare was more than a little defiant. She drove around Maine on a Vespa, after all, the least safe, least conventional form of transportation he could imagine.

He was finding it hard to think.

Her smile. Her curves in that black coat, blue sweater dress, and tall boots. Her trademark vitality. On top of all that, she smelled ridiculously good.

Every fiber of him wanted to swerve this car to a curb and pull her into a private space and draw her body against his. He wanted to feel the texture of her dress beneath his fingers. He wanted to run his hands into her hair. Then taste her lips and breathe her in—

This line of thought was extremely unprofessional. A lot was riding on Operation Scent-sible and from now until they parted from Cedric and Vincent, he needed his brain to be *very* sharp.

Ten more minutes. He had to endure ten more minutes shut inside the car with her before they reached the restaurant.

They'd talked on the phone for an hour last night and he was as confident as he could be that Gemma was ready. Even so, to get their minds—*his mind*—focused, he started quizzing her on the backstory of their supposed romance. She answered every question with ease, then quizzed him in return. He breezed through the answers.

"Cedric is not a particularly observant man," she said, ending the game. "It's his henchman-slash-bodyguard-slash-friend-slash-assistant Vincent who's as observant as they come. He misses nothing and he's the one we'll have to convince."

"We'll convince Vincent."

"Are you wearing a wire?"

"No." Technically true since no one had worn an actual microphone wire for decades. He was recording, though, thanks to a microscopic device in what looked like a car key fob. "We're almost there. How are you feeling?"

"Earlier I was nervous, but now I'm fine."

"Yeah?"

"No need to worry about me. I typically do very well under pressure."

There were numerous things he wanted to say to her in these final seconds but he kept them all back. Gemma seemed to be in the right headspace. He refused to risk saying more and potentially throwing her off her game.

He brought the Mercedes to a stop in the parking lot behind the restaurant and killed the engine, leaving them in dense silence. "When we step out of this car, we're a couple."

"Right. And you're not going to act all ruffled and stiff about it."

He glanced across at her. "I'm going to act only as ruffled and stiff as I do with my actual girlfriends."

"You told me at our first meeting that you do not have an actual girlfriend at present. Has that changed?"

"No."

"Good. This is complicated enough as it is. Selfishly I'm glad that I'm queen of your heart."

"Jude Camden's heart is not involved." At least, he wished to heaven and back that it wasn't.

"Right but *Jude McConnell's* heart is enraptured with me—"

"Enraptured is overstating it—"

"I'm queen of Jude McConnell's heart," she said firmly.

He checked his watch. "Time to go." He gave her an expression like, *You sure you're good?*

Gemma looked at him dead-on. "I'm good, boyfriend of mine."

He exited the car.

She did the same.

Before they'd gone two steps, she interlaced her fingers with his.

It rocked him—the intimacy of holding hands with her. Her fingers were delicate and confident. She looked one hundred percent comfortable with herself, just as she always did, just as she should for this assignment.

It was only when he opened the restaurant's door that she broke the contact of their hands to precede him inside.

A hostess showed them to their reserved table. One quick scan as they walked informed Jude that Cedric and Vincent had not yet arrived.

They settled at their four-top, which had a small bouquet of spring flowers in the center and linen napkins. The whole place was decorated in tones of beige. Expensive fixtures gave off warm, flattering light. Almost every table was already full at this hour, yet the acoustics and spacing were such that the conversations of other diners were muted—festive but not deafening.

Gemma moved to slip off her coat.

He reached out to help. "Would you like me to hang this up for you?" He'd left his coat on the rack by the entrance.

"Thanks, but no. I'll keep this draped behind me in case I get cold, which I'm likely to do on and off during the meal."

"Shame this restaurant doesn't hand out throw blankets."

"You've noticed my affinity for throw blankets?"

"Impossible not to notice. You leave a trail of them like breadcrumbs everywhere you go."

Dimples dug into her cheeks. "It's not terrible to have a boyfriend who notices things about me." Already, she was playing the role of girlfriend convincingly. She took a deep breath. "I love how it smells in here. What do you smell?"

He thought about it. "Maybe beef cooking?" That seemed more obvious and also safer than saying, *your perfume.*

"Yes. I also smell figs and brown sugar and butter and rosemary. Very promising smells."

They'd arrived five minutes prior to their reservation time. Not so early that it would seem strange to Cedric. But early enough to give them time to pretend to study the menu, even though they'd already accessed it online and decided which dishes they'd order. When Cedric got here, they'd be able to give him their full attention.

By 5:10 Cedric still hadn't showed.

Gemma had warned Jude that her cousin tended to run late, on what he jokingly called "Cedric time."

Gemma was talking about how much she enjoyed it staying light later at this time of the year because winter sometimes gave her a case of the seasonal blues. And he was admiring her freckles and how her gray irises were darker around the rims—

Her words suddenly broke off and she raised her hand to wave. "Here he is!" Gemma stood and approached her cousin with open arms.

Jude rose, giving Gemma and Cedric space as they did that triple-air-kiss thing that French people did. They followed that up with a hug.

Parting from Cedric, Gemma addressed Cedric's friend. "Vincent, welcome back to America." She and Vincent went through the three kisses but not the hug.

Gemma stepped back. "I'd like to introduce my boyfriend, Jude."

Jude shook hands with both men.

Cedric smiled affectionately at Gemma. "C'est bon de te revoir, cousin." *It's good to see you again, cousin,* Jude translated in his head.

"C'est bon de te voir aussi," Gemma replied smoothly.

"Vous êtes ravissante."

You look lovely, Cedric had said.

"Merci."

Cedric's attention shifted to Jude. "Do you speak French?"

"Only a little." Gemma had already told him that she and her cousin spoke almost entirely in English since the mediocre French she'd picked up through her high school classes didn't serve her as well as did Cedric's excellent English.

They took their places at the table and their server—a middle-aged woman with blond bangs and a tight ponytail—approached to take drink orders.

Both Cedric and Vincent looked exactly as Jude had anticipated based on the photos he'd viewed and the copious biographical information he'd studied. Nonetheless, it always took him a few minutes to adjust to the realities of a subject when face-to-face.

Cedric had on a collared white shirt, the top few buttons open. His tweed blazer, black pants, and leather loafers communicated wealth. He had brown hair and deep-set eyes beneath straight brows. His prominent nose curved out slightly from top to bottom.

Cedric's focus strayed to the other diners, as if to assure himself that he was the best-looking and most important person in the room. It was Cedric's sidekick who kept a close eye on Jude, clearly sizing him up.

Vincent, wearing all black, looked tough and shifty—with a shaved head, beard, and small, hard eyes. Lines permanently grooved the skin between his brows and veins were visible at his temples.

"So," Cedric said to Gemma in accented English, "this is your mysterious boyfriend."

"This is him." Gemma placed her hand on Jude's forearm.

"Gemma is so secretive about her love life," Cedric complained to Jude.

"With good reason," Gemma shot back. "My family has run off a few of my past boyfriends."

"I think it was *you* who ran them off," Cedric teased. "It was easiest for the boyfriends to blame your family."

"Never! My family is the only difficult thing about me. I'm an angel."

Jude made a scoffing sound.

She swung toward him, round-eyed. "Jude! You traitor."

"That sound I made? That was just me clearing my throat. Something got stuck in my windpipe."

"Was it disdain for my claim that I'm an angel? Is that what stuck in your windpipe?"

Vincent remained straight-faced, but Cedric seemed to appreciate the verbal exchange. "Does it bother you that Gemma hasn't introduced you to her family yet?" he asked Jude.

"No, but only because she's convinced me it's not because she's ashamed of me."

"I have three nosy brothers, parents, and several grandparents who are all very much involved in my life. I'm trying to protect Jude from them for as long as possible."

"How did you two meet?" Cedric asked.

Jude could feel his face reddening as she recounted how she'd fallen into the canal at The Venetian hotel in Las Vegas. Yet the outrageous story made her glow from the inside out. Her enthusiasm for it was believable.

"You seem embarrassed by this," Cedric said to him when she finished.

Jude gave a small shrug. "Because I am. She embellished it. But that *is* how it went down."

"What is this word *embellished*?"

"It means," Gemma answered, "that I added to the tale of our meet-cute to make it sound more dramatic than it was. But it felt plenty dramatic to me. It was infatuation at first sight, and Jude here has been devoted to me ever since."

Why did he have to be the lovesick one in this fake romance?

"Devoted?" Cedric asked. "Give me some examples of how he is devoted. Maybe I need to take notes."

"You do not have any difficulty with the ladies, Cedric."

He spread his hands. "But I do not have a girlfriend. So I can improve. Give me some examples of how Jude is devoted."

Cedric was putting Gemma on the spot, and she was going to have to come up with quick answers.

"Well"—Gemma squeezed the hand that remained on his forearm—"as you can see, Jude's adorably introverted, polite, old-fashioned, noble. He often sends me notes in the mail. Imagine, in this digital age. His notes are swoony."

"What do you write in these notes?" Cedric asked Jude.

"Simple things like how much I miss her." He looked down at Gemma. Her eyes met his. "How beautiful she is to me. Sometimes, I'll send lines of poetry."

"Your own poetry?"

"No. The poetry of people much more talented than me."

"For example?"

"Cedric, you're officially prying now," Gemma said. She was plainly trying to save him from being caught in a lie. He was grateful to her for running defense for him, but he wouldn't have mentioned poetry unless he was equipped to back up his claim.

"It's fine," Jude told her. "I remember several of the lines I sent you."

"For example?" Cedric prompted.

"'You need but lift a pearl-pale hand,'" Jude quoted to

Gemma. "'And bind up your long hair and sigh; And all men's hearts must burn and beat; And candle-like foam on the dim sand, And stars climbing the dew-dropping sky, Live but to light your passing feet.'"

"Who wrote that?" Cedric asked.

"William Butler Yeats," Jude answered.

"Another," Cedric encouraged.

"'The spring sun shows me your shadow, the spring wind bears me your breath, you are mine for a passing moment, but I am yours to the death.' That's by Rosamund Watson." And people said English wasn't practical. He'd majored in literature as an undergrad.

"I'm melting all over again." Gemma kissed him on his cheek, then smoothed back a few strands of his hair.

She was only touching him in the ways they'd agreed on in their meeting with his FBI superiors. Her physical affection toward him wasn't real but it *felt* real and affected him as if it were. The dynamic between them inside this restaurant was . . . great. Somehow, deeply right. Except, it wasn't right. It was an act. The thing he'd been warned about repeatedly in under-cover training—reality blurring with fiction—was happening.

Their server arrived with a tray of drinks.

Gemma removed her hand from him in order to accept her glass from the woman and the rational part of him was relieved. The irrational part of him was sorry.

They kept up exactly the type of conversation he would've expected for a girlfriend and boyfriend out to dinner with her cousin and her cousin's friend.

Cedric asked about Jude's life and job, but only in the most general way. At no time did he pry into Jude's knowledge of the perfume business or appear to be in a hurry to sell his secrets. It seemed Cedric's goal for this outing was simply to get to know Jude.

If Cedric was giving out pass/fail grades, Jude suspected he'd get a pass. Jude had established a good rapport with the Frenchman.

Vincent, on the other hand, didn't appear to like him or anyone.

Hopefully Jude had done enough with them both to make Cedric feel comfortable communicating directly with him going forward. If so, Gemma wouldn't need to remain in the mix, which would be simpler for Jude and safer for her.

Once they'd paid, the four of them walked into the now-dark, now-cold air and congregated next to a standing heater while the valet jogged off to retrieve Cedric's car. Jude asked for Cedric's number.

"Sure. Let's exchange." Cedric unlocked his phone, opened a blank contact screen, and passed it over.

Jude did the same. They entered their details and passed their phones back.

"I'm going to extend my schedule and stay a couple more days," Cedric announced. "How long are you in town?" he asked Jude.

Gemma had mentioned that Cedric typically returned home on Sunday. But he'd just used the phrase *"a couple more days."* "Until Tuesday," Jude said to be safe.

"I can't remember, Gemma. Did you say you two are free Sunday night?" Cedric asked. Fortunately, Cedric wanted to see them again. Unfortunately, he wasn't ready to move forward with Jude alone.

"Ronan's receiving a photography award at his college that night. I was planning to have dinner with the family after but since Jude's now in town, I'll skip the dinner part this time. All that to say, we'll be free to meet you at eight." She'd handled that like a pro.

"Good. Eight then. Let's go to that little Italian place in Bayview."

"Pasta Bella is tiny."

"I'm hungry for their Bolognese meatballs," Cedric said.

"The service is slow," Gemma countered.

"You love that place."

"In theory, yes. I'm just not in the mood for it at the moment."

"I want to go to Pasta Bella with you and Jude," Cedric said in the stubborn tone of someone used to getting his way.

"I'd also like to eat there," Jude said easily. Gemma was attempting to steer Cedric away from a restaurant in her hometown where they'd be more likely to see people she knew. But if they resisted too much, they might lose the chance for another meeting with Cedric before he returned to France.

The valet pulled up in Cedric's rented Ferrari. "Will I be seeing you at Pasta Bella or not?" Cedric asked Gemma with a persuasive smile.

Gemma shook her head like, *You rascal you.* "You'll be seeing us there."

"I like it"—Cedric snapped his fingers—"when I get my way."

"Yes," Gemma said wryly. "I'm aware. Where are you two staying?"

"An Airbnb. Bangor *still* hasn't built a decent hotel." Cedric slipped into the driver's seat. Vincent took the passenger seat. With a roar of the expensive engine, they were gone.

Gemma's hand looped around Jude's elbow and they stayed in character while walking to the Mercedes. He tried to imprint the sensations on his memory—her beside him, her arm around his, their shoulders rubbing.

Too soon, they reached the car. Once they'd snapped their seat belts, he eased the car into motion. "You did very well."

"Thank you. You also did very well. Did I overdo it with the physical affection?"

"I think you hit just the right note."

"It seemed necessary in order to make our pretend romance look genuine. The poetry was a nice touch."

"Thank you."

"You should know that I'm very susceptible to eighteenth-century poets."

"Nineteenth-century poets you mean."

"I'm very susceptible to *historical romantic* poetry! I cannot be responsible for my actions if you look at me and quote poetry like that again. So please refrain."

He smiled.

"Will you refrain?" she pressed.

"I'm not making any promises."

"You're playing with fire!"

Light from passing streetlamps fell into the car at regular intervals as they passed a block, then two.

"I know you were hoping I wouldn't need to be in the mix with Cedric again," she said. "It didn't go down that way."

"Right. I'm sorry that you'll have to continue this over dinner on Sunday." That was both a lie and the truth. He was selfishly glad that he'd get to see her again on Sunday because he wanted her in his life and also, physically, just plain wanted her. But he'd never act on those feelings because doing so would violate everything he stood for professionally. So he was sorry that seeing her again could only bring him misery.

And a lot of joy, a voice within him pointed out.

But mostly unemployment and, thus, misery.

He'd never been more certain that the sooner she was gone from his life, the better for them both.

Chapter Twelve

The following morning, several states to the south, Fiona sat on a sidewalk bench wearing her favorite calf-length Burberry puffer coat. This particular bench was positioned outside a luxury apartment building called The Dorchester. And The Dorchester was positioned on the Upper East Side of Manhattan.

As always in Manhattan, all types and ages of people were striding busily past. Only Fiona and the potted miniature pine tree with red pansies encircling its base were still in this city of perpetual motion.

She'd flown in from Maine last night and dressed to the nines today in wool-lined leather gloves, a magenta scarf and matching cap from Jimmy Choo, and what they'd called a "power suit" back in the eighties.

Oh, how she'd loved the eighties.

She'd been here for forty minutes, sipping from a to-go cup of coffee. If need be, she could remain here comfortably for quite some time, though she didn't think she'd have to wait much longer for her sister Isobel to emerge.

Their younger sister Alice had always kept Fiona apprised of Isobel's address but determining when Isobel might come and go from her apartment building had been more difficult.

Last week, Fiona had found an article highlighting the Pilates instructor of famous model, Isobel O'Sullivan. The piece mentioned that Isobel enjoyed private sessions at the woman's studio. She was quoted as saying she particularly enjoyed her Saturday morning session because she found it a great way to begin her weekend. Fiona had called the studio, pretended to be a prospective client, and inquired about the instructor's schedule. They'd told her she taught private sessions from eight to ten on Saturdays, followed by group classes.

Which meant Isobel either had the 8:00 or 9:00 a.m. slot.

Fiona had arrived on the park bench at 6:45.

Draining the last of her coffee, she lobbed her empty cup into a black metal trash can. She'd skipped breakfast because her stomach was too busy wrestling with angst, guilt, predictions over how Isobel would respond, doubt about whether this approach was best.

Fiona was a decisive person. A conflicted mental state was neither her norm nor her preference.

She was putting herself through this out of sheer determination. Determination had motivated her to book a ticket to New York. Determination was keeping her bottom situated on this bench.

She was fifty-eight, plenty old enough to have learned that achieving goals did not come easy. If you wanted something, it would require sacrifice from you. And she wanted to reestablish communication with her sister.

Several taxis came and went. At 7:35, a limo pulled up to the curb. The doorman exchanged a few words with the driver, making it clear that they were familiar with one another.

The limo waited.

Fiona waited.

The doorman opened the door and a tall, thin woman with brown-gold hair caught back in a ponytail emerged. She wore large Cartier sunglasses, but Fiona didn't need to see her face without them in order to make a positive ID. She'd know that body, that bearing, that profile anywhere.

Fiona rose, standing tall in her high heels. "Isobel," she said calmly but loudly.

Isobel's head turned toward the sound, then her gait sliced to a halt, and she faced Fiona. From the pink laces of her Nikes to the fashionable bag slung over her shoulder, every inch of Isobel's workout look spoke of good taste.

She was still a great beauty. Her bone structure was so in-your-face amazing that it almost dared you not to acknowledge it. Her sister would always be more attractive than Fiona and a full five inches taller—truths that still rankled.

"I'm here to tell you that I'm sorry," Fiona said.

Isobel didn't reply.

They hadn't looked each other in the face in thirty-five years and Fiona felt an ocean of memories shift between them. Holding hands as they ran into the living room Christmas morning to see what Santa Claus had brought for them. Making mud pies on the driveway. Fiona, watching Isobel dance in the part of angel in *The Nutcracker*. Lying side by side on the hood of their dad's car, stargazing as he pointed out the constellations and planets. Fighting over a sweater Fiona had worn without Isobel's permission. Laughing uncontrollably during Mass when their brother had belched. Both of them leaning toward the small bathroom mirror to put on their makeup before school.

"I'm sorry," Fiona repeated. "What I did was terrible. I betrayed you and our relationship and . . . there's nothing I can say to defend myself because my actions weren't defensible. I was jealous of you. And obsessed with Felix. I regret my actions deeply."

People flowed around them on both sides. The limo's motor ran. Fiona's heart beat fast.

"I returned your letter unopened," Isobel said in a dignified voice that shook slightly, "because I don't want communication between us."

"Okay."

"Yet here you are. Outside my home."

"Yes."

"Why?"

"Because right after the eclipse in Suriname, we pinky-promised each other that we'd experience the eclipse coming to our hometown, far in the future, together. That eclipse will occur this fall and I'm asking you to consider watching it with me."

"You traveled here because you want to fulfill a pinky-promise?"

"Yes."

Isobel regarded her with disbelief. "Decades have passed. I divorced Felix and married again. I raised my children. I built my career. But you realize, right, that thanks to your actions, I'm still mostly known as the wife who was wronged by my husband and sister. That's how I will always be known."

When it came out that Felix had cheated on Fiona, too, God had forced her to taste some of the pain she'd inflicted. It had been soul-destroying. She wouldn't claim to comprehend Isobel's experience, though. Because, while the housekeeper Nicole had been Fiona's best friend, the housekeeper had not been her sister. And unlike the situation between Isobel, Felix, and Fiona—Felix had not gone on to marry Nicole.

"I know I can't have a sister relationship with you ever

again," Fiona said. "But Mom and Dad are in their mid-eighties. I'm not sure how much longer we'll have them." It might be a low blow to play the mom-and-dad card. Yet the mom-and-dad card was also one hundred percent valid. "I think it would mean a lot to them if we could exist in the same room together from now on."

"I don't think you have the right to ask me for anything." Isobel's knuckles showed white where she gripped her bag. "Don't come here again. Don't ambush me anywhere."

Fiona dipped her head in silent agreement.

Isobel disappeared into the backseat of the limo. Seconds later, it slid away, and Fiona was left on the sidewalk in her power suit.

That had been stomach-churning, emotion-heaving, pride-shredding awful.

Yet, she'd broken the stalemate between herself and her sister. She'd addressed the scariest of the crouching lions in her life, the lion she'd been avoiding and pretending to ignore all these years. The one that stirred the most shame inside her.

The next move was Isobel's.

Fiona scanned the oncoming traffic for a cab with its top lights lit. She'd go home to Maine now and see Burke. It surprised her how much that appealed. She could sit on his sofa in front of the fire with a glass of wine. He would listen, empathize, encourage.

By late this afternoon. She could be there. With him.

○ ○

Gemma sank low in the water of her nightly bath, until only her face hovered above the water line.

She had died—died!—when Jude had spoken poetry so solemnly while looking right at her last night. When she'd pulled up to his car in the strip mall, she'd thought that he looked like a poet. And then he'd *spoken poetry to her*. The line about how he was hers unto death had tempted her to drag him to the nearest altar for a rush-job wedding.

She knew he'd only quoted romantic poetry because he was being a good little soldier and trying to perform his undercover role with excellence. Still. That had been reckless!

Gemma. Divert yourself with thoughts of your actual boyfriend.

More and more with Chaz, out of sight was becoming out of mind.

She sloshed upward in the bath. Opening the Photos app on her phone, she found pictures of them the last time they'd been together, in New York in early February. He was six years older than she was, which she liked because those extra years had given Chaz time to establish his career. He didn't have the tang of a boy bouncing from job to job because no one deigned to hand over the respect or salary he "deserved." He was independent. Not needy. And with his sunny disposition, not given to pouting.

She flicked over to her text messages and pulled up their most recent exchange. He'd sent her more gym selfies and another pun.

CHAZ

A pirate's favorite workout is the plank.

Lately, he'd been lobbying her to come and see him in New York again even though she'd made it clear that it was his turn to come and see her. He'd remained noncommittal and she hadn't pressured him.

Dating Chaz was just so easy.

There had been times in her life when she'd experienced mountain peaks of infatuation, like the time that had inspired her to create Hope and Spice. Her boyfriend then had been named Garrett—a guitarist with long hair and a penchant for bomber jackets. He'd been bold and intense and creative, and she'd been absolutely crazy about him for a time.

But her infatuation for him and the others had eventually come to a stop on the downhill side of the mountain. A few relationships she'd ended because it had become apparent that her boyfriend was a jerk, as had been the case with Garrett. A few relationships had ended because they'd fizzled into boredom. Two relationships had ended because her boyfriend had broken her heart. Those two times, she'd wallowed in drama and sorrow.

Then her father had been arrested and her mother had suffered a stroke and for the first time in her life she'd tasted *real* pain. It had been awful. She had the capacity to feel emotions deeply. And though she wasn't afraid of much, she *was* afraid of setting herself up for that level of pain again because she understood that it could ruin her.

For that reason, Chaz had seemed like the ideal boyfriend. What Gemma had with him cost her almost nothing and scared her not at all. No giddiness, no goosebumps, no spikes of neurosis or crushing disappointments or risking her own downfall.

There was a lot to be said for things that were light. Light books. Light movies. Light meals. Sometimes you just needed something that wouldn't bring bad surprises or tears. But she was realizing that at this particular time in her life, she did not need or want a light boyfriend.

Her feelings for Chaz had become completely insubstantial. She cared a lot more about Jude, her not-boyfriend, her business associate.

Should she end things with Chaz?

She weighed the question. In response came a flood of *yes*.

It wasn't doing Chaz any favors for her to take up space as his barely-there girlfriend. And she earnestly didn't want to continue this anymore.

She dialed his number.

"Hey, babe."

"Hey." She didn't like the nickname *babe*. "Listen, I think we should have a talk."

Long pause. "Uh-oh. Are you breaking up with me?"

"Actually, yes," she said gently. "I am."

In Gemma's dream, Jude was standing in her kitchen, smiling down at her. The dancing tenderness in his eyes assured her that he found her irresistible.

He found *her* irresistible. He saw her. Appreciated her. Desired her. He was a golden boy. One of the most intelligent people she'd ever met. He could date socialites or beauty queens and yet—marvelously, unbelievably—*she* was the one he wanted.

He pulled her against him with a palm at the small of her back. She gasped, a thrill arrowing to her belly.

He swung them and leaned her against her refrigerator door, his actions strong and sure. Her breath left her as his free hand tunneled slowly into her hair. Slowly. Slowly.

Hungry anticipation crackled between them. Then he was taking her lips in a kiss. He tasted like chocolate. He felt like expensive clothing and clean hair. He smelled like smoky cologne and *him*. Jude. And she wanted to burrow into that scent and make it her home.

Their chemistry mounted high, quickly high, beyond her control. She gloried in the kiss, curving her arms around his neck to lock him against her. She never wanted this to end—

Instantaneously, it *did* end.

She came awake on an uneven inhale. Her eyes opened to reveal her living room. She was curled on the sofa under a throw blanket, a decorative pillow beneath her head. It was a stormy Sunday afternoon. She'd been rereading Gracie and Paul's letters when she'd gotten sleepy.

She closed her eyes and relaxed her body and willed the dream to sweep her away again. She could pinpoint the details of it with clarity. How Jude had looked. How he'd made her feel.

Minutes passed. She concentrated harder than a fan trying to shoot a million-dollar shot during halftime at a basketball game.

C'mon, she begged. *Let me return to the dream—*

Her phone alarm chimed, announcing that it was time to get ready for Ronan's photography award ceremony followed by dinner with Jude, Cedric, and Vincent at Pasta Bella.

She growled as she pressed herself upright. Disoriented and groggy, she scowled. Had breaking up with Chaz given her subconscious the go-ahead to dream about Jude? Also, how come nightmares always went on too long but truly excellent dreams ended too soon?

She was still cranky after the awards ceremony.

Upon leaving the auditorium, Gemma hurried across the campus of her brother's community college toward the parking lot where Jude had told her he'd be waiting.

It was full dark now, but numerous lights brightened the pathways and numerous students were out and about. The earlier rain had passed, leaving glistening puddles. Now that March was almost over, the air was finally smelling of spring.

By the time she spotted Jude, leaning against the Mercedes, he was already watching her. A warm zing went through her, which she angrily cut off half-formed. It was disconcerting to see Actual Jude while Dream Jude was so fresh in her mind. He was dressed much as he had been Friday and looked wonderful, which was frustrating, because Actual Jude was not available to kiss against her refrigerator.

This whole situation was messing with her head.

For Jude, this operation was just another day on the job. When it ended, he'd move on to the next case without breaking his stride. She, though, would be left with the consequences of her alliance with the FBI. For one thing, a lot of French Bettencourts who would have strong opinions about her role in all of this. For another, a blank space in her life where Jude had been.

She was very afraid of how much she'd miss him.

"Good evening," he said.

"Hi." She opened the passenger door before he had a chance to do it for her.

On the way to the restaurant, they spoke less than usual, mostly chitchat initiated by him. She had the sense that he was trying to feel out her mood.

Following her conversation with Chaz last night, it had occurred to her that Jude might've wanted her to run her decision to end things with Chaz by him before she'd gone ahead and spontaneously done the deed.

But see? That made her grumpy, too. She was still an autonomous person capable of making her own choices and worthy of privacy. Chaz had been in little danger of interrupting the FBI's mission before. Now he was in zero danger of doing so. Gemma wasn't going to mention the break-up to a single friend or family member, so everything was fine, just as it was. She'd done nothing to upset the case.

This time, when she and Jude walked from the parking lot to the restaurant's door, she did not reach for his hand.

They entered Pasta Bella's bar, then trailed the hostess down a staircase. The restaurant's nine tables were located in a stone-walled room that had once been a wine cellar belonging to a ship's captain. Nicks and scratches gave character to the wood floor. Sconces cast honey-colored light, as did the glowing wicks fed by glass pots of oil on the tables. This had been her family's place for decades and she relished its familiar scent—bubbling tomato sauce, basil, and welcome.

Once again, she and Jude had arrived five minutes early. Once again, Cedric and Vincent were not waiting for them when they settled at their table.

Gemma selected a crunchy breadstick from the basket and bit into it with fervor. "Yummy," she said sharply, then gnawed it down like a beaver would a branch while hiding behind her menu.

Silence from Jude.

They'd pre-selected the items they were going to order. Also, she'd told him about her family's connection to this place, so he knew that she knew this menu by heart. Since she couldn't get away with hiding behind the menu for long, she lowered it.

Jude lifted tawny eyebrows.

Those lips of his, chiseled yet soft, had been excellent to kiss in the dream. How well would they measure up in real life? Very well, by the look of them.

"You okay?" he asked.

"Yes."

The heating vent blew a gust of warm air over them, which nudged a lock of Jude's hair toward his eye. He raised a hand with the clear intent of fixing it.

"Allow me," Gemma said, sweeping the lock into place. For

a split second she stilled, ordering herself to behave. Then ignored her own order by delving her fingers into his hair, rustling her hand, and disordering all the strands.

She returned her hand to her lap. "Sorry." Truth be told, she wasn't sorry.

He tilted his expensive head in a way that asked, *Really?*

"I couldn't resist," she said. "I really do try very hard to listen to the angel on my shoulder."

"Do you really try *very hard?*" he asked dryly, but without animosity.

Her phone pinged. She extracted it from her purse.

CEDRIC

I apologize for the late notice. I've been busy and just remembered that I should have let you know sooner that Vincent and I won't be able to join you and Jude for dinner. Business matters called me home. We're on the jet back to France.

With a sigh, she handed Jude the phone so he could read it.

Jude had the best poker face of all poker faces. This information had to come as a setback to him, but he didn't telegraph that outwardly. He passed her phone back.

"Sounds like we don't need to stay for a full dinner," she said. "I wouldn't want to leave so quickly, though, that the employees here will hold a grudge. I come here a lot and I'd like to stay on good terms with everyone."

"How about we order appetizers, then go?"

"That will work, especially if you leave our server a really big tip to apologize for the fact that we're not staying for entrées and dessert."

"Deal."

After they'd placed their orders—a Caesar salad for Gemma, minestrone soup for Jude—she excused herself and went to find shelter in the women's restroom. She took the longest possible amount of time washing her hands, lotioning them, freshening her makeup, and giving herself a pep talk along the lines of, *Go out there, be a professional, and stop feeling so contrary.*

Returning to their table, she gave Jude a fake-affectionate gaze, which he fake-affectionately returned. He'd clearly tried to tidy his hair while she was away. But she'd made such a spectacle of it that his attempts hadn't fully succeeded. It was slightly mussed, and the joke was on her because it looked irresistible that way.

"Gemma!" A woman's voice.

Oh no.

Gemma knew that voice well.

Her face jerked up in time to see Grandma Colette finish descending the stairs, followed by Gemma's three brothers, her mother, Grandpa Stevie, and Great-Grandma Gracie.

Chapter Thirteen

At the close of Ronan's award ceremony, Gemma had purposely stayed for her family's *Where should we go for dinner?* conversation. She hadn't left to meet Jude until they'd definitively decided on the Gastro Pub and moved on to other topics.

So *why? WHY* were they here?

Colette, with her puff of tangerine hair and poker player's observant eyes, set her hands on ample hips and addressed Gemma. "You said you couldn't join us for dinner because you had to catch up on some orders for Perfumes by Gemma Clare."

The others congregated around her, their ringleader. Everyone stared avidly at Gemma then Jude, Jude then Gemma.

"And you said," Gemma returned, "that you were going to eat at the Gastro Pub."

"We went to the pub, but the Corvette Club of Maine was having a social night there. The place was packed. So we came here. Why are *you* here?"

"Because of me," Jude said. Pressing to his feet, he smiled at her family. "She called to say she was on her way to the shop, and I convinced her to eat with me instead."

"And you are?" Colette asked.

"Jude McConnell, Gemma's boyfriend." Her family members were related to Cedric. So, to them, Jude must be Jude McConnell.

"Gemma's boyfriend!" Colette crowed.

"Yes." He gave handshakes to them one by one as they provided their names.

Gemma wholeheartedly wished she could bolt out of here screaming. She'd not battled guilt over lying to Cedric about who Jude was to her. The end definitely seemed to justify the means in that situation. But lying to her closest family members about Jude? She hadn't planned to do so and didn't want to do so.

"Jude," Mom said. "What a wonderful name. That rings a bell with me, for some reason."

"It's a book of the Bible," Gracie announced.

"Gemma is tight-lipped about her boyfriends," Mom continued in an apologetic tone to Jude. She rested a hand on her chest and peered at him like a Swiftie at Taylor Swift. "I don't know why. We're always very supportive."

"I'm tight-lipped about my boyfriends because you people are like the Spanish Inquisition." No one was paying attention to her.

Colette ordered the others to push Gemma and Jude's table against the bigger, empty one next to it. They'd been coming here so long that no one thought twice about rearranging furniture without permission.

Next thing she knew, Jude was seated at the head of the table, her mother and grandmother on either side of him. Then came Stevie and Gracie. She and her brothers were relegated to the far end, Gemma facing Jude down the long rectangle.

"Jude! Tell us about yourself," Colette ordered.

Jude went into a recitation of his curated background.

"He's a step up from your usual caliber of boyfriend," Hugo whispered.

"What'd you do to get him?" Nicolas wondered.

"Pay for a sponsored ad on Tinder?" Ronan joked.

"If I did, I wouldn't waste my breath telling you three about it because you're so hopeless a sponsored ad would do you no good."

"You work in the perfume industry!" Gracie was saying to Jude. "How wonderful. My late husband, Paul Bettencourt, was a member of the family who owns and makes Rhapsodie perfume."

"We're only getting appetizers," Gemma told them all. "And then we have to go."

"To work on orders for Perfumes by Gemma Clare?" Colette jabbed. "Jude, how did you and Gemma meet?"

"I really am sorry that we don't already know these things," Mom said to Jude.

Jude gave Gemma an expectant look like, *Go ahead and tell them how we met.*

She swished a hand. "I told the story to the last person who asked. You can tell it this time."

Their fictional meeting was a whole lot more hilarious when she told it. But he looked uncomfortable enough at having to relay the fantastical tale that she was pleased with herself for making him do it. She was also pleased with herself for suggesting they set their fictional meeting during a real-life trip to Vegas her family knew she'd taken for a perfume conference.

"So then there he was," she added after the part where he'd

saved her from the canal water and given her his sweater, "without a shirt, and I couldn't help noticing that though he's somewhat reserved, he does have a fantastic upper body."

Her brothers snickered.

"What?" Stevie asked.

"Jude has a fantastic upper body," Gemma called loudly to Stevie.

Mom laughed nervously. "Gemma's teasing you, Jude. Don't let it bother you."

Colette craned her neck. "I need a drink."

Gemma's family was *a lot*. For anyone. For her, even. Jude was about to spend time earning his paycheck the hard way.

"So, Jude," Mom said, "I'd love to know what it is that you appreciate most about Gemma."

Jude shrugged. "Everything."

Mom waited hopefully.

Jude met Gemma's eyes. "She's creative and brave. Independent, confident, talented, funny."

Mom bestowed the Swiftie look on him again.

"I don't recognize the person he's describing," Nicolas murmured.

"Who's he talking about?" Hugo whispered.

"I'd like to meet this person," Ronan added.

"It's nice to hear that you've noticed Gemma's strengths," Mom said to Jude. "Did you know she's currently trying to help Gracie track down details of her past?"

"Yes, she mentioned that to me."

"Gemma has some flaws as well as strengths," Colette confided to Jude. "She ran away from home when she was six. Once, she marched in a one-person picket line demanding that she never be served honeydew melon again. And we couldn't keep clothes on her when she was three."

"I learned to accept clothing," Gemma pointed out.

"Good thing, otherwise I'd have been traumatized," Ronan muttered.

"I still hate honeydew," Gemma said, "and still maintain that running away from home is an acceptable form of non-violent protest."

"You're not a mother," Mom said, "so you have no idea how terrifying it is when you can't find your child."

"I went two houses down and climbed into the Whittakers' doghouse," Gemma explained to Jude.

"When you have children, hopefully with Jude here, you'll find out how scary it is when one of them runs away," Colette said.

"Are you thinking of having children?" Gracie inquired of Jude with a look of extreme optimism.

"No," he answered.

"We haven't ruled it out for the future, though," Gemma added.

Jude swallowed as if a wasp had just flown down his windpipe.

Colette gave Jude her full attention. "We don't know much about you, but Gemma did mention to me a while back that you're a big NASCAR fan. So are Stevie and I."

"Oh?"

Gemma's eyes widened as if looking at an oncoming train. Chaz was a NASCAR fan. NASCAR was not part of Jude McConnell's persona.

"Who's your favorite driver?" Colette asked him.

A beat of silence. "Ricky Bobby," he said. "From *The Ballad of.*"

That drew a laugh.

"No, really." Stevie chuckled. "Who's your favorite driver?"

"The great Dale Earnhardt," Gemma inserted, naming Chaz's fave. She was not a NASCAR person herself but had picked up enough from Colette, Stevie, and Chaz to talk the talk.

"Gemma," Colette scolded. "Quit it. You're acting like an old married lady and answering questions for him. We want to hear your boyfriend talk."

"Gemma's right," Jude said. "Dale Earnhardt is my favorite."

"And which of his races sticks out most in your memory?" Stevie asked. "I have a hard time remembering to get eggs and bread at the grocery store, but I remember all his races."

"I don't have a good memory, myself," Jude said humbly, no doubt paving the way should he struggle to pull up NASCAR details. Gemma had noted that his memory was, in fact, exceptional. "I guess the race that sticks out most in my memory is Dale's most recent win."

"Back in 2000?" Colette asked. Jude would have been under ten years old.

"That's right," Jude said without blinking. "Thank goodness for YouTube."

"Thank goodness," her brothers echoed in unison, all having grown up in the YouTube era.

"I remember that race well!" Stevie declared happily. "The 500 at Talladega."

"As soon as our appetizers get here," Gemma announced, desperate to change the subject of NASCAR, "Jude and I will need to eat and go."

"How come you're so stingy about sharing your boyfriend with us?" Nicolas teased.

"Yeah, Gemma." Hugo followed Nicolas's lead. "It's weird how you're insisting on having him to yourself."

"Sharing is caring," Mom said feebly, voicing the refrain she'd repeated one million times when raising them.

"It's great to finally get to talk with all of you," Jude said.

"Gemma's told me how close you are and what a wonderful family she has."

"Thank you." Gracie beamed, clearly taking his words as a compliment to herself, seeing as how she was the family's matriarch.

"Yes," Colette said. "We're so wonderful that Gemma's been hiding us from you. If I'd ever had a boyfriend like you, I'd have put him on a float and sent him down Main Street in a parade."

"Let's not assume Gemma was the one hiding us from him," Hugo said. "It's just as likely that Jude here was reluctant to meet us. If so, I get it, man."

"Why would he be reluctant to meet us?" Colette asked.

"I can't imagine why," Ronan whispered with faux innocence.

"I wasn't reluctant," Jude replied smoothly. "In fact, I've been waiting for the chance to meet you."

And with that brush, he'd painted himself as the good cop and Gemma as the bad cop who'd been withholding him from her family.

Her relations grumbled and shot her accusing looks.

She'd just been valiantly trying to rescue Jude from the NASCAR quicksand and he'd blithely thrown her under the bus! Her destructive mischievous streak reared its head and she heard herself saying, "When you were giving your bio earlier, Jude, you failed to mention how much you love collecting butterflies. Why don't you tell them more about that?"

The group turned blank faces to his end of the table.

He gave a thin smile. "Not much to tell, really. It's a *very* small pastime of mine."

"Not that small," Gemma said. "One whole wall of his New York apartment is filled with glass-fronted display boxes of butterflies. You know, the boxes with the black velvet backs?"

A pause.

"How do you catch them?" Gracie wanted to know. "With a net?"

Gemma grinned at the mental picture of Jude leaping around in a meadow, butterfly catcher in hand.

"No," Jude said, "not with a net."

"Do you kill the butterflies?" Mom winced.

Jude shook his head. "I collect my specimens after they're dead. I'm not someone who kills animals."

"What about mosquitoes?" Stevie asked.

"And scorpions?" Gemma wondered.

"I haven't really found scorpions to be much of an issue in my life," Jude answered.

"Lucky you," Colette said.

"What?" Stevie said.

"How did you get interested in butterflies?" Hugo asked.

Everyone quieted.

"I got interested in butterflies through my mother. She's a big fan."

"It doesn't seem a little creepy to you?" Colette asked. "To have a wall of dead insects in your apartment?"

"Did you pin the butterflies to the velvet yourself?" Stevie asked, blinking.

Jude set both palms on the table. "To be honest, I really don't enjoy talking about myself. I would much rather spend the time we have learning about you."

"We're not very interesting," Mom told him apologetically.

"In my eyes, you're very interesting." Then he began showing off the knowledge of her family members he'd gained when preparing for their operation. He knew that Gracie had lived in D.C. during World War Two. That Colette still made money as a poker player. That Mom was a gifted knitter. That Stevie had retired from a career in waste management administration. That Hugo played fantasy baseball. That Nicolas loved Vietnamese food. And that Ronan was getting a degree in video game design.

Not his messed-up hair, nor NASCAR, nor butterflies had thrown him off his game. He was the boy in childhood photos who wore pressed shirts and new shoes. She was the girl in childhood photos with a hand-me-down dress and scratched knees.

She resented him and at the same time liked him far too much.

Their appetizers arrived, a tremendous relief, and Gemma tore into her salad like an inmate at a Russian prison.

Jude ate more slowly. When he finally finished his soup, Gemma jumped to her feet. "This has been great! So much fun."

"I detect sarcasm," Hugo said.

"Sorry," *not sorry*, "to steal him away."

"I'd love to snap a picture of the two of you before you go," Mom said.

"No pictures." Gemma crossed to Jude and took hold of his hand. "Good night, everyone!"

The chorus of goodbyes from her family was so noisy that it interrupted the conversation of the other diners. Jude inclined his chin like a Prince Regent, telling them how nice it had been to talk with them.

When she finally got him upstairs, he waylaid their server and paid their bill and a tip. Minutes later, they were accelerating away from Pasta Bella in the Mercedes.

He'd been a paragon of good manners at the restaurant. But now she could feel rays of anger shooting off of him. His profile was like slate. The silence prickly.

"It was reckless and unnecessary," he said, "to mention butterflies."

"Yes," she agreed. She was a big enough person that she could already admit to herself that she shouldn't have done that.

"Why'd you say that? Because you were irritated with me?"

"Yes. I was irritated."

"Why?"

"You told them you'd been eagerly waiting to meet them, which makes me the selfish shrew who was too ashamed of them to introduce you."

"That's no excuse. You cannot let irritation cause you to react in a way that jeopardizes my identity."

"Do you really think, after regaling my family with your extensive knowledge of their professions and hobbies, that any of them thought to themselves, *I don't think that was actually Gemma's boyfriend because I don't believe he collects butterflies?* No. Only a boyfriend would know the things you knew about them. You gave them far more evidence to support the fact that you're my boyfriend than any of my actual boyfriends ever have."

"You were out of line. Never forget that this is a deadly game we're playing."

"Last I checked, Grandpa Stevie's not very deadly with a bread knife."

"What about Vincent, Gemma?" he asked tightly. "Do you think he's harmless?"

Stubbornly, she said nothing.

He cut a look across at her, then turned back to the road.

When he pulled to a stop beside her Vespa, she exited the car without a word.

She waved for him to drive off while she fumbled with her helmet.

He did not. He waited, steadfast.

She found her keys and adjusted her purse cross-body so

that the bulk of it rested at her lower back. Then she put on her gloves and her night-driving glasses.

Gemma was going to be the death of him.

Jude remained motionless inside the Mercedes, watching her Vespa's taillights disappear.

Enormous emotions roiled within him. Frustration and admiration. Longing and desire. He wasn't used to . . . *feeling* this much. Gemma had the power to take lighter fluid to his self-control.

He rubbed his thumb against the steering wheel repeatedly.

He regretted that her family had shown up at the restaurant. His mother was from a big, loud family similar to Gemma's, so he had a soft spot for families like hers. If tonight had merely been a social outing for him, he'd have enjoyed them. He'd have been amused by all the redheads. He'd have spent time identifying each person's resemblance to Gemma. He'd have laughed at their antics.

As it was, he'd been painfully aware that Operation Scentsible was riding on his shoulders. That Shannon and others were listening to the audio. That several agents were inside Pasta Bella and nearby.

Putting himself forward as Jude McConnell had been the only option, given the situation. However, the more people you introduced yourself to while utilizing your alias, the more complexity that could bring to a case. Gemma came from a family of long-time Mainers. The Camdens were long-time Mainers. He'd been concerned about the outside possibility that one of them might recognize him as a Camden. Those pressures had made juggling them all—Colette, especially—feel difficult.

He needed to stay clear on the fact that Gemma's family's discovery of them was not Gemma's fault. He'd been the one who'd relented to Cedric's assertion that they eat at her family's favorite restaurant. The run-in with her relatives was just one of those things that unexpectedly happened during UC ops and that an agent had to roll with.

Gemma's fragrance still lingered in the interior of his car.

With every breath he drew it in.

Hope and Spice.

The following day, Gemma received a text from Cedric.

CEDRIC

I enjoyed dinner the other night. Wanted to let you know that I've reconsidered, about Rhapsodie. Decided not to move forward with a deal at this time.

Chapter Fourteen

Max Cirillo was the biological son of Felix Camden. That was the truth of Max's DNA.

But he was no Camden. Not in practice and not by name. He'd been born to a single mother, and she'd given him her surname at birth.

From his earliest memories, Max had understood his position in the Camden household. He was the son of the housekeeper. His mom, a first-generation American born to Greek immigrants, was raising him on a modest salary. They lived in the servants' house of an estate, Maple Lane, focused on grooming two young American princes. To be fair, even the servants' house had been ridiculously nice. Yet there'd been a huge difference between Max and his best friend, Jude. A difference far larger than the short distance that had separated the mansion from the servants' house.

For his first fourteen years, Max had been a normal kid.

Then his mom and Fiona had a fight. Temper blazing, Mom had called a journalist and informed the man that Felix Camden was the father of her son.

Hours later, she'd realized the full scope of what she'd done. But by then, it had been too late. His "normal" was over. Her "normal" was over.

Scandal had broken like a storm cloud.

They'd been banished from Maple Lane. Public opinion had settled on them like a fiery spotlight. He'd hated its glare and cruelty. No one had sympathy for them. Everyone judged his mother harshly. Though Max had been illegitimate from the beginning, that had never been something he thought about much. It hadn't been even close to the main thing about him. But overnight, America boiled down his mother's identity to "the other woman" and his identity to that one word. *Illegitimate.*

He'd been disgusted to learn he was the result of an affair between his mom and Felix, outraged with her for sleeping with Felix, and betrayed by her for never telling him the truth about his origins.

He'd started a lousy new school in a lousy new town. His mother and Jude's mother had taken up opposite sides of the battlefield.

Giving his head an impatient shake in an attempt to scatter the memories, Max walked up to the Federal Building in Bangor.

MAX

I'm here. I'll wait outside.

JUDE

Be right down.

He was meeting Jude for lunch, as he did every time he came this direction.

After all these years, Jude was still his best friend. No thanks to Max. When he'd been fourteen and bitter, he'd been ready to cut Jude out. His short life experience had led him to believe that friends were easy things to acquire. Jude was the one who'd been unwilling to let their parents' mistakes ruin their friendship. Now, at the age of thirty-two, Max owed Jude for that because he'd discovered that true friends were a rare commodity. A best friend like Jude? The rarest, most valuable commodity of them all.

Too often for his taste, he was surrounded by people, employees, acquaintances. But hardly any of them really knew him. It was good for him to be known the way he and Jude knew each other. It was necessary.

Sliding his hands into the pockets of his jeans, he faced the drizzly Monday weather.

Jeremiah, Jude, and he had all responded differently to the scandals they'd been raised under.

Jeremiah had seized control of his story and proved to everyone why he was, in his own right, worthy of attention by becoming the most successful American Formula One driver in history.

Jude had retreated from the public eye. When he'd finished holding his family together after Felix and Fiona's divorce, he'd taken steps toward a career that would enable him to hold the world together by righting its wrongs.

As for him? Max had clawed to prove his worth independent of the Camdens. For the past decade, he'd worked tirelessly to build an empire of his own. And succeeded.

Footsteps sounded behind him, and he twisted to watch Jude exit the building.

They exchanged their usual brief hug.

Jeremiah and Jude were the sons of two blond people. Both of them were light skinned with dark blond hair. Max's mother had olive skin and thick, black hair. Max, too, had an olive skin tone and dark hair. If someone were to look at the three brothers, they'd immediately note that he was the one who didn't belong. Fitting because Max had viewed Jeremiah and Jude as friends when they were kids and still viewed them much more as friends than as brothers.

"How are you?" Jude asked.

"I'm well. You?" It had been a month since they'd seen each other.

Jude nodded. "Also well. Ready for lunch?"

"Starving." Max took his keyring from his pocket and spun it on his index finger as they walked toward his car. "I'll drive."

"Ah, good. Nausea for an appetizer."

Max smiled. "I'm shallow and want to flaunt my car."

"Fine by me."

"I'd like it better if you were insecure enough to argue and demand a chance to flaunt your car." Max gave a long-suffering sigh. "Your self-assurance is the kind that doesn't need a sports car to prop it up. It's infuriating."

"How can I be infuriating when all I said was 'fine by me'?"

"You manage."

"Also, why would I flaunt a Ford Bronco?"

"The bigger question is why are you driving a Ford Bronco when you could be driving a Ferrari?"

"I'm assuming that question is rhetorical."

"Jeremiah has the sense to drive a Ferrari."

"Jeremiah and you are equally shallow," Jude joked. "I'm the only one with substance."

No need to ask Jude where they were going for lunch because they always ate at the same place in Bangor—a lobster pound on the river at the edge of town.

When they got there, they approached the walk-up window side by side. Live lobster moved around in a tank on the left. At this time of year, they'd be hard-shell, caught offshore. To the right, a tall kettle of seawater bubbled above a wood fire. They ordered what they always ordered. Whole lobster with melted butter, a dinner roll, an ear of corn, and a scoop of coleslaw.

Soon the weather would begin to turn warm enough to eat at the large outdoor area when they came here. For now, though, they settled at the last empty indoor table. Maine travel posters and enlarged photos of customers eating here in the seventies and eighties curled and turned yellow from where they'd been stapled to the walls. Beyond the room's picture window, the gray-blue Penobscot flowed. It, like the bay, a town, and a slew of businesses, had been named for Maine's indigenous people.

Jude asked questions about Max's work and Max's mom. Max asked for the same work and family updates from Jude.

Jude answered in the usual type of way, but something was off in his demeanor. He was pretending his typical calm, but Max wasn't buying it. "What's bothering you today?" Max asked.

Jude took a sip of ice water. "A woman."

When Jude didn't immediately offer more information, Max concluded, "A woman you like."

"A woman I want to help."

Jude wanted to help most people. But Max could see this was a woman he liked *and* wanted to help . . . much more uncommon. "Her name?"

"Confidential."

"How did you meet her?"

"Through work."

"Is she FBI?"

"No."

"What kind of help does she need?"

"Assistance handling debt collectors. Her father was incarcerated several years ago, and her mom suffered through an expensive medical condition. Her mom went back to work as a secretary as soon as she was able, but the family never recovered financially. And won't, at this rate."

"She asked if you'd intervene?"

"No. In fact, she doesn't know I'm aware of the situation or that I've been reading her mail, and I'd like to keep it that way."

Max lifted an eyebrow. "You've been reading her mail?"

"I have a warrant to do so."

Since Jude had a warrant, she must be connected to one of his cases. A suspect? Surely not. Then maybe an informant or cooperating witness? Max had *never* known Jude to mix something personal with FBI business. Help handling debt collectors was definitely personal. "What's stopping you and me from paying the debts off?"

"She's proud. She'd never accept that. What her family really needs is someone on their side who has knowledge of the laws pertaining to debt collection."

"And you want to be that person but can't because . . . ?"

"It's beyond the purview of my job."

Thinking on it, Max took a bite of coleslaw, then another. "I hate the tactics some of those collection agencies use. One of them badgered my mom—calling at all hours of the day and night—when I was in high school. The stress of it was hard on her. She ended up selling a lot of her stuff and using that money to pay them off because she was desperate to get out from underneath them."

"Right." Jude frowned. "The stress of this has to be getting to . . . the woman I know. She's been dealing with this for years."

"Is she as hot as she is self-sacrificing?"

Jude gave Max a warning look.

"That's a yes," Max said. "Fascinating."

Jude's attention shifted to the river. The lines of his profile communicated strain.

"Your conscience isn't going to rest until you step in and help this family." Max crossed his arms. "You're discreet and careful. Be extra discreet and extra careful with this and it'll be fine."

Jude scratched the back of his neck, considering. "The FBI . . ."

"Doesn't have to know who you give advice to on your nights and weekends."

For the next few minutes, they worked at polishing off the last of their food.

"I heard from Sloane yesterday." Jude pulled free a hunk of claw meat.

Max stopped chewing. Every muscle stilled.

Jude flicked a knowing glance at him.

Max forced himself to start chewing again and made an impatient, *Tell me more* gesture.

"She's moving back to Groomsport this summer to take care of Ivy for four months."

Max's brain reeled. "Why does she need to take care of Ivy?"

"Ivy's parents took an assignment overseas. Ivy doesn't want to go, so Aunt Sloane is coming to the rescue. With Sloane as her chaperone, Ivy can start her sophomore year with all her friends."

Max had acquired a long list of enemies. Even though he hadn't talked to Sloane in years, he still viewed her as the person at the top of that list. She was the only one who'd continued as a source of annoyance—like a piece of popcorn stuck in his teeth—long after his communication with her had ended.

Jude was fair and impartial and had kept in touch with Sloane even though Jude was *his* friend, a fact that had irritated Max in the past but was serving him well now that he was receiving an insider tip. "When exactly is she arriving in Groomsport?"

"Early July," Jude answered.

And just like that, Max started scheming.

The next day, Jude once again spent far too long preparing a simple text to Gemma.

JUDE

I've met with Dixon and Shannon. May I come by your place tonight to briefly discuss how to proceed with Cedric?

GEMMA

Yep. Time?

JUDE

It should be dark by 7:30. Is that okay?

GEMMA

See you then.

Technically, he could have relayed how to proceed with Cedric through a text or phone call. But now that Cedric had communicated to Gemma that he'd changed his mind about selling Rhapsodie's secrets, and Jude had begun to absorb that setback, a new worry was emerging. He might never have a reason to see Gemma again.

Night before last, she'd gotten out of his car mad. He

couldn't leave that as their last in-person exchange. He needed one last interaction with her, if only for a few minutes.

Tonight, he'd go in with the awareness that this meeting might be their last and he'd make sure it ended on a better note.

Jude looked inside Gemma's mailbox as soon as he arrived. No letters for him to riffle through and steal this time.

She answered his knock and beckoned him to step from the night into the glow of her house and nearness.

Her T-shirt was printed with the pine tree and blue star of Maine's historic flag. Socks with stars on them poked out from beneath the hems of her bell-bottomed yoga pants. She'd caught her hair, the color of orange-red autumn leaves at the peak of brightness, in a casual knot at the back of her neck.

There was something more approachable, more vulnerable about her dressed like this, in her after-work clothes.

He wanted to be with her. He wanted her to be with him. Hunger for that lifted in Jude. She brought *life* with her effortlessly. He needed her companionship and acceptance and sense of humor.

He wished . . .

Well. It didn't matter what he wished.

"I ate dinner a while ago," she said, "but I have leftovers and I'm more than happy to heat them up for you."

It had been a long, difficult day at work. He hadn't managed to fit in dinner yet. Only now that he felt a twist of disappointment at the news that she'd eaten earlier did he realize he'd unconsciously started equating coming here with food. "No, that's okay. Thank you, though."

She moved through the space, turning on lights.

On the kitchen island, she had five Hope and Spice candles

burning. Five. The scent was almost liquid in the air. He was certain now that she knew exactly how the scent affected him. He'd rubbed her the wrong way the other night and this fragrance was her revenge. It was working.

"I'm sorry," he said, "that I inferred to your family that you were the one keeping them from meeting me. I should have handled that better."

She came to a stop a few feet from where he stood and studied his face like she would a game board.

"Are you sorry that you told them I have a butterfly obsession?" he prompted.

"Yes?" she said in a tone that meant *no*.

"Gemma."

She laughed, deep and amused.

His chest had been tight for two days since they'd parted. The sound of her laugh loosened the tension.

"I am sorry," she said. "But please admit that your butterfly obsession is a little bit funny."

"I admit no such thing."

"You. Trotting through fields holding aloft a butterfly catcher. This is a visual I love."

He scowled at her like a disapproving schoolteacher.

Which made her laugh again. Their eye contact lengthened. She cleared her throat. "What step does the FBI want for me to take next with Cedric?"

"Text messages." He unfolded a piece of paper from his suit jacket and handed it over.

She set a hip against the kitchen island and stacked one foot on top of the other, read it, then lifted her face. "You know, I thought we did as well as we possibly could have with Cedric. I don't know why he backed away from the idea of selling his secrets. Whatever his reason, I can't fathom that it had anything to do with you or me."

"I agree." He'd been over and over the conversation at dinner multiple times in his memory but couldn't pinpoint anything that would have caused Cedric to get cold feet. "We both did our part to make good on the resources and hours the FBI has dedicated to this. Maybe Cedric reconsidered because of something that's going on with his personal life or family dynamics or the Bettencourt company."

In Jude's line of work, operations occasionally stalled and agents didn't always receive a clear reason why. People were fickle. People were indecisive. "Our only move at this point," he continued, "is to leave the door open to Cedric in case he decides to change course."

She nodded and indicated the paper she still held. "Do you want me to keep the gist of what you have written here but edit it to make it sound like it's coming from me?"

"Yes. Show it to me for approval, please, before hitting send."

She bent her head to tap on her phone.

He found himself looking down at the perfect bridge and tip of her nose. He was crazy about the curves of Gemma. Whether the curve of cheek, chin, shoulder, fingertips, waist, hips—you name it. Pick a curve on Gemma Clare and it was beautiful to him. Either because it was generous or soft or sweet or firm.

She finished typing and passed the phone over so he could read what she'd written.

GEMMA

No problem! Jude's contact is definitely interested. So if you change your mind, reach out. He'd be more than happy to talk with you or meet with you anytime. It was so much fun to see you the other night! Hope to hang out again soon.

"Good," he said.

"Really?"

"Are you surprised?"

"Your perfectionistic standards are sky-high."

He handed the phone back. "Maybe I'm not as perfectionistic as you believe."

"Oh, you most certainly are. May I send?"

"Send," he confirmed.

She did so and set her phone aside.

"It's late in France," he said. "I don't expect Cedric to reply anytime soon but I'll stick around for ten minutes just in case he does."

"'Kay. Ice cream?"

"No, thanks."

She pulled a carton of Rocky Road out of the freezer, served herself a scoop, and took a bite.

His stomach growled.

She shot him an expression that said, *You should have taken me up on my food and ice cream offer when you had the chance.*

Her phone rang face-up on the counter. The caller ID read *Debt Collection.*

She made a sound of frustration and silenced the call.

Several seconds passed and the same company called again. "Slow to take a hint," she murmured and silenced it.

When they called a third time, Jude swiped the phone and answered. "This is Gemma Clare's attorney. Are you calling to collect on a debt?"

"Yes," a man answered.

"What is the address of your workplace?"

A pause. "Did Gemma consent for you to speak on her behalf?" the man asked.

He held the phone toward Gemma. "Please give him verbal confirmation that I can speak with him on your behalf."

She looked unsure.

"Trust me," he said.

She didn't take the phone from him, just leaned over close to the microphone. "This is Gemma Clare, and he does have permission to speak with you on my behalf."

Jude brought the phone back to his ear. "What is the address of your workplace?"

The debt collector cursed.

Gemma slid a notepad and pen in his direction.

"The Fair Debt Collection Practices Act prohibits you from using profane language," Jude said. "The address of your workplace, please?"

The man grudgingly rattled off the address.

Jude wrote it down. "Expect a letter from me dictating at what hours you are permitted to contact my client by phone." He completed the call, folded the piece of notepaper, and slipped it into his pocket.

Gemma regarded him with wide, gray eyes. "Did you just defend me?"

He couldn't tell her that he'd defend her to anyone at any cost. When he'd seen who was calling, picking up the call had been instinctive, unstoppable. "Let's talk about something else—"

"You just defended me!"

"I don't like it when companies badger people unlawfully," he said stiffly.

She positioned herself in front of him, angling her chin up. "You care about me."

"We're colleagues. I do this type of thing for colleagues—"

"You. Care. About. Me."

"Don't read anything into it. I—"

She gripped the lapels of his suit jacket. "Thank you."

He braced against the need that surged through his veins. "You're welcome."

She flipped the end of his tie over his shoulder.

"We are not undercover at the moment." He smoothed his tie back into position. "No need to pretend."

"Who's pretending?"

She was smiling up at him and he was staring down at her as their dynamic turned quiet and serious. Her attention dropped to his mouth. Then her lashes skimmed slowly up as she met his eyes once more. She was so close that he could see the gradient of color in her irises.

Move, he told himself. *Say something.* But he was rooted to the spot. Riveted.

She slid a finger along his bottom lip.

He held his breath. Afraid to stop this moment. Afraid not to stop it.

She rose onto her tiptoes and then her lips were on his, warm.

He couldn't believe this was happening. *Gemma.* Everything about her was delicious and his body was demanding that he kiss her for hours. But he could not—*could not*—let himself do so.

Belatedly, his muscles obeyed his brain, and he stepped back.

They peered at each other. She licked her bottom lip, and he almost had a heart attack.

"You can't kiss me," he said, hoarse. This was against FBI rules. Plus, she had a boyfriend.

"I just did."

"We're involved in a Bureau operation."

"It looks to me like our operation might have come to an end."

"We're not the ones who decide when it comes to an end." His hands were trembling, so he fisted them at his sides.

She gave him an expression of compassion.

"What?" he said tightly, his heart thumping.

"It must be difficult to always stop yourself from getting upset. I get upset sometimes. I don't mind if you get upset. Want to throw something? I can supply a pillow."

"I do not want to throw a pillow."

"It might help. It helps me to throw pillows."

"No."

"Suit yourself." She resumed eating ice cream.

"I'll need to report what just happened."

She cocked her head. "From where I'm standing, that seems like an overreaction. It was just a peck on the lips. Pretty chaste, actually."

It had not felt chaste to him.

"And I'm the one at fault," she continued. "You did nothing wrong. I didn't plan to kiss you, but I did. It was an impulsive type of thing and I take full responsibility—"

The doorbell sounded. They both stiffened.

"Who's here?" he asked, low.

"No idea."

Gemma knew better than to have company over while he was at her house. This must be a friend or family member stopping by unannounced.

Gemma couldn't pretend not to be home because when Jude had arrived, he'd seen her scooter parked out front. No doubt, this visitor had seen it, too. Thankfully, his car was, as usual, parked blocks away.

"What should I do?" she whispered.

"Answer and make them go away as quickly as possible. I'll wait over there." He nodded toward the section of wall separating the foyer from the living room. Standing behind that, he'd be out of sight of the door.

"All right."

The person on the threshold knocked again. Jude and Gemma moved into place.

Jude heard the door pull open. Gemma gasped. Was that a happy gasp or a frightened one? He was on the verge of going to her in case she needed him when she said, "Chaz?"

Chapter Fifteen

"Gemma!" Chaz said.

"This is a surprise."

"Good! I wanted to surprise you."

A rustling sound followed that had to be the sound of them hugging because the thought of them kissing was flatly unbearable to Jude. Two minutes ago, Gemma had been kissing *him*.

He grabbed Gemma's laptop from the coffee table. Silently, he took a seat on a chair, laptop open on his legs. If Chaz spotted him, he didn't want Chaz to spot him hiding.

"You look great," Chaz said.

"Thank you . . . What are you doing here?"

"Do you remember me mentioning my business trip to Boston? It wrapped up earlier today and Teddy encouraged me to take a few days off. I was already halfway here so I made a spur-of-the-moment decision to drive up and see you."

"Um—"

"I'm hungry and dying of thirst. Can I hit you up for a drink—"

"Actually, let's go out. I hardly have any food in the house. I'll just grab my purse and coat and we'll be off."

Gemma appeared in Jude's line of sight as she scooped her purse off the table. Chaz came into view behind her. He swept up her coat and held it for her while she pushed her arms into it.

This wasn't good. Chaz was going to see him.

They both turned toward the door, which meant turning toward Jude. Chaz startled when he met Jude's gaze.

Jude raised a hand in greeting. "Hello."

"This is Mike Ferguson," Gemma said to Chaz. "He's the one who owns the label-printing company I use for my perfume bottles." He had to hand it to Gemma for thinking fast on her feet. Jude shut the laptop and held it under an arm as he approached them.

"I know you've heard me mention him before," Gemma went on. "Right?"

"Yeah. I think so. I'm Chaz."

"Good to meet you." Jude made himself shake the guy's hand.

"We were just finishing up a meeting," Gemma said.

"How come you didn't mention that someone was here?" Chaz regarded her with amusement.

"My brain got scrambled when I saw you. Besides, Mike's an old friend. He doesn't mind letting himself out."

Chaz wrapped an arm around Gemma's shoulders.

Hot jealousy flooded Jude. Chaz and Gemma were in a relationship and Chaz had every right to wrap an arm around her. Even so, Jude had to set his back teeth together to keep himself from saying, *Get your hands off of her.* He revealed none of that outwardly, though. He'd been practicing the art of appearing impassive for a long, long time. He was a master at it now. Master of a miserable skill.

He understood with burning clarity why Chaz was drawn to Gemma. Men would always be drawn to Gemma like surfers to waves. That would never change. Everywhere she went all day long, at work, at the gym . . . men would pursue her.

"Sorry that we ignored you for a bit there, man," Chaz said to him. "I only saw the scooter parked outside so I had no idea you were here."

"I caught an Uber here and another one's on its way to pick me up," Jude explained. "It's my anniversary. I'm meeting my wife at a restaurant in fifteen minutes, and I plan on celebrating so much that I won't be able to drive home after."

Chaz chuckled, his demeanor relaxing now that he'd learned Mike was married. "Congrats."

Jude had researched Chaz. He knew Chaz was about as serious as cotton candy and had had one girlfriend after another—all many years younger than he was—since his divorce. Jude's research had given him a mild, impersonal distrust of Chaz.

But now? His reaction to the guy in person was far worse, far stronger. Angry heat was racing up Jude's throat. His tie felt like it was choking him. Chaz did not deserve Gemma.

Jude might find a way to deserve her if he was free to try. He was coming to loathe that he had to place his job and his honor before his feelings for her. His stomach churned. "I'll get out of your way." Jude pretended to check his phone. "My driver is just three minutes away."

"It was a productive meeting," Gemma said to him. "Thanks for coming by—"

The sound of a car arriving reached Jude. *Who is this?* He hadn't heard Chaz's arrival. But this car was loud. Impossible to miss.

"That's my mom's car," Gemma said. "I'd know that muffler anywhere."

The word *no* silently filled Jude's head. He couldn't simultaneously be Mike to Chaz and Jude McConnell to Simone.

"I'd be happy to meet her—" Chaz started.

"This is *not* the time to introduce you to my mom," Gemma stated firmly.

Outdoors, the engine went silent. Jude's blood pressure and anxiety shot upward.

"Will you do me a favor and wait in my bedroom while I spend two minutes getting my mom turned around and back on her way?" Gemma asked Chaz.

Chaz hesitated, clearly confused.

"Please," Gemma said. "As a favor to me?"

"Sure, babe. I'll wait in the bedroom." He winked at Jude.

Yeah, Jude couldn't stand him.

Dragging Chaz by the hand, Gemma hurried him upstairs.

Jude set the computer on the island. The laptop had added believability to the idea of a business meeting, but it was an awkward prop to be holding when greeting Gemma's mom.

The song "Shut Up and Dance" erupted from above, then Gemma ran down the stairs. "I turned on music so Chaz can't hear what's being said out here. Sorry about all this. I didn't know—"

A key turned in the door and Gemma's mother appeared in the opening. Her mouth fell open with joy at the sight of the two of them together.

He'd always been excellent with his girlfriends' mothers. They'd all loved him. It appeared his fake girlfriend's mother felt the same. Wonder how she'd react if she knew Gemma's real boyfriend was stuffed in the bedroom?

"Jude!" Simone said. "You're still in town?"

"I am." He moved forward and hugged her.

She released him from the hug, beaming. "Is that your car outside?"

"Yes." Improv was part of undercover work. That didn't mean he relished scenarios like this one. He might as well be riding a passenger train derailing in slow motion.

"He's about to head to the airport to fly back to New York." Gemma interlaced her hand with his. "So, so sad. We're having our last few minutes together before he goes."

"I won't intrude. I just stopped by to drop off some of the cannelloni I made earlier." She pulled a container from her large purse and passed it to Gemma.

"Thank you."

"You're welcome." Simone fiddled with her car keys. Music blared from the bedroom. "Is it a little loud in here?" she asked Gemma. "It's hard to hear myself think."

"It's just the right amount of loud in here," Gemma answered. "Jude loves this song." She sang along with the chorus, pounding one hand into the air in sync with the beat. "Shut up and dance with me."

He definitely did not love this song, but he did love the sight of her singing it to him.

"Well." Gemma blew a strand of hair out of her eyes. "Just a few minutes left before Jude will have to leave." She leaned the side of her face against his shoulder and it felt . . . right. Real. Good in all the ways that seeing her with Chaz had felt awful.

"It's terrible to be separated from the one you love. I should know." Simone headed toward the door, then stopped and looked back at him. "I saw a butterfly the other day and thought of you."

"Oh?"

"It was black. There were blue dots at the edges of its wings and a yellow outline. What variety do you think that was?"

Gemma's posture tightened.

"That sounds like a mourning cloak," he answered.

"They're one of the species that overwinters in Maine and emerges in the spring." If Jude McConnell liked butterflies, then give Jude Camden any amount of time at all, and butterfly information would be studied. As it had been.

"My favorite butterfly expert," Gemma said affectionately.

"I didn't know what to make of that hobby when I first heard about it," Simone admitted. "But now that I've had time to contemplate, I think it's wonderful. It's always good for men to get in touch with their gentler side."

He didn't want a gentler side that had to do with butterflies. In fact, if he never had to hear or speak another word about butterflies, he'd be happy.

"Bye, Mom!" Gemma said.

"Jude, it's wonderful to see Gemma with a man like you. Some of her past boyfriends . . ." Simone winced.

"Mom," Gemma warned.

"I'll be off, then."

Once Simone had gone, Gemma clicked the door closed and broke contact between them. "Now you can go, and I'll release Chaz from captivity."

"I can't go until your mom's out of sight. We made her think we wanted a few minutes together."

She made a face. "Right." She groaned. "It's getting hard to keep all these narratives straight, Mike."

He stashed her computer in the pantry. "I'm putting this away so it will look to Chaz like Mike took his laptop with him."

She expelled a shaky breath. "Are we actually going to make it through this evening, do you think, without blowing your cover?"

"Yes, we're going to make it through." He'd just been treated to living proof that she had a boyfriend who wasn't him. His thoughts and emotions were in the worst kind of turmoil. But if she needed reassurance, he would always give it. If he was drowning, and she was in a raft, he'd give it.

"I thought we were screwed about ten different times," she said.

"We're fine."

"Radioactive" by Imagine Dragons now played from her room.

Her mom's muffler rumbled away to silence.

"Reach out to me when and if Cedric responds," he said.

"I will."

"And please tell Chaz you've changed your mind and want to stay in now that you have cannelloni. We can't allow neighbors to see the two of you out together as a couple, seeing as how your family now knows me as your boyfriend."

"Got it."

"If you could convince Chaz to return to New York, that would be best." For the op and for Jude personally because he couldn't take the idea of Chaz staying in town, spending time with Gemma. "You might be spotted out with him at any point during his stay."

"I'll convince him to return to New York ASAP."

He nodded, then made himself go. He wasn't going to get the relaxed and friendly goodbye with her he'd come tonight to get. He wasn't going to eat cannelloni. He wasn't going to see Gemma smile one last time.

He walked through shadows to where he'd parked his distant car.

Alone.

Leaving Gemma behind with her real-life boyfriend.

That was a debacle, Gemma thought.

She massaged her temples, needing a minute to herself before dealing with Chaz.

Three's Company with John Ritter and Suzanne Somers was her mom's TV version of comfort food. When she'd been incapacitated after her stroke, Mom had escaped into *Three's Company* often. Watching it with her had given Gemma a way to provide company and solidarity when there'd been no words to articulate the depth of the difficulty.

What had played out just now? It had felt like an episode of *Three's Company*, except a lot more nerve-racking and a lot less funny when you were not a paid actress yet found yourself having to play a role.

The one part that had not been acting? The part before Chaz's arrival when she'd kissed Jude.

She was accustomed to following her spontaneous curiosity. *Chase that smell around a corner to see where it's coming from. Reach out and feel that sweater hanging on the rack. Order that pink drink to find out what it tastes like.*

She'd taken hold of Jude's lapels and he'd been so close and looked so handsome and untouchable. Her instincts had whispered, *Discover what it feels like to kiss him.*

Turned out that the intimate, fleeting seconds of their kiss had been *stellar* seconds. Like the seconds when you're chewing a chocolate truffle or breathing in the perfect fragrance or sinking into a bubble bath. During those seconds, she hadn't felt the weight of the FBI operation. Or the heaviness of her mom's health issues. Or the stress of the bills that needed to be paid to keep her family afloat.

But then Chaz had arrived. As soon as she'd comprehended the risk he presented to Jude's alias, she'd suddenly felt every ounce of the weight of the FBI operation. Thank God she'd not made a mistake that had ruined all of Jude's careful work.

She started up the stairs.

Should she have mentioned to Jude that she'd broken up with Chaz? There'd been a moment, in the midst of all that, when she'd considered it. She'd decided against it because things had been fraught after Chaz's arrival as it was. She'd not wanted to thrust another surprise on Jude. Additionally, selfishly, she hadn't wanted to risk Jude criticizing her for ending things with Chaz without consulting the FBI.

Inside her bedroom, she found Chaz sitting on the end of her bed, scrolling on his phone. Gemma flipped off the music, leaving reverberating silence. "My mom's gone. The coast is clear."

"I haven't been hidden away by anyone since I was twenty-one," Chaz said happily, pressing to standing. "I was dating a woman at the time whose divorce wasn't final. Her husband came in unexpectedly." He waggled his eyebrows.

Irritation toward him stabbed through her. What had he been thinking, coming here? She gestured for him to follow. "My mom dropped off homemade cannelloni, which might as well have been prepared by angels. Plus, I remembered that I have some bread rolls and probably enough veggies to scrounge up a salad. How about I feed that to you and we stay here?"

"Yeah! Sounds great."

He'd been driving for hours and professed to be starving, so she'd get some food in him. The conversation they were about to have would go down better on a full stomach. She set to work fixing him a plate. It didn't take long before he was sitting on a tall stool at her kitchen island, lifting his first bite of pasta. He pointed to the red sauce speckled with seasonings. "Thyme is money."

She dredged up a weary smile. "Yep. I get it."

He chuckled, then dug into the food with gusto. When he'd eaten about a third of it, he slowed and stated the obvious. "You look displeased."

"I broke up with you. So I'm a little mystified about this surprise visit."

"Okay, okay. I hear you. I get why you'd be mystified." He blotted his mouth with his napkin. "After our last talk, I missed you. I remembered that it had been my turn to come here, to Maine, but that I'd tried to talk you into coming to New York instead. I felt bad. That wasn't fair. So this is me, showing you that I'm willing to do my part. And saying that I'm sorry I dragged my feet about coming here. I'm really into you, Gemma. I'd like to give this thing between us more time."

Right here and now she could instantly transport herself back to the courtroom where she'd stood next to her mother and brothers, her heart ripping in half when someone she truly, truly loved had been taken away in handcuffs.

The Chazes of the world had not put her heart at risk. But that wasn't enough anymore to entice her to keep on dating them. Something had shifted inside her since she'd met Jude.

"Babe?" Chaz asked.

"I haven't changed my mind. I don't want to get back together."

Chapter Sixteen

Jude never drank too much.

In fact, ordinarily, he hardly drank at all. He was too much of a perfectionist to let his guard down. Too responsible to allow alcohol to make a fool of him. Too worried that he'd be drunk right when someone needed him.

Tonight, though, after leaving Gemma at her ancient lake house with Chaz, he'd called Jeremiah and asked if he'd meet him for drinks at the sports bar Jude went to from time to time with FBI friends. It was a Tuesday, not exactly a night of the week known for socializing. And Jeremiah lived an hour away from Bangor. Even so, his older brother hadn't paused before telling him he was on his way.

Jude was the person in the family everyone relied on. He never asked the others for anything. Clearly, Jude requesting that Jeremiah meet him had told Jeremiah all he needed to know.

Jeremiah had the faster car, but Jude had the advantage of proximity. He arrived first and took a seat at the bar.

When Jude joined his buddies here, they ribbed each other while playing pool, or darts, or shuffleboard on a raised table.

Tonight, Jude had no interest in games. He began by downing what he intended to be the first of many shots. Then he ordered hot wings—not as healthy as his usual dinners. While waiting for Jeremiah, he divided his focus between the Celtics and Red Sox games playing on the mounted TVs. He only wished he could divert himself by concentrating on the games, even a little. His thoughts sabotaged him by remaining fixed on Gemma.

No need to watch the door for Jeremiah because he'd know when his brother entered without having to look. He had lots of experience with the response Jeremiah's famous face generated.

Even before Jeremiah had been famous, their family had received attention everywhere they'd gone. When he'd been very young and shy, the interest of others had been like warm light, making him feel remarkable and special.

But during his late elementary school years, he'd comprehended that people didn't view Mom or Dad as normal, like he did. His parents were the ones who took care of Jeremiah and him, fed them, drove them places, ensured they took showers and did their homework, read to them at bedtime. No one was more familiar to him.

Yet strangers saw Dad as a quarterback and an unfaithful husband. They saw Mom as his mistress. Once he'd understood the reason behind everyone's awareness of their family, he'd started to feel the animosity and sharp curiosity in it. Turned out, he was a circus attraction. That had been doubly true when the second scandal hit them. Jude had gone to ground.

When he'd applied to college, his self-esteem demanded that he do so on his own merits. Same with law school and later, the FBI. His accomplishments were his own, which brought deep satisfaction.

It had been years since he'd advertised his connection to his parents or to Jeremiah. He didn't want to wonder whether people liked him because of him or his family's notoriety. He didn't want to fuss with the questions people asked him about the Camdens. And he definitely didn't want to be anyone's circus attraction.

A stir worked its way through the atmosphere of the place. Jeremiah had arrived. Sure enough, seconds later Jude's brother clamped a hand on Jude's shoulder, then took the barstool next to him. "Hey."

"Hello."

Jeremiah looked Jude over, pushing his tongue against the inside of one cheek. "Hmm," he finally said.

A female bartender rushed up to take Jeremiah's order. He, too, ordered the chicken wings. She thanked Jeremiah as if he'd given her a gift and peered at him with starstruck wonder before moving off. Universally, this was how women treated Jeremiah. When they'd both been single in their twenties, Jude had benefitted from going out with his brother even though he was the not-quite-as-handsome, younger, not-racecar-driver one. So many women had flocked around them that it had been like having chocolate drop in Jude's lap just because he was standing close to the main attraction.

"What's the matter?" Jeremiah asked.

"A case." He downed his second shot.

"You've had difficult cases before, but this is the first time you've asked me to meet you at a bar."

Jude said nothing.

"Is this case particularly violent or disturbing or something?"

"No."

"Then what is it about it that's bothering you?"

"It's messing with my emotions."

"Emotions?"

Jude caught a bartender's eye and tapped on his empty glass like, *I'll have another.*

"Is there a woman involved?" Jeremiah asked.

Jude combed his fingers through his hair.

"There's a woman involved in your case," his brother stated.

"It's confidential."

Jeremiah held his tongue for a minute straight, then said, "Occasionally, when I was falling in love with Remy, you'd mention how miserable I looked. Remember?"

Jude had never named what he felt for Gemma as love. Never thought to himself, *I'm falling in love.* Truthfully, he didn't know what this was. He hadn't permitted himself to examine it because it could go nowhere. But now that he had an opportunity to tell his brother that he *wasn't* falling in love, the words wouldn't come. "Are you here to gloat?"

"If you're miserable because you're falling in love then yes, absolutely. I'm here to gloat. But I'm also here to be your designated driver and to eat chicken wings and to say that I haven't forgotten how much it sucked when I thought Remy would never have me."

One of the Celtics slam-dunked the ball. A cheer went up around them.

"Are you not allowed to be with this woman because it's against procedure?" Jeremiah asked.

Jude nodded.

"Would she want to be with you if not for that?"

"I don't know. She has a boyfriend."

The conversations and laughter of others crowded in.

"She's the one for you," Jeremiah said. "Isn't she?"

"She can't be."

"You'd think, once you find the right person, that the road to happiness would be straight. For me, it wasn't. But I can tell you that it was worth all the stress it cost me."

He was glad his brother was here so he didn't have to drink alone. But his misery hadn't lessened. It was intolerable. More alcohol needed.

An hour later, he made his way back to the bar from the restroom, bemused to note that the lights in the building were all slightly fuzzy and the edges of things blurry.

"Jude?" a feminine voice asked.

He came to a stop, his brain sloshing in his skull.

Riley from work darted up from where she'd been sitting at one of the tables. "Hi. Wow! How are you?"

"Fine. You?"

"Great, especially now that I've run into you." She blushed. "My brother's here with me tonight." She motioned to a guy sitting at her table who was the male version of her. Blond, thin, pale.

"Ah." Jude's vocabulary had gone missing.

She introduced him to her brother, then pulled Jude out of earshot. "It's really wonderful to see you outside of work."

"Ditto."

"Would you like to join us?"

"Thanks, but I'm here with my own brother. I think I'm about to leave."

"Would you . . . like me to come along with you? Wherever you're headed?" She was very pretty. And hopeful. She was clearly into him. Gemma . . . terrible Gemma had a boyfriend. So what would it hurt if he said yes to Riley? He opened his mouth to tell her yes right when Jeremiah slung an arm around his shoulders.

"Is this the woman from your case?" Jeremiah whispered against his ear.

Jude answered with an expression that said, *Are you crazy? No.*

"Hello there," Jeremiah said to her. "I'm the brother."

"I'm Riley. Jude and I work together."

Then Riley's brother asked Jeremiah for his autograph and Jeremiah got busy charming them both. "Well," he announced after a few minutes, "Jude and I are going to call it a night."

"I'm happy to drive Jude home," Riley offered with the expression of a puppy waiting at the door for a bathroom break.

That would save Jeremiah a lot of time on his drive back to Groomsport. The *O* of okay was all Jude got out before Jeremiah interrupted.

"Thanks so much for offering, but I'm going to take him. Now that I'm retired, I don't have many chances to show off my driving skills to my little brother."

"I'm tired of watching you show off your driving skills," Jude said.

Jeremiah chuckled. "Which is why I love chances to force him to admire them. Good night, guys. Great to meet you."

Once they were in Jeremiah's Ferrari speeding through Bangor, his brother looked across at him several times. Jeremiah was checking on him. Which was rich. Jude was the person who checked on Jeremiah. And Mom and Dad and Max. And their grandparents.

"You should have let Riley drive me," Jude said.

"No way. She's obviously crazy about you. You're too noble to take advantage of that."

"No, I'm not."

"Yes, you are. At most, you'd have let her make out with you. But even then, you'd be angry with yourself in the morning. Plus, you'd have an awkward situation to clean up with her at work. So, no."

"You're the worst."

"Actually, I'm feeling like a prince among brothers right now."

Jude closed his eyes and let the car veer and turn beneath the dead weight of him.

"You want to come with me to Appleton tonight and crash there?" Jeremiah asked.

"Can't. Work tomorrow."

"You can take one of my cars to work tomorrow."

"I want to go home. Mabel's waiting." He'd brought her home from doggie daycare this afternoon, but no way was he leaving her alone at the house overnight.

Once they arrived at the cabin and he finally got Jeremiah to leave—why had he thought it was a good idea to invite him in the first place?—Jude stepped into the shower.

Weaving a little, he scrubbed shampoo into his hair and congratulated himself on his decision to go to the bar. He felt great.

Nothing bothered him. Definitely not Gemma.

Once he was dry and he'd let Mabel out for the final time and given her bedtime treats, he fell heavily onto his mattress.

He dreamed of Gemma.

He was holding her hand. Her red hair fanned out as she swung her head to smile at him tenderly. They were walking across a field at the time of day when the sun was dying and darkness rising. She was relaxed and he could feel the glow of her happiness. But when he looked forward, he saw a group of men walking toward them. He knew they were coming to take her from him.

Fear pierced him deep. He and Gemma began running toward where he'd parked his car.

The men sprang into motion, chasing. He and Gemma sprinted as fast as they could go but the men were faster. One of them lunged and caught her wrist. She cried out as she jerked to a stop. Jude fought them with all the strength and fury he had, but they yanked her away.

She screamed. Some of them were pulling her from him. Some of them were holding him in place. He couldn't get free. "Gemma!"

Hopeless. There were too many of them. His heart was shattering, his horror rising—

Gasping, he woke. Then struggled to differentiate what was dream and what was reality.

His dark bedroom was reality.

The field, Gemma looking at him with love, the attack, the struggle. That was dream.

Gemma was safe tonight. At her house. With her boyfriend.

Mabel snored softly from her dog bed. He was under a down comforter, the sheets around him soft. Yet he felt *rotten*. His pulse pounded sickly. He was hot, sweaty, nauseous.

He had family and he had friends and he had his dog. He had the privacy from the media he wanted. He had a job he loved. A house he loved. Money. He'd made his work the biggest part of his life, yes. But he still had time to be as social as he wanted to be.

So why did he feel as profoundly lonely now as he had lying in his high school bedroom back when he'd been in charge of his mother and terrified that he'd lose his battle for her mental health? The loneliness then had been aching—a physical thing that had stalked him like a predator, caught him, and gnawed on him.

It was stalking him like a predator again.

The following morning, Gemma checked her phone upon waking and found a text from Cedric.

CEDRIC

I don't plan to change my mind, but I want you to know that I liked Jude. It was nice to see you with a good guy.

Heavy-hearted, she took a screenshot of Cedric's text and sent it to Jude.

Jude updated Shannon, Scent-sible's case agent, on Cedric's text to Gemma, then hesitated before leaving her office.

"Is there something else?" Shannon shot him a quizzical look from where she sat behind her highly organized desk.

"Gemma kissed me last night."

Her lips flattened but she did not appear surprised.

"It was brief," he continued, "but I should've stopped her before it happened." Gemma had given him plenty of time to prevent the kiss when they'd been inches apart, locked in physical awareness of each other.

"Did you fail to stop her because you're attracted to her?"

"I am attracted to her," Jude admitted. "But I can keep that from interfering with the job."

"It sounds like Ms. Clare can't keep it from interfering with the job, however."

"I think this was a one-off. She indicated that it was unplanned."

Tense quiet. "I'm not thrilled," Shannon finally said.

"I apologize."

"Overall, I've been very impressed with your work on Scent-sible."

"Thank you."

"But if a cooperating witness develops feelings for an agent during a UC op, it's the responsibility of the agent to ensure nothing inappropriate happens."

"Yes."

"Despite how a cooperating witness says they'll behave, we have to be aware—all the time—that they might not adhere to that behavior. It's up to us to enforce the standards."

"Right." He hated failing at any aspect of his work. He hated letting himself and others down. And all of that was making his hangover worse. He felt physically terrible and would rather die than drink another shot as long as he lived.

"That seems like an overreaction," Gemma had said after he'd told her he'd need to report the kiss. *"It was just a peck on the lips."* Maybe so, but he wouldn't have been able to live with himself if he'd remained silent. Doing the right thing was still right even when it cost you. Especially when it cost you.

Shannon stacked her palms on the desktop. "I'm going to suspend Operation Scent-sible for the time being."

His muscles clenched.

Her shrewd eyes seemed to note the change in his body language. "I'm suspending it mostly because our subject, Cedric, has indicated that he is no longer willing to continue. But I'm also suspending it in smaller part because I cannot condone a relationship between you and a cooperating witness during the course of an active operation."

"I understand."

"Now that the case is suspended, I can't dictate the choices you make in your personal life. But I strongly suggest that you keep your distance from Ms. Clare. That's what will go best for your reputation here and for your continued employment. You're too good an agent to throw your career away, Jude."

He let himself out of her office and returned to his desk. As always, he faced more work than work hours. Yet he sat unseeing, struggling to accept that Scent-sible had been suspended. Partially because of him. Guilt and blame sank talons into him.

How was he supposed to accept anything less than a successful resolution of this case?

He'd researched every detail of Rhapsodie's history. From the herbalist in the convent through the twists and turns of time, it had endured. Rhapsodie was Gemma's family's legacy.

He'd researched Cedric extensively. He was convinced of Cedric's long list of crimes and yet, up until now, Cedric had evaded the law. He needed to be brought down. Not just because he couldn't be trusted with Rhapsodie's formula and process but because of the laundry list of felonies he'd committed and would continue to commit. Scent-sible had been Jude's chance, Gemma's chance, to have a hand in putting him behind bars.

He picked up his phone and forced himself to type a text to Gemma.

JUDE

Operation Scent-sible has been suspended.

Her reply was almost instantaneous.

GEMMA

What? Why?

JUDE

Because Cedric has expressed his decision not to pursue the selling of his proprietary information.

For sixty full seconds he watched scrolling dots. His headache throbbed and he checked the time to see if he was okay to take more medicine. He still had to wait an hour for that.

GEMMA

Did you tell your boss that I kissed you?

JUDE

Yes.

GEMMA

Jude! Did she suspend this case because I
kissed you?

JUDE

She said that was a small part of the reason.
The larger part was about Cedric. We can't
bait him into selling his secrets because we
must avoid entrapment.

GEMMA

Jude!

JUDE

Gemma. There's nothing more you or I can
do at this juncture. If he doesn't want to sell
Jude McConnell his secrets, then that's it.

GEMMA

That's it?

JUDE

That's it.

GEMMA

Just because Cedric's not going to sell
secrets to you at this point, that doesn't mean
he's not going to sell them to someone else
now or later. Rhapsodie isn't safe. Cedric
would put his mother up for auction for the
right price.

JUDE

I agree with you. However, I can't stop him unless he reinstates communication with Jude McConnell.

JUDE

Thank you for your participation.

GEMMA

Please don't use formal Bureau-speak with me. This is you, cutting me out of your life, isn't it?

JUDE

This is me letting you know the case has been suspended.

GEMMA

Am I supposed to tell my family that I broke up with Jude McConnell?

JUDE

Yes, but not yet. There's a chance Cedric might change his mind. If you can pretend to continue dating Jude McConnell long-distance for the next two months or so, that would be ideal.

GEMMA

Okay.

JUDE

Thanks for your work. It really is appreciated.

He waited and waited.

She did not reply.

Chapter Seventeen

Fiona and Remy had very little in common. So little, that Fiona had grasped early on the importance of cultivating any overlap between herself and Jeremiah's girlfriend.

One area of overlap? They both harbored affection for Remy's elderly friend Wendell.

Which explained why Fiona was spending the first Saturday in April scurrying around Groomsport's dock, working to stage a wedding proposal on a sailboat.

Wendell had told Remy and Fiona privately last month that he wanted to propose to Marisol. Not only that, but he dreamed of doing so on a sailboat.

Initially, they'd settled on the idea of him proposing to Marisol while he sailed her around the bay. Wendell was a bookish sort and though he'd lived on a remote island most of his life, he'd never learned to sail. Remy had suggested lessons.

Wendell had quickly flunked his first three lessons. After his instructor had been hit with the boom during his fourth and final lesson, Wendell and Remy had seen the brilliance of proposing on a sailboat moored to the dock.

As the only talented hostess in the group, Fiona had volunteered to rent a sailboat and to prepare all the engagement "swag." A picnic lunch, balloons, champagne.

She checked her watch. Goodness! Just ten minutes left before Burke would be dropping off Wendell and Marisol. She and Remy would have had everything ready by now if it wasn't for the wind. Though today's temperature had reached the high fifties, the wind kept impishly trying to fling things overboard. At the moment it was threatening to lift her dolman top over her head and expose her bra.

Clamping down her mint-green shirt with one hand, she placed items on the boat's built-in outdoor table. A heavy crockery vase filled with flowers. Porcelain plates. Fabric napkins held down with flatware. Then she and Remy stuffed the remaining items into the space below deck.

According to Wendell's plan, she and Remy were to wait out of sight until after he proposed, then pop into view. Which brought to mind scantily dressed women exploding out of the tops of life-sized cakes.

As she and Remy jammed into the tiny interior it became abundantly clear that Fiona's flair for the dramatic had led her astray. She'd purchased just two clusters of silver, cream, and gold balloons. But each cluster contained an enormous number of balloons.

Now every inch of cubic space inside the sailboat was taken up by females or balloons. The smell of latex was dizzying. The scent reminded her of when she was a girl, tasked with blowing up balloon after balloon for her siblings' parties and how sore that had made her cheeks.

I'm doing this for an excellent cause, she reminded herself. Remy loved Wendell. And Fiona was very fond of him and Marisol, both of whom were so kind and endearing. She only wished this good deed hadn't resulted in balloons pressed against her temples and butt. Hyperventilating down here did not appeal.

"I now know what a gumball feels like when it's waiting in a gumball machine," Remy murmured.

Fiona started giggling.

Then Remy started giggling.

"I should have purchased more balloons," Fiona said sarcastically. "Why was I so stingy? What was I thinking?"

"*Stingy* is not a word I associate with you, Fiona."

"Well, that's one thing I can be glad of in this highly uncomfortable moment."

Balloons squeaked against each other. "Don't mind me," Remy said. "I'm just trying to adjust my position so I can see out the window." *Squeak squeak.* "Wendell and Marisol are coming. I think. I'm looking through ivory-encased helium, so I'm not sure."

Turned out, Remy was correct. Soon, thank God, the sound of Wendell and Marisol's voices reached Fiona through the thin door in front of her. It had a window set into it, covered by a slightly see-through shade. "Do you want to come and stand in this spot, so you'll have a view of the big moment?" Fiona asked.

"I wouldn't be able to trade places with you unless I popped seven hundred balloons."

Fiona released another slightly hysterical giggle. Was she getting high?

"What a beautiful boat," Marisol was saying as she walked ahead of Wendell down the gangplank toward the deck. Wendell's balance wavered and Fiona caught her breath in terror, afraid he'd pitch into the water below. He wrapped his palm around the handrail and steadied himself.

Marisol continued forward, oblivious. "Who does this belong to?"

"A friend. They said that we were welcome to come and sit

for a time and . . . and enjoy the best view in the world." When Wendell reached the deck, he stood stiffly, wringing his hands.

"It's wonderful. I've always loved Groomsport's harbor. So picturesque."

A slight pause followed. "I'm sorry that it's a little windy," Wendell stated.

"I enjoy a breeze." The wind whipped Marisol's white hair out of its bun and flung it in front of her face like an opaque mask.

"Marisol," Wendell stated abruptly.

"Yes?"

"I have something to ask you."

She waited. When he didn't go on, she said, "Yes?"

He moved to lower to one knee but didn't get far before gripping the table for support. It took a full ten seconds for him to make his slow-mo descent. When he got there, he winced. "My kneecap," he wheezed.

Marisol passed him a throw pillow.

He levered up partway to place the throw pillow below his kneecap, which cost another several seconds for a repeat slow-mo descent. Once he had his legs situated, he attempted to remove his hand from the table. He started to tilt and clamped the table once again. "Marisol."

"Yes, Wendell?" She cleared a space in the hair mask to look through.

"I love you so much. You have added joy and companionship back into my life. You are the most giving . . . the sweetest person. I can't believe that God has brought you to me again. I don't deserve it, but He is good, and I'll forever be grateful. I wonder . . . That is to say . . ." He cleared his throat. "I wanted to know if you would consider doing me the great honor . . . the biggest honor of them all . . . of becoming my wife?"

Even the hair in her face couldn't obscure the brightness of her smile. "*Yes.* I'd love to marry you, darling." Marisol reached down to help him up.

Then they were kissing, embracing, laughing.

Fiona grinned. Happiness for them welled buoyantly within her. Wendell and Marisol wholeheartedly treasured one another.

Fiona had once believed that Felix treasured her like that. He had not. In fact, she now understood that he wasn't capable of treasuring anyone that way. As a consequence, she was no longer capable of telling herself fairytales about love and calling them non-fiction.

"Did he give her the ring?" Remy whispered.

"Either he forgot about the ring, or it wasn't physically possible to extract it without him crashing to the deck."

"Should we make ourselves known now? Or is it too early?"

"Too early. They're kissing."

"Let's wait until they transition to talking. I don't want to interrupt."

"Or scare Marisol so badly we send her into cardiac arrest."

After a few minutes had passed, Wendell and Marisol stepped apart, hands still linked.

"Okay," Fiona said. "I think this might be the time to make ourselves known."

"Good. If I stay down here much longer, I'm afraid I'll pass out and no one will be able to find me in order to resuscitate."

Fiona turned the knob, thrust forward, and immediately found herself wedged into the opening.

Marisol jumped and turned toward the sound with a gasp.

Fiona heaved her body forward again. She was squeezed as narrow as the Flat Stanley character she remembered from picture books when her boys were small. With a wail of latex, she freed both herself and dozens of balloons. It must have looked to Marisol and Wendell like the boat was vomiting festivities.

"Congratulations!" Fiona exclaimed, keeping a death grip on the velvet ribbon cinching her bunch of balloons. The wind yanked at them, bumping them together furiously and tangling all of their ties.

"Thank you!" The couple hugged Fiona as Remy wrestled free from below deck. They greeted Remy, too, with hugs.

Remy and Fiona's manic balloons were becoming a hazard, making it difficult to see, hear, or think.

"We can let these two bunches of balloons go," Fiona announced loudly on a wave of inspiration, "to commemorate the love you have for each other lifting to the heavens."

"Oh, how perfect," Marisol said.

"I'll count up to five," Remy told them. "One, two, three"—they all joined in—"four, five!"

They released the balloons and Fiona had never been so glad to see two expensive bundles of decorations fly away to become somebody else's problem. She knew that was terrible of her. Too selfish toward the environment and animals. When she got home, she'd write a check to World Wildlife.

Fiona located her purse and passed out hair ties to the females. She never ordinarily lowered herself to a ponytail, but desperate times and all that.

Fiona and Remy were unpacking the picnic basket as Burke made his way down the gangplank. Fiona smiled with relief at the sight of him. His low-key vibe made every situation better.

Burke congratulated the newly engaged couple, easily drawing them into conversation, always knowing the right things to say.

The stars hadn't been aligned for her and Burke to become gold-level friends back when they'd first met. At that time, they'd both been married with young kids. In this season, however, the stars *had* aligned in their favor. There was just something so comforting about a gold-level friend whom you earnestly liked and fully trusted.

Fiona finished preparing plates of chicken salad sandwiches, fruit, nuts, pretzels, and pickles. She waved them all into seats at the table.

Remy held aloft her champagne flute. "Here's to true love."

"To true love," they all echoed. Their glasses clinked.

Happy chatter flowed around Fiona. She soaked in the details of dusky blue sky, deep blue water, and brave spring fighting to make itself known on the branches of the trees hugging the bay. She drew salty air into her lungs, held it for a few beats, and gradually released it. Her shoulders relaxed. They'd pulled off Wendell's memorable engagement. He and Marisol were as thrilled as any two people could be. Jeremiah had his memories back and he was doing incredibly well because Remy had breathed life back into his heart. Jude was killing it with his career. She hadn't seen Felix for a blessed three straight weeks. Her accountant had informed her yesterday that her business was on track to reach its highest quarterly earnings in history.

This moment would have felt artificially ideal without the wind. But the wind was here. And the one imperfect aspect of this day made all the other aspects sweeter.

"Want to come by my place?" Burke asked when they'd finished the meal and were cleaning up.

"Yes, please. I have something I want to discuss with you."

Fiona had many favorite spots. The living room inside her storybook house. The dining table of the home where she'd grown up when it was packed with family. Bistro Pierre, the impeccable French restaurant in downtown Groomsport where she'd shared hundreds of dinners with her sons. Lying on a table at her spa, receiving a facial. A lounge chair overlooking the teal-blue Caribbean at her favorite resort.

One of her new favorite spots? The leather sofa inside Burke's comfortable, masculine house. He always lit a fire in the fireplace for her because he knew she liked it. She always took off her heels. And he always had wine stocked for her.

The atmosphere here was beguilingly cozy. Mostly because of *him*.

After she'd returned from her conversation with Isobel in New York, she and Burke had discussed at length how to proceed. Isobel had asked Fiona to respect her boundaries. At this point it wouldn't be kind or productive for Fiona to force another meeting.

"I've decided to send Isobel a piece of mail." She rustled inside her purse and brought out the envelope she'd not yet sealed. "I haven't tried to disguise my handwriting or my return address this time." She passed it over. "Isobel will know who it's from and be free to open it or return it unopened."

She watched as he gently took out the contents and looked through them. A twinge of vulnerability assailed her. She hoped he approved.

"Since most everything has been articulated between us," she went on, "I've only included photographs and an article. The photos are of the two of us on the trip to South America when we were girls and saw the eclipse together."

He smiled fondly at the pictures. "Remind me how old you were here?"

"Eight."

"You look like a mini version of your adult self. Same beautiful face. Your bravery and confidence are obvious in every inch of you, even at this age." He turned the photo toward her.

In the snapshot, Isobel stood with perfect posture, feet together. Already then, she'd been a lady. By contrast, Fiona had plunked her hands on her bony hips. One leg bent to the side, feet placed wide. The photo could have been titled, *Serene Older Sister and Feisty Younger Sister*.

He continued studying the items.

"The article's a lyrical piece," Fiona explained, "about the wonder and awe that the coming eclipse will bring to Maine." At the end of the article, Fiona had simply scrawled a heart and her initial *F*—which was how she'd signed all her notes and letters to Isobel before they'd become enemies.

"I think this is a good approach," he said.

"Excellent. I'll send it on Monday."

He handed the envelope back and their fingers touched, giving her a pleasing jolt of awareness.

Back in late November, when he'd expressed his interest in dating her, they'd been sitting in these same seats in this same room.

Since then, she'd replayed the words he'd spoken again and again.

"I'm crazy about you, just the way you are."

And then, *"I want you to know that with patience and time . . . I think I'll be able to win your heart."*

He hadn't raised the subject of dating since then. But that sentiment—*I'm crazy about you*—was in his eyes . . . eyes not of a boy or a young man. On the contrary, Burke had the wise eyes of a man who'd lived a long time and loved his people very, very well.

I'm crazy about you was also in the way he showed up for her faithfully.

I'm crazy about you was in the laughter they shared.

She had the sense that Burke was biding his time, like a woodsman coaxing an injured fox to come inside the warmth and safety of his home.

A week and a half after Jude's last communication with Gemma, he arranged a meeting with her mother.

Because he'd arrived early at the Bayview coffee shop mid-morning on this April Saturday, he was waiting for Simone Clare by the door when she arrived.

Gemma's mom greeted him warmly, hugging him longer than expected.

They chatted while they placed drink orders. A vanilla steamer for her, a latte for him. He paid, then they carried their to-go cups to a booth. Seeing Gemma's mom in person was satisfying and tortuous. Satisfying, because he was finally doing something about his compulsion to help the Clares. Tortuous because he couldn't look at Simone—with her red hair and the elements of her features that echoed Gemma's features—without thinking of her daughter.

He missed Gemma. Constantly. So much his chest burned with it.

"Hearing from you was a wonderful surprise," she told him when they were settled. "You're back in town so soon!"

"Yes. Just a quick trip this time." She still knew him as Jude McConnell. Which was tricky but not insurmountably so.

"You said over the phone that you wanted to chat about how you might be able to assist our family. I've been eager to learn what you meant by that ever since."

"I'm an attorney." He and McConnell both were. "I'm hoping that my law background might be helpful to you."

"Oh? How so?"

"In the area of law that pertains to debt collections. The more time I've spent with Gemma, the more aware I've become of the debt collectors who send her mail and call her."

He watched Simone's shoulders slowly sag. "That's my fault."

"No," he said, unequivocal. "It's not your fault."

"I should have made sure long ago that I was the one receiving the calls and the mail from the debt collection agencies. I'll fix that right away." Anxiously, she smoothed her bangs to the side. "I let Gemma bear the brunt of things after her father went to prison. That was wrong of me. She was so young."

"Gemma wanted to take on all that she did. She's persuasive and strong. She wouldn't have had it any other way and you couldn't have stopped her if you'd tried." Gentle Simone was no match for Gemma in terms of willpower. "I reached out to you because, if you'd like, I can explain to you your rights and also how to keep the debt collectors in line using the laws already in place."

Surprise smoothed her features. "I . . . Really?"

"Yes."

"That would be amazing. This is timely because a few weeks ago, I received a complaint one of the collectors filed against me in court. I didn't know what to do."

"How old is the debt specified in the complaint?" Jude asked, frowning.

"All of my debts originated seven years ago, when my husband went to prison. I've made payments on them. As much as I was able. It was never enough."

"The statute of limitations in Maine is six years. Debts older than that, like yours, are referred to as time-barred debts. They can't take you to court for them."

"They can't?"

"No. If you'll furnish me with a copy of the complaint you received, I'll read over it and let you know how to respond to the court."

"*Thank you.* I—I'll need to pay you for your time."

"Definitely not. This is just me sharing what I know with a friend. We can spend as much time as you'd like talking through this today. And you can call me with additional questions anytime. I'm also going to put you in touch with a debt counselor who will be able to advise you, free of charge, on debt modification and debt consolidation." Either he'd find a counselor who provided services free through a non-profit, or he'd hire one for her. "Together, you can come up with a strategy. Which should take off a lot of the pressure."

Moisture sprang to her eyes.

He had a soft spot for mothers, like his own mother, who'd had to go it alone when their husbands walked off stage. "Are you all right?" he asked gently.

"I just—I can't believe you'd do all of this for us."

I would do anything to make Gemma's life better. He woke up every day remembering the agonizing sight of Gemma with Chaz. He went to sleep thinking about it. The possibility that he'd never see her again was a thorn in his side. But here was one small thing, the only thing, he could actively do for Gemma. A stampede of horses couldn't have kept him from this.

"You must care about Gemma," she said. "A lot."

"I do."

"How can I ever thank you?"

"No thanks needed. I do have one request, though."

"Anything."

"Can we please keep my involvement in this confidential?"

"You . . . don't want me to tell Gemma?"

"No. I spoke with a debt collector when he called her, so

she knows I stepped into that one situation. I'd like to leave it at that for now."

"But why? She'd be so grateful to you."

"That's just it. I don't want her to feel obligated to be with me." Gemma wasn't with him. Even if she was, she wasn't the type to keep a boyfriend around due to a sense of obligation.

Her thin brows rose. "I can't imagine, Jude, that any woman would feel obligated to be with you."

"Gemma might. Also, I don't want her to spend any more time thinking about debt collection."

Simone nodded thoughtfully. Sniffed. Gave him a tremulous smile. "Jude? You have a deal."

Chapter Eighteen

One week later, the silence and solitude of Gemma's house closed around her like a cage. Her restlessness spiked. *I can't be trapped in here right now or I'm going to go stark raving mad.*

She flipped up one corner of the living room rug, then unlatched and opened the trap door. A series of metal rungs bolted to one of the stilts provided her most direct route to the lake.

Gemma draped a throw blanket over her shoulders, wearing it the way Vikings on TV shows wore fur pelts, and climbed down. Her rowboat bobbed on the water, secured with a loose loop so that it could raise or lower with changes in the height of the lake. She climbed in the boat, released it from its moorings, and began to row.

She'd been in a blue mood ever since Jude had informed her that Operation Scent-sible was at an end, then abruptly dismissed her from his life as if she were a magazine subscription he was eager to cancel. Though he'd been perfectly polite —politeness was woven into the fabric of Jude Camden's soul—

the way he'd severed their connection left her feeling as though he'd delivered a slap.

Every time she thought about it, which she'd been doing ceaselessly, she experienced a spurt of annoyance followed by a gloomy feeling of loss.

Two and a half weeks had come and gone since she'd heard from him. Two and a half weeks! Instead of his absence becoming easier to bear with every passing day, it was becoming harder.

She'd known, of course, that her conversations and meetings with Jude had taken up a large chunk of her time over the past two months. What she'd failed to recognize until now was just how much *value* she'd come to attach to the time she spent with him. He'd entered her life as an interruption. But as they'd been preparing for their operation, he'd become much more to her than that. She loved sparring with him, she loved looking at him, she loved hearing his voice over the phone. He entertained her. He could make her swoon with a glance.

And now he'd been wiped from her calendar.

Gone.

Though she'd enjoyed an active life before Agent Jude Camden had walked into her shop, his absence had left a void bigger than she would have dreamed. It was shocking and dismaying, the size of the void.

Her breath came faster as she put more muscle into the movement of the oars.

Maybe this empty feeling was magnified because Chaz had disappeared from the scene around the same time as Jude?

Chaz had taken her decision not to get back together in stride—likely because he hadn't been much more invested in her than she'd been in him. He'd stayed at a hotel the night he'd arrived at her house unannounced, then driven back to New

York the following day. He'd texted once to say he'd returned home safely. Nothing else.

So. Did some of this emptiness have to do with Chaz?

Listening to the rhythmic splashing sounds of water, she pondered that.

No. All of it, every bit of the emptiness, had to do with Jude. The failure of their operation, yes. But mostly the end of their relationship.

Via their last text message exchange, Jude had made it clear that they were colleagues in his eyes and nothing more. In the days between then and now, he'd verified that with his silent detachment. Yet before he'd distanced himself from her there had been times when he'd looked at her with heat and softness. She'd thought . . .

What? That he was attracted to her?

Well. *Yes*.

She was positive she hadn't been generating the chemistry between them all by herself with wishful thinking. She'd bet Jude had felt a tug toward her. But maybe the FBI's rules preventing agents from entering into romantic relationships with witnesses were still in play even now? Or maybe whatever tug Jude had felt for her was smallish and had died a quick death after the case was suspended?

Gemma, what had you expected would happen with Jude? It's not as if she, a small-time perfumer and daughter of a convict, had ever been fated to capture the heart of the Camden family's most elusive son.

With a groan of irritation she yanked the oars into the boat.

Her view from this spot on the lake was as peaceful as her internal state was not. The sky had gone a dreamy, dusky shade of blue. The buildings and trees on the shore cast long reflections on the water. The shadows were deepening, the sun sinking toward the horizon in a puddle of gold.

Her phone rang. Listlessly, she checked the screen, intending not to answer. It was her mom calling. Ever since she'd received the news that her mother had suffered a stroke and was suddenly and unexpectedly hanging on to life by a thread, Gemma answered when Mom called. "Hello?"

"Hi. Remember me saying that the name Jude rang a bell with me, back at Pasta Bella the night we met him?"

"Yes. Vaguely." She pulled the throw blanket snugly around herself.

"The famous quarterback Felix Camden has a son named Jude!"

Oh no. Cold clutched Gemma's chest and squeezed.

"As you know," Mom went on, "I watched Felix marry that model Isobel O'Sullivan on TV decades ago. Since then, I've always kept an eye on them both. Anyway, Felix had two sons with that awful woman—his wife's sister—that he married after Isobel. Those sons are a few years older than you and they're named Jeremiah and Jude."

"I see."

"Just now, when I remembered Felix Camden had a son named Jude, I looked online for pictures of him. There are hundreds of pictures of Jeremiah Camden because he went on to become a racecar driver. But there are hardly any of Jude Camden at all. He's a child with his family in one of the few pictures I could find of him. Is that strange that there aren't more photos available?"

"Not all that strange." Gemma tried for a cavalier tone. "These days, I think a lot of celebrity parents fight for their children's privacy and don't allow photos of them to be made public."

"But Jude Camden would be in his early thirties now. Not a child."

"He probably wants to stay away from the media. With his parents' history, I can't blame him."

"I took a photo of the picture of Jude Camden I found. I'm going to text it to you. Here." Scuffling sounds.

Gemma held her phone away from her ear, bracing herself for the incoming text. When the picture arrived, she enlarged it. Jude's parents appeared to have been in their thirties when this family photo had been taken at an outdoor event. Both were physically stunning. Debonair Felix and sophisticated Fiona with the crystal smile and gleaming ash-blond hair. Felix wore a navy blazer and the boys had on blazers that matched his, plus madras shorts and leather loafers.

Both sons' tanned faces contrasted with their glittering pale eyes and towheaded blond hair. Jeremiah, age approximately ten, smiled directly at the camera with confidence. However, Jude looked reticent. His smile was there, but small and cautious as if asking the photographer, *Can I trust you?*

Gemma's heart gave a swift throb.

"Did the picture come through?" Mom asked.

"Yes."

"Jude Camden looks like Jude McConnell."

"I don't see it," Gemma lied.

"Gemma! There's a strong resemblance."

"Really?"

"That little face looks like it could have become your boyfriend's adult face."

How was she going to put a stop to this? "Mom, I'm sure a lot of men looked similar to this when they were kids. Hundreds of thousands."

"Yes, but how many of them are named Jude? Gemma. I think your Jude *is* Jude Camden."

"*What?*" she squawked. "No. My Jude grew up in Rhode

Island. His dad's name is Henry and his mom's name is Harriet."

"What if your Jude uses a different last name because he wants to find someone who loves him for him? And not for his family's fame and fortune?"

Mom was striking terrifyingly close to the truth. "Google Jude McConnell and you'll see pictures of my boyfriend."

"Remember that movie *Coming to America*? How the prince masqueraded as a commoner? Maybe Jude Camden is masquerading. And you're his princess."

"No—"

"Imagine if you're dating Jude Camden, Gemma. *I would die.* I would be so starstruck. Felix Camden's son! Imagine."

"*Mom. Google Jude McConnell and you'll see pictures of my boyfriend.*" She loathed lying to her mother. Loathed. But even worse would be bearing the blame for ruining Jude's alias, which had been so painstakingly created.

This situation called for Gemma's no-nonsense school-teacher voice. She'd had to use it a lot on her younger brothers. "This is a fun fantasy but just that, a fantasy. You haven't told anyone else about this theory, have you?"

"No."

"I need for you to promise that you'll keep it to yourself."

"Why do you need me to promise that? *Is* your boyfriend Jude Camden? Are you covering for him?" Excitement bubbled through her words.

"No! As Google will prove, if you'll take two minutes to find Jude there. I need you to promise to keep it to yourself because you know how our family is. This theory will spread faster than a pandemic and if it does, everyone will pummel me with questions."

"Hmm." She sounded pleased with herself.

"Promise?"

"Yes. I promise."

"I'm your loving daughter who, we can both agree, has done a lot for this family. I don't ask for many favors, but I'm asking for this one. I'm dating Jude McConnell from Rhode Island and he's great."

"He *is* great."

"And yourself? How are you doing?"

They chatted in the usual way for several minutes, then ended the call. Gemma's nerve endings buzzed. Did she need to tell Jude about her mom's suspicions?

Yes. Which gave her a valid reason to restore communication between them.

She lifted her phone to call or text him—

Then stopped. Why call or text when Mom's suspicions provided her with an excuse to pay him a visit tomorrow?

She'd never been to his house. In fact, she'd have to do some digging to locate his address but was confident she could overcome that obstacle.

A sense of rightness was gathering inside.

Finally—an excuse to see Jude.

"It's almost impossible for people to separate God from the hurt the church caused them." That's what Gemma had said to him once.

It had been a long time since she'd spoken those words. But Jude remembered them exactly. They'd been slipping into his head in unprotected moments ever since.

Other things had been dredging this subject up, too. Twice this week when he'd hit the scan button on his radio, it had landed on Christian worship music. He'd driven by a billboard he'd never seen before advertising John 3:16. Yesterday he'd talked to his mom on the phone and she'd brought up the subject of church and encouraged him to find one in Bangor.

Mabel ran to where he was standing outside his house and dropped her tennis ball. Panting, she grinned up at him.

"How you doing, sweetheart? Well? Yeah?"

Her wagging tail assured him she was doing very well. He heaved her ball into the trees and she streaked after it.

He'd spent his Saturday wisely. After sleeping in, he'd taken Mabel to a bakery that served excellent chocolate chip croissants. He'd played a round of golf with Jeremiah. He was about to settle in for an hour of reading before meeting friends for dinner.

And yet.

And yet he hadn't been right since he'd said goodbye to Gemma. And thinking about his issues with God made things even less right. So though he was doing all the things that should add up to a great Saturday, he was miserable inside.

Mabel returned. He spent time giving her a good scratch, then sent her ball flying again.

Without his permission, his mind slid back in time, pushing a memory at him that he hated revisiting.

He'd been sixteen and the owner of a brand-new driver's license. In those days, he'd made it to parties rarely because he was needed at home. But that night, Mom had been doing well, so he'd gone to a party.

Things had been in full swing when he'd arrived at Charlie DuPont's house. Music pounding, girls in tiny skirts, drinks flowing, dancing, laughter. His friends had welcomed him enthusiastically. Instead of feeling grateful about that, he'd envied them. Their lives were so much simpler. They weren't responsible for their parent's welfare. Max, his best friend, no longer lived in Groomsport. The guys that were left were better friends with each other than he was with any of them. He didn't party as hard as they did. He'd turned down two spring break trips in a row with them. They had stories about things they'd done together when he hadn't been there. They had inside jokes.

Resentful over the things he'd missed and angry at the pressure he constantly felt to keep his mom together, he'd downshifted into a serve-me-all-the-alcohol-you-have type of mood. Soon, his worries had disappeared on a sea of drunkenness.

It had been unbelievably stupid. Rebellious. Self-destructive.

The remaining details of that night were hazy. There'd been a pool glowing pale blue in the night. A brunette he'd made out with. A choice not to return home. He'd ended up tossing his phone into a bush and passing out on Charlie's sofa.

Rays of sunlight had woken him the next morning.

Instantly, consciousness crashed in. *He'd slept at Charlie's.* He'd been here *all night.* Without telling his mom. Without even letting her know where he was going.

She'd be furious. She'd be terrified.

Sick—nauseous, weak, his head throbbing—he found his shoes where he'd thrown them. Stepping over a couple of sleeping kids, he stumbled, blinking, into the morning. It took him three tries to successfully get his key into the ignition of his truck. His conscience criticized him violently as he drove. He was selfish. Bad. The worst son. How could he have made a mistake this big?

When he reached the gate that led to the house he lived in with Mom, it was open. Which caused his stomach to drop like concrete released by a crane. This wasn't normal. They always kept the gate closed.

Anxiety pushed acid up his throat. As he neared the house, he saw a police car parked outside. *A police car.*

Had something happened to his mother? The fear was so

paralyzing he couldn't move for several excruciating seconds. Eventually, he forced himself to approach the front door.

A middle-aged policeman with a stern face sat at their outdoor table. "Jude?"

"Yes, sir."

"Your mom is going to be fine."

"What . . . " He swallowed with effort. "What's happened?"

"She became extremely agitated when she couldn't get in contact with you. She called us. You'd only been gone five hours at the time. We weren't overly concerned because we're plenty familiar with teenagers. But we were very concerned about your mother. We came out to check on her and found her in such a state that my partner thought it best to take her to the emergency room. She was suffering from a severe panic attack. They've sedated her and stabilized her vitals."

Jude hated himself too much to speak.

The policeman indicated the brown sack sitting on the table. "My wife likes to pack my breakfast. I figured I'd take a break and eat it while I waited for a bit to see if you'd show."

"Thank you. I'm so sorry."

"It's your mother you need to apologize to. These days, with cell phones, if parents can't reach you right away, they begin to worry. If they can't reach you for hours, some of them, your mother included, panic."

"Yes, sir."

The policeman placed the food back in his sack and carried it forward until he was facing Jude, eye to eye. "From now on, answer your cell phone when your mother calls you. Do not stay out all night without letting her know where you are. Obey your curfew."

Jude closed his eyes for a moment, the regret crushing. "I will, sir. Is she at the hospital in Rockport?"

"Yes. You'll find her there."

And he had. The whole episode had been a living nightmare. Until then, he hadn't known guilt could twist your insides and turn your world gray.

He'd been a careful child. But since Charlie DuPont's party, right up to the present, he'd taken extraordinary care with people and with decisions. He deeply feared making a mistake.

Forgiving himself did not come easy. He'd never thought of himself, though, as someone who had a hard time forgiving others. Yet following his conversation with Gemma about faith, he was realizing that he'd been so fixed on what church members had done wrong toward him, that he'd failed to notice the thing *he* was doing wrong.

Refusing to forgive.

For years, he'd been stewing in unforgiveness and bitterness toward the church community who'd abandoned them. And because he'd conflated that abandonment with God, he'd been stewing in unforgiveness and bitterness toward God, too.

Which smacked of pride, didn't it? He'd been a self-righteous jerk, secretly viewing himself as superior. Viewing himself as someone who was above failing the way he'd judged those Christians to have failed. Yet he was the idiot who'd just handled his feelings for Gemma the same way he'd handled his feelings at Charlie DuPont's party. By getting drunk.

Not so superior now, was he? It was sickeningly humbling.

Crossing to his outdoor table near the grill, he lowered into one of the chairs. His elbow planted on the table's surface and he leaned his forehead into his hand. Mabel came to a stop at his feet, looking at him with concern and compassion.

He'd made good decisions his god. He'd been trying to find his worth in his degrees and career. His contentment in recognition and excellence. And after all this time he'd discovered that none of that was a firm foundation on which to build a life. He'd given that route a sincere shot. But none of it was capable of real joy or real peace.

He didn't yet know what to make of all this. What to do. How, even, to pray. It had been so long.

But at least now he was being honest with himself. He was looking hard at the perfection he'd attempted. And he didn't like what he saw.

His perfection was rotten inside.

Chapter Nineteen

The next afternoon, Gemma piloted her Vespa along a ribbon of road on the outskirts of Bangor. Tufts of white starflowers marked wooded land that rose and fell. A few cabins watched her pass as she eyed the numbers on the roadside mailboxes. The numbers climbed and climbed until she finally spotted the box for number 221. Jude's mailbox.

She turned. No gate blocked her progress along the gravel drive. *How welcoming of you, Jude.*

She drove through the forest for five minutes before glimpsing a modern black cabin through the foliage. Nearing it, she saw that two cars were parked outside. A Bronco—which must be Jude's car because this was the same one she'd seen at their meeting with his bosses in the meadow. Also a metallic-gray Porsche 911 that looked as if it had just driven off a showroom floor.

She eased to a stop.

She'd known her best shot at catching Jude at home would be on a weekend. But until now, she hadn't known if she'd get lucky on this particular day or if she'd have to sit on his doorstep and wait for him to show. It appeared that he was home. But the Porsche signaled he might have company.

What if this Porsche belonged to a woman? And Gemma was showing up unexpectedly while Jude was in the middle of a date?

Goodness gracious, she thought, her heart twisting. *Let that not be the case.*

Hopefully, the Porsche was either Jude's second car or belonged to a male friend or one of his relatives.

She stood, set aside her helmet, and shook out her hair.

The new and angular lines of Jude's cabin were inset with large panes of glass. Trees surrounded the structure on every side except the side facing the picturesque Penobscot River, which swept past in an indentation of land.

Given all his Camden wealth, she'd expected Jude to live somewhere enormous. This place was impressive, but not enormous. It seemed he'd opted for expansive view over expansive house.

"Gemma?"

She swung toward his voice.

Framed by his open front door, Jude held his lean body motionless. His clothes were more casual than any she'd seen him wear. A gray crewneck shirt and worn-in jeans. His feet were bare. Though he kept his expression guarded, his eyes glowed with alert intensity.

Pleasure *inundated* Gemma. Seeing him here was more thrilling than seeing a movie star at rest in their dressing room. She made her way forward, coming to a halt a few feet in front of him. "I wouldn't have believed it if I wasn't seeing it for myself."

"Wouldn't have believed what?"

"You in relaxed clothing. I'm shocked. I thought that combination was like vampires and daylight." She grinned.

His lips hitched higher on one side.

A yellow Lab came up beside him, wagging its tail.

"Relaxed clothing and a dog!" The animal approached her, and she bent to give it a rub. "Your dog?"

"My dog."

"Name?"

"Jude Camden." Dimples grooved his cheeks.

"Name of your dog?"

"Mabel."

She straightened. "May I come in, relaxed-clothes-wearing, dog-owning Jude?"

He slanted his body to the side for her to pass. "How did you find out where I live?"

"I did some FBI-style investigating."

"What kind of investigating?"

"You're listed as the owner of this property at the real estate tax assessor's website."

As she entered the open-concept living area, her attention intersected with a handsome black-haired man rising from the sofa. "What a crafty way to find an address," the stranger said with appreciation. "I heartily approve."

"This is Max Cirillo," Jude said.

Max. Recognition clicked in her brain. She'd seen photos of him online and now here he was in the flesh. Felix's son with the housekeeper Nicole. Max, who was just three months younger than Jude. "I'm Gemma Clare. Nice to meet you."

"Likewise."

Jude and Max had grown up together on the same piece of property. They'd been in the same grade in school. Best friends. Meeting Max felt like scratching off a winning lottery ticket.

Jude and Max had similar (excellent) builds and the same pale green eyes. Both had larger-than-life magnetism. But that's where the similarities ended because Max's coloring—

the olive skin and very dark hair—was so different from Jude's.

"I wondered whose car that was outside," she said, trying not to stare impolitely at the half-brothers.

"If you're referring to the interesting car," Max said, "that one's mine."

"We did some fishing earlier," Jude said. "Max was just leaving."

"Was I?" Max asked.

"Yes."

"I've heard about you," Max said to Gemma. Bizarrely, he seemed as interested in her as she was in him. "It's excellent to have the chance to put a face to a name."

"Ditto. Are you the owner of Libri?"

"I am."

"My mom's a subscriber. She loves it." Libri was a digital library packed with more than a million items. Mom used it for books, audiobooks, magazines. When Gemma had realized that Jude was a Camden, and done her deep dive into his family, she'd learned that Max's company was valued at a *billion dollars*. Which was crazy and awe-inspiring.

"Please tell your mom thank you for me," Max said.

"I will."

Max's eyes crinkled in an appealing way. Smooth confidence radiated from his posture, voice, expression.

"See you later, Max," Jude said.

Max chuckled. "He's kicking me out, but I don't care because I stayed long enough to get to meet you, Gemma. So I'm the luckiest man in Maine."

"Nice to meet you, too."

Max moved toward the door. "You've made my day." He gave her a practiced smile that likely stupefied most women, then was gone.

The door shut behind him.

"Any chance he's a ladies' man?" Gemma asked.

"The worst," Jude confirmed. "He was always a flirt but then he had his heart broken. Since then, he's cynical and he has no problem using women. I'm waiting for the day when the right woman will prove to him that he still has a heart in there."

"Fascinating."

Jude did not look fascinated or amused. He looked worried. "Are you here because something's wrong? Did anything happen—"

"I'll get to that in a second. First, a tour? I'd like to snoop around." She was avidly interested in his house.

He looked conflicted. On the one hand, tension hardened the lines of his jaw. On the other, he hadn't stopped giving her that hungry look since she'd arrived. Whatever he might be feeling, one thing was sure. Jude was *seeing* her deeply. More deeply than anyone had seen her since she'd been with him last.

"Tour?" she repeated.

"There's not much to show you."

"I'll be the judge of that." She wandered farther in. "Did you have this cabin built?"

"I did."

"I guessed as much. It feels like you, like it was made for you."

"I wanted something simple that was focused on nature."

"You achieved that." The more details she noticed, the more she appreciated his home's genius. "There are windows everywhere, which means you don't need art because the views are the art. Did you keep the size small because you didn't want to leave a giant footprint on the land?"

"That's part of the reason." His hands delved into his pockets. "Also, it's just me and Mabel. We don't need a bigger house."

Humble Jude. Never one to call attention to himself or his money.

"How long have you lived here?"

"Three years."

She wasn't crazy about cabins with wood on the floors, walls, and ceilings because that brought to mind thoughts of burial in a pine coffin. He hadn't made that error. Here, the floors were wood as were the ceiling beams, which came to a point high above. White-painted sheetrock covered the rest.

The kitchen cabinets wore a coat of neutral dark green paint. Black stone countertops complemented the black free-standing fireplace that loosely divided the kitchen and dining area from the living room. His furniture was contemporary but warm. Sophisticated lines, wood accents. Shades of caramel brown, black, green, pale blue. She saw zero clutter. And though her own decorating style leaned toward happy chaos, she could admit that his more minimal style did make this place feel like a retreat.

Nosy to see more, she ambled down the hallway.

"There are only bedrooms and bathrooms down there," he said in a *that's private* tone.

"One can hope." She continued forward.

"I've been to your house several times, and I've never looked into your bedrooms or bathrooms."

"Yes, because you're circumspect. I'm not."

His sunny bathroom looked as organized as the rest of the house. Based on the products in his shower, he was loyal to the Kiehl's line for men. Pricier than grocery store stuff, but far less expensive than he could afford.

She could feel him behind her as she made her way to his bedroom. A wooden headboard gave way to neatly made white linens. The chair by the window had a matching footrest and a book about the history of the FBI open over the armrest.

This was where he slept and the air smelled like him, addictively wonderful.

"I'm inspired," she announced.

"Inspired?"

"To create a scent based on you." She met his gaze. "It would sell more than Hope and Spice." Which she'd liberally applied before traveling here today.

"People don't want to smell like me."

"How wrong you are. I'm an expert in this field and, trust me, they do want to smell like you. It's not just your cologne, either. It's that, plus your soap and your shampoo. Your detergent. Your toothpaste. And . . . *you*."

The space between them turned thick and hot with attraction. Gemma rolled her bottom lip inward and sank her teeth into it. She was with him again, finally. She wanted to taste him. She wanted to feel his lips on hers and his hair between her fingers. She wanted his arms around her. She wanted to make a move even though she'd told herself, quite firmly, after initiating their first kiss, that if they ever kissed again, it would be because he initiated.

He led her through two more bedrooms joined by a bathroom, then back to the living area. They faced one another. "Will you tell me now what brings you here?" he asked.

"My mom suspects that you're Jude Camden."

He winced.

"The name Jude was familiar to her," she went on, "and she recently realized that's because it's the name of Felix Camden's second son. She dug around and found a picture of you online as a child and she called me to say that she thinks the child in the picture is you."

"How did you respond?"

"I told her she was wrong, that you're Jude McConnell from Rhode Island and that the internet would verify that. She promised me she wouldn't share her suspicions with anyone else in my family." She scratched behind her ear. "Should I go ahead and tell her the truth about what's going on with the operation?"

"No. We'll need to depend on her promise that she won't tell anyone else. If she brings up this subject again, please continue to say that she's mistaken, that the boy in that picture is not your boyfriend."

A pause unwound like a spool of thread.

"Okay." Gemma had no plans to leave now that they'd gotten that behind them. "While I'm here, I wanted to say sorry again. About Chaz showing up to surprise me the way he did that night at my house. Because I haven't seen you since, now's my chance to tell you that it felt weird to me and maybe a little demeaning to you that I had to pass you off as a label maker."

"Pretending to be your label maker was just part of my job."

"Huh." He was never going to budge off the company line, was he? He was never going to discuss real, not-FBI things with her unless she forced him to do so. "Part of your job."

"Yes."

"How much of what's between you and me is business and how much is personal? Because you were very quick to cut me out of your life when our operation was suspended. I wouldn't have cared that you'd cut me out if everything between us was business. But I did care. I *do* care. I've missed you."

Some of his composure cracked and she saw raw yearning beneath. "I didn't cut you out of my life, per se. I stopped communicating with you because there was nothing left to say after our op was suspended."

"I think there's a lot more to say." She placed her fists on her hips. "I no longer have a boyfriend and so I'm now free to tell you I like you."

He didn't move. Just studied her, unblinking. "You no longer have a boyfriend?"

"No. I broke up with Chaz."

Jagged quiet expanded. "Why?"

"Because I realized that I didn't care that much about him. It became clear to me that I wanted to date my fake boyfriend a lot more than I wanted to date my real one."

Muscles braced all the way up Jude's frame.

"So," she went on, "do you see me only as a work colleague? Or as more?"

"I see you as more," he said, hoarse. "But I can't act on that. Doing so would be strictly against FBI policy."

"And you highly value your reputation and career."

"Highly."

"You've made that clear every step of the way. But our operation was suspended. Did Shannon Bailey tell you that you couldn't be with me even though we're no longer, technically, working together?"

"She doesn't have the power to prevent us from being together now that we're no longer working together. She did warn me against it, though. Strongly."

Gemma studied his serious lips. The defined nose. The thick, dark blond hair. She began to smile. "You know what that sounds like to me, Jude?"

"What?"

"A loophole. To my way of thinking, loopholes are meant to be exploited."

"To my way of thinking, they're meant to be avoided. Too much gray area."

"I'm no longer dating Chaz. We're no longer working on an operation. I'm free. You're free. Not much gray area there."

"You came over here to make me crazy, didn't you?"

A thrill sizzled down the backs of her legs at the low rasp of his tone. She took a step closer to him. "No. I came over here to tell you about my mom's suspicions and to see you again. If I'm making you crazy, that's just a side benefit." She lifted her chin challengingly.

"You're making me crazy."

"Good. I'm not afraid to see the lid blow off all that towering control of yours." Her voice was slightly winded, as if she'd been running instead of simply standing near him. "Do you want to kiss me? Because I would very much like to kiss you."

His irises went smoky, but he remained still.

"How about you be honest," she whispered, "and tell me what you're afraid of?"

"You. Gemma."

"You're afraid of me? I'm sunshine and fun. Ask anyone."

"Sunshine and fun with the power to destroy me."

She couldn't get enough oxygen into her lungs. Her senses were like pinwheel fireworks. "I won't destroy you."

"You already have."

"No."

"Yes." Then his hands were in her hair, and he was kissing her passionately. No preamble. No warming up to it.

But, of course, the last two months had been preamble. This entire conversation had been preamble. He had her running a temperature of one hundred and fifty.

She drank in the textures of his clothes, his hair, his mouth, the sound of his breathing. All of that and more flooded into her—a feast. With it came satisfaction and desire and something more . . . a deep sense of *fit*. She fit with him.

They were not strangers. They'd spent many hours together or talking over the phone. Usually she let physical combustion lead the way into romances. This time, she'd put the horse before the cart and gotten to know him. He was the reliable second son. The one who picked up the broken pieces of things his family had shattered. The one full of goodness and duty. Firmly ethical.

Her renegade soul had come to appreciate who he was.

Through their kiss, he showed her the depths of what he felt for her. His touch communicated intimacy and tenderness. Jude had kept everything so tightly under wraps until now. The full onslaught of him—of them—was overwhelming in the best way.

He gentled the kiss as he walked her backward until her spine came up against wall. "You're beautiful," he murmured against her ear. Then kissed down her throat. When he straightened, he slid a lock of her hair between his fingertips.

She watched him with dumbstruck infatuation. She should be taking advantage of these seconds and using them to run her fingertips along his cheek, his neck, his shirt collar. All of it screamed for exploration. Instead, she gave a slow blink. Simply looking at him was all that she could handle.

With her red hair and outgoing personality, people often commented on how colorful she was. But it turned out that, in this pairing, *he* was the vivid one. Many facets of him weren't out there in the open. If you wanted to see Jude's vivid facets you had to put in work, you had to dig for treasure. She was enormously glad she'd gone digging. Beneath the surface lived more emotion and passion than she would have believed.

Impatiently, she tugged his mouth back to hers.

Hard to know how long their kisses went on. She couldn't get enough. He couldn't get enough. For all she cared, the sun could set and rise again. Everything in the universe that mattered was right here—

His dog's bark caused Jude to startle. He pulled back,

looking toward the sound. One of his hands was interlaced with hers, his other burrowed in her hair.

Mabel gave her an expression that said, *Really, lady? I was trying to be tolerant but now you've hogged too much of his time.*

"I think she's jealous," Gemma said.

"She only barks when she wants to go outside."

That showed how little he understood females.

He separated from her and went to let Mabel out.

Without him, she felt immediately cold and wobbly-legged. She waited impatiently for him to return and resume.

He returned but didn't resume. His hair was messy from where she'd run her fingers through it. His shirt askew. And he'd never looked more painfully desirable.

He scrubbed his hands down his face, and she understood that he-of-the-responsible-soul was beginning to second-guess what had just happened between them.

Which caused her own fear to stir. She'd been in no jeopardy of falling very hard for Chaz. But she was in enormous jeopardy of falling very hard for Jude. If she invested her heart in him and things didn't work out, the pain would be crushing. Debilitating.

She was afraid of pain just as Jude was afraid of wrecking his career. Her empathy toward him pricked. Kissing him was dangerous to her emotionally, but it didn't put her career on the line. It didn't put at risk the years of sweat, blood, and tears she'd invested in Perfumes by Gemma Clare.

Jude loved his work just as much if not more than she did. She thought of how he'd shown up for their first meeting at her house. In his suit—all brainy, and formal, and prepared. He was wise and measured. If that hadn't been the case, he wouldn't be Jude and she wouldn't respect him as much as she did.

If she could gather enough courage . . . if he gave her

reasons to think that banking on him might pay off . . . then she might be willing to take the plunge with him. But the next step —for her peace of mind and his—wasn't force or pressure. The next step was to give them both room.

The silence grew long. She could've jumped off a high platform and executed a dive into that silence, swum down into it, touched bottom, then stroked toward the surface of it.

Like an addict, one dose of the closeness and fire they'd just generated had sealed her fate. She had to squash a greedy urge to yank him back to her.

"That was . . . well . . ." She pulled her hair forward over her shoulder and twisted it once, twice. "That was *fabulous*. But we both probably need time to think about . . . things."

He stared at her, a notch between his eyebrows, his color high.

"You'll want to ponder the impact that a connection between the two of us might have on your career. Let's tap the brakes," she said as lightly as she could manage. "Is that cool with you?"

He nodded once.

"Are you going to confess what just happened between us to Shannon Bailey?"

"No. Scent-sible isn't active, so I'm not obligated to do so."

"Well, you can certainly count on me not to confess this to anyone. So your job won't take a hit." She moved toward the door.

"Gemma."

She stopped, focused on him, and lost herself. *I'm trying to be noble here, Jude, but don't start kissing me again or I'll crumble faster than a dry cookie.*

"I missed you, too," he said. "A lot."

"You did?"

"You are like light . . . to me. Because of you, everything inside me, everything in my life is brighter."

God, help me! She cleared her throat, curled her fingers in so she wouldn't reach for him. "That sounded a lot like poetry, and I've already warned you. I cannot control myself if you quote poetry to me."

"'This perpetual jar of earthly wants and aspirations high. Come from the influence of an unseen star. An undiscovered planet in our sky.'"

"You're playing with dynamite," she warned.

He gave her an unexpected, whimsical smile. Endearing.

"Moist!" she shouted. It was the equivalent of bursting through an emergency exit. She had to create a quick separation between them so she could zoom off on her scooter and catch her breath. "Jiggle! Scuttle! Congealed! Greasy!"

He gritted his teeth comically.

She ran all the way to her Vespa.

By the time Jude followed her out of his house, her scooter was already spitting gravel. He watched her go, long strands of red hair flapping in the wind below the bottom edge of her helmet.

Somehow, he'd screwed up. He should have taken her in his arms right away after he'd let Mabel out. He should have done a better job explaining to her how much she meant to him. He should have told her that the last weeks had been a wasteland without her. He should have tried to convince her to stay longer.

Because those kisses had changed everything for him. He'd lived thirty-two years and never experienced anything close to it.

Hearing Gemma say that he'd want to ponder the impact that a connection between the two of them might have on his career had been a strange role reversal, as if he was suddenly standing in an alternate universe. It had taken him off guard, made him unsure what to do. So he'd done nothing. Then she'd said she wanted to tap the brakes, at which point he'd had no option other than to accept what she wanted. However, hearing her say she wanted to tap the brakes had made him sure that he did not.

As always, Gemma was a force of nature. He felt as if he'd just been picked up by a tornado, spun around, and thrown to Earth. Dazed.

He was a disciplined person. But he found that he *needed* to indulge in this one thing.

Her.

He'd earned this single indulgence. Deserved it. Was coming to not care at all what a relationship with her might cost him.

SUNDAY NIGHT

MAX

Are you and Gemma together?

JUDE

No.

MAX

Have you two kissed?

JUDE

No comment.

MAX

That means yes because you'd have said no
if the answer was no. So why aren't you
together?

JUDE

I'm working on that.

MONDAY AFTERNOON

GEMMA

I'm experimenting with fragrance notes
inspired by you.

JUDE

You're kidding, right?

GEMMA

I'm as serious as a funeral. I'm thinking about
calling it Elegance and Oak.

JUDE

I'm not the kind of person who serves as
anyone's muse.

GEMMA

You're exactly that kind of person. It boggles
my mind that you haven't noticed you're
muse-worthy. At the same time, I'm glad you
haven't noticed because if you had you'd be
insufferable and would go around dating
beautiful actresses.

JUDE

There's only one woman I want to date. She's
beautiful, but she's not an actress.

TUESDAY MORNING

JUDE

I saw this ad for an antiques fair and thought of you. I don't think you have an inch of counter or shelf space left for more antiques, but maybe you could start stacking them on the floor.

GEMMA

I'm going to ignore the subtle jab regarding my clutter and focus instead on the fact that an ad made you think of me.

JUDE

Everything makes me think of you.

WEDNESDAY MIDDAY

GEMMA

A butterfly flew past on my lunch break and I took the below picture of it. Do you have this species in your gallery of dead butterflies in New York? And if not, is its life in danger?

JUDE

That's a Milbert's Tortoiseshell. It's part of the brush-footed butterfly family. Its larval host plant is a nettle, and it likes to eat sap. I already have twenty-five of these pinned to velvet in my collection, ensuring they'll spend their eternity with me. So the butterfly you saw is safe from me.

THURSDAY MORNING

MAX

Are you and Gemma together now?

JUDE

No.

MAX

What? You said you were working on it. That was four days ago.

JUDE

Still working on it.

MAX

Do not hesitate. Do not get in your own head. If you don't make a move, someone else will. Then she'll marry another guy and you'll never forgive yourself.

JUDE

Gemma was the one who asked to slow things down.

MAX

I know you and it's 80% likely she said that because she worried you were having second thoughts.

Chapter Twenty

On Friday morning, Gemma's leopard-print flats struck the sidewalk leading from her shop to City Hall with a determined *tap tap tap tap*. She checked her watch. Perfumes by Gemma Clare wouldn't open for another forty minutes but Bayview's City Hall had already been up and running for more than an hour.

In her purse, she carried Gracie and Paul's marriage certificate and her parents' marriage certificate. Her mission: find an expert who could shed light on her concerns regarding Gracie and Paul's certificate.

All around her, Gemma's town was coming lazily awake. The sky was sunny but so raw with chill that not a single cloud had ventured to disturb it. Light glimmered and slipped lovingly along historic storefronts and the shingles hanging above doorways.

Helen, owner of the paper store, called a greeting to ceramic-store-owner Ron. Two young twenty-somethings hurried past carrying to-go trays of coffees, likely for employees at their workplace more senior than they were. Don swept the landing outside his barber shop.

The stout breeze whisking against Gemma's face carried a tinge of pine. By the smell of it, Cinnamon and Spice Bakery had blueberry muffins baking. The scent of tobacco lilted from the cigar shop, which made her think of Jude because his cologne included a tobacco note.

The days that had come and gone since their kiss had brought her to the conclusion that she was ready for more with him. But *only* if he was definitively ready for more with her. She wasn't sure that he was. Thus she'd found their text exchange delightful and, at the same time, slightly painful. Painful because he'd stirred a longing in her that wouldn't quit or abate.

Upon entering City Hall, she informed the employee in the lobby that she'd come to inquire about marriage certificates. She was directed to the office of the municipal clerk where a young man wearing glasses glanced up as she approached. At the moment, only the two of them and the smell of lemon Pine-Sol inhabited the space.

He listened patiently, looking emaciated and in desperate need of carbs, as she filled him in on her discovery of her great-grandparents' marriage certificate and her suspicions about its authenticity, especially as compared to her parents' marriage certificate.

Gemma extracted both documents from her purse. "I'm wondering if this one"—she lifted Gracie and Paul's certificate —"is handwritten and missing the seal because of its age?"

"That's easy to check. Excuse me. I'll locate another marriage certificate from the forties."

"Thank you."

A few minutes later, he returned. "Here you are. This

certificate was issued the very same month as your relatives' certificate." He set it before her.

Gracie and Paul's certificate did not match. The one he'd brought out had the seal and only the signatures were hand-written. The decoration and fonts were different. The color and weight of the paper was different.

"Your certificate," he proclaimed, "is a fake."

Her world tilted slightly. Did this mean that Gracie and Paul had never been married? No, *surely* they had been.

"Someone," the employee pointed out, "went to a bit of trouble to make this look believable to the untrained eye."

He was right. It wasn't the document itself that had caused her to doubt its authenticity. It looked official-ish. It was the date of their supposed wedding that had tripped her up. Had Gracie and Paul created the fake? If so, for what purpose?

"Do you have the ability," Gemma asked, "to search your records for a valid marriage certificate for my great-grand-parents?"

"Anyone may place an open record request for marriages that occurred fifty years ago or more. Which this one did."

"Excellent. Here are their names." She pointed them out on the fake certificate.

"Hang on." He typed into his computer. Paused. Scrolled. Typed. "Your grandparents were married October 4, 1945, in Caribou, Maine."

In October of '45, not January of '45.

Gemma remembered attending Gracie and Paul's sixtieth anniversary celebration. She'd been a kid in her late elementary school years at the time. Plenty old enough to remember the event well, even now. It had been held in January when the Maine weather was raw and cold, at their church. They'd chosen a winter wonderland theme for the party. The cake had been decorated with edible snowflakes and icicles. She recalled stealing a mini-icicle when no one was looking and taunting her brothers with it.

Gracie and Paul had told everyone, had always lived, as if their wedding had taken place on the January date specified on their fake certificate.

"Do any other marriages come up for either Paul or Gracie?" Gemma asked. While she was here, might as well be thorough.

More typing. "No."

"Is it possible for me to get a copy of their real marriage certificate?"

"Certainly. For a non-certified copy you'll need to fill out a form and pay a small fee. You'll receive it in the mail."

With his assistance, Gemma completed those steps. Then she exited City Hall, stopping halfway down its wide steps. She could breathe and think better here in the fresh air.

Gracie and Paul had actually married in October of 1945. But they'd gone to the trouble of forging a certificate saying they'd married in January of that year. What would have motivated them to make people believe they'd married earlier than they had?

Across the road, a man entered a Pilates studio. A woman strode by talking on her cell phone, a baby tucked into a carrier strapped to her chest.

An idea struck Gemma, sending chills streaking over her skin. *A baby*.

It was almost opening time when she reached Perfumes by Gemma Clare. Aunt Stella's car was parked in the alley, God bless her, which meant the shop was covered. Free to run an errand, Gemma climbed onto her Vespa and motored off.

Ten minutes later, she turned into Bayview's cemetery. Her family came here every Memorial Day to pay their respects, pray, and reminisce about their loved ones who'd passed away.

She knew in general where to find her family's section—no, she'd taken a wrong turn. She backtracked and found the right spot.

Leaving her Vespa and helmet behind, she walked until she reached Paul's gravestone.

Now that she'd read his letters to Gracie, she had a new window into the man he'd been. Paul Bettencourt no longer existed in her mind only as the old man, the cherished great-grandfather. She'd now glimpsed the heart of the youthful, handsome man wearing a cable-knit sweater and trousers in a photo. His love for Gracie had burned like a comet in the pages and pages he'd written and mailed across the Atlantic while Europe and America and the Pacific raged with war.

"Hi, Great-Grandpa." She knelt and swept her fingers over his name. "I love you so much. I miss you."

Beside Paul's plot was the plot that awaited Gracie. And next to that lay the flat gravestone she'd come here to see. She rose and came to a stop above it. This was where Warren, their eldest child, was buried.

WARREN THEODORE BETTENCOURT
PFC US ARMY
VIETNAM
OCTOBER 14, 1945 – JUNE 24, 1966

Gemma's hands raised to cover her mouth. Warren had been born just ten days after Gracie and Paul's legitimate marriage. Which meant he'd been conceived around January, when Paul had been in France and when Gracie had been an unmarried Code Girl living in D.C. Paul was not Warren's biological father, but they'd forged a marriage certificate to make it seem as though he was. Then they'd raised Warren as the firstborn of their happy marriage.

Her great-grandparents and Grandma Colette had always spoken of Warren with deep love. What had they told her about him over the years? She racked her brain.

She knew Warren had been excellent at math like his mother. Quiet, introverted, kind. His parents had served their countries in World War Two, and so he'd stepped up to serve his country too, in Vietnam. He'd been killed in action.

Gracie had been right on the day of her birthday when she'd insisted that there was more to her love story during the war years than the rest of them knew. But she hadn't remembered that the full story contained a secret she and Paul had perpetuated for decades. In asking Gemma to unearth her whole love story, she'd unknowingly asked Gemma to uncover a secret that younger Gracie wouldn't have wanted uncovered.

Maybe the strip of paper on which she'd written the code had looked new because she'd scribbled it down after her Alzheimer's diagnosis two years ago. Back when she'd learned that her memories might be stolen from her, it was plausible to believe she'd left a trail of breadcrumbs for herself. Breadcrumbs she alone could follow that would remind her of her full history with Paul.

Gemma wrapped her arms around herself. She'd been waiting to tell her relatives about her findings until she had kinder and more conclusive facts to share.

She had a few answers now, but they'd opened an even bigger question.

Namely, *what in the world* had happened between the date of Gracie and Paul's final letters and the date of their real wedding?

Gracie was the only person alive who held the answer. It was contained in her brain, but locked away there in an area that could no longer be accessed by anyone, including Gracie herself.

Gemma needed to find Gracie's missing diaries.

Max was observant and Max had known Jude all his life. Which meant he knew things about Jude that Jude might not even know about himself.

For example, Max knew that Jude was in love with Gemma.

Jude had said very little to Max about her. The day they'd met for lunch at the lobster pound, he'd suspected that Jude had deep feelings for the woman he'd said he wanted to help. But Jude likely wouldn't have disclosed even her name to Max had Gemma not shown up at Jude's house while Max had been there. Within seconds of seeing Jude with Gemma, Max's suspicions about Jude's feelings had been confirmed.

Gemma was beautiful. However, Jude had known many, many beautiful women. Some of them had loved him but Jude had loved none of them. This one, he loved. The fact of it was in his protective posture. In the way he looked at her. In the palpable chemistry between them.

Max had told Jude via text that Gemma had likely mentioned slowing things down because she'd believed Jude was having second thoughts. He'd put that theory forward because Jude hesitated when he was uncertain of the right choice. Also, when Jude was thinking hard, which he almost always was, his face could look troubled and serious. If a man hesitated, looking troubled and serious, after kissing a woman, that woman was going to think the man was having second thoughts. If that woman was smart enough to see Jude's worth and love him back, she was smart enough to know to give him room.

Jude was too humble to see the accuracy of Max's theory.

Humility was admirable, perhaps, but also infuriating. Max didn't want to spend the rest of his life with Jude if Jude was going to spend the rest of his life mourning Gemma.

Max was not burdened by humility.

Nor was he above stirring this pot. His intrusion might make Jude mad, but making Jude mad in the short term would be in Jude's best interest in the long term.

Max entered Perfumes by Gemma Clare near close of business on Monday. Gemma stood behind the counter, gift-wrapping a box, in conversation with a female customer. She gave him a bright, welcoming smile.

He nodded at her, then began browsing.

The customer talked on and on about how the moon's phases affected her mood before finally leaving with her purchase.

Gemma made her way to him.

"Remember me?" he asked.

"How could I forget you, Max?"

"And how could I forget you, Gemma?"

"No one can." She shrugged, amusement in her expression. "You know, I'd have gambled a great deal on the fact that I'd see Jude before I'd see you again. I'd have lost that bet."

"Life lesson for you. Always bet on me."

She groaned.

He chuckled.

"Are you here to buy something for the woman in your life?" she asked.

"Don't you mean *women*? You do me a disservice to assume there's only one."

"Businessperson to businessperson, I have no issue with selling you products for multiple women, instead of just one."

"Sell me several things, then. Take all my money."

"Happily."

She explained that if he were to smell everything in her product line, his nose would fatigue. Even if a fragrance was perfect for him, if it was the tenth one he smelled, he'd be unlikely to recognize its perfection. So she provided a verbal summary of the scents and asked which three or four sounded most appealing.

Max rattled off the ones he wanted to smell.

When she gave him a scent strip for Hope and Spice, he narrowed his eyes at her. "That should be illegal. It's . . . downright underhanded. Were you wearing this the other day when I met you?"

"I was."

"No wonder I was devastated when Jude made me leave. Maybe I'll just buy it and douse my sheets in it."

"I won't argue with that plan."

In the end, he bought two bottles each of three different perfumes. By then, his admiration for her skill as a perfumer and salesperson had grown exponentially. "What are you doing when you get off work?" he asked when she was ringing him up.

"Heading home. No plans."

"How about you come to a clam dig with me and Jeremiah and others from Jude and Jeremiah's family?"

"Where?"

"Sears Island."

She said nothing for a few seconds. "Will Jude be there?"

"We invited him and he turned us down. Work, he said." Max rolled his eyes, which was misleading, seeing as how he was far more of a workaholic than Jude. "But if Jude knows you'll be there, he will come."

"I'm not sure that he will."

"If he knows you'll be there," Max repeated, "he will come."

She peered at him as if using X-ray vision to understand his brain. "Why are you inviting me to a get-together of Jude's family that Jude will not be attending?"

"Because I like you. Because I think it will be fun. And because Jude *will* be attending."

She paused, then finally said, "I do love a clam dig."

"Then come." She seemed like the type of person who wasn't afraid of a challenge. He gave her a look that communicated, *I dare you.*

She dipped her chin. "Okay."

"Outstanding. Please text Jude to let him know that you accepted my invitation to the clam dig."

"I've known you five minutes and you're already ordering me around," she murmured wryly, lifting her phone.

"I only boss people I like."

She closed the shop and soon they were shooting toward the coast in his Porsche. "Jude hasn't texted you back?" he asked.

"Nope."

"That means he's in a meeting and hasn't seen your text."

Jude was going to blow a fuse when he did see her text. It was wrong of Max, seeing as how Jude was his best friend, to relish that idea as much as he did.

It wasn't easy for Fiona to interact with Max. He was, after all, a living and breathing reminder of Felix's affair with Nicole while Felix had been married to her.

Fiona hadn't spoken with Nicole even once since the truth of Max's parentage had come out. But Max was a different story. Max was her sons' close friend. Max had had no say in his conception. In fact, Max was sensible enough to have made it clear that, if he'd had a say in things, he wouldn't have chosen Felix as a father.

After the scandal, Jude had needed his best friend. And Fiona loved Jude too much to deny him that. So her home had been open to Max all these years. Since Jeremiah, Jude, and Max had become adults with their own places, Max hung out with her sons apart from her much more than he hung out with her sons in her vicinity. Even so, she still saw and chatted politely with him a handful of times a year—at birthday parties and the like. Never effortless, but certainly doable.

When Jeremiah had called her earlier today, he hadn't asked if Max could bring the woman Jude was interested in dating to tonight's clam dig. In Jeremiah's charming way, he'd informed her that Max *would* be bringing the woman Jude was interested in dating.

"Why would Max bring the woman Jude is interested in dating to my family's clam dig?" she'd asked, baffled.

"Just trust us, Mom. Max and I think this is in Jude's best interests. Plus, I'm sure you'd enjoy meeting this woman that Jude likes. Yes?"

"Yes! Of course!" They didn't tend to let her in on the ground floor of their relationships.

"Same. I'm curious about her."

"What's her name?"

"Gemma."

"If Jude's serious about Gemma— *Is* he serious about Gemma?"

"My intuition says yes."

"Okay, so since he's maybe serious about Gemma, wouldn't it be better to plan something later this week at my house, for a smaller group? Then Jude himself can bring her."

"Nah. When Max called to talk with me about this, we agreed it would be best to move fast. The clam dig was already on the calendar, so the clam dig it is. Remy and I will also see you there."

"Wonderful!" she'd said. Because when your adult child—who you did not get to see as often as you wanted—suddenly invited himself, his half-brother, his girlfriend, and Jude's prospective girlfriend to a family clam dig he'd earlier declined, you responded with upbeat enthusiasm.

Two hours had passed since that phone call and Fiona paused her clam digging on the beach to watch Max and a redhead make their way toward her. Sears Island was one of Maine's many "bridged" islands, meaning it could be reached from the mainland by bridge without having to take a boat or plane. Sears Island did not, however, allow cars. So if you wanted to visit, you parked on the causeway and either walked or biked to your destination on the island. Max and Gemma had walked.

Fiona's sister Elizabeth was in the middle of interpreting Fiona's dream from last night in which she'd been falling. Elizabeth was spouting some rubbish about how Fiona must be feeling unsupported.

"Excuse me, please," Fiona cut in. "I need to go and welcome the newcomers." She hurried forward in her giant sun hat, pulling her rolling basket behind.

Before reaching Gemma, Fiona spotted several promising characteristics. Gemma wore wide-legged jeans and a gorgeous ivory crewneck sweater. She liked her style. And that red hair! That skin! Gemma's body looked as though it could handle childbearing with ease—ideal because (should Gemma turn out to be wonderful for Jude) Fiona wanted grandchildren.

For reasons that were incomprehensible to Fiona, Remy was not in a rush to marry Jeremiah even though it was abundantly clear to everyone that he was ready for that step. Remy didn't seem to have a functioning biological clock. If Gemma did, that would be stellar because many of Fiona's siblings were besting her on the grandparent front. Which was completely unjust seeing as how Fiona's two children were the most attractive in the bunch.

"Welcome," Fiona said, a little breathlessly. She pulled off her clam-digging gloves and tossed them in her basket. "I'm so pleased that you were both able to join us."

"Thank you for having us," Max said smoothly. "I'd like to introduce Gemma Clare."

"I'm Fiona, Jeremiah and Jude's mother." They shook hands. Fiona piled her free hand on top of their joined ones and gave a few extra affectionate pats before they stepped apart.

"Gemma's a perfumer," Max said.

"A perfumer!" Fiona exclaimed.

"And a business owner like yourself," Max told Fiona. "We've just come from her shop in Bayview, where she sells her own line. It's called Perfumes by Gemma Clare."

"Why, that's extraordinary. I've heard of your line. All good things." Had Jude told her the whole truth when he'd said he wanted to learn about exclusive perfumes for "a case"? Maybe he'd been learning about perfumes because of Gemma. "We have something in common because I deal with fragrances at work, also. I own a company that sells scented hand creams."

"I know all about Lavish," Gemma said. "I have one of your creams in my purse right now! I'm a big fan."

"Thank you." Well, that was gratifying. A child-bearing body *and* good taste in hand creams. "I'll freely admit to you, though, that I didn't design the fragrances. I worked with a nose."

"Your collab was a great success."

"I like to think so." She turned to Max. "Earlier, when my

father learned you were coming, he mentioned how much he was looking forward to chatting with you."

"I'll head over and say hello to him." He took Fiona's unsubtle hint and moved off.

Now that Max was no longer eyeballing her, Fiona had a golden opportunity to be as honest as she wanted to be with Gemma. "How about we get you fixed up with boots, gloves, and a basket?"

"That would be great."

They made their way to the carts containing supplies. Gemma exchanged her shoes for rubber boots, collected gloves, and set a hoe into a rolling basket identical to Fiona's. Fiona led her to a quiet patch of beach.

Harvesting clams this way required little expertise. Spot a hole in the sand, dig down about a foot, get clam. Fiona was no stranger to it. Nor was Gemma, based on the ease with which Gemma went to work.

"Jeremiah tells me that you're a friend of Jude's," Fiona said.

"I am."

"How long have you two known one another?"

"More than two months."

And Fiona was just now meeting her? Slightly insulting. "Has Jude told you much about his childhood and teenage years?"

"I'd love to know more. But no. He's not told me much."

Again, that ruffled her feathers. But if she let everything ruffle her feathers that threatened to ruffle her feathers, she'd be a very agitated chicken. "We just met, so what I'd like to say to you may seem like oversharing. But I've no idea when I'll get you alone again and I'm not one who likes to miss my chances."

Gemma laughed. "I don't like to miss my chances, either.

And both the giving and receiving of oversharing comes naturally to me. Feel free to say whatever's on your mind."

"Details of Jude's upbringing that might give you insights into him. That's what's on my mind."

Gemma stilled with her hoe in the sand, her attention sharp with interest. "Okay."

They both resumed digging. "When my marriage to Felix ended, Jude was just a freshman in high school. Very young."

"That *is* young. I remember my three brothers at that age."

"Jude and I moved out of Maple Lane, our old house, and into a new one. Jeremiah came back from Europe for a few weeks and would have stayed longer, but Jude and I assured him that he should return to racing. He did, which I still believe was the right call. He went on to great success."

"Yes."

"But that meant that Jude was the only one home with me during the darkest time of my life. For two years, I wasn't very functional." She placed a clam in her basket. Gemma did the same, then they moved down the beach a few steps. "It felt like I was surrounded by a black fog that made it hard to move, to breathe, to think. I couldn't get to the bottom of my grief and betrayal."

Fiona lifted her face and took a moment to let the beauty around her temper the memories. Today's late-April high had reached sixty-two. But here on the water, the wind was cooler and stronger than it had been in Groomsport. With just an hour of daylight left, the massive sky peered down on them moodily. The sun shot upward through clouds ranging in color from bright white to opaque gray.

"I became a bit of a hermit." Fiona burrowed her hoe into the sand. "For one thing, I couldn't motivate myself to go out. For another, I was embarrassed. It didn't help that the majority of people were delighted that I'd gotten what they viewed as my comeuppance." Fiona had given this type of speech to Jude's past few long-term girlfriends. She viewed it as her penance for what she'd put Jude through. Additionally, though, this was her way of testing the girlfriends. Her version of placing a pea under a stack of mattresses, like in the fairytale. The woman who was sensitive to this information, who liked him even more and treated him even better because of it . . . That would be the right person for her son.

"During his early high school years, Jude parented me. Insisting that I eat. Lecturing me into taking showers. Going to the grocery store. He went on walks with me so I'd get fresh air and exercise. He held my hand when I cried. That he graduated high school is a testament to how smart he is because he missed a lot of classes on my behalf. He quit sports. He didn't date. He hung out with friends rarely."

Using her wrist to hold her hair back from her eyes, Gemma looked directly at Fiona—something most people didn't have the nerve to do. "My mom had a stroke many years ago. My brothers and I had to step up to help. I know my mom harbors guilt because of that. But the truth is, my brothers and I are better people because of it."

A gust of emotion caught Fiona by surprise, squeezing her throat. "That's an excellent perspective to take. I do believe that Jude emerged an even better person but that doesn't stop me from regretting that he had to grow up so very fast. He became cautious during those hard years, worried about making mistakes. If you see evidence of that in him, now you'll know why."

"Thank you for sharing that with me."

"You're welcome." Fiona added another clam to her basket. "I was much better by the time Jude was a senior in high school. I'd started my company and was feeling like myself again. I insisted Jude apply to any college he wanted, no matter how far away. He was able to have a normal college experience."

"It all worked out."

"Yes." Nearly so, anyway. Fiona could go the rest of her life without love and marriage. But she did not want that for Jude. After all his sacrifices for her, it was imperative that Jude get his happily ever after. Maybe then the score between her and her younger son would be closer to settled and the scales of justice would hang fair.

Jude left a meeting that had run long, made his way toward his desk, and saw Riley hovering there. His steps slowed as he approached. Most of the office had already cleared out for the day. He wished Riley had gone with them.

"Anything I can do for you before I go?" she asked.

"No, thanks."

Her hands twisted together. "It was so much fun to see you at the sports bar and meet your brother."

"Yeah." His time at the sports bar was fuzzy in his memory. Mostly, he recalled how desolate he'd felt over Gemma.

"Do you have plans to go again any time soon?"

"No, no plans."

"When you do decide to go, please let me know."

"All right," Jude said while thinking *no way*. He indicated his desk. "If you'll excuse me, I have some things I need to address."

She seemed to go into a little trance. Snapping out of it, she said, "Of course! See you tomorrow?"

"Yep."

She paused for an awkward amount of time before leaving.

Sitting, he pulled his phone from the drawer and found a text from Gemma waiting.

GEMMA

Max stopped by my store just now. He invited me to a clam dig on Sears Island this evening with some of your relatives. I said I'd go. Join us if you're free!

For a few prolonged, agonizing seconds, Jude was pretty sure he was experiencing a brain aneurysm.

Was Gemma trying to kill him? It felt like she was trying to kill him.

And what about Max, the traitor? What in the world was Max doing, inserting himself between Jude and Gemma?

She'd sent this text an hour and twenty minutes ago. That knowledge landed like a rock in his gut. Gemma and Max would already be at the clam dig—his family's clam dig— without him.

It was terrifying to think what his mother might say to Gemma and how Jeremiah would pry. The O'Sullivan relatives on his mom's side of the family were quirky. He should be the one introducing Gemma to them. For one thing, he was the one who formed the connection between his family and Gemma. For another, his presence would have kept his family on their best behavior.

This made no sense.

Gemma and Max had shared a two-minute-long conversation at Jude's house. And now Max had invited her to the clam dig? Max's motives . . . God only knew what his motives might be.

Jude had a pile of work waiting. He'd been planning to eat dinner at his desk. Yet he didn't hesitate before tossing that plan aside, grabbing his keys, and striding toward the exit.

Chapter Twenty-One

Don't *look a gift horse in the mouth.*

That phrase summed up Gemma's feelings toward her current surroundings. She could not explain the events that had landed her in the center of Jude's family's gathering. But she was savoring this unexpected backstage pass.

She and Fiona had been digging for clams and chatting for thirty minutes straight, and it still felt surreal to be in conversation with this glamorous and infamous person that Gemma had read about in multiple articles online.

Fiona had a Jane-Fonda-in-her-fifties vibe. Jude's mother was *that* polished, *that* impeccable. Her outfit seemed like something chosen by a clothing brand for a clam-dig photoshoot.

Gemma would have expected rich, cultured Fiona to be as close-lipped as Jude. Instead, she was as forthright as her son was private—which had come as a juicy surprise.

If Jude's mom had confided in Gemma in order to deepen Gemma's sympathy and admiration for Jude, then—mission accomplished. Jude had told her the big brushstrokes of his bio, but she'd had no idea that some chapters of his story had been so brutal.

When she'd first met Jude, she'd assumed that he'd lived a charmed life. She'd jumped to that conclusion in part because he didn't show his scars. But also because he honestly *had* received big advantages in terms of looks, smarts, wealth, and education. Parts of his life had been charmed. But it hadn't been only that. Was anyone's life *only* that? It was easy to think so when you were someone who'd always had to scrape for money looking into the face of someone who'd never had to scrape for money.

She saw now that Jude's life was more complicated than she'd initially made it. Her heart went out to the teenage boy he'd been, a boy who'd carried his mother's well-being on his shoulders. The more she learned about him, the higher protectiveness toward him flamed within her. And the more she understood why he was the man he was. The clean-shaven jaw and wrinkle-free shirts were a symbol of the integrity inside.

Fiona introduced her to a blur of family members as conversation and the tide eddied around Gemma. At least twenty were out on the beach and, apparently, more would be joining them at the house of Jack, Fiona's older brother, where they'd be cooking and eating dinner.

So far, Gemma had not seen hide nor hair of Jeremiah. And she assumed Felix was persona non grata in the eyes of Fiona's family, so if she ever had the chance to meet the family's arch villain, it would have to be another time.

Most importantly, though, where was Jude? Almost here, hopefully. She kept catching herself scanning the distance for him. Jumping every time she saw the figure of a man. Then sighing internally when the figure turned out not to be Jude.

The sun slid halfway behind the hills and the sky began to darken, at which point Fiona's eighty-something father organized the packing of the gear and clams. A female cousin of Jude's gave her bike to Max. Then the cousin and Gemma were loaded onto one of several carts towed behind bikes. Their caravan reached the cars, and everyone dumped the clams into two coolers filled with icy saltwater.

After a short ride in Max's car over the causeway and back to the mainland, they reached Jack's house—a small, rustic cottage on a prime piece of land. She and Max followed others around the side of the structure to a stone patio at the back. A combination of mounted exterior lights and burning tiki torches gave the space a magical feel and revealed a strip of sand dotted with tall grass and, beyond that, rocks descending to ocean.

The group gathered at outdoor tables to inspect the clams. Chipped and open clams, they discarded. The rest, they cleaned. That done, they moved en masse to an indention that had been dug in the sand. Jack had clearly started burning wood some time ago, because it had already reduced down to smoldering remnants. Once a layer of seaweed had been laid, they placed the clams on top, as well as corn still in its husks, tinfoil-wrapped potatoes, and onions. More seaweed followed, then a soaked tarp that would act as a lid to steam the food.

Gemma drew in and teased apart the familiar scents of a clam dig—bracing ocean, salty seaweed, wood fire.

Still no Jude. Max had been certain he would show. But Jude had yet to reply to her text and that likely meant Jude was slammed at work. Jude prioritized his job. If he was slammed at work, it was a stretch to imagine him leaving that in the lurch.

Her earlier elation over being included in this gathering was dissolving into unease. If Jude didn't come tonight . . . Well. That was going to be very telling. And depressing. Plus, Max would see that Jude's feelings for her were not as deep as Max supposed. Which was humiliating to contemplate.

Had she been wrong to come? Sometimes her tendency to say yes to spontaneous adventures came back to bite her.

She retreated to the patio to grab a glass bottle of Coke from a bucket of ice and drinks. Immediately after she popped its top, a couple rounded the side of the house nearby.

Gemma knew the man on sight and found herself instantly starstruck. This was unmistakably Jude's older brother, Jeremiah.

His gait hitched when he spotted her, but almost at once his stunning face broke into a smile. "You must be Gemma."

"Yes." It was strange in the extreme that he, the famous one, would recognize *her*. What had been going on behind the scenes that resulted in him knowing her name?

He introduced himself and the blond woman next to him as Remy, his girlfriend.

Remy was lovely in a very natural way. Her long hair looked as if it had dried in tousled waves without the aid of a curling iron. Her overalls, turtleneck, and lace-up boots were adorable on her.

"No need to fear, Gemma," Jeremiah said. "We're here to rescue you from this eccentric bunch."

"That sounds chivalrous," Remy said. "But those are empty words because he's the most eccentric of them all."

"Remy's always been strangely resistant to my appeal."

"Not as resistant as I should've been, seeing as how I consented to date you." Remy winked at Gemma.

"Opposites really do attract," he said.

"But enough about us," Remy said.

"Exactly. Enough about us." Jeremiah concentrated on Gemma. "Tell us what's going on between you and my brother."

Remy elbowed him. "That was a nosy way to phrase that."

"I prefer to think that was an honest way to phrase that."

For the first time, a gap opened in Jeremiah and Remy's rapid-fire banter. "Um," Gemma said. They were expecting her to answer. What could she say that Jude would condone? "Jude and I are still figuring out what's going on between us. So I suppose my answer is: unsure."

"Hmm." Jeremiah took her measure. "What can we do to convince you to take a chance on him? I know. There's a house on the tip of Islehaven Island I can offer you—"

"That's my family's house!" Remy interrupted, laughing. To Gemma, she said, "Jeremiah would like me to spend even more time than I do in Groomsport so that he can stay in the lap of luxury in his ridiculous house—"

"You know very well I'll stay on Leigh's waterboard of a mattress on Islehaven whenever I need to be near you—"

"—but I love my cottage on Islehaven. So that's that."

"Are you saying," Gemma joked, "that taking a chance on Jude will not earn me a house?"

"It will," Jeremiah vowed. "Free of charge—"

"Jude has a lot to recommend him," Remy said, "even without the perk of my house. He's principled, has a great sense of humor, and best of all, he's not a celebrity. Between you and me, I would not have started falling for this one here if I'd realized he was well known—"

"All around the world—"

"To a *small* circle of F1 fans. As you can see, his conceit is tiresome. Jude is not conceited."

"No. He's not conceited," Jeremiah agreed. Some of the teasing melted from his face. "I think he really likes you, Gemma."

"You do?"

"Yeah."

"He's not here tonight."

"Sure about that?" Jeremiah's focus centered behind Gemma's shoulder and he angled his chin forward.

Gemma's pulse leapt. She swiveled, holding her still-full bottle of Coke. Her vision intersected with Jude's. They both froze.

He wore a charcoal suit and one of his spotless white business shirts, one button released at the throat. He must have discarded his tie somewhere between the office and here. The simplicity of the clothing was a perfect foil for his handsomeness. He looked as elegant as always. Yet, uncharacteristically, he also looked faintly frazzled, as if he'd rushed to get here.

The memory of kissing him swamped her. It felt impossible to believe. *This* sophisticated man had kissed her? *No.* And yet, yes. He had.

The sight of Gemma poleaxed Jude.

He'd been thinking about her for so many days now. Not just the last eight since she'd visited him at his house. But for weeks and weeks, since the first time they'd met. Now here she was, lifting a hand to keep her hair from tangling with her eyelashes. That didn't stop the strands from drifting against her pale, graceful neck. Her sweater looked soft and warm, and he wanted to fold her against his chest and nuzzle his nose into the place where her shoulder curved up to her throat.

"Jude," Jeremiah said, "we've been getting to know your friend Gemma."

"I see that." He walked the rest of the way to their group. He hated arriving at things late. Nor was he a fan of feeling like an afterthought at a party comprised of his own family members. "Hello," he said to Gemma, cursing himself for not having a better opening.

"Hello."

The recollection of what they'd done the last time they'd seen each other was enormous—the elephant in the room. He was also hugely aware of Jeremiah and Remy, watching them avidly. He shook hands with his brother and greeted Remy.

"We'll give you two some privacy." Remy interlaced her fingers with Jeremiah's.

"Think about my offer, Gemma," Jeremiah said.

Then Remy tugged him away.

"Should I ask what his offer was?" Jude asked.

"I wouldn't recommend it."

"Okay. Sorry about them."

"You're kidding, right? They're fabulous."

It surprised him, how much it meant to hear her say that.

"This whole clam dig so far has been fabulous," she continued. "You should be charging me a fee to attend this party."

He should be paying everyone here to back off and let him have her to himself. "Has your mom raised her suspicions about me again?"

"Yes, one other time." She took a sip of Coke. "When we were out shopping. Once again, I told her she was mistaken and she looked at me with this dopey, hopeful, knowing smile. So I'm not sure where her head is at on all that. The main thing is that she's kept quiet."

He needed something else to say. "How . . . are things going with your research into your great-grandmother and grandfather's love story?"

"In order to solve the rest of the mystery, I have to find my great-grandmother's diaries." She straightened. "In fact, here's a question for you, Mr. Expert Investigator. If the diaries aren't in the house where Gracie lived, which it seems they are not, where might Gracie have hidden them?"

"Would she have stored them where she lives now? Or placed them in a storage facility?"

"No to the storage facility. I helped her move into Marigold Manor and she definitely didn't unload them there, either."

"The first clue led to a box. Could the box or its contents hold another clue?"

"We unpacked the box. There wasn't a slip of paper with a code on it inside."

"A second clue might be more subtle."

"I returned the box to Gracie. Next chance I get, I'll go by and take another look at it—"

"Gemma," Max called as he walked up, butting in without remorse. "Come sit down. Both of you."

Jude curbed the urge to do what he wanted to do—wrap his hands around Max's throat and squeeze. So far, he and Gemma hadn't had the chance to exchange any meaningful words.

Gemma took a seat next to Max on lawn chairs forming a half circle around the fire pit facing the Atlantic. Jude went around, hugging his mother, his grandparents, and the others.

Several conversations were happening among the group, and when Jude took his seat on Gemma's other side, Gemma and Max were busy having the type of conversation Max excelled at with women. A mix of flattery and outrageous boasts. *Max* was flirting with *Gemma*.

How had he become the third wheel in this group?

Jude wanted Gemma to be his. Gemma, who he'd do anything for. Hike across mountains. Sail across seas. Sacrifice his job, if she wanted him.

"Do you have any Jude stories from your younger years for me?" Gemma asked Max.

"So many."

"Pick one, please."

"Well, there was the Easter when Jeremiah and I thought it would be hilarious to throw four dozen confetti eggs at the gardener's greenhouse. We tried to convince Jude to be our accomplice, but he wouldn't, of course."

"He was eight going on thirty-eight," Jeremiah put in from where he sat on Max's far side.

The whole Jude-is-an-uptight-bore theme was wearing thin.

"What are confetti eggs?" Remy asked.

"Empty eggshells filled with confetti," Max said.

"You weren't into destruction of property?" Gemma asked Jude.

"No. Nor really any of the stupid things elementary school boys are into."

"Jeremiah and I," Max continued, "hid behind the bushes near the greenhouse and threw the confetti eggs one by one. When we were done, we started back toward Jeremiah and Jude's house. On our way we passed Jude, heading toward the greenhouse with a broom, a dustpan, and a trash bag."

"We heckled him," Jeremiah said, "but he walked past us with his chin up, like he was too dignified to respond. Which he was."

"You were going to clean up their mess?" Gemma asked.

Jude hefted a shoulder. "I didn't want the gardener to have to do it."

"So what happened then?" she asked. "You cleaned it up and tattled on Jeremiah and Max?"

"No," Max said.

"He should have tattled on me a million times, but never did," Jeremiah confessed.

Max leaned his elbows against his knees. "Jude cleaned up the mess but didn't say a word about it. Because of him, Jeremiah and I didn't get in trouble."

A softening moved across Gemma's face as she looked at Jude. Her cheeks and lips were pink. Sandy smudges marked her jeans. Every inch of her body glowed with health and vitality.

He held her gaze. She was brave, feisty, funny, and bold.

At Undercover School they'd repeatedly said, *Remember who you're lying to and try your best to be honest with yourself.*

This was him, being honest with himself . . .

He loved her. Exactly as she was.

Precisely because that's how she was.

He wouldn't change anything about her. None of it. Every aspect of her made up the whole. And the whole was worth more than anything to him. Priceless.

Jeremiah asked Max a question and Jude took the opportunity to lean toward her. "Come inside with me?"

"Sure. Why?"

"My grandfather asked me to bring out some . . . stuff," he lied.

"Stuff?"

"Stuff," he confirmed.

She followed him into Jack's cottage, which was absent of people but filled with rag rugs, plaid sofas, and enough nautical details (ropes, buoys, signs that said things like *Life Is Better at the Beach!*) to choke a gift shop.

"What stuff—" she began.

"There's no stuff." He didn't know what to do with his hands, so he pressed them into the pockets of his suit pants. "Please, please tell me that you're not interested in Max. If you are, I'll have to kill him. And I'd have a hard time explaining that to his mother."

Slowly, her lips curved. "I am not into Max."

"Thank God."

"But I'd love to hear why you'd have to kill him if I was." She'd put him on the spot.

"I'd have to kill him," he said bluntly, "because I desperately want you to be with me."

Her brows lifted.

"I'm crazy about you," he went on. "I can't remember ever wanting anything in my life as much as I want for you to be my girlfriend."

"Your job . . ."

"My job is secondary to you. I'm going to let that sort itself out. If I'm with you, then anything that happens with that is fine."

Moisture collected in her eyes, but she was still smiling.

"You told me," he said, "back at my house, that you wanted to tap the brakes. Do you still feel that way?"

"I said that mostly because I wanted to give you time to think so you could be certain of our next step. And partly because I needed a little more time myself."

"I don't need any more time."

"Me neither. I just . . ."

He waited. Worry fought with hope.

"I'm scared of a relationship between us ending in disaster and the"—she blew out a shivering breath—"desolation that would bring me. But what you've said just now has gone a long way toward giving me a reason to hope that it might not end in disaster. That it's worth the risk."

"If you'll give me a chance, I'll do everything in my power to make sure this ends well for both of us. For you, even more than for me, because I'll put you first."

She dashed her fingertips under her eyes. Beamed at him.

"Will you give me a chance?" he asked.

"Yes."

"You will?"

"Yes."

He moved toward her, then halted as his grandmother and aunt walked past the window, talking.

Jude took hold of her hand and drew her into the galley kitchen, out of sight of the windows. They looked directly at each other. His blood rushed hot and then they were kissing, and his hands were delving into her hair. She drew him closer. He could feel her pulse, smell her perfume and the sea spray in her hair.

"You're all I think about," he whispered.

She pulled back enough to meet his eyes.

They were both breathing hard, his profile tilted down, her arms locked around him.

Her features held honesty and an aching tenderness that mirrored how he felt about her. "I'm amazed that I've been promoted from fake girlfriend to real one."

"I like to do everything well, but I was mediocre at the role of fake boyfriend."

"Only because you viewed the role like a test you had to ace instead of like an acting gig that was mainly about pretending to be obsessed with me."

"And look what happened. I'm obsessed with you."

She laughed, relaxed and heartfelt.

"Just you wait, Gemma. I plan to dedicate myself to excellence at the role of real boyfriend."

Electricity built between them, rising and rising. Their mouths met, and it was so unbelievably good to kiss her now that this thing that existed between them had been spoken about and recognized.

Minutes later, he was deep in sensory bliss when the sound of the door opening and closing reached him. Gemma leapt away from him as if they were about to be caught robbing a bank.

Chapter Twenty-Two

Gemma watched Max amble into view. "I heard you mention getting some things for your grandfather, Jude. Since you've been gone a while, I thought I'd come see if I could help." He spoke the obvious lie with a sly glint in his eye. Max was quite the plotter. And completely cool and shameless about it. Jude had told her he was waiting for the right woman to prove to Max that he still had a heart. But Gemma had to wonder if that was possible. There might not be a heart in there.

"I made up the thing," Jude said, "about getting stuff for my grandfather. To get Gemma alone."

"Oh?" Max looked between them smugly. "How did that ploy go?"

"Very well, thanks," Jude answered, brisk.

"God cursed me," Max said to Gemma, "when He put me in competition with Jeremiah and Jude. Women always prefer them to me."

"Somehow I think your ego will survive," Gemma said.

"But, if you like, I'll place a hold on you in case this thing with Jude doesn't pan out."

"*Gemma*," Jude growled.

Max grinned.

"Let's go eat clams," she said.

So they did.

Beneath a star-studded night sky, Gemma feasted on seafood and veggies and sipped her second icy bottle of Coke. The wind picked up. Voices rose and fell like musical notes. And the whole time she buzzed with the newfound understanding between herself and Jude. Their magnetism was so tangible, it gave her goosebumps.

This was happening. Jude had said that he was crazy about her. More than any man she'd known, he could be trusted. He wouldn't have said all those extraordinary things to her if he hadn't meant them.

They left the party as soon as politely possible. They talked and teased and snuck heavy glances at each other while he drove them back to Bangor.

They went to his house instead of hers because he had Mabel. However, they quickly outlasted Mabel, who snoozed while the two of them stayed up until two in the morning. Gemma didn't want to leave and Jude definitely didn't want her to leave, but she finally insisted she had to go home so they could both get a few hours of sleep.

When her head finally hit her pillow, she realized she wasn't going to be able to achieve the sleep she'd advocated for. Wide awake and goofy, she smiled into the darkness remembering once, twice, thirty-five times how he'd looked when he'd said, "*I desperately want you to be with me.*"

When Jude told his FBI superiors that he was going to pursue a dating relationship with Gemma, they responded with grave silence.

He was closed into Dixon's office with both Dixon and Shannon. The older man half-sat against the front edge of his desk. Shannon stood next to Dixon, arms crossed. Jude kept his posture tall, his back near the door, which he hoped to leave through as soon as possible.

"You know I have your best interests at heart, yes?" Dixon asked Jude.

"Yes, sir."

"Then hear me when I say that I advise you to end things immediately with Ms. Clare. Find yourself a different girl-friend. Any girlfriend will do so long as she's unconnected with our casework. There are a lot of wonderful women in the world."

"Not for me," Jude replied. He didn't enjoy speaking about his personal life with Dixon and Shannon. But in this situation, it couldn't be helped. "Gemma is the one for me. I know it would have been better for me, career-wise, if that wasn't true. But it is true."

The older agents frowned.

"The FBI takes a hard stance on this, Jude," Dixon stated.

"I know, sir."

"We can't have agents compromising themselves or others because of love or lust."

"I told him not to go this route weeks ago," Shannon said.

"The fact that Scent-sible is currently inactive is a techni-cality," Dixon said. "That won't give you a get-out-of-jail-free card."

"I understand."

"Think of all that you've invested to get where you are," Dixon said. "The application and selection process. The academy. Years of work. Undercover training. You're an outstanding agent. You have a bright future ahead of you at the Bureau. I'd hate to see you jeopardize all that."

"Think of all the good you can do with us here in the years to come," Shannon added.

"I'd like to do good here in the years to come," Jude acknowledged. "But I won't give Gemma up. Whatever consequences there are for that, I'll accept."

"I'll have to speak with those higher up the food chain." Dixon sighed. "This doesn't give me any pleasure, Jude, but until a decision about your future with the FBI has been reached, I'm placing you on administrative leave."

Jude's gut hardened.

He hated this.

Yet he regretted nothing.

In Bayview, Gemma entered Marigold Manor with a two-fold goal: spend time with Gracie; search for a clue.

She purposely arrived forty minutes before Gracie's beloved arts and crafts session. That way, they had plenty of time to catch up before they escorted her great-grandmother to arts and crafts.

Once again, Gracie asked if Gemma had learned what had gone wrong between herself and Paul all those years ago. Again, Gemma had told her she was still working to find out.

After Gracie left, it didn't take Gemma long to locate the cardboard box in Gracie's closet. She set the box in the middle of the rug and went through each piece of Gracie and Paul's wedding clothes. Tie, gloves, pocket square. Slip, crinoline, wedding dress. When possible, she turned the dusty items inside out. In every case, she went over them inch by inch, sneezing occasionally. She found no clues.

Turning the box and opening every flap, Gemma searched the cardboard itself for a clue. Maybe a code written in faint pencil? But no.

Disappointed, she repacked the things into the box. The letters and photos weren't with the other items, so she peeked inside Gracie's bedside dresser and found them in the second drawer. Gemma switched on a lamp, and held each letter up to it, eyeing both sides like a customs inspector eyes passports. No clues.

She peered at the first photo, turned it over. Then the second photo. When she turned that one over, she saw again the hand-drawn border around the date. Very ornate. Hearts, flowers, leaves, and . . . She held it even closer to the lamp light. Symbols?

What looked like a number two emerged from the design. Impossible to tell if that was an intentional two or just a creative flourish. She noticed that the border didn't close on the top left corner. If she started there and moved to the right—

Oh! An oval was camouflaged in the doodle. That oval could be a zero. She moved farther along the border and found a seven.

Her heartrate picked up speed.

She pulled out her phone and typed each digit she discovered into a note.

By the time she'd made it around the border, she had a line of nine numbers. She typed parentheses around the first three digits. Two-zero-seven was Bayview's area code. She didn't have enough remaining numbers, however, to complete a full phone number. Which hopefully meant she'd overlooked a number that was still hiding in the design.

Running her fingernail along the border, she went back

over it, and found a number four she'd missed the first time. "Gotcha," she whispered. She added the four where it fell in the order, then input a dash in the right spot.

A phone number. Gracie loved puzzles. Embedding numbers in a hand-drawn doodle was right in Gracie's wheelhouse.

Gemma popped to her feet, dialed, then paced while the phone rang.

"Hello?" the voice of an elderly woman answered.

"Hello, this is Gemma Clare. I'm Gracie Bettencourt's great-granddaughter."

"Gemma. Of course. Is everything all right?"

"Everything's perfectly fine. Gracie's well. I found your number among her things and reached out because I have a question for you. But I'm afraid Gracie didn't leave a name next to this number. I'm at a bit of a disadvantage because I don't know who I'm speaking with."

"Oh! This is Wanda."

Gracie's long-time friend. A mental image populated of a five-foot-tall woman with a stooped back and short, light pink hair. When Gemma was young, she remembered Wanda coming by Gracie's several times for coffee, cake, and conversation. And Gemma had been with Gracie a handful of times when they'd stopped by Wanda's house to pick up or drop off items. "Wanda!"

She gave a warbling laugh. "Yes, doll."

"This question might seem strange. But did Gracie, by any chance, leave her diaries with you?"

A brief silence. "Why, yes. She dropped them off with me a few years back."

Elated surprise bubbled up in Gemma.

"Gracie told me," Wanda continued, "that she might want

to come back to look at them from time to time. After she dies, though, she asked me to dispose of them."

Ah. Crafty. Gracie had left a clue in code within her desk that led to her cardboard box of memories. Then she'd left another clue in the doodle that would lead her from the box to the rest of the story—recorded in the diaries. The fact that she'd stored the diaries with Wanda and asked her friend to dispose of them after she passed away confirmed Gemma's theory that Gracie had left this trail of clues for herself alone following her Alzheimer's diagnosis.

"A few months ago," Gemma said, "Gracie told Grandma Colette and Mom and me that she'd forgotten the early stages of her love story with Paul. She was distressed about that and asked for our help. We've figured out some of her story, but the rest is in the diaries."

"Do you think she'd want the three of you to know what's in the diaries?" Wanda asked doubtfully.

"I don't think the Gracie of two years ago would've wanted that," Gemma answered honestly. "But the Gracie of today definitely does. She knows there are details she can't remember."

Wanda made a thoughtful sound but didn't go on to invite Gemma over to her house to collect the diaries. Clearly, Wanda was unsure how to remain loyal to her friend in this situation.

"We love Gracie," Gemma said. "A tremendous amount. We won't judge her for anything in her past. Our aim here is simply to reunite her with her own history so she'll know how much she was loved by Paul then and how much she's loved by us now."

"In that case, doll, come on by and see me when I get back from my trip."

"You're traveling?"

"I'm in Oregon with my daughter and her husband. I'll be back in three weeks."

"I'll call you then."

Just as they were saying their good-byes and ending the call, Gemma's phone pinged.

JUDE

If you're free, will you come over and have dinner with me tonight?

If you're free. Darling! As if she'd go to kickboxing class or out antiquing instead of having dinner with him. A hurricane of epic proportions could not keep her from having dinner with him tonight.

JUDE

Not to brag, but I'm pretty good at grilling sausages on the barbecue.

GEMMA

I'll bring bread and salad! What time?

JUDE

As soon as you can get here.

GEMMA

Be there at 5:45.

Lucky her. Usually he worked late.

During the rest of the workday at her shop, she checked the time every thirty seconds. Gemma hadn't been this eager when she'd been twelve and counting the days until her family's trip to Disney World.

At last, closing time arrived.

Stopping at the grocery store, she picked up French bread

and a pre-made green salad and—on a wave of inspiration—a bar of good-quality chocolate.

As soon as she reached his cabin, she detected the smell of barbecue smoke. Following her nose, she rounded the side of his house, carrying her grocery sack.

He must've heard her because when he came into view, he was already facing in her direction with hopeful expectation. He had the grill open and a pair of tongs in his hand. A wide grin spread across his face, making him so breathtaking that she almost couldn't bear it.

It was chilly and blustery out today. He wasn't wearing a hat or gloves with his casual clothes and green pull-over fleece, so his fingers and cheeks were red.

"You're finally here," he said.

"Finally? I said I'd be here at 5:45 and it's 5:41."

He set down the tongs and moved toward her. "The hours between 2:00 a.m. last night and 5:41 tonight were the longest hours I've ever lived."

She knew exactly what he meant.

His hands came up to support the sides of her face and jaw. "Hello." His voice was a sexy caress.

She dropped the sack and placed her palms on his chest. "Hello."

Then he showed her just how much he'd missed her through their kisses. She loved the taste of him, the texture of his cheeks at this hour of the day after he'd shaved this morning. Loved his assurance—

Mabel's barking interrupted them once again.

His forehead rested against hers. "I might need to call a dog trainer."

"And also check to make sure the sausages aren't burning?"

"The sausages!"

She followed him to the barbecue and sure enough, one

side of the sausages was going to be toastier than the other side. "That's exactly how I like them," she said truthfully.

"And here I was trying to impress you by cooking the only thing I cook well."

"I'm already as impressed by you as a person can be."

He glanced at her. Their eye contact lingered.

"How did it go at work today?" she asked. He'd told her last night that he intended to tell his bosses about them today. She'd tried to convince him not to do so. To wait, at the very least. He'd responded with laid-back ease, defusing any irritation she might have felt over the fact that he wasn't going to take her advice. After all, she'd been in no mood then or now to let anything bother her.

"They put me on administrative leave," he said as nonchalantly as if he'd just said, *These sausages are made of pork.*

It took her a few seconds to digest his sentence. When she did, each word landed hard—clanging. "They . . . suspended you because you're dating me?" She did not sound as calm as he'd sounded.

"Yes. Dixon is going to discuss things with his superiors and then they'll make a determination."

"A determination about what?"

"About whether I'll be able to continue with the FBI, and if so, under what circumstances."

Her hands fisted at her sides. *"What!"*

"It's all right, Gemma. Their response is not unexpected and I'm at peace with my actions. I wouldn't do anything differently."

"Excuse me?" *How dare the FBI do this to him?*

You knew all along, her conscience pointed out, *that a relationship with Jude was against their rules.* It's true. It's just . . . the news that she'd actually gotten him suspended was awful. Guilt rose in her, a painful tide.

He took hold of her elbows. "I wouldn't do anything differently," he repeated. "It's always been important to me that I do the right thing. There's no doubt in my mind that I did the right thing. So I'm good."

"*I'm* not good with this. You're terrific at what you do. If you're on the job, then I still have hope that you'll be able to stop Cedric. But mostly, Jude, I can't have you lose your position because you're with me."

"Whatever happens with my job, I'll deal with it. Losing you—that's the thing I couldn't stand." He rubbed her upper arms, giving her a persuasive smile. "Remember that I'm a Camden. I'm not going to starve."

She socked him in the shoulder.

"Ow," he said amiably.

"Don't joke about this!" She retreated two steps.

"I have a law degree and an excellent résumé. I could always go back to work for the DA's office."

"You didn't like working for the DA's office. You love being an FBI agent."

He lifted one shoulder in a way that indicated his love for his job was no big thing.

She didn't buy that. Her love of her job accounted for a good chunk of her satisfaction in life, and she knew it was the same for him. Gemma drew close, curling her fingers into the fabric of his fleece. "At the clam dig, your mom told me—"

"That's a terrifying way to start a sentence."

"—that you spent some of your high school years giving things up for her. I do not want you to give up . . ." Her voice ambushed her by trembling. She cleared her throat. "I do not want you to give up anything for me."

He pulled her in and hugged her. Strong arms, warmth, and reassurance circled her. His cheek rested against the top of her head. "I'll sacrifice anything I have to for you."

"No."

"Yes. This is my job we're talking about. My choice."

"Tell them we'll break up."

He leaned back to look at her. "Never."

"Yes!"

"Never."

"You can't stop me from breaking up with you." She could hear Mabel rustling through foliage in the quiet that followed.

"Gemma." His tone had lost its levity. "Please don't talk about breaking up with me. My heart can't take it."

She rolled her lips inward. She did not want to break up with him, of course. She'd rather do anything than that. But this *sucked*. "I've known, academically, that this was a possibility. But now that it's happened, it seems ridiculous that they've punished you for this reason. It makes me feel rotten."

"This might be temporary. They might not fire me, so there's no reason for us to get riled up about something that hasn't even happened yet."

"If the FBI fires you, they're the stupidest organization in the history of the world."

His grip tightened. "In the future, we'll both have to give up some things now and then for the other. For example, you're going to have to give up your dignity within your family."

"Why's that?"

"Because you have a boyfriend who's a butterfly collector."

She chuckled. "Now I'm angry at you for making me laugh."

"Your laugh is my favorite sound."

She straightened the collar of his fleece. "Speaking of our relationship and my family, how do we proceed from here?"

"In their eyes, your relationship with McConnell continues as it has been."

"For how long?"

"McConnell is an FBI alias in an FBI case. How long they'll want to keep that alias active is up to them. But keeping that alias active shouldn't be too prohibitive. If it's okay with you, we'll do most of our outings in public away from places where we're likely to run into your family members."

"That's okay with me."

"If we do run into your family like we did at Pasta Bella, that's not a problem. We'll just say McConnell's here for a visit from New York and I'll interact with them as McConnell like I've done in the past."

"What's the end game? When the FBI shuts your alias down, we tell them the whole truth?"

"We tell them everything that's not classified. Fine by you?"

Her family was going to go bonkers when they found out his real identity. In a way, it was lovely to have this chance to keep him, *them*, insulated from her family for a while longer. She and Jude would be free to do what she'd long preferred to do with boyfriends—see where things led away from the scrutiny of her brood. "Fine by me."

JEREMIAH

What's going on with Gemma? Are you two a couple?

JUDE

I'm happy to report that Gemma is now, officially, my girlfriend.

MAX

The clam dig was the ball and Jeremiah and I were the fairy godmothers. You can pay us back by buying us both a new boat.

Gemma did not let the subject of Jude's FBI suspension go. For the first three days of their romance, she unselfishly pointed out to Jude the wisdom of them parting ways so that he could tell his idiot bosses he was free to go back to work for the idiot FBI. Each time, he kindly let her know that he would never, not under any circumstances, do what she was suggesting he do.

How did she make sense of his willingness to give up his job for her hours after they'd started dating?

Her attempts at martyrdom kept meeting with abject failure. So, at the end of those first three days, she had to resign her quest for martyrdom. At which time, she and Jude became inseparable.

His schedule was open, and she delegated the perfume shop to Aunt Stella as much as possible. He brought Mabel to her house. They hung out at his cabin. They posed for a photo with the Paul Bunyan statue and saw *Little Shop of Horrors* at the Penobscot Theatre Company. They watched numerous old movies and tried to one-up the other with their knowledge of movie trivia. They visited a farmers' market near the coast, where he bought a confusing number of red chilies, and she found a butter churn and a milk-glass serving bowl to add to her collection. They took Mabel for long walks on the Orono Bog boardwalk.

They introduced one another to their favorite places to eat beyond the borders of Bayview (to reduce their likelihood of running into her family). She took him to holes-in-the-wall and he took her to fancy spots she'd never ventured to before because of their price tag.

He joined her for a kickboxing class, where he poured sweat, which made his T-shirt stick to his body in intriguing ways and turned his hair wet and spiky. For a kickboxing beginner, he was ridiculously good at it. That conclusion left her both irritated and swoony.

Once, she attempted to join him for his usual cardio-and-weightlifting routine. Before they'd completed it, she announced her intention not to repeat the experience for the rest of her days.

They hiked through forests. They kayaked on his river. They took her rowboat out on her lake.

And things were altogether perfect for three weeks straight.

Until the day Cedric called Jude.

Chapter Twenty-Three

Jude had upped his grocery game now that he was lucky enough to feed Gemma at his house a few nights a week.

Standing in the pasta aisle at the grocery store, he was scrolling through the results from his phone search for *Easy Pasta Recipes*. Gemma liked pasta and he liked to make her happy. Problem was, her father's side of the family was Italian and he didn't know if Google's *Easy Pasta Recipes* were going to be up to her standards—

His phone rang. The caller ID on the screen read *Cedric Bettencourt*.

Adrenaline shot through him. It was quickly moderated by his training, which came online to steady his body's response. The same night he'd exchanged numbers with Cedric, he'd programmed his phone to "always record" conversations to and from Cedric's number. This incoming call was unexpected, but the preparation for it had been laid long ago. "Hello?"

"Jude? This is Cedric Bettencourt calling." Cedric's accented English was easy to recognize after having spent a long meal across the dinner table from him.

"It's good to hear from you." Jude covered his free ear with his hand, trying to drown out grocery store distractions.

"Several weeks back, Gemma indicated that you might know someone interested in making a purchase from me. Still interested?"

"Yes. Absolutely."

"Excellent. I'll be flying to New York in two days. You live in New York, yes?"

"Yes. Would you like to meet to discuss the deal?"

"*Non. En fait* . . . We can discuss now and meet then so I can give you the things I told Gemma were for sale."

Cedric was obviously smart enough not to transmit Rhapsodie's secrets electronically. A computer expert would be able to trace his actions, which would generate evidence against him. Secrets written on paper left no digital footprint.

"When we're talking about the things you have for sale," Jude said, "we're talking about a recipe, correct? Ingredients and process?"

The FBI monitored Cedric's phone communications. Whether verbally or via text, Cedric always kept his language vague. He knew that vague communication did not make for strong evidence against him. Jude had kept his language equally vague just now, but a real representative would ask for clarity, so he'd asked.

"Correct."

"You will write every detail down for my buyer?" Part of the tradition around Rhapsodie: the fact that its specifics were to be passed down orally and never written down.

"I will."

"Do you have terms in mind?" Jude slid his cart backward to make room for a woman who reached for a bag of penne.

"My price is thirty-two M."

M was a slang term for million. Quick agreement would strike Cedric as suspicious. He and his sidekick Vincent would be expecting Jude to negotiate. Also, Jude's "buyer" was the FBI. Just as if he was representing a perfume magnate, he couldn't agree to any price without his buyer's approval. He'd need to use real dollars for this transaction, provided by the FBI. "I'll check with my buyer to confirm what they're willing to pay and get back to you."

"I'll be honest." Cedric's tone communicated cavalier, take-it-or-leave-it ease. "I'll come off my number a very slight amount. Very slight because my product will not be hard to sell. Please call me back with your best offer in the next five hours. If your buyer provides a number I can accept, I will see you in New York."

"You'll hear from me within five hours."

"Very well. And Jude?"

"Yes?"

"Are you still dating my cousin Gemma?"

"I am, yes."

"I do not want her or any of my family members involved in this from now on."

"Agreed."

"You'll keep this secret from Gemma?"

"I will."

"Good day."

"Good day."

Click.

Jude rushed through the rest of his grocery shopping. When he was back in his car, he called Shannon.

"Bailey," she said when she picked up the call.

"Cedric Bettencourt just reinstated contact and told me that he wants to sell his secrets."

"Was the call recorded?"

"Yes. I'll send the recording to you now."

"Come into the office. We'll meet with Dixon."

It felt like longer than three weeks since Jude had walked through the FBI bullpen. His fellow agents greeted him, but it wasn't the same. Either pity or mistrust now tinted their faces—which was hard to see, hard to accept.

When he and Shannon had taken seats in Dixon's office, the older man rested his forearms on his desk. "Shannon and I listened to the call several times while you were en route. It seems clear that Cedric asked for thirty-two million because what he really wants is the round number of thirty million. I suggest you call him back and tell him that's your client's highest offer."

"All right," Jude said.

"Please suggest that the two of you meet at your New York apartment," Dixon said. "So that we can prep a location." The FBI's Tech Squad were experts at audio and video recording. Agents out of the New York office would first have to secure an apartment for use, then the squad would need to get it fitted out with equipment. Two days was a tight timeline, but it could be done.

"And if Cedric doesn't agree to meet at my apartment?" Jude asked.

"In that case, we'll have to accept his proposed location," Dixon answered. "Of course, the sooner he provides that location, the better for our purposes."

Jude nodded.

"I'm temporarily revoking your administrative leave," Dixon continued, "but only to work on this operation."

Uncomfortable quiet lengthened.

"Any other questions?" Shannon asked.

"No."

"Ready to call Cedric back?" Dixon asked.

"Yes."

Dixon made a *go ahead* motion.

Jude dialed. On the third ring, Cedric picked up. "Jude?"

"Yes. I spoke with my buyer. His highest offer is thirty M."

"Hmm."

Jude waited, staring intently at the corner of the wooden desk.

"Accepted," Cedric said. "Be prepared to transfer the funds during our meeting. As soon as I see the money in my account, I'll hand over your buyer's purchase."

"That will be fine. Would you like to meet at my apartment? It's conveniently located and private."

"*Non, merci.* We'll meet at my hotel."

"Very well. Which hotel?"

"I haven't decided. Let's plan on Friday at four o'clock, New York time. I'll let you know my hotel forty-five minutes before."

"Sometimes it takes more than forty-five minutes to get around the city."

"I'll be in Midtown Manhattan. If you're in that part of town when I call, you'll have plenty of time. Yes?"

"Yes," Jude was forced to concede.

"See you soon." The call disconnected.

Jude placed his phone face-up between Dixon and Shannon. He played back the exchange for them.

Shannon gave the older man a concerned look.

The FBI subscribed to the idea that haste makes waste. Their standards of professionalism were extremely high and they frequently invested months and large sums of money in laying groundwork. That and foreseeing every possible complication enabled the best chances of success.

Had it been within their control, none of them would have chosen this scenario. Cedric had not given them the name or address of his hotel. They had just forty-eight hours to prepare and gain approval for the temporary use of thirty million dollars.

"Cedric told you he hasn't decided on a hotel but that might not be true," Dixon said. "It's possible he has or soon will reserve a room. We need to know the name of his hotel." With that information, they'd gain advance access to his hotel room to set up audio and visual equipment.

"If we're able to search the reservation information of hotels in Midtown," Jude said, "we might be able to pinpoint Cedric's name."

Shannon made a note in her phone. "If we can narrow the search to one or two hotels, we should be able to get an order from a judge to access reservations information."

"Do you think Gemma will know where in Manhattan Cedric likes to stay?" Dixon asked.

"Maybe."

"Let's you and I converse with Gemma as soon as she gets off work today."

Foreboding gathered in Jude, dark and icy. He was more than willing to fulfill his role in this operation but the best thing about his conversation with Cedric had been Cedric's insistence on removing Gemma from the equation. He didn't want her anywhere near Cedric or Vincent. He couldn't do his job if she was in even the smallest amount of danger.

Dixon's attention transferred to Shannon. "Please contact the New York office and bring them up to speed."

"Got it."

"We'll need transportation to New York and lodging there for the three of us. I want us on a plane out of here tonight."

It was the middle of May and springtime weather blanketed Maine in green splendor. The last time Gemma had met the FBI in the meadow outside Bangor, snow had prevented her from steering her Vespa along the private drive. This time she made it almost all the way before the road began to disappear into thick grass and the ruts made it impossible to continue.

When Jude had texted, asking if she could meet him and Dixon here, she'd immediately responded with a barrage of questions. He'd been reticent to say much more. Consequently, her brain had run rampant through anxious possibilities.

Did this have to do with Scent-sible? If Cedric had changed his mind and regained interest in selling the secrets, Cedric would've told her first. Wouldn't he?

Was Dixon calling her and Jude to a meeting to officially announce that their operation was over and that Jude had been fired?

Could Dixon be calling them in to lecture them?

Was he calling them in to say that Jude was being transferred to an office far away?

She rounded the final corner to her destination on foot and saw Dixon and Jude waiting for her in the same spot as before next to a black Suburban. As always lately, her heart swelled at the sight of Jude. Forget exercise and chocolate. Jude was the best source of endorphins.

He wasn't wearing work clothes in the older man's presence, which was odd. He had on the same type of clothing he'd been wearing since they'd put him on leave—today, jeans and a navy T-shirt. He watched her approach with all of his usual affection, but she also detected a guardedness in his face that she hadn't seen for quite some time. Was he bracing for bad news? Trying to warn her silently?

"Hello, Ms. Clare," Dixon said as she came to a stop before them.

"Hello." Animosity toward him over how he'd treated Jude turned inside her like the Death Star of *Star Wars* fame. But she knew better than to let that show. This was Jude's boss, not hers. His work relationships were his to navigate.

"Your cousin Cedric," Dixon told her, "contacted Jude today and reinstated his interest in selling the secrets behind Rhapsodie."

"Oh?" She looked between them inquiringly. "I'm surprised. I would've expected him to reach out to me first in relation to selling the secrets."

"From my perspective," the older man replied, "it makes sense that he chose to communicate directly with Jude. You introduced Jude to Cedric, which gave Jude immediate credibility in Cedric's eyes. But now that Cedric is ready to do business, it's understandable that he wants to keep you and every other family member in the dark about the transaction. The more people who know, the more dangerous for Cedric. Far better, from his point of view, for you to think that he changed his mind and never pursued selling the secrets."

"So I won't be involved in the operation from here on out?" Gemma asked.

"You can assist as an advisor to us on Cedric, which is why I called you here today."

She cut a peek at impassive Jude before looking back to Dixon. "How can I help?"

"Cedric will be meeting with Jude to make the purchase two days from now in Midtown Manhattan. He proposed they meet at his hotel but refused to reveal the name of his hotel. Do you know where in New York Cedric typically stays?"

"Yes. He and his parents and grandparents always had a fondness for The Plaza. Back in the day, they were very loyal to it. Then fifteen or so years ago, they started staying at The Lowell, which is smaller and has more of a boutique feel. The last time I met up with Cedric in New York he was staying at a very modern hotel . . ." She'd joined Cedric there for drinks once. She racked her brain. "I can't recall its name, but it has a central atrium. It's a new building, not historic. Here. I can look it up—"

"Allow me." Jude tapped his phone screen. "The Mod?"

"That doesn't ring a bell. May I see pictures?"

He handed over his phone and she glanced through images of The Mod. "No, this one isn't right."

He brought up more options. None were right.

Finally, on the fourth try, she recognized the photos. "Yes. This is the one where he stayed. Henry House."

"Excellent," Dixon said. "That's helpful. What else can you tell me about his travel preferences when in New York City? How does he get around? Spend his time? Are there any restaurants he prefers?"

Gemma relayed every piece of information she knew, surprising herself with the quantity of it.

Dixon listened. Jude took notes on his phone.

"Thank you," Dixon told her when he'd exhausted his questions. "Agent Camden and I will be leaving for New York immediately. It's of utmost importance that you have no contact with Jude whatsoever and that he have no contact with you over the next several days until this operation has reached its conclusion."

The words impacted her like a fist to the lungs. No contact?

While Jude was risking himself to meet with Cedric and Vincent?

"It will be fine." Solemn lines etched Jude's forehead. It didn't look to her like he really believed no contact would be fine.

"I can come to New York," she said quickly to Dixon. "I can be an advisor to you there regarding Cedric."

"No," Jude said.

She frowned at him, stung.

"I'll feel much better if you're here, Gemma," Jude said. "Where it's safe."

"He's right," Dixon agreed. "Continue with your usual rhythms. Post on your shop's Instagram account about things you're doing in Bayview. That way, if Cedric checks your feed, he'll see that you're at home, oblivious to the illegal deal he's striking with your boyfriend."

She hadn't been out of contact with Jude for so much as two waking hours across the last three weeks and didn't want him going dark at such a pivotal time. "I really think I can be of value in New York—"

"No," Dixon said, not unkindly. "I can't allow anything or anyone to cloud Jude's judgment. In this situation, under my watch, cooler heads *must* prevail. Do you understand, Ms. Clare?"

She bit her lip. "I do."

"If I have further questions for you, I'll call." Dixon opened the passenger side of the Suburban. "I'll wait in the car for the next few minutes so that you two can say goodbye to one another."

As Dixon shut himself inside, Jude took Gemma's hand and led her behind the SUV's tailgate, as out of sight as possible.

"I don't like this," she stated.

The thumb of his free hand swept along her cheekbone,

then tucked her hair behind her ear. "What part don't you like?"

"All of it. *Now* they're welcoming you back? Now that you're useful?"

"I'm glad to be useful to them."

"I don't like that we can't be in contact. I don't like that Cedric cut me out of this. I don't like that Cedric won't tell you the name of his hotel. That means he might be suspicious."

"We always knew that Vincent was street smart."

"Right, and you can bet that Vincent will be with Cedric in New York. I don't like that you'll be outnumbered—meeting both of them without much time to prepare. Most of all, I don't like that this will put you in danger."

"This is my job," he said gently. "This is the meeting we've been hoping for all along."

He was the one going to face Cedric and he was calm. It wouldn't be fair to shove more stress or drama onto this good-bye. And make no mistake, this was—suddenly, unexpectedly— goodbye. Never had she wanted to say goodbye to someone less than she wanted to say goodbye to him. How to act? What to say? Dread and protectiveness were jumbling inside, making it hard to think straight. A memory of Gracie and Paul's goodbye on that train station platform in the 1940s skated through her memory . . . The photo of them from that day. The heartbreak that followed.

She wanted more time, more privacy. But had none of either. "I'll take care of Mabel while you're gone."

"Thank you. She'd like that better than boarding overnight at daycare, which is what I was thinking I'd do."

"Be safe."

"I will."

"I'll miss you." He was so beautiful to her. Inside and out.

"I'll miss you." He spoke the words back to her like a vow.

"These . . . these last weeks have been the best of my life because of you."

It felt as if she should confess everything that was in her heart. The words bottled up and formed an internal pressure like a pop can that had been shaken. Yet this was hardly the place to share intimate emotions. For pity's sake, they were standing behind the SUV where his boss was waiting. "I won't be able to contact you," she told him, "but know that I'll be thinking about you and praying for you the whole time. Come home soon."

"As soon as I can," he promised. "You're here and you're the best reason I could ever have to come home."

He gave her a kiss laced with unexpressed words and the sorrow of parting. Then they looked into each other's eyes.

Something was off. This felt all wrong. What was bothering her?

Maybe that all the power seemed to be Cedric's? Maybe that Cedric was her relative and she felt responsible for his maddening choices? Maybe that she hadn't forgotten what had happened the last time someone she cared about—her father—had gotten involved with Cedric. That had ended terribly for Dad and their whole family.

Though Jude was a Camden who had the might of the FBI behind him, he was as vulnerable to injury as any other human being. She honestly couldn't stand the thought of him getting hurt.

They kissed again, a reverent whisper of pressure.

"Do you want a ride back to your Vespa?" he asked.

She'd rather this be their final interaction because she didn't want Dixon witnessing their last moment. "You and Dixon go on. My scooter's parked right around the corner."

"Sure?"

No. "Yes. I'll see you soon."

His touch parted from her and cold whooshed across her skin. He paused at the driver's door to look back. Smiled.

Miraculously, she managed a return smile.

Then he was driving off in the SUV.

Then the SUV was out of sight.

Chapter Twenty-Four

Exhaustion and anxiety—Gemma's least favorite combo—pounced on her the moment she came awake the following morning after the world's worst night of sleep.

She was scheduled to swing by the house of Gracie's friend Wanda, newly returned from Oregon, at seven this morning. Today's gloomy weather might as well have been holding up a *stay in bed* sign. But, for Gemma, there was no better time to leave her house to retrieve Gracie's diaries than this. She was desperate to occupy her body and mind with any activity that might distract her from worries about Jude.

Following her stop at Wanda's, she planned to read the relevant diary passages before meeting up with Gracie, Colette, and her mother at Marigold Manor for brunch.

"Gemma!" Wanda crowed when she answered Gemma's knock. "Come in, come in."

"Thank you." Wanda's place looked just as she remembered it. Lots of lace and needlepoint, the fragrance of an orange-scented cleaning product suspended in the air.

"Gracie's diaries are just in here." Wanda's pale pink head

led the way down the hallway. She swept open a closet door and gestured to the collection of diaries. They stood upright, spines out.

As Gemma searched for the volumes she sought, Wanda regaled her with a list of the ways her son-in-law had annoyed her during her recent visit with her daughter.

Satisfaction swept through Gemma when she spotted the diaries embossed with 1944 and 1945. She slid them free. Thanking Wanda profusely, Gemma gave the diminutive woman a hug.

"You're welcome, doll. I adore Gracie. When she asked me if I'd keep her diaries safe, I jumped at the chance. She's been a dear friend to me."

With the diaries stowed in her backpack, Gemma steered to Cinnamon and Spice Bakery through swaths of fog. The bakery only had three high-top tables with stools, but Gemma was able to score one of them after purchasing a chocolate, chocolate chip muffin.

The muffin was incredibly good. Jude would love it, chocolate enthusiast that he was. The thought gave her a pang. She earnestly wished that he was here with her, tasting this, gazing at her in the way that made the backs of her knees tingle.

If anything happened to him—

Don't go there, Gemma.

It didn't take her long to locate the point in time in the diaries when Paul had been sent from D.C. back to France. June 1944.

She skimmed pages and pages of tidy cursive, stopping several times to read the most revelatory sections.

Gemma arrived at Gracie's room to find her three red-headed female ancestors busy with brunch prep.

Colette was pouring Bloody Marys from a thermos that no one would drink but her. Her mother was opening store-bought fruit salad and apologizing because she hadn't brought something homemade. Gracie was placing napkins and silverware on the small, round table in one corner of her room. Gemma set muffins from the bakery next to the eggs and bacon Colette had cooked at home and transported here.

Once Colette had squeezed in a satisfying amount of telling the others what to do and once Mom had squeezed in a satisfying amount of fretting, they settled around the table.

Gracie had drawn her curtains wide to reveal a view of pine trees and, beyond that, road. Fog still clung to the ground, giving the earth a fairytale quality. White below, white-gray above. Gemma noted that the overcast sky was lightening subtly as the day went on, as if its glum mood first thing this morning was improving by degrees.

"Drink up!" Colette said, eagerly following her own order. After draining a third of her Bloody Mary, she smacked her lips with a sigh.

Fondness for the circle of women—*her women*—overcame Gemma. They'd known her and cared for her all her life. The sense of belonging she felt with them was a powerful, matchless thing.

"Mom," Colette said, "are you looking forward to the reason behind this brunch? Learning the missing part of your love story?"

"Very much, yes."

"I am too," Simone concurred.

"You were secretive over the phone, Gemma," Colette scolded. "Everyone who knows me knows I'm not good at being kept in suspense. So now that we're all assembled, can you spill the beans?"

"I can. After we found the cardboard box in the northwest corner of the attic, I began reading Gracie and Paul's love letters." While they ate, she brought them up to speed, explaining how a careful examination of the dates of the letters made her suspicious of the marriage certificate and how a trip to City Hall had verified their certificate to be a fake. She pulled a document from her backpack and handed it to Gracie. "This is a copy of your real marriage certificate. I ordered it and it came in the mail."

No one was eating now. Nor moving. They were all just watching her, alert.

"We had . . . two certificates?" Gracie asked, obviously confused.

"Yes. I wanted to understand why and remembered you writing in your diaries. I realized the diaries would fill in the blanks, but where were they?" Gemma crossed to Gracie's bedside dresser and returned with the photo that had the doodled border on the back. "Turns out the code you left in the desk drawer wasn't the only clue associated with this treasure hunt. You left a clue to the location of the diaries hidden in plain sight here in this drawing." She handed it to her mom.

"I don't see anything except hearts and flowers," Mom said.

"I didn't either at first," Gemma acknowledged.

Colette took the photo and squinted at it. "I think I see a number seven in here. Is there a seven?"

"Yes."

Colette pointed out the seven to Simone, then Gracie. Gracie accepted the photo from her daughter. It didn't take long for her face to light up. "Ah. There are several numbers here."

"Yes," Gemma confirmed. "Ten, to be exact."

"Ten?" Colette demanded, swirling the ice and liquid in her glass. "What do you do with ten numbers?"

"You dial them, when you place a phone call," Gracie said, her trademark mastery of puzzles shining through.

"Exactly," Gemma said. "I dialed the numbers and your friend Wanda answered. I asked her if she had your diaries, and she said she did. You'd left them nearby with someone you trusted for a situation exactly like this one. A situation in which you wanted to jog your own memory and answer your own questions."

"Because sometimes I forget things?"

"I believe so, yes. I believe, a few years back, you antici-pated that you might forget things you'd want to remember." Gemma drew the two diaries from her backpack and set them next to her plate. "I went by Wanda's house earlier and borrowed these. The answers are all here. Would you like to read them yourself? Or would you like me to fill in the pieces of your love story?"

"I'd like for you to do it, sugar. I'm too impatient to hunt through the diaries now, though I will certainly read them later."

"Hear, hear!" Colette barked as if she was a member of the British Parliament.

Gemma took a few bracing bites of bacon and a sip of coffee. "Well." She set a hand on the diaries. "You and Paul were deeply in love when he was sent back to France by the French Committee of National Liberation. You were both determined to reunite as soon as possible after the war and spend the rest of your lives together. You both promised to write. Which you did faithfully and which he did faithfully. But, unfortunately, after the first few months, you stopped receiving his letters and vice versa. I think that was due to your job as a Code Girl. International letters would have posed a security risk for someone like you who had access to such sensitive information."

"Makes sense," Colette said.

"The letters that survived from him are heartbreaking," Gracie said. "He didn't understand why I wasn't writing."

"And you didn't understand why he wasn't writing to you. In the diaries you talk about continuing to write to him again and again despite hearing nothing from him in return. After five months with no word, you came to the conclusion that he no longer loved you and had moved on once he returned to France."

"I was the one who gave up on him?" Gracie asked, looking deeply disappointed with her younger self.

"In your diary, you admit that was motivated by fear. At the time, you were scared that the pain of continuing to love him was more than you could take." Reading that earlier in the diary and speaking it again now, conviction struck Gemma. She and Gracie were similar in personality. Both of them, passionate. Both of them, afraid of the pain their big hearts and big emotions could cost them. "You were devastated and lonely and overwhelmed with the grief of war. In January of 1945, you entered into a rebound romance with a soldier named Theodore Cook. He fell in love with you right away. It's clear from the diaries that you were fond of him in return, but that your heart belonged to Paul."

"Still does," Gracie whispered.

"You and Theodore conceived a child, but you didn't know about the pregnancy when Theodore shipped off for war in the Pacific in February of 1945."

Gracie went still.

"Wait," Colette said. "Is Warren the child we're talking about?"

"Correct," Gemma answered. "Warren's biological father,

339

Theodore Cook, died in May of 1945 during the Battle of Okinawa. Right around that same time, you were no longer able to hide the pregnancy at work, Gracie. The military discharged you. You went to live with your sister in the town of Caribou, Maine." Gemma's mind spun when she tried to think how difficult that season must have been for her great-grandmother. An unwed, expectant mother in the 1940s who had lost both Paul, her great love, and the father of her child. She'd been fired from her job, forced to move out of her government-provided housing. She hadn't returned to her hometown because she'd been afraid her pregnancy would break her parents' hearts.

"Was it my sister Hazel?" Gracie asked feebly. "In Caribou?"

"That's right," Gemma confirmed. "As soon as the war ended in early September of that year, Paul started trying to book passage for himself back to America so that he could find you. He made it to D.C. first. When you weren't there, he went to the post office and discovered that you'd had your mail forwarded to an address in Caribou, Maine. He traveled north and knocked on your sister's door one fall afternoon when you were at the house alone."

"Imagine," Mom murmured, "what it must have been like to have him show up like that after so long."

"More than a year had passed since you'd seen each other," Gemma said to Gracie. "He found you shortly before your delivery date."

Gracie inhaled audibly, then lifted shaking hands to cover her cheeks. Clarity banished confusion from her expression. "I remember," she said, then began to cry. "*I remember*."

The rest of them got up and congregated around her. They embraced her in a group hug where she sat, reassuring her as she wept.

"I'm so grateful," Gracie said after a time. "So humbled by his love."

"What happened," Simone asked, "after Paul arrived at your sister's house?"

"I believe I need some tissues," Gracie said. "Then I'll tell you."

Gemma ran to retrieve the tissue box. Simone and Colette got Gracie situated on the sofa, Simone on one side holding her hand, Colette on the other side, a strong arm on the back of the sofa behind her mother. Gemma perched on the coffee table and handed over tissues.

After mopping at her face, Gracie composed herself enough to pick up the story. "He found me pregnant with another man's child. It was his right to be angry. To reject me. I didn't feel that I deserved his love, but he showed me the most beautiful thing in this world."

"Which is?" Mom asked.

"Grace." She blotted beneath her eyelashes. "He told me how very much he loved me. How sick with worry he'd been that he'd lost me forever, how incredibly thankful he was to have finally found me. He wept with relief. I wept too. Because I loved him very deeply, you see. I told him so and we clung to each other for hours. We never did let go, for the rest of our lives."

"He's with us still," Colette said gruffly. Of them all, she was the least comfortable voicing emotions. "I'm his daughter and yours. Simone, his granddaughter. Gemma, his great-granddaughter."

"I still feel surrounded by his love," Simone said.

"As do I." Gemma nodded. "He and his legacy are all around us."

"He wanted to marry me," Gracie said, "right away. And, of

course, I wanted the same. So we married just as soon as we could get a license, and soon after, Warren was born."

"I noticed on Warren's gravestone that you named him Warren Theodore Bettencourt," Gemma said. "The Theodore, I presume, in honor of his biological father."

"Quite right. I worried some over the years that I did a disservice to poor Theodore because I never acknowledged his role in Warren's life in any way except through that middle name. I didn't tell Theodore's family about Warren. And not even Warren himself, God rest his soul, knew about Theodore." She pursed her lips, balled the tissue in her free hand. "It's hard to explain how difficult it was in those days, for the mother and the child, if a baby was conceived out of wedlock. Paul wanted to protect us both and had the best of motives when he suggested we tell everyone we married in January. If we did that, we could raise Warren as our child. His and mine."

"Did any of the rest of your family, besides Hazel, ever learn the truth?" Mom asked.

"No. No one except Hazel. The whole time I was in Caribou, my family believed I was still in D.C. Hazel and I were very close. She was . . . God's gift to me."

"Dad was an excellent father," Colette stated, "to Warren and the rest of us."

"That's true," Gracie agreed. "He couldn't have loved Warren more or grieved for Warren more when he died, had he been his biological father."

A sweet, pensive silence moved between them.

"Are you disappointed in me?" Gracie asked.

"No," they said in unison.

"For a long time, years, I was disappointed in myself for the mistakes I'd made," Gracie confessed. "But Paul had forgiven me completely. He loved me every day without reserve. He assured me that God did not want me crushed by guilt. And so, eventually, I forgave myself. And now . . . Now it's freeing to tell you all the truth. No more secrets."

"I love you, Mom," Colette said.

Simone and Gemma echoed the sentiment.

"I love you all." Gracie cupped a hand around Colette's cheek. "My daughter." Then Simone. "My granddaughter." Then Gemma. "My great-granddaughter. Love the people in your life with all that you have and all that you are. Show them grace. Forgive."

They promised her that they would.

Fear had almost kept Gracie from living out her life with Paul. Fear had kept Gemma from telling Jude how she felt about him. That had been a mistake and the next time she saw him, she was going to shove fear away with both hands.

"Thank you all, from the bottom of my heart," Gracie said, "for giving my love story back to me. I feel complete again." She smoothed a tendril of ginger-white hair toward her bun. "If I forget again . . . ?"

"We'll be here," Gemma said. "And your diaries will be here. To retell your story to you."

Chapter Twenty-Five

Yesterday, Jude had arrived in Manhattan. Today, he and many others had put in a long day of preparation for tomorrow's meeting with Cedric. It was after nine, dark out, and he'd just let himself into his hotel room. It echoed with loneliness.

He switched on a lamp. Stripped off his suit jacket and tie. Emptied his pockets. Removed his holster and weapon. Moving to the window, he peered out at the scene. Tall buildings all around stacked with people. Lights in windows. Cars jammed into rare parking spots below. Strangers hurrying past.

He should probably eat something, but his body had gone past hunger and now he had no appetite.

If everything went according to plan, Cedric would sell Jude his secrets tomorrow. Then Jude could wrap things up here and return to Gemma, hopefully in under a week. Already, he couldn't wait to get back to her.

Memories populated in his mind. How she'd looked that first day when he'd walked into her shop. The frozen moment before she'd pressed her lips to his in her kitchen. How her gray eyes sparkled when she wrinkled his shirts or tugged his tie out of place. The way she felt in his arms when he hugged her. Gemma laughing, cheeks pink, hair twining around him in the breeze.

It was as if his chemical makeup had shifted irrevocably. He had no hope of feeling whole or at peace until he was with her again.

The FBI had received approval to scour reservation records for Cedric Bettencourt and Vincent Dumas at the three hotels where Gemma had told them Cedric had stayed in the past—The Plaza, The Lowell, Henry House. They'd located a reservation for two rooms under Vincent Dumas's name at Henry House.

They'd have recording devices on Jude. But thanks to an order signed by a judge and the cooperation of Henry House management, their Tech Squad had also planted audio/visual equipment in Cedric and Vincent's rooms. The FBI was thorough. They'd learned over their decades of experience to prepare layers of surveillance.

In the room next door to Cedric's, they'd assembled monitors and speakers so that Shannon, Dixon, and more would be able to supervise the meet in real time and so that backup agents would have a place to wait until the buy was accomplished. As soon as that occurred, backup would move in to arrest Cedric and Vincent.

When Cedric had changed his mind about selling his secrets, it had seemed this op would remain unfinished. Now, thankfully, it looked like they might be able to see it through to completion.

Even so, low-level anxiety had begun to thrum in his veins, just as it had prior to his other UC ops. Trying to squash it was pointless, so he sought instead to coexist with it. It would sharpen his nerves and keep him alert. The anxiety meant he had a realistic understanding of the seriousness of the thing he was about to do.

Gemma was gazing out a window of her own. On the far side of the glass, light from her house gleamed on the night-dark surface of the lake.

All afternoon and evening, she'd been talking herself out of the idea of driving to New York. She had the strongest feeling that she should be there. Her intuition kept saying, *Go.* Over and over. This whole dangerous mess had fallen into Jude's lap because of *her* cousin.

Yet it would be crazy of her to drive to New York, right?

Right. There was nothing she could do to help the operation there. New York wasn't close by. And the FBI had expressly forbidden her from going. Jude himself had told her he wanted her to stay here.

Her phone rang, signaling a call from her mother.

"Hello?"

"I've been thinking, since our brunch with Gracie, that there's something I should tell you."

"Oh?" *God, let me not be the biological daughter of another man.*

"Gracie shared her secrets with us, which made me feel sheepish because I've been keeping a little secret of my own from you."

"Which is?"

"Jude met with me a while back and offered to advise me on the laws around debt collection. It's been the best thing ever. A game-changer. I've called him with questions several times and he's always so patient. Plus, he set me up with a debt counselor and I've had four meetings with her. Gemma, I feel as if I can breathe again."

Gemma had been living with her family's debts for many years now. She knew exactly how heavy they were to carry. There was nothing more meaningful Jude could have given them. "I . . ."

"Gemma?"

"I'm blown away that he'd do that for us."

"It's incredibly generous, what he's doing."

"When was it that he volunteered to help in this way?"

"Hmm . . . I wrote my meeting with him on my calendar. Let me just look back and find the day." Crackling sounded on the line. "April ninth."

It was now May nineteenth. On April ninth, Gemma and Jude hadn't been a couple. That date had fallen after their operation had been suspended and before they'd resumed their relationship. While completely out of communication with her, when she'd been tempted to think he didn't care, he'd met with her mother? And been busy ever since, behind the scenes, using his knowledge of the law on their behalf?

When was the last time she'd gotten a call or a letter from one of the debt collectors? Weeks. Her life with Jude had been so full and happy recently, the lack of those debt-collection calls and letters hadn't even registered.

"Jude asked me not to tell you that he was helping me," Mom said. "He didn't want you to feel obligated to be with him."

Gemma loved him. And not just a little.

In a dive-in-the-deep-end way, she *loved him*. She wished she'd told him that before he'd left. She should have told him that.

"He's such a good man, Gemma," Mom said.

"Yes. He is."

They wrapped up the call.

Mabel tilted her head and studied Gemma quizzically.

Go to New York, her intuition whispered.

The time on her phone screen read 9:40. It would take her seven hours to drive to New York. If she got on the road shortly, she'd get in around 5:00 a.m.

Crazy! She wasn't going to New York. She was staying in Bayview, exactly as instructed.

The following day, Jude sat inside a Midtown coffee shop, awaiting contact from Cedric. He'd purchased coffee so that he had the right to sit at a table. However, his stomach wasn't in the mood for even one sip.

Cedric had said he'd contact Jude forty-five minutes before four o'clock to let him know the name of his hotel. Jude Camden already knew the name of Cedric's hotel, but he was Jude McConnell now, waiting at a coffee shop for Cedric to tell him where they were meeting.

He stared at the time—3:12—on his phone screen. It was unbelievable how slowly a minute could pass.

The numbers finally switched to 3:13. When Cedric texted him, this buy would go into motion. Once it did, Jude was committed.

3:14.

3:15. The awaited text came. It jarred Jude, even though he'd been sitting here expecting this very thing.

CEDRIC

> Can you meet me in the lobby of the Henry House Hotel in 45 minutes?

After reading the text, Jude waited a couple of minutes

because that's how long it would've taken him to check his GPS route if he hadn't known his destination until now.

After taking a screenshot of the text exchange, he forwarded it to Dixon, who immediately responded to say he'd received it.

Jude tossed his full coffee in the trash, exited onto the sidewalk, and walked in the direction of the meet. As he went, he deleted his text thread with Dixon from his phone.

Like several other pedestrians, he was dressed as a businessman. He wore a navy suit, pale blue shirt, gray tie. Details mattered so he'd put on the same ring he'd worn to dinner with Cedric. A messenger bag rested against his lower back, its strap a diagonal across his chest. He intended to transfer funds via his phone but had brought a laptop with built-in WI-FI as an alternative option. Everyone on his team knew that technology sometimes glitched or failed. They always had a plan B.

Criminals were smart. They all wanted independent proof from their own bank that money had landed before they'd finalize a sale. It wasn't enough to prosecute a suspect for *intending* to do a deal. A UC agent had to see the deal all the way through by paying for illegal items in order to secure evidence that would hold up in court. Later, the FBI would recoup their money, but an actual transfer was a necessary first step.

Far above, the sun hung in a pale blue sky. Its light struggled to reach him through the canyon of buildings. Except at cross-streets. There, sun flashed over him as he passed through.

Jude spun the ring around and around his finger, using its motion to ground himself in Jude McConnell's life. He'd spent his childhood in Rhode Island. Attended Tufts. Worked for perfume giant House of Cordell. Had met Gemma in Las Vegas. Jude McConnell was ambitious, greedy, and willing to skirt the law to benefit himself. He'd be cautious because of the illegal nature of the sale, but also very keen for it to go through so he could collect his broker's fee from his buyer.

He was dialed-in by the time he reached Henry House, and spotted Cedric and Vincent right away. The two were dressed in suits and occupying luxurious chairs near the lobby fireplace. Standing as Jude approached, they exchanged handshakes.

"Did you have a nice flight?" Jude asked.

"We did, absolutely." Cedric went on to list the reasons why he always enjoyed visiting New York and Jude made the expected responses.

After a few minutes, Cedric pulled his sleeves into place with two small tugs. Metal cufflinks caught the light. "Shall we get to business?"

"Yes. Whenever you're ready."

Cedric nodded at Vincent.

Vincent strode to the front doors and left.

Strange.

"Shall we?" Cedric gestured for him to follow where Vincent had gone.

"Are we leaving?"

"I thought we would go a short distance, yes. The weather is pleasant. We can talk about this further outdoors. Is that agreeable?"

Warning arrowed through Jude. "Certainly."

Cedric made his way toward the street and Jude fell in step with him.

Did they suspect their rooms were under surveillance? Is that why they didn't want to conduct the meeting here?

No. If Cedric or Vincent suspected their rooms were under surveillance, they'd have called off the meeting. Likely this was just more of the overall defensive strategy they'd exhibited when they'd refused to provide the name of their hotel in advance.

No matter what, this was a blow to Jude and the FBI. He had audio and video recorders on him as well as a tracker so that his team could pinpoint his location. But now the painstaking preparation of Cedric and Vincent's hotel rooms was worthless. The plainclothes agents in the lobby and in the unmarked cars outside would need to follow in order to provide Jude with backup.

Outside, Vincent opened the front and back passenger doors of a black Mercedes sedan.

Jude's concern deepened. Walking to their destination would have been better. It was dangerous for undercover agents to get into a car driven by a suspect. Two New York City UC policemen had been killed that way a few years back while attempting to buy illegal guns. Even so, the protocol here was to go along. Not doing so risked blowing his cover. Jude got into the backseat.

As Vincent steered them into the flow of traffic, Cedric asked Jude conversational questions about his work.

Jude matched Cedric's demeanor, answering in a relaxed tone, asking Cedric similar questions in return.

"If you and Gemma get more serious, are you going to move to Maine or is she going to move here?" Cedric wanted to know.

Jude bit down on his back teeth. He'd been highly motivated to get Gemma involved in this at the start. Now he wanted her *nowhere* near this. So much so, he hated hearing Cedric say her name. On top of that, he had to keep his wits about him and the mention of her had the potential to shatter his focus. "Gemma and I are having fun. For now, I think we both enjoy our long-distance relationship. It gives us each our own space."

"Possibly for the best. Like me, she doesn't seem to take her relationships seriously."

"Yeah, that's kind of the stage of life I'm in, too." A lie. Jude was going to do everything in his power to ensure that Gemma took him very, very seriously.

Near the northern end of Central Park, Vincent pulled up to a hotel and left the Mercedes with a valet. Cedric thrust one arm through the strap of a leather backpack. No doubt this held the physical documents Jude was buying.

The three of them took the crosswalk to the park. Cedric led them down one pathway after another as if he knew exactly where he was headed. They entered the forty-acre North Woods. The deeper they went into nature, the fewer people they saw. Central Park had a fair number of police cameras. But Jude spotted none in this area.

Cedric turned off the wider trail onto a thin trail mostly hidden by vegetation. It ended inside a circular grouping of trees that sheltered a stone bench covered in pollen and leaves. From here Jude had a partial view of the ravine on one side, an obstructed view of the trail on the other side.

Cedric pulled a handkerchief from his suit jacket and used it to clear the bench of debris. "Shall we sit?"

Jude and Cedric sat. Vincent remained standing in the lookout position. Mostly concealed by foliage, he peered in the direction from which they'd come.

"I have my banking information ready," Cedric said.

"May I first have a look at what I'm purchasing?"

"A brief look, yes." From his backpack, Cedric extracted a dark green folder and handed it to Jude.

Jude took a few minutes to page through the contents. It contained the precise recipe for Rhapsodie, as well as the specialized steps involved in the process of making the herbalist's centuries-old perfume. Jude closed the folder and set it on the bench between them.

"I trust that's satisfactory?" Cedric asked.

"Yes."

"Ready for my banking information?"

"One moment." Jude brought out his phone and logged on to the app that would allow him to transfer funds. "Ready."

A man and woman jogged by their alcove. Likely agents.

Cedric handed him a piece of paper that listed his bank account details. Jude plugged them into his app. Double-checked that he'd gotten everything right. Then hit the button to transfer the funds from Jude's client's bank to Cedric's. The cell signal was weak here. A spinning circle appeared.

Go through, Jude demanded silently. *Go through.*

After what felt like five minutes but had probably only been five seconds, a green checkmark appeared. The transaction had been completed. He showed his screen to Cedric.

Wordless, Cedric opened his account on his own device and refreshed it a couple of times. When he saw the money arrive there and that the balance of his account now equaled their agreed-upon price, he tucked away his phone and smiled. "Excellent."

Jude slid the folder into his messenger bag and looped the strap across his body to secure the evidence.

"It was nice to do business with you," Cedric said.

"Likewise."

"Do you expect your buyer will create their own version of this perfume?"

"I do—"

Vincent made an angry, whistling sound through his teeth.

Cedric looked up alertly with a frown.

Vincent spoke French in a low undertone. Jude rapidly translated in his head. *"The man who is about to pass by was driving the car that pulled onto the street behind us when we left Henry House."* Vincent pulled free a Glock with a suppressor attached.

Cedric and Jude rushed to their feet. They all watched a man in his fifties walk by at a leisurely pace, hands clasped behind his back. He disappeared from view.

"Are you sure," Cedric asked Vincent in French, *"he was the one who followed us in his car? It wasn't someone else?"*

"I'm sure."

Jude's heart contracted painfully with each beat, but he'd trained his body well. He blocked outward signs of agitation, allowing only confusion to show.

Cedric glared at Jude with accusation. "Is that man with you?" he asked in English.

"No. I've never seen him before." He spoke with steely calm.

Backup should have swarmed the scene as soon as the transfer had gone through. Instead, they'd given Vincent time to draw his weapon. Maybe Jude's audio wasn't transmitting well. Maybe there was a problem communicating real-time information to the plainclothes agents.

Vincent pointed his gun at Jude. "Who's with you?" he asked furiously.

Jude raised his palms. "No one."

"I don't believe you." Vincent closed the space between them and pointed the Glock at Jude's chest. "Who's with you?"

"No one."

The raw anger of a trapped animal flared in Vincent's eyes. *"He set us up,"* Vincent said to Cedric in French, keeping his focus and gun on Jude.

He started calling Jude obscenities in French. White formed against the pad of Vincent's trigger finger as he exerted pressure.

No.

Jude's life whirred in front of him like a runaway train, stopping on the memory of Gemma's face.

From yards away, sounds reached them. People—agents—moving fast through the woods in their direction.

"Non," Cedric hissed at Vincent. He shoved Vincent's arm just as the gun fired.

A bullet ripped into Jude's flesh.

Chapter Twenty-Six

The explosion staggered Jude back. He looked down dumbly, stunned, as blood wet the front of his shirt.

Vincent hurried Cedric toward the ravine. Moving fast, they were out of sight in seconds.

Jude crumpled to one knee, then planted a palm on the rugged earth. He pressed his other palm against the injury and felt warm blood ooze down his side.

Am I going to die?

Agents flooded in from both sides. The man and woman in exercise clothing. The fifty-something guy. More.

"They went that way," Jude rasped with a jerk of his head.

Several took off after Cedric and Vincent. Three remained behind with him.

His voice had sounded strange when he'd spoken just now and their voices sounded strange, too. They were saying things and lifting the messenger bag from him and administering pressure and calling on their cell phones and giving him encouragement. They covered the wound and helped him lie down on that side of his ribs.

Fear climbed like an evil beast up his insides toward his heart, its claws digging in.

He'd done the right things. Made the right decisions. Caught Cedric. He didn't—he didn't regret his work.

But he did regret, deeply, the way he'd turned his back on God.

God, he thought. *God.*

He'd been a fool. He'd gotten caught up in unimportant things and ignored matters of life and death. Remorse coursed through him. *I forgive everyone who's hurt me. All of them. Every one.*

The thing he'd been so reluctant to do—forgive—was shockingly easy in this moment.

God, please forgive me. I'm so sorry. Please forgive.

Into the chaos and pain came a clean wind. And that clean wind chased away the ashes of his mistakes. It brought strength and reassurance.

Love for his brothers and mother and father tugged at him. He could bear that, though. There was only one thing he could not bear, one thing that was breaking his heart.

Gemma. He hadn't gotten enough time with Gemma.

God, if you can, give me more time with her. I beg you.

He grabbed the shirt of the male agent next to him. "I need Dixon to call . . ." He pulled in a breath. "Gemma Clare."

"Of course."

"Tell her . . . that I . . . love her." It was becoming hard to form words. They slid around, not cooperating.

"I will, but you'll be able to tell her yourself soon—"

"Tell her," Jude repeated.

A verse whispered through his soul. *Not my will, but thine.* He put his last conscious moments into that prayer, surrendering.

Then his vision grayed.

Gemma's first thought upon waking this morning had been, *Today's the day Cedric will sell Jude the secrets behind Rhapsodie. Today's the day.*

Instantaneously, worry had leapt onto her. It hadn't let go. It had been with her all day at work. On and off she'd spent time praying. Spent time pacing. More time praying.

She was cleaning her studio in preparation to go home for the day when her phone rang. Caller ID announced an unknown number.

Her nerves pulled taut. "Hello?"

"Miss Clare?" The caller had the voice of an older man.

"Yes?"

"This is Agent Dixon Martin with the FBI. Agent Camden has been injured."

Her stomach dropped and her pulse spiked. *Injured.*

"It's serious," he continued. "A gunshot wound. At the scene he insisted that you be notified. He wanted to tell you something."

"Yes?" Her ears were ringing.

"He wanted you to know that he loves you."

She squeezed closed her eyes. With her free hand, she supported her forehead to keep the weight of it, of this situation, from snapping her neck. *Injured.* She'd said goodbye to Jude the day before yesterday and he'd been fit, healthy, strong. It was hard to hold that memory of him up against the word picture Dixon had just relayed. Yet she knew with bone-deep conviction that Jude had, indeed, been shot. *This* was why her instincts had told her to go to New York. "Where is he?" she rasped.

"Manhattan Valley Hospital. They just took him back for

surgery. He's receiving the most outstanding medical care possible."

Memories of the day of her mother's stroke circled like angry black crows—dive bombing, pecking her with lethal beaks. "Please tell me everything you know."

"He was shot in the side. The bullet tore through the bottom edge of his left lung. It missed major blood vessels, thank God. Right now they're cleaning the wound and repairing the tissue."

"How long will surgery take?"

"I don't know."

"Prognosis?"

"They haven't said."

"Has his family been notified?"

"No, but Shannon has put in a request for his next-of-kin details. She should receive phone numbers soon."

"I can try to reach his mother." She did not want to be the one to relay this devastating news to Fiona. But someone needed to do it. Immediately. "What went wrong that resulted in this?"

"Cedric took Jude to a remote location. We had trouble receiving immediate information."

"Did you arrest Cedric and Vincent?"

"We did. They're in custody."

"I'm on my way to New York." She wished she hadn't over-ruled her intuition. Now she needed to do her best to fix that bad decision. She'd ask her Mom to pick up Mabel. Then she'd catch a car, plane, train—whatever would get her to New York soonest.

They ended the call. Her hands were shaking as she ran a search for the phone number of Lavish in Groomsport.

Gemma dialed.

Answer, she urged the employees. It was 4:56 now. They would likely quit for the day in minutes if they hadn't already.

A receptionist answered cheerfully. "Lavish."

"This is Gemma Clare. I'm Jude Camden's girlfriend and I need to be connected to Fiona Camden immediately. Her son has been injured in New York and is in surgery."

The woman on the other end made a sound of dismay. "Fiona isn't here at the moment."

"Please do whatever you have to do to get through to her and give her my number."

"You said your name was?"

"Gemma Clare." She rattled off her cell phone number.

When Fiona received the worst phone call a mother can receive, the one that informs you your child has been injured, her heart stalled, then set off at a panicked pace. She clutched Burke's arm for support.

"What is it?" Burke asked, his own face turning white. He'd been privy to her half of the brief conversation with her receptionist.

They'd been walking through town on their way to enjoy a glass of wine together. She'd been obliviously happy, trusting that her sons, wherever they were in the world this evening, were thriving and fine. The news that Jude *wasn't* thriving or fine had frozen Earth on its axis. "It's Jude. He's been hurt. In New York. I need to call Gemma."

He led her to a window seat on the exterior of a shop.

Fiona's phone pinged with a text from her receptionist containing Gemma's number. She dialed it.

Her imagination was flying to the very darkest places.

Her Jude. Her Jude.

Gemma answered and began explaining and Fiona could hear Gemma's own worry in her voice, but she was speaking with so much compassion for Fiona.

Burke held her hand, his warm steadiness flowing into her.

"Felix has a plane," Fiona told Gemma. "We'll take it to New York. As soon as possible. If you're able to drive to Rockland Airport right now, you can go with us."

"I'll meet you there."

When they disconnected, Fiona relayed the basics to Burke in a voice that seemed to belong to someone else.

"Are you okay?" he asked.

She shook her head.

"What can I do to help?"

"I . . . need to tell Jeremiah and Felix. Then I need to get to the airport to meet up with the others."

"Do you want to stop at your house and pack a bag first?"

She shook her head.

"I'll drive you to the airport," he said, "while you make calls."

Max didn't let himself spy on Sloane's social media very often. Once a month or so, ordinarily. But since Jude had told him that she was moving back to Maine, he'd been scrolling her feed more often.

He was sitting in his expansive office, feet crossed on his desk, paused on a picture she'd posted yesterday to Instagram. In it, she was staring into the camera with a small smile, straight brown hair highlighted with shades of caramel. Long eyelashes. Wide mouth. There was a sweetness to her face. She didn't look like anyone's enemy, but she was his. And he was already planning how best to bring her into his orbit when she returned.

Finally, he was going to get closure from her. She'd never allowed him that and over all these years he'd never stopped wanting it.

His phone alerted him to an incoming call from Jeremiah.

Slightly unusual. Jude called him much more than the oldest Camden sibling. He answered. "Jeremiah?"

"Jude's in surgery. He was shot during an FBI operation in New York."

Max's feet hit the floor as he sat upright. "Shot? How bad is it?"

"The bullet caught the edge of his lung. I'm worried."

Max swore.

"Can you get to the airstrip in the next twenty minutes? We'll take Dad's plane to New York."

"I'll be there." He ran toward the parking garage, ignoring the startled questions of his employees.

Jude was the best friend he'd ever had. He'd go anywhere, do anything necessary, for Jude.

Gemma rushed into the waiting area for the operating rooms of Manhattan Valley Hospital like a steamship at full speed, eyes narrowed, red hair flying around her shoulders.

Dixon and Shannon were there, conducting a hushed conversation with numerous other people. All FBI, no doubt. When Dixon saw Gemma arrive flanked by Felix, Fiona, Jeremiah, and Max, he broke away and crossed to them. He introduced himself and told them Jude was still in surgery.

It had taken Gemma and the others only an hour in the air

to travel here on Felix's private plane. Everyone had been grim and mostly silent both on the plane and in the limo that had been waiting for them when they'd landed. Gemma had wanted to meet Felix and now she had, but that event had barely penetrated, given the circumstances. Felix had a plane. And she'd been invited onto it. That's what had been relevant today.

Dixon answered the Camdens' questions the same way he'd answered Gemma's earlier. No new information to report. And almost zero information about who had shot Jude or why. Dixon could not, he explained, share any active investigative information with the family.

Gemma perched on an indestructible-looking chair, separate from the Camdens, separate from the knot of agents. Alone. Terrified.

When a nurse entered to say that the surgery was going well and that she'd be back in forty-five minutes with another update, Gemma excused herself and sought out the hospital's chapel. It had a large skylight and a round stained-glass window that glimmered behind the altar.

She was the only one here.

These chairs did not feel indestructible, she noted as she sat on one. And neither did she.

Clenching her hands in her lap, she bowed her head.

Of all the things Jude could have been thinking about in the moments following his injury, he'd been thinking about her and had asked a fellow agent to tell her he loved her. That request was intensely bittersweet. *He loved her*. That was the sweet part. But it was also bitter because he'd tapped someone else to speak this very private thing to her, which meant he'd feared he would die and be robbed of the chance to tell her himself.

How was she supposed to continue on if she didn't get the

chance to tell him she loved him, too? Her mind shut down at the question. It was too impossible to imagine.

He could not die. For a million reasons.

God, she prayed with a ragged heart. *Fight for him. Save him.*

The fear was vicious and yet she wasn't alone. God was with her in it. Vast love. Bottomless compassion. Unending grace.

God, I love him. Please, please don't ask me to part with him.

Just . . . no. She refused to part with Jude. Even if parting meant heaven for him and heaven was better than this difficult, painful life.

Golden sunset light moved from behind a cloud, coating the space, warming her shoulders and bent head.

I am here, she sensed in that space.

Not, *He will be well.*

But **I am here.** It was enough to pull her back from the edge of a cliff and enable her to make it through two more minutes of this awful day. Then two more minutes. Then two more.

Gradually, Jude became aware of strange and confusing things.

An unfamiliar male voice. Then the sensation of a warm sheet on top of him. A soft surface below him. His sluggish body seemed to weigh a thousand pounds.

"Ms. Clare," the male voice said in a friendly way. "Feel free to talk to him."

Ms. Clare was Gemma. *Gemma* was here? Anticipation pushed against the heavy mud of his brain.

"Jude." *Her* voice. Unbelievably, her voice. "You're doing great. Everything is well."

"Jude," the male voice said, "you asked specifically for Gemma a couple of minutes ago and so I went and got her. Gemma's here. Can you wake up for us?"

He had no memory of asking for Gemma, but he was so glad he had.

"Can you open your eyes and talk to me?" she asked.

He struggled to open his eyes. He was really out of it. This wasn't like him. Why was he so out of it? With effort, he squinted into the light.

"That's it," she said. "I'm next to you. Do you see me?"

He was finally able to open his eyes fully. Gemma was standing next to him, holding his hand. He was reclining in some sort of bed with rails.

She smiled encouragingly and her eyes glowed with warmth. Freckles dotted her ivory skin like sprinkles on a cupcake. Her copper hair . . . so beautiful.

"Gemma?" he rasped. His throat felt like someone had gone after it with a scrub brush.

"Yes." She was bright, lit from the inside. "Hello."

"Hello." Moisture fuzzed his vision because he was so grateful to see her. "You were . . . in Maine."

"Correct. But I caught a plane here with your family this evening. They're out in the waiting room. And now you and I are both in New York." She bent and kissed the top of his hand, then straightened.

"Thank God you're here. You . . . okay?"

"Yes, I'm perfectly okay."

Jude turned his head. He wished he and Gemma were alone—he had a lot he wanted to say to her—but they weren't alone. A middle-aged man in scrubs watched from the end of the bed. Curtains and machines lined parallel sides of the space. An IV had been implanted in his arm.

Fractured memories dribbled in. Cedric. Vincent. The circle of trees. The gun. "What happened to me?" he asked Gemma.

"You were shot in the side." The reality of that started to sink in on him like a cave collapsing, but Gemma held the rubble back by squeezing his hand. "You came through surgery and are in recovery at Manhattan Valley Hospital in New York. You're going to be fine."

Surgery? He'd missed a chunk of time. The circle of trees was the last thing he remembered. Now surgery was behind him?

"How are you doing?" the nurse asked.

"Considering I was shot and had surgery, I guess I'm doing all right." He felt terrible. Stupidly groggy, with a body too fragile and weak to move.

Gemma filled him in on what had happened after he passed out using details she said Dixon had given her. The nurse provided medical information.

He recalled now that after Vincent had shot him, he'd thought he might die. The idea that he wouldn't get more time with Gemma had devastated him.

She was here. She was here all the way from Maine, happy and whole. And he wasn't going to die. At least not yet.

God had given him more time.

He'd have a chance to live out the rest of his days with her and he'd never, *never* take that for granted. It was a gift of grace.

Privacy was a luxury, Gemma silently concluded. A luxury beyond her grasp at present.

She and Jude had spoken for only a few minutes before his relatives had joined them in the recovery area. They had every right to Jude. More right to him than she had, certainly. She didn't begrudge them their spots at Jude's bedside. On the contrary, she'd forever be grateful to them for allowing her—the newcomer—a seat on their plane.

It's just that she *couldn't wait* to be alone with Jude. In part so the two of them wouldn't have an audience. In part because then she wouldn't feel the way she felt now—like she was intruding on their family time. It must be awkward for the Camdens to have an almost-stranger inserted into this gathering at such a critical time.

Jude had improved enough that the staff was about to move him to a room on the tenth floor. "I'll be back a little later and will meet you up there," Gemma said to Jude, gathering her purse.

His focus zeroed in on her. "You don't have to go."

"I know. I'm not going far, but there's something I need to do. I'll be back in an hour or so."

She went straight to Dixon, still in the waiting room where she'd left him, and made a request.

The FBI had taken Cedric to their local Federal detention facility. The multi-story brown-brick building was as imposing as a muscular bouncer with a broken nose.

Gemma waited in a small room enclosed by sliding, see-through doors on both sides. From her chair, she watched as Cedric was led in. Neither she nor her cousin nor the guard spoke as Cedric was pressed into the opposite chair. They affixed his handcuffs to a ring mounted on a metal table bolted to the ground.

The burly guard retreated to the far side of the doors behind Cedric, which whooshed closed.

Wrinkles and dirt marred his suit. His face looked pale and tired. His usually perfect hair was oily and unkempt—like he'd been running his hands through it and tugging.

She hoped he pulled it all out.

"Why are you in New York?" he asked.

"I'm here because Jude got shot today." She spoke with preternatural calm.

"Is he alive or dead?" The coldness in his eyes assured her that he only cared about Jude's living or dying because of the effect that might have on *his* future. Not because he had an ounce of concern for Jude.

"Alive."

"The FBI learned of my deal with Jude, Gemma. Either they were monitoring us and Jude and I are both under investigation. Or Jude's an undercover agent working with them. Which is it?"

"He's an undercover agent."

He cursed. "Were you aware of that?"

Gemma stacked her palms on the table, registering its chill. "I've known that Jude's an undercover agent for three months. Ever since he came to me and informed me that the FBI was aware of your willingness to sell Rhapsodie's secrets. Jude asked if I'd help bring you down. I told him that I would."

Cedric's head pulled back—disgust and fury evident.

"Everything that followed—my communication with you about Jude, our dinner at the restaurant. It was all part of an FBI operation. I came by to tell you face-to-face that I couldn't be prouder of my part in it, especially now that you've injured Jude. I'd do it ten times over again."

"How could you?" he sneered.

"How could *you*?" she shot back, icy. "The Bettencourts have been Rhapsodie's protectors for four hundred years."

"You traitor. My own flesh and blood—"

"You're the traitor." She looked him directly in the eyes. "I remember the boy you were, and I still have fondness for him. But your actions as an adult have done far too much damage. We both know you've left a wake of crimes behind you. My father's in jail for some of them. And now you're willing to betray Rhapsodie for money? *No.* It's time for you to pay for what you've done."

He hurled venomous French words at her.

She rose. "If Jude had died, I'd have come after you with grenades." She walked toward the sliding door and the guard.

He rattled his handcuffs in their ring and tried to lunge for her. It was no use. He was trapped.

She left with her head held high.

Chapter Twenty-Seven

When Gemma reached Jude's hospital room, she found the Camden contingent still present.

This was New York City. One square foot of interior space cost more here than anywhere else. Even guests of honor at hospitals, like Jude was, did not get huge single rooms. So it was wall-to-wall bodies when Gemma entered. They all turned toward her.

"Hi." She addressed the group. "I came back to check on the patient." Her eyes met Jude's and she watched as relief came over his face and relaxed his shoulders. She had that outsider feeling again in this company, but it was plain to see that he viewed her as his favorite insider.

"The patient is doing very well," Felix said. "And you're right on time to vote in the debate we're having."

"Oh?"

"We're arguing," Felix continued, "over which of the four of us guys looks the best in a hospital gown."

That elicited a surprised laugh from Gemma. The day had

been so fraught that humor felt rusty but welcome. Like a green sprout pushing its way up through scorched earth.

"It's pure ridiculousness." Fiona rolled her eyes.

"It's a serious dispute," Felix maintained. "I, of course, think I should win. When I had my rotator cuff fixed twenty-eight years ago, I looked fantastic in my hospital gown. I made extra effort to put on this type of accepting, calm, and courageous face." He demonstrated the expression to Gemma.

"I was married to you at the time," Fiona said, "and I remember you as pouting and irritable before and after that surgery."

"I had to wear a hospital gown last fall when I had a chest infection and, no question, I rocked it the best of anyone in this room." Jeremiah crossed his arms, lips curving. "I'm an international sex symbol."

"So am I," Felix said.

"You're a senior citizen," Jeremiah pointed out.

"I'm a silver fox," Felix corrected. "More seasoned than you youngsters."

"I vote Jude," Fiona said. "You look gorgeous right now, darling."

"I also vote Jude," Max said. "But only because I can't vote for myself seeing as how I'm too smart to have needed a hospital gown."

"You're only voting for Jude," Jeremiah said to Max, "because he's the one in a hospital gown right now. That's a pity vote."

"I have a gunshot wound, so I deserve a pity vote," Jude said.

"Gemma," Felix entreated, "see sense and vote for me."

"No." Jeremiah pointed to himself. "Me."

She felt like a contestant on *The Voice* forced to choose between the coaches. "You can split my vote between the two of you. Jude still wins because it's now two votes Jude against a half point each for Felix and Jeremiah."

Felix and Jeremiah tipped their heads back in mock agony.

"We're both athletes—" Jeremiah grumbled.

"—And terrible at accepting defeat," Felix finished.

"I love you all," Jude broke in, raising his voice. "But if your name isn't Gemma, please go to a hotel for the night and get some sleep."

Everyone answered with good-natured affirmatives except for Fiona. "I thought I'd stay here tonight to help. That is . . . I'll give you two some time alone. Then come back in a bit?"

"No, thank you," Jude said to his mother. "I'll rest better knowing that all of you are resting, too."

This was vintage Jude. He was a caretaker at heart, and it probably wasn't natural for him to receive so much care. He'd be far more comfortable giving care to these people.

Fiona looked like she wanted to argue but then said, "All right," and kissed him on the forehead. "I'll be back in the morning."

Felix, Jeremiah, and Max approached Jude one by one and took turns squeezing his shoulder.

"I'm proud of you," Felix told him.

"My life wouldn't be half as good without you in it, so thanks for sticking around," Jeremiah said. "But next time, sidestep the bullet."

"Glad you've got a scar on you now," Max said. "You were too perfect before."

"I wasn't even sure whether he actually worked for the FBI until now," Jeremiah said to the others on their way out. "I thought he might have made it up to seem cool."

All at once, the rest were gone. It was blessedly quiet and surprisingly still.

Gemma cataloged Jude's appearance. His breathing was

mildly labored, and he was no doubt existing in a soup of heavy pain meds. But she was mollified to see that his color was better. His eyes were a clearer green than they'd been earlier. His hair, adorably disheveled.

Did he remember that he'd asked Dixon to tell her that he loved her? Regardless, she was not leaving here until he was good and certain that she loved him.

"Finally," he said with satisfaction, "it's just you and me."

She drew closer to him. "And I'm free to confide my opinion that no man since the beginning of time has ever looked as good as you do in a hospital gown."

"A hospital gown *and* an IV," he boasted. He lifted his eyebrows like, *What do you think about that irresistible combo?*

"I'm undone."

"Yeah. The female nurses have been swirling around me like groupies."

"I knew that if I left on an errand, I'd have competition."

"Where'd you go?"

"To give Cedric an earful."

He regarded her questioningly.

She relayed the exchange she'd had with her cousin. "I may have said something about coming after him with grenades if he hurt you."

"Have you ever seen a grenade?"

"No. But I'm committed to learning how to use them on him if he ever causes you more harm and I wanted to make sure he knew it."

"Sit with me?" He patted the mattress beside his hip.

She lowered the bar, sat, then kissed him gently. The contact of their lips blazed with power despite its softness. The chance to kiss him again was an affirmation of life. His heart was beating. He had breath in his lungs. They'd survived.

They rested their foreheads together. She could feel their

unique alchemy and the soul deep connection of their emotions.

When she sat back up, she intertwined her hand with his to keep a link between them. He was looking at her like she was a priceless jewel, and he the explorer who'd spent a lifetime searching for it.

He lifted his other arm, the one on his injured side, and winced subtly.

"Careful," she whispered.

Resolute, he ran his fingers into her hair, smoothing it to the side. "When I thought I was dying, everything about living became clear. I was proud of the things I'd done, but I hated that I wouldn't get to spend my life with you. Worst of all, I hadn't told you how I felt."

"I was mad at myself over that, too. Not just today but ever since you left Maine, I've regretted not telling you how I felt. And now I want the chance to tell you how I feel first."

"No way. I'm the one who had surgery today. I get first dibs."

"We'll play rock, paper, scissors to decide it."

"I had *surgery today*."

"Scared I'll trounce you in rock, paper, scissors?"

"Fine." They both fisted their hands.

"Rock, paper, scissors," they chanted in unison as their fists bobbed in time, "shoot." They both showed paper.

"Again!" Gemma demanded.

This time they both showed scissors.

"Again!"

This time they both showed rock.

"I'm taking this as confirmation that we're incredibly compatible," Jude said.

"I'm taking this as a sign that the game has ended in a tie, and we should tell each other how we feel simultaneously. "Ready?"

He gave a nod.

"One, two," they said in unison, "three. Shoot."

Then they both said, "I love you," at the same moment.

He blinked once, concentrating on her. "What was that you said?"

"I love you."

His eyes blazed even as a lopsided smile slowly overtook his mouth. "I love you," he said.

Her lips parted with wonder. Those words!

"I think I fell in love with you long ago," he said somberly. "Maybe the day you insisted that I rescued you from a canal at The Venetian and I agreed. I'd never have agreed if I hadn't loved you."

She laughed.

"I love you, Gemma. I'll spend my life making sure you know how much."

Her feelings billowed, tightening her throat and threatening tears. "I don't think I deserve you," she confessed in a low voice.

"Gemma—"

"—But that's not going to stop me from taking every bit of you that I can get."

Epilogue
SIX WEEKS LATER

"I think you're overdoing it," Gemma stated.

Jude secretly relished all the ways she'd cared for him since his injury. Sometimes she coddled him, like when she stuck pillows under his feet in the early days or brought him chocolate. Sometimes she nursed him, like when she'd changed his bandage or brought him dinner. Sometimes she scolded him, like now. He treasured all of it. But accepting her opinion too quickly in this case would rob him of the chance to banter with her.

"The doctors let me do a rowing machine at the gym," he pointed out. "This is easier than a rowing machine." They were out on Pushaw Lake on a perfect summer day. He maneuvered her rowboat's oars rhythmically through the water, Gemma facing him and Mabel behind him.

Gemma gave a disdainful sniff. "The doctors don't know you as well as I do, and I say that's enough already."

"It feels great, actually."

"Stop at once."

"You know who's really easy to get along with right now? Mabel. She's too busy enjoying my efforts to grumble at me."

"Mabel is a dog. Are you comparing me to a dog?"

He was way too smart to answer that one.

"Stop rowing," she demanded. "This is far enough."

"Just a little farther—"

"This is my last warning before I use your word aversions against you."

He pulled the oars into the boat, then moved toward her swiftly, catching her face in his hands.

She released a squeak of surprise.

He grinned. "Fine, because what I really want to do right now is kiss you." His universe was right here, in his hands. He loved Gemma with every breath, every minute of his day. She'd overrun into all the corners of his life and improved them all.

He'd broken FBI protocol by falling in love with her. However, his actions in New York had swung the higher-ups in his favor. Sustaining an injury in the line of duty tended to have that effect. He'd resumed his role at the Bureau and appreciated his second chance to work as a special agent even more than he'd appreciated his first chance.

With the completion of Scent-sible, Cedric and Vincent had been charged and were awaiting trial while Jude worked with prosecutors to build the government's case. The physical documents containing Rhapsodie's secrets were safely stored in the evidence vault. At the conclusion of the trial, they'd be returned to their rightful owner—the CEO of the Bettencourt company, Cedric's father. Based on family tradition, he'd almost certainly opt to destroy them.

Jude and Gemma had come clean to her family about his real identity and the reasons for their charade. Upside: Her family had been extremely supportive. Downside: He hadn't attended a Clare family gathering yet in which one of her brothers hadn't made a crack about his butterfly collection.

"You presume you can kiss me now after flagrantly ignoring my orders?" Gemma asked. But her hands gripped his knees and tugged him forward an inch, bringing his profile closer to hers.

"Hmm. I can see that I'm going to have to bring out the big guns."

"Please do."

"'How do I love thee? Let me count the ways.'"

He watched her eyes go dreamy, then kissed her. His senses rushed with the feel of her lips, her taste—

She pulled back. "I believe there's more to that poem."

His chest was hitching in and out, even after just a five-second kiss. He could smell that infernal perfume of hers that always scrambled his head.

He adjusted their position, speaking the next words against her lips. "'I love thee to the depth and breadth and height. My soul can reach, when feeling out of sight. For the ends of being and ideal grace.'" He trailed kisses along her jaw before meeting her eyes.

She gazed at him, and he saw her love for him there, faithful and true.

Then she brought her mouth to his and thoughts were lost as the boat rocked, Mabel barked, and the Maine sun glittered all around.

"For God gave us a spirit not of fear
but of power and love and self-control."
2 Timothy 1:7

Catch up with Max Cirillo (and Fiona & Burke, too) when Max comes face to face with Sloane in Uneasy Street, the romantic conclusion of the Sons of Scandal series!

Acknowledgments

In early 2023, I went in (without any concerns) for my annual, routine mammogram. That mammogram found a cancerous tumor. For me, and so many other women, early detection made a world of difference. Sweet readers, I encourage you to stay current with your mammograms.

God showed His love and provision to me in a hundred ways before, during, and after surgery and radiation therapy. One of those ways? He gave me this particular book to write in 2023. *Rocky Road* will always occupy a special place in my heart because Jude and Gemma's story provided me with such a delightful, imaginary place to escape. Books are good company on hard days, aren't they? This novel was the best of company to me on the hardest of days.

Heartfelt thanks to the people who keep me going behind the scenes . . . . My family—I love you. Katie Ganshert and Courtney Walsh—for sharing both writing and life with me every step of the way. Dani Pettrey—for your friendship and prayers.

Enormous appreciation to the excellent team who worked with me on this novel . . . . Editor Charlene Patterson. Proofreader Sophia Walsh. Literary Agent Kristy Cambron. Fantastic beta readers Joy Tiffany, Crissy Loughridge, Amy Watson, Shelli Littleton, Jennifer Major & Kay Whitton. I can't thank you enough for volunteering your time to read and provide feedback on an early version of this book. Narrators

Reba Buhr and Ryan Hudson—I'm thrilled with the way you brought *Rocky Road* to life via its audiobook.

And finally, a bouquet of gratitude to the following readers for your amazing support of me and my books . . . . Kim Ann, Holly Bleggi, Emily Packer, Lisa Kelley, Cindy Viehmann, Andi Tubbs, Melissa Romine, Cindy Case, Kimberley Endicott, Kim Wong, Theresa Pihl & Carolyn Robinson. Thank you!

About the Author

Becky's a California native who attended Baylor University, met and married a Texan, then settled in Dallas with their three children. She loves writing sweet contemporary romances filled with sizzling chemistry, twisty plots, faith, banter, and humor. She's the Christy and Carol Award–winning author of thirteen novels. When she's not writing, you'll find her power-walking her neighborhood, driving carpool, eating chocolate, doing yoga, or admiring her Cavalier spaniel.

To learn more about Becky and her books, visit her website at www.beckywade.com. While you're there, subscribe to her free quarterly e-newsletter for updates about upcoming books, exclusive giveaways, and more!

You'll find Becky on Facebook as Author Becky Wade and on Instagram as BeckyWadeWriter.